*He seduced her
with his touch and*

D0483632

"Miss Bowman," Westcliff said coldly, *"Queen Victoria herself could not drag someone like you along the path of respectability."*

"I thought you might say that." Taking a deep breath, she stepped closer to him. "Very well, you leave me no choice. If you don't agree to help me, Westcliff, I will tell everyone about what happened this afternoon. I daresay people will find no small amusement in the fact that the self-possessed Lord Westcliff cannot control his desire for a bumptious girl with atrocious manners. And you won't be able to deny it—because you never lie."

Westcliff arched one brow, giving her a look that should have withered her on the spot. "You are overestimating your attractions, Miss Bowman."

"Am I? Then prove it."

"How?"

Even in her present spirit of throwing caution to the wind, Lillian had to swallow hard before answering. "I dare you to put your arms around me."

By Lisa Kleypas

Lisa KLEYPAS

It Happened One Autumn

AVON BOOKS
An Imprint of HarperCollinsPublishers

This is a work of fiction. Names, characters, places, and incidents are products of the author's imagination or are used fictitiously and are not to be construed as real. Any resemblance to actual events, locales, organizations, or persons, living or dead, is entirely coincidental.

AVON BOOKS
An Imprint of HarperCollins*Publishers*
10 East 53rd Street
New York, New York 10022-5299

Copyright © 2005 by Lisa Kleypas
Excerpt from *Devil in Winter* copyright © 2006 by Lisa Kleypas
ISBN-13: 978-0-06-056249-6
ISBN-10: 0-06-056249-8
www.avonromance.com

First Avon Books paperback printing: October 2005

Avon Trademark Reg. U.S. Pat. Off. and in Other Countries, Marca Registrada, Hecho en U.S.A.
HarperCollins® is a registered trademark of HarperCollins Publishers Inc.

Printed in the U.S.A.

10 9 8 7 6 5 4 3 2 1

To Christina Dodd,
my sister, friend and inspiration.

Love, L.K.

Prologue

London, 1843

Two young women stood at the threshold of the perfumery, one tugging impatiently at the arm of the other. "Do we *have* to go in there?" the smaller one was saying in a flat American accent, resisting as the other pulled her forcibly into the quietly lit shop. "I'm always bored to tears in these places, Lillian—you stand there and smell things for *hours*—"

"Then wait in the carriage with the maid."

"That's even *more* boring! Besides, I'm not supposed to let you go anywhere alone. You'd get into trouble without me."

The taller girl laughed with unladylike gusto as they entered the shop. "You don't want to keep me from getting into trouble, Daisy. You just don't want to be left out if I do."

"Unfortunately there's no adventure to be found in a perfume shop," came the surly reply.

A gentle chuckle greeted the statement, and the two girls turned to face the bespectacled old man who stood behind the scarred oak counter that stretched along the side of the shop. "Are you entirely certain of that, miss?" he asked, smiling as they approached him. "There are some who believe that perfume is magic. The fragrance of a thing is its purest essence. And certain scents can awaken phantoms of past love, of sweetest reminiscence."

"Phantoms?" Daisy repeated, intrigued, and the other girl replied impatiently.

"He doesn't mean it literally, dear. Perfume can't summon a ghost. And it's not really magic. It's only a mixture of scent particles that travel to the olfactory receptors in your nose."

The old man, Mr. Phineas Nettle, stared at the girls with growing interest. Neither of them was conventionally beautiful, although they were both striking, with pale skin and heavy dark hair, and a certain clean-featured appeal that seemed indigenous to American girls. "Please," he invited, gesturing to a nearby wall of shelves, "you are welcome to view my wares, Miss . . ."

"Bowman," the older girl said pleasantly. "Lillian and Daisy Bowman." She glanced at the expensively dressed blond woman whom he had been attending, seeming to understand that he was not yet at liberty to assist them.

While the indecisive customer hovered over an array of perfumes that Nettle had brought out for her, the American girls browsed among the shelves of perfumes, colognes, pomades, waxes, creams, soaps, and other items intended for beauty care. There were bath oils in stop-pered crystal bottles, and tins of herbal unguents, and tiny boxes of violet pastilles to freshen the breath. Lower shelves held treasure troves of scented candles and inks, sachets filled with clove-saturated smelling salts, potpourri bowls, and jars of pastes and balms. Nettle noticed, however, that while the younger girl, Daisy, viewed the assortment with only mild interest, the older one, Lillian, had stopped before a row of oils and extracts that contained pure scent. Rose, frangipani, jasmine, bergamot, and so forth. Lifting the amber glass bottles, she opened them carefully and inhaled with visible appreciation.

Eventually the blond woman made her choice, purchased a small flacon of perfume, and left the shop, a small bell ringing cheerfully as the door closed.

Lillian, who had turned to glance at the departing woman, murmured thoughtfully, "I wonder why it is that so many light-haired women smell of amber . . ."

"You mean amber perfume?" Daisy asked.

"No—their skin itself. Amber, and sometimes honey . . ."

"What on earth do you mean?" the younger girl asked with a bemused laugh. "People don't smell like anything, except when they need to wash."

The pair regarded each other with what appeared to be mutual surprise. "Yes, they do," Lillian said. "Everyone has a smell . . . don't say you've never noticed? The way some people's skin is like bitter almond, or violet, while others . . ."

"Others have a scent like plum, or palm sap, or fresh hay," Nettle commented.

Lillian glanced at him with a satisfied smile. "Yes, exactly!"

Nettle removed his spectacles and polished them with care, while his mind swarmed with questions. Could it be? Was it possible that this girl could actually detect a person's intrinsic scent? He himself could—but it was a rare gift, and not one that he had ever known a woman to have.

Withdrawing a slip of folded paper from a beaded bag that hung from her wrist, Lillian Bowman approached him. "I have a formula for a perfume," she said, handing him the paper, "though I'm not quite certain of the proper proportions for the ingredients. Might you be able to blend it for me?"

Nettle opened the paper and read the list, his graying brows lifting slightly. "An unconventional combination. But very interesting. It could work nicely, I think." He glanced at her with keen interest. "May I ask how you obtained this formula, Miss Bowman?"

"It came from my head." An artless smile softened her features. "I tried to think of what scents might be most effective with my own alchemy. Though as I said, the proportions are difficult for me to figure out."

Lowering his gaze to conceal his skepticism, Nettle read the formula once more. Often a customer would come to him requesting that he mix a perfume that contained a predominant scent like roses or lavender, but no one had ever given him a list like this. More interesting still was the fact that the selection of scents was unusual and yet harmonious. Perhaps it was an accident that she had managed to choose this particular combination.

"Miss Bowman," he said, curious as to how far her abilities extended, "would you allow me to show you some of my perfumes?"

"Yes, of course," came Lillian's cheerful reply. She

drew close to the counter as Nettle brought forth a small crystal bottle filled with pale, glittering fluid. "What are you doing?" she asked, while he shook out a few drops of the perfume onto a clean linen handkerchief.

"One should never inhale perfume directly from the bottle," Nettle explained, giving her the handkerchief. "You must first aerate it, to float off the alcohol . . . and then one is left with the true fragrance. Miss Bowman, what scents are you able to detect in this perfume?"

It required great effort for even the most experienced perfumers to separate the components of a blended perfume . . . minutes or even hours of repeated inhalations to discern one ingredient at a time.

Lillian lowered her head to breathe in the fragrance from the handkerchief. Without hesitation, she astonished Nettle by identifying the composition with the nimble finesse of a pianist running through practice scales. "Orange blossom . . . neroli . . . ambergris, and . . . moss?" She paused, her lashes lifting to reveal velvety-brown eyes that held a glint of puzzlement. "Moss in perfume?"

Nettle stared at her in open astonishment. The average person was severely limited in his ability to recognize the components of a complex smell. Perhaps he could identify a primary ingredient, an obvious aroma like rose, or lemon, or mint, but the layers and refinements of a particular scent were far beyond most humans' ability to detect.

Recovering his wits, Nettle smiled faintly at her question. He often graced his perfumes with peculiar notes that gave the fragrance depth and texture, but no one had ever guessed at one of them before. "The senses delight in complexity, in hidden surprises . . . here, try another." He produced a fresh handkerchief and moistened it with another perfume.

Lillian performed the task with the same miraculous ease. "Bergamot . . . tuberose . . . frankincense . . ." She hesitated, inhaling again, letting the rich spice fill her lungs. A wondering smile touched her lips. "And a hint of coffee."

"Coffee?" her sister, Daisy, exclaimed, and bent her head over the flask. "There's no coffee smell in there."

Lillian threw Nettle a questioning glance, and he smiled, confirming her guess. "Yes, it is coffee." He shook his head in admiring surprise. "You have a gift, Miss Bowman."

Shrugging, Lillian replied wryly, "A gift that's of little use while searching for a husband, I'm afraid. It's just my luck to have such a useless talent. I would do better to have a fine voice, or great beauty. As my mother says, it's impolite for a lady to like to smell things."

"Not in my shop," Nettle replied.

They proceeded to discuss aromas as other people might have discussed art they had seen in a museum: the sweet, murky, living odors of a forest after a few days of rain; the malty-sweet breeze of the sea; the musty richness of a truffle; the fresh acrid snap of a snow-filled sky. Quickly losing interest, Daisy wandered to the cosmetic shelves, opened a jar of powder that made her sneeze, and selected a tin of pastilles that she proceeded to crunch noisily.

As the conversation continued, Nettle learned that the girls' father owned a New York business enterprise that manufactured scents and soaps. From occasional visits to the company's laboratory and factories, Lillian had gained a rudimentary knowledge of fragrance and blending. She had even helped to develop a scent for one of Bowman's soaps. Her training had been nonexistent, but it was obvious to Nettle that she was a prodigy. However, such talent would go forever undeveloped because of her gender.

"Miss Bowman," he said, "I have an essence that I would like to show you. If you will be so kind as to wait here while I locate it at the back of my shop . . . ?"

Her curiosity piqued, Lillian nodded and leaned her elbows on the counter, while Nettle disappeared behind a curtained doorway that led from the shopfront to the storeroom in back. The room was filled with files of formulas, cupboards of distillations and extracts and tinctures, and shelves of utensils and funnels and mixing bottles and measuring glasses—everything necessary for his craft. On the highest shelf reposed a few linen-wrapped volumes of ancient Gallic and Greek texts on the art of perfumery. A good perfumer was part alchemist, part artist, and part wizard.

Ascending a wooden stepladder, Nettle procured a small pine box from the top shelf and brought it down. Returning to the front of the shop, he set the box on the counter. Both the Bowman sisters watched closely as he flipped open the tiny brass hinge to reveal a small bottle sealed with thread and wax. The half ounce of near-colorless fluid was the most costly essence that Nettle had ever procured.

Unsealing the bottle, he applied a precious drop to a handkerchief and gave it to Lillian. The first inhalation was light and mild, almost innocuous. But as it traveled up the nose, it became a surprisingly voluptuous fragrance, and long after the initial rush had faded, a certain sweet influence lingered.

Lillian regarded him over the edge of the handkerchief with patent wonder. "What is it?"

"A rare orchid that gives off its scent only at night," Nettle replied. "The petals are pure white, far more delicate even than jasmine. One cannot obtain the essence by heating the blossoms—they are too fragile."

"Cold enfleurage, then?" Lillian murmured, referring to the process of soaking the precious petals in sheets of fat until it was saturated with their fragrance, then using an alcohol-based solvent to draw out the pure essence.

"Yes."

She took another breath of the exquisite essence. "What is the orchid's name?"

"Lady of the Night."

That elicited a delighted chuckle from Daisy. "That sounds like the title of one of the novels my mother has forbidden me to read."

"I would suggest using the orchid's scent in place of the lavender in your formula," Nettle said. "More costly, perhaps, but in my opinion it would be the perfect base note, especially if you want amber as a fixative."

"How much more expensive?" Lillian asked, and when he named the price, her eyes widened. "Good Lord, that's more than its weight in gold."

Nettle made a show of holding the little bottle up to the light, where the liquid glittered and shimmered like a diamond. "Magic is not inexpensive, I'm afraid."

Lillian laughed, even as her gaze followed the bottle with hypnotic fascination. "Magic," she scoffed.

"This perfume will make magic happen," he insisted, smiling at her. "In fact, I will add a secret ingredient to enhance its effects."

Charmed but clearly disbelieving, Lillian made plans with Nettle to return later in the day to collect the perfume. She paid for Daisy's tin of pastilles as well as the promised fragrance, and walked outside with her younger sister. One glance at Daisy's face revealed that her younger sister's imagination, always easily stirred, was running rampant with thoughts of magic formulas and secret ingredients.

"Lillian . . . you *are* going to let me try some of that magic perfume, aren't you?"

"Don't I always share?"

"No."

Lillian grinned. Despite the sisters' pretend rivalry and occasional squabbles, they were each other's staunchest ally and closest friend. Few people in Lillian's life had ever loved her except for Daisy, who adored the ugliest stray dogs, the most annoying children, and things that needed to be repaired or thrown out altogether.

And yet for all their closeness, they were quite different. Daisy was an idealist, a dreamer, a mercurial creature who alternated between childlike whimsy and shrewd intelligence. Lillian knew herself to be a sharp-tongued girl with a fortress of defenses between herself and the rest of the world—a girl with well-maintained cynicism and a biting sense of humor. She was intensely loyal to the small circle of people in her sphere, especially the wallflowers, the self-named group of girls who had met while sitting at the side of every ball and soiree last season. Lillian, Daisy, and their friends Annabelle Peyton and Evangeline Jenner had all sworn to help one another find husbands. Their efforts had resulted in Annabelle's successful match with Mr. Simon Hunt just two months ago. Now Lillian was next in line. As of yet, they had no clear idea about whom they were going to catch, or a solid plan for how they were going to get him.

"Of course I'll let you try the perfume," Lillian said.

"Though heaven knows what you expect from it."

"It's going to make a handsome duke fall madly in love with me, *naturally*," Daisy replied.

"Have you noticed how few men in the peerage are young and nice-looking?" Lillian asked wryly. "Most of them are dull-witted, ancient, or possess the kind of face that should have a hook in its mouth."

Daisy snickered and slid an arm around her waist. "The right gentlemen are out there," she said. "And we're going to find them."

"Why are you so certain?" Lillian asked wryly.

Daisy gave her an impish smile. "Because we've got magic on our side."

Chapter 1

Stony Cross Park, Hampshire

"The Bowmans have arrived," Lady Olivia Shaw announced from the doorway of the study, where her older brother sat at his desk amid stacks of account books. The late afternoon sun streamed through the long, rectangular stained-glass windows, which were the only ornamentation in the austere, rosewood-paneled room.

Marcus, Lord Westcliff, glanced up from his work with a scowl that drew his dark brows together over his coffee-black eyes. "Let the mayhem begin," he muttered.

Livia laughed. "I assume you're referring to the daughters? They're not as bad as all that, are they?"

"Worse," Marcus said succinctly, his scowl deepening as he saw that the temporarily forgotten pen in his fingers had left a large blot of ink on the otherwise immaculate row of figures. "Two more ill-mannered young women I have yet to meet. The older one, particularly."

"Well, they are Americans," Livia pointed out. "It's only fair that one should give them a certain latitude, isn't it? One can hardly expect them to know every elaborate detail of our endless list of social rules—"

"I can allow them latitude on details," Marcus interrupted curtly. "As you know, I am not the kind to fault the angle of Miss Bowman's pinkie finger as she holds her teacup. What I do take exception to are certain behaviors that would be found objectionable in every corner of the civilized world."

Behaviors? thought Livia. Now, this was getting interesting. Livia advanced farther into the study, a room that she usually disliked, because it reminded her so strongly of their deceased father.

Any recollection of the eighth Earl of Westcliff was not a happy one. Their father had been an unloving and cruel man, who had seemed to suck all the oxygen from the room when he entered it. Everything and everyone in his life had disappointed the earl. Of his three offspring, only Marcus had come close to meeting his exacting standards, for no matter what punishments the earl had meted out, no matter how impossible his requirements or unfair his judgments, Marcus had never complained.

Livia and her sister, Aline, had been in awe of their older brother, whose constant striving for excellence led him to get the highest marks in school, to break all records in his chosen sports, and to judge himself far more harshly than anyone else ever could. Marcus was a man who could break a horse, dance a quadrille, give a lecture on mathematical theory, bandage a wound, and fix a carriage wheel. None of his vast array of accomplishments, however, had ever earned a word of praise from their father.

In retrospect, Livia realized that it must have been the old earl's intent to drive every lingering touch of softness or compassion out of his only son. And it had seemed for a while that he had succeeded. However, upon the old earl's death five years ago, Marcus had proved himself to be a very different man from the one he had been reared to be. Livia and Aline had discovered that their older brother was never too busy to listen to them, and that no matter how insignificant their problems seemed, he was always ready to help. He was sympathetic, affectionate, and understanding—miraculous, really, when once realized that for most of his life, none of those qualities had ever been shown to him.

That being said, Marcus was also a bit domineering. Well . . . *very* domineering. When it came to those he loved, Marcus showed no compunction about manipulating them into doing what he thought was best. This was not one of his more charming attributes. And if Livia were to dwell on his faults, she would also have to admit that Marcus had an annoying belief in his own infallibility.

Smiling fondly at her charismatic brother, Livia wondered how it was that she could adore him so when he bore the physical stamp of their father so strongly. Marcus had the same harsh-hewn features, broad forehead, and wide, thin-lipped mouth. He had the same thick, raven-black hair; the same bold, broad nose; and the same stubbornly jutting chin. The combination was striking rather than handsome . . . but it was a face that attracted female gazes easily. Unlike their father's, Marcus's alert dark eyes were often filled with glinting laughter, and he possessed a rare smile that flashed startling white in his swarthy face.

Leaning back in his chair at Livia's approach, Marcus laced his fingers together and rested them on the hard surface of his stomach. In deference to the unseasonable warmth of the early September afternoon, Marcus had removed his coat and rolled up his sleeves, revealing muscular brown forearms lightly dusted with black hair. He was of medium height and extraordinarily fit, with the powerful physique of an avid sportsman.

Eager to hear more about the aforementioned behaviors of the ill-bred Miss Bowman, Livia leaned back against the edge of the desk, facing Marcus. "I wonder what Miss Bowman did to offend you so?" she mused aloud. "Do tell, Marcus. If not, my imagination will surely conjure up something far more scandalous than poor Miss Bowman is capable of."

"Poor Miss Bowman?" Marcus snorted. "Don't ask, Livia. I'm not at liberty to discuss it."

Like most men, Marcus didn't seem to understand that *nothing* torched the flames of a woman's curiosity more violently than a subject that one was not at liberty to discuss. "Out with it, Marcus," she commanded. "Or I shall make you suffer in unspeakable ways."

One of his brows lifted in a sardonic arch. "Since the Bowmans have already arrived, that threat is redundant."

"I'll make a guess, then. Did you catch Miss Bowman with someone? Was she allowing some gentleman to kiss her . . . or *worse?*"

Marcus responded with a derisive half smile. "Hardly. One look at her, and any man in his right mind would run screaming in the opposite direction."

Beginning to feel that her brother was being rather too

harsh on Lillian Bowman, Livia frowned. "She's a very pretty girl, Marcus."

"A pretty facade isn't enough to make up for the flaws in her character."

"Which are?"

Marcus made a faint scoffing sound, as if Miss Bowman's faults were too obvious to require enumeration. "She's manipulative."

"So are you, dear," Livia murmured.

He ignored that. "She's domineering."

"As are you."

"She's arrogant."

"Also you," Livia said brightly.

Marcus glowered at her. "I thought we were discussing Miss Bowman's faults, not mine."

"But you seem to have so much in common," Livia protested, rather too innocently. She watched as he set the pen down, aligning it with the other articles on his desk. "Regarding her inappropriate behavior—are you saying that you did *not* catch her in a compromising situation?"

"No, I didn't say that. I only said that she wasn't with a gentleman."

"Marcus, I don't have time for this," Livia said impatiently. "I must go welcome the Bowmans—and so must you—but before we leave this study, I demand that you tell me what scandalous thing she was doing!"

"It's too ridiculous to say."

"Was she riding a horse astride? Smoking a cigar? Swimming naked in a pond?"

"Not quite." Moodily Marcus picked up a stereoscope that was poised on the corner of the desk—a birthday gift that had been sent from their sister, Aline, who was now living with her husband in New York. The stereoscope was a brand-new invention, fashioned of maple wood and glass. When a stereo card—a double photograph—was clipped on the extension behind the lens, the picture appeared as a three-dimensional image. The depth and detail of the stereo photographs were startling . . . the twigs of a tree seemed likely to scratch the viewer's nose, and a mountain chasm yawned open with such realism that it seemed you might fall to your death at any moment. Lifting the stereoscope to his eyes, Marcus examined the view of the Colosseum in Rome with undue concentration.

Just as Livia was about to explode with impatience, Marcus muttered, "I saw Miss Bowman playing rounders in her undergarments."

Livia stared at him blankly. "Rounders? Do you mean the game with the leather ball and flat-sided bat?"

Marcus's mouth twisted impatiently. "It occurred during her last visit here. Miss Bowman and her sister were cavorting with their friends in a meadow on the northwest quadrant of the estate, when Simon Hunt and I happened to be riding by. All four of the girls were in their undergarments—they claimed that it was difficult to play the game in heavy skirts. My guess is that they would have seized on any excuse to run about half naked. The Bowman sisters are hedonists."

Livia had clapped her hand over her mouth in a not-very-successful effort to stifle a fit of laughter. "I can't believe you haven't mentioned it before now!"

"I wish I could forget," Marcus replied grimly, lowering the stereoscope. "God knows how I'm going to meet Thomas Bowman's gaze while the memory of his unclothed daughter is still fresh in my mind."

Livia's amusement lingered as she contemplated the

bold lines of her brother's profile. She did not fail to note that Marcus had said "daughter," not "daughters"—which made it clear that he had barely noticed the younger one. Lillian was the one he had focused on.

Knowing Marcus as she did, Livia would have expected him to be amused by the incident. Although her brother possessed a strong sense of morality, he was the farthest thing from a prig, and he had a keen sense of humor. Although Marcus had never kept a mistress, Livia had heard the rumors about a few discreet affairs—and she had even heard a whisper or two that the outwardly straitlaced earl was decidedly adventurous in the bedroom. But for some reason her brother was disturbed by this red-blooded, audacious American girl with raw manners and new money. Shrewdly Livia wondered if the Marsden family's attraction to Americans—after all, Aline had married one, and she herself had just wed Gideon Shaw, of the New York Shaws—was holding true for Marcus as well.

"Was she terribly ravishing in her underclothes?" Livia asked craftily.

"Yes," Marcus said without thinking, and then scowled. "I mean, *no*. That is, I didn't look at her long enough to make an assessment of her charms. If she has any."

Livia bit the inside of her lower lip to keep from laughing. "Come, Marcus . . . you are a healthy man of thirty-five—and you didn't take one tiny *peep* at Miss Bowman standing there in her drawers?"

"I don't peep, Livia. I either take a good look at something, or I don't. Peeping is for children or deviants."

She gave him a deeply pitying glance. "Well, I'm dreadfully sorry that you had to endure such a trying experience. We can only hope that Miss Bowman will stay fully clothed in your presence during this visit, to avoid shocking your refined sensibilities once again."

Marcus frowned in response to the mockery. "I doubt she will."

"Do you mean that you doubt she will stay fully clothed, or you doubt she will shock you?"

"*Enough,* Livia," he growled, and she giggled.

"Come, we must go and welcome the Bowmans."

"I don't have time for that," Marcus said curtly. "You welcome them, and make some excuse for me."

Livia stared at him in astonishment. "You're not going to . . . oh, but Marcus, you must! I've never known you to be rude before."

"I'll atone for it later. For God's sake, they're going to be here for nearly a month—I'll have ample opportunity to placate them. But talking about that Bowman girl has put me in a foul mood, and right now the thought of being in the same room with her sets my teeth on edge."

Shaking her head slightly, Livia regarded him in a speculative way that he did not like. "Hmm. I've seen you interact with people that I know you dislike, and you always manage to be civil—especially when you want something from them. But for some reason Miss Bowman provokes you excessively. I have a theory as to why."

"Oh?" Subtle challenge lit his eyes.

"I am still developing it. I will let you know when I've come to a definitive conclusion."

"God help me. Just *go,* Livia, and welcome the guests."

"While you hole up in this study like a fox run to ground?"

Standing, Marcus gestured for her to precede him through the doorway. "I'm leaving through the back of the house, and then I'm going for a long ride."

"How long will you be away?"

"I'll be back in time to change for supper."

Livia heaved an exasperated sigh. Supper this evening would be a heavily attended affair. It was the prelude to the first official day of the house party, which would begin in full force tomorrow. Most of the guests had already arrived, with a few stragglers due to arrive soon. "You had better not be late," she warned. "When I agreed to act as your hostess, it was not with the understanding that I was going to handle everything by myself."

"I am never late," Marcus replied evenly, and strode away with the eagerness of a man who had suddenly been spared from the gallows.

Chapter 2

*M*arcus rode away from the manor, guiding his horse along the well-traveled forest path beyond the gardens. As soon as he crossed a sunken lane and ascended the incline on the other side, he gave the animal its head, until they were thundering across fields of meadowsweet and sun-dried grass. Stony Cross Park possessed the finest acreage in Hampshire, with thick forests, brilliantly flowered wet meadows and bogs, and wide golden fields. Once reserved as hunting grounds for royalty, the estate was now one of the most sought-after places to visit in England.

It suited Marcus's purposes to have a more or less constant stream of guests at the estate, providing ample company for the hunting and sports that he loved, and also allowing for quite a bit of financial and political maneuvering. All kinds of business were done at these house parties, at which Marcus often persuaded a certain politician or professional man to side with him on important issues.

This party should be no different from any other—but for the past few days, Marcus had been deviled by a growing sense of unease. As a supremely rational man, he did not believe in psychic premonitions, or any of the spiritualist nonsense that was becoming fashionable of late . . . but it did seem as if something in the atmosphere at Stony Cross Park had changed. The air was charged with expectant tension, like the vibrant calm before a storm. Marcus felt restless and impatient, and no amount of physical exertion seemed to pacify his growing disquiet.

Contemplating the evening ahead of him, and the knowledge that he would have to hobnob with the Bowmans, Marcus felt his unease sharpen into something approaching anxiety. He regretted having invited them. In fact, he would gladly forgo any potential business deal with Thomas Bowman if he could just be rid of them. However, the fact was that they were here, and would stay for well nigh a month, and he might as well make the best of things.

Marcus intended to launch into an active negotiation with Thomas Bowman about expanding his soap company to establish a production division in Liverpool or, perhaps, Bristol. The British soap tax was almost certain to be repealed in the next few years, if Marcus's liberal allies in Parliament were to be trusted. When that happened, soap would become far more affordable for the common man, which would be good for the public health and, conveniently, also good for Marcus's bank account, hinging on Bowman's willingness to take him on as a partner.

However, there was no escaping the fact that a visit from Thomas Bowman meant enduring his daughters' presence as well. Lillian and Daisy were the embodiment

of the objectionable trend of American heiresses coming
to England to husband-hunt. The peerage was being set
upon by ambitious misses who gushed about themselves
in their atrocious accents and constantly angled for pub-
licity in the papers. Graceless, loud, self-important
young women who sought to purchase a peer with their
parents' money . . . and often succeeded.

Marcus had become acquainted with the Bowman sisters on their previous visit to Stony Cross Park, and had
found little to recommend either of them. The older one,
Lillian, had become a particular focus of his dislike when
she and her friends—the wallflowers, they called themselves (as if it were something to be proud of!)—had engi-
neered a scheme to entrap a peer into marriage. Marcus
would never forget the moment when the scheme had
been exposed. "Good God, is there nothing you won't
stoop to?" Marcus had asked Lillian. And she had replied
brazenly, "If there is, I haven't discovered it yet."

Her extraordinary insolence made her different from
any other woman of Marcus's acquaintance. That, and
the rounders game they had played in their drawers, had
convinced him that Lillian Bowman was a hellion. And
once he had passed judgment on someone, he rarely
changed his opinion.

Frowning, Marcus considered the best way to deal with
Lillian. He would be cool and detached, no matter what
provocation she offered. No doubt it would infuriate her
to see how little she affected him. Picturing her irritation
at being ignored, he felt the tightness in his chest ease.
Yes . . . he would do his utmost to avoid her, and when
circumstances forced them to occupy the same room, he
would treat her with cold politeness. His frown clearing,
Marcus guided his horse over a series of easy jumps; a

hedge, a fence and a narrow stone wall, rider and animal working together in perfect coordination.

"Now, girls," Mrs. Mercedes Bowman said, regarding her daughters sternly as she stood in the doorway of their room, "I insist that you nap for at least two hours, so that you will be fresh for this evening. Lord Westcliff's dinners usually start late, and last till midnight, and I don't want either of you to yawn at the table."

"Yes, Mother," they both said dutifully, regarding her with innocent expressions that did not deceive her in the least.

Mrs. Bowman was a rampantly ambitious woman with an abundance of nervous energy. Her spindle-thin body would have made a whippet look chubby. Her anxious, hard-edged chatter was usually directed toward advancing her main objective in life: to see that both her daughters were brilliantly married. "Under no circumstances are you to leave this room," she continued sternly. "No sneaking about on Lord Westcliff's estate, no adventures, scrapes, or happenings of any kind. In fact, I intend to lock the door to ensure that you stay safely in here and *rest.*"

"Mother," Lillian protested, "if there is a duller spot in the civilized world than Stony Cross, I'll eat my shoes. What possible trouble could we get into?"

"You create trouble from thin air," Mercedes said, her eyes slitted. "Which is why I am going to supervise the pair of you closely. After your behavior on our last visit here, I am amazed that we were invited back."

"I'm not," Lillian rejoined dryly. "Everyone knows that we're here because Westcliff has an eye on Father's company."

"*Lord* Westcliff," Mercedes corrected with a hiss.

"Lillian, you must refer to him with respect! He is the wealthiest peer in England, with a bloodline—"

"—that's older than the queen's," Daisy interrupted in a singsong tone, having heard this speech on a multitude of occasions. "And the oldest earldom in Britain, which makes him—"

"—the most eligible bachelor in Europe," Lillian finished dryly, raising her brows with mock significance. "Maybe the entire *world*. Mother, if you're actually hoping that Westcliff is going to marry either of us, you're a lunatic."

"She's not a lunatic," Daisy told her sister. "She's a New Yorker."

There were an increasing number of the Bowmans' kind back in New York—upstarts who could not manage to blend with either the conservative Knickerbockers, or the highly fashionable crowd. These parvenu families had garnered massive fortunes from industries such as manufacturing or mining, and yet they could not gain acceptance in the circles that they aspired to so desperately. The loneliness and embarrassment of being so thoroughly rejected by New York society had fueled Mercedes's ambitions as nothing else could have.

"We're going to make Lord Westcliff forget all about your atrocious behavior during our last visit," Mercedes informed them grimly. "You will be modest, quiet, and demure at all times—and there will be no more of this wallflower business. I want you to stay away from that scandalous Annabelle Peyton, and that other one, that—"

"Evie Jenner," Daisy said. "And it's Annabelle Hunt now, Mother."

"Annabelle did marry Westcliff's best friend," Lillian pointed out idly. "I should think that would be an excellent reason for us to continue seeing her, Mother."

"I'll consider it." Mercedes regarded them both suspiciously. "In the meantime, I intend for you to take a long, quiet nap. I don't want to hear a sound from either of you, do you understand?"

"Yes, Mother," they both chorused.

The door closed, and the outside key turned firmly in the lock.

The sisters regarded each other with a shared grin. "It's a good thing that she never found out about the rounders game," Lillian said.

"We would be dead now," Daisy agreed gravely.

Lillian fished a hairpin from a small enameled box on the vanity table and went to the door. "A pity that she gets so upset about little things, isn't it?"

"Like the time we sneaked the greased piglet into Mrs. Astor's parlor."

Smiling reminiscently, Lillian knelt before the door and worked the pin into the lock. "You know, I've always wondered why Mother didn't appreciate that we did it in her defense. *Something* had to be done after Mrs. Astor wouldn't invite Mother to her party."

"I think Mother's point was that putting livestock in someone's house does little to recommend us as future party guests."

"Well, I didn't think that was nearly as bad as the time we set off the Roman candle in the store on Fifth Avenue."

"We were obligated to do that, after that salesman had been so rude."

Withdrawing the pin, Lillian expertly crimped one end with her fingers and reinserted it. Squinting with effort, she maneuvered the pin until the lock clicked, and then she glanced at Daisy with a triumphant smile. "That was my fastest time yet, I think."

However, her younger sister did not return the smile. "Lillian . . . if you do find a husband this year . . . everything's going to change. You'll change. And then there will be no more adventures, or fun, and I'll be alone."

"Don't be silly," Lillian said with a frown. "I'm not going to change, and you won't be alone."

"You'll have a husband to answer to," Daisy pointed out. "And he won't allow you to be involved in any mischief making with me."

"No, no, no . . ." Lillian stood and waved a hand in a dismissive gesture. "I'm not going to have *that* kind of husband. I'm going to marry a man who either won't notice or won't care about what I do when I'm away from him. A man like Father."

"A man like Father doesn't seem to have made Mother very happy," Daisy said. "I wonder if they were ever in love?"

Leaning back against the door, Lillian frowned as she contemplated the question. It had never occurred to her before now to wonder if her parents' marriage had been a love match. Somehow she didn't think so. They both seemed entirely self-contained. Their partnership was at best a negligible bond. To Lillian's knowledge, they seldom argued, never embraced, and rarely even spoke. And yet there was no apparent bitterness between them. Rather they were indifferent to each other, with neither evincing any desire or even aptitude for happiness.

"Love is for the novels, dear," Lillian said, trying her best to sound cynical. Easing the door open, she peeked up and down the hallway, and glanced back at Daisy.

"All clear. Shall we slip out the servants' entrance?"

"Yes, and then let's go to the west side of the manor, and head into the forest."

"Why the forest?"

"Do you remember the favor that Annabelle asked of me?"

Lillian stared at her for a moment of incomprehension, and then she rolled her eyes. "Good God, Daisy, can't you think of something better to do than carry out a ridiculous errand like that?"

Her younger sister gave her an astute glance. "You just don't want to because it's for Lord Westcliff's benefit."

"It's not going to benefit *anyone*," Lillian replied with exasperation. "It's a fool's errand."

Daisy responded with a resolute stare. "I'm going to find the Stony Cross wishing well," she said with great dignity, "and do as Annabelle asked of me. You may accompany me if you wish, or you can do something else by yourself. However"—her almond-shaped eyes narrowed threateningly—"after all the time you've made me wait while you browse through dusty old perfume shops and apothecaries, I should think that you owe me just a little forbearance—"

"All right," Lillian grumbled. "I'll go with you. If I don't, you'll never find it, and you'll end up lost in the forest somewhere." Looking out into the hallway again, and ascertaining that it was still empty, Lillian led the way toward the servants' entrance at the end of it. The sisters tiptoed with practiced stealth, their feet noiseless on the thick carpeting underfoot.

Much as Lillian disliked the owner of Stony Cross Park, she had to admit that it was a splendid estate. The house was of European design, a graceful fortress made of honey-colored stone, cornered by four picturesque towers that stretched toward the sky. Set on a bluff overlooking the Itchen River, the manor was surrounded by terraced gardens and orchards that flowed into two hundred acres of parkland and wild forests. Fifteen generations of Westcliff's family, the Marsdens, had occupied the manor, as any of the servants were quick to point out. And this was hardly the full extent of Lord Westcliff's wealth. It was said that nearly two hundred thousand acres of England and Scotland were under his direct control, while among his estates were numbered two castles, three halls, a terrace, five houses, and a villa on the Thames. Stony Cross Park, however, was undoubtedly the jewel in the Marsden family crown.

Skirting the side of the manor, the sisters took care to keep close to a long yew hedge that sheltered them from view of the main house. Sunlight glittered through the canopy of interlaced branches overhead as they entered the forest, populated with ancient cedars and oaks.

Exuberantly Daisy threw her arms into the air and exclaimed, "Oh, I adore this place!"

"It's passable," Lillian said grudgingly, though she had to admit privately that in this full-flowered early autumn, there could hardly be a more beautiful part of England than this.

Hopping onto a log that had been pushed to the side of the path, Daisy walked carefully along it. "It would almost be worth marrying Lord Westcliff, don't you think, to be mistress of Stony Cross Park?"

Lillian arched her brows. "And then have to endure all his pompous pronouncements, and be expected to obey his every command?" She pulled a face, wrinkling her nose in distaste.

"Annabelle says that Lord Westcliff is actually much nicer than she originally thought."

"She would *have* to say that, after what happened a few weeks ago."

The sisters fell silent, both reflecting on the dramatic events that had occurred recently. As Annabelle and her husband, Simon Hunt, had been touring the locomotive works that they owned along with Lord Westcliff, a horrific explosion had nearly claimed their lives. Lord Westcliff had dashed into the building on a near-suicidal mission to save them, and had brought them both out alive. Understandably, Annabelle now viewed Westcliff in a heroic light, and had actually said recently that she thought his arrogance was rather endearing. Lillian had replied sourly that Annabelle must still be suffering the aftereffects of smoke inhalation.

"I think we owe Lord Westcliff our gratitude," Daisy remarked, hopping off the log. "After all, he did save Annabelle's life, and it's not as if we have a terribly large array of friends to begin with."

"Saving Annabelle was incidental," Lillian said grumpily. "The only reason that Westcliff risked his life was so he wouldn't lose a profitable business partner."

"Lillian!" Daisy, who was a few steps ahead, turned to view her with surprise. "It's not like you to be so uncharitable. For heaven's sake, the earl went into a burning building to rescue our friend and her husband . . . what more does the man have to do to impress you?"

"I'm sure Westcliff couldn't care less about impressing me," Lillian said. Hearing the sullen note in her own voice, she winced, even as she continued. "The reason I dislike him so, Daisy, is that he so obviously dislikes *me*. He considers himself to be my superior in every possible way; morally and socially and intellectually . . . oh, how I long for a way to set him back on his heels!"

They walked along in silence for a minute, and then Daisy paused to pluck some violets that were growing in thick clusters on the side of the path. "Have you ever considered trying to be nice to Lord Westcliff?" she murmured. Reaching up to tuck the violets into the pinned-up garlands of her hair, she added, "He might surprise you by responding in kind."

Lillian shook her head grimly. "No, he would probably say something cutting, and then look very smug and pleased with himself."

"I think you're being too . . ." Daisy began, and then paused with an absorbed expression. "I hear a sloshing sound. The wishing well must be near!"

"Oh, glory," Lillian said, smiling reluctantly as she followed her younger sister, who was scampering along a sunken lane that was sided by a wet meadow. The swampy meadow was thick with blue and purple asters, and sedge with its bottlebrush flowers, and rustling spikes of goldenrod. Close to the road, there was a heavy thicket of St. John's wort, with clusters of yellow blossoms that looked like drops of sunlight. Luxuriating in the balmy atmosphere, Lillian slowed her pace and breathed deeply. As she approached the churning wishing well, which was a spring-fed hole in the ground, the air became soft and humid.

At the beginning of summer, when the wallflowers had visited the wishing well, they had each thrown a pin into its frothing depths, in keeping with local tradition. And Daisy had made some mysterious wish for Annabelle that had later come true.

"Here it is," Daisy said, producing a needle-thin metallic shard from her pocket. It was the metal filing that Annabelle had pulled from Westcliff's shoulder when exploding debris had sent bits of iron flying through the air like grapeshot. Even Lillian, who was hardly disposed to have any sympathy for Westcliff, winced at the sight of the wicked-looking shard. "Annabelle told me to throw this into the well and make the same wish for Lord Westcliff that I did for her."

"What was the wish?" Lillian demanded. "You never told me."

Daisy regarded her with a quizzical smile. "Isn't it obvious, dear? I wished that Annabelle would marry someone who truly loved her."

"Oh." Contemplating what she knew of Annabelle's marriage, and the obvious devotion between the pair, Lillian supposed the wish must have worked. Giving Daisy a fondly exasperated glance, she stood back to watch the proceedings.

"Lillian," her sister protested, "you must stand here with me. The well spirit will be far more likely to grant the wish if we're both concentrating on it."

A low laugh escaped Lillian's throat. "You don't really believe there's a well spirit, do you? Good God, how did you ever become so superstitious?"

"Coming from one who recently purchased a bottle of magic perfume—"

"I never thought it was magic. I only liked the smell!"

"Lillian," Daisy chided playfully, "what's the harm in allowing for the possibility? I refuse to believe that we're going to go through life without *something* magical happening. Now, come make a wish for Lord Westcliff. It's the least we can do, after he saved dear Annabelle from the fire."

"Oh, all right. I'll stand next to you—but only to keep you from falling in." Coming even with her sister, Lillian hooked an arm around her sister's slim shoulders and stared into the muddy, rustling water.

Daisy closed her eyes tightly and wrapped her fingers around the metal shard. "I'm wishing very hard," she whispered. "Are you, Lillian?"

"Yes," Lillian murmured, though she wasn't precisely hoping for Lord Westcliff to find true love. Her wish was more along the lines of, *I hope that Lord Westcliff will meet a woman who will bring him to his knees.* The thought caused a satisfied smile to curve her lips, and she continued to smile as Daisy tossed the sharp bit of metal into the well, where it sank into the endless depths below.

Dusting her hands together, Daisy turned away from the well with satisfaction. "There, all done," she said, beaming. "I can hardly wait to see whom Westcliff ends up with."

"I pity the poor girl," Lillian replied, "whoever she is."

Daisy tilted her head back in the direction of the manor. "Back to the house?"

The conversation quickly turned into a strategy-planning session, as they discussed an idea that Annabelle had mentioned the last time they had talked. The Bowmans desperately needed a social sponsor to introduce them into the higher tiers of British society . . . and not just any sponsor. It had to be someone who was powerful and influential, and widely renowned. Someone whose endorsement would have to be accepted by the rest of the peerage. According to Annabelle, there was no one who fit the bill more than the Countess of Westcliff, the earl's mother.

The countess, who seemed fond of traveling the continent, was rarely seen. Even when in residence at Stony Cross Manor, she chose to mix very little with the guests, decrying her son's habit of befriending professional men and other nonaristocrats. Neither of the Bowman sisters had ever actually met the countess, but they had heard plenty. If the rumors were to be believed, the countess was a crusty old dragon who despised foreigners. Especially American foreigners.

"Why Annabelle thinks there is any chance of getting the countess to be our sponsor is beyond my comprehension," Daisy said, kicking a small rock repeatedly before them as they walked along the path. "She'll never do so willingly, that's for certain."

"She will if Westcliff tells her to," Lillian replied. Picking up a large stick, she swung it absently. "Apparently the countess can be made to do something if Westcliff demands it. Annabelle told me that the countess didn't approve of Lady Olivia marrying Mr. Shaw, and she had no intention of attending the wedding. But Westcliff knew that it would hurt his sister's feelings terribly, and so he forced his mother to stay, and furthermore, he made her put on a civil face about it."

"Really?" Daisy glanced at her with a curious half smile. "I wonder how he did that?"

"By being the master of the house. Back in America the woman is the ruler of the home, but in England everything revolves around the man."

"Hmm. I don't like that much."

"Yes, I know." Lillian paused before adding darkly, "According to Annabelle, the English husband has to give his approval of the menus, the furniture arrangement, the color of the window hangings . . . *everything*."

Daisy looked surprised and appalled. "Does Mr. Hunt bother with such things?"

"Well, no—he's not a peer. He's a professional man. And men of business don't usually have time for such trivialities. But your average peer has much time in which to examine every little thing that goes on in the house."

Leaving off her rock kicking, Daisy regarded Lillian with a frown. "I've been wondering . . . why are we so determined to marry into the peerage, and live in a huge crumbly old house and eat slimy English food, and try to give instructions to a bunch of servants who have absolutely no respect for us?"

"Because it's what Mother wants," Lillian replied dryly. "And because no one in New York will have either of us." It was an unfortunate fact that in the highly striated New York society, men with newly earned fortunes found it quite easy to marry well. But heiresses with common bloodlines were desired neither by the established blue bloods nor by the nouveau riche men who wanted to better themselves socially. Therefore, husband hunting in Europe, where upper-class men needed rich wives, was the only solution.

Daisy's frown twisted into an ironic grin. "What if no one will have us here either?"

"Then we'll become a pair of wicked old spinsters, romping back and forth across Europe."

Daisy laughed at the notion and flipped a long braid over her back. It was improper for young women of their age to walk about hatless, much less with their hair hanging down. However, both of the Bowman sisters had such a wealth of heavy dark locks that it was an ordeal to pin it all up in the intricate coiffures that were so fashionable. It required at least three racks of pins for each of them, and

Lillian's sensitive scalp literally ached after all the tugging and twisting required to make her hair presentable for a formal evening. More than once she had envied Annabelle Hunt, who had light, silky locks that always seemed to behave exactly as she wished them to. At the moment Lillian had tied her hair at the nape of the neck and allowed it to fall down her back in a style that never would have been allowed in company.

"How are we going to persuade Westcliff to make his mother act as our sponsor?" Daisy asked. "It seems very unlikely that he would ever agree to do such a thing."

Drawing back her arm, Lillian flung the stick far into the woods, and brushed the flecks of bark from her palms. "I have no idea," she admitted. "Annabelle has tried to get Mr. Hunt to ask him on our behalf, but he refuses on the grounds that it would be an abuse of their friendship."

"If only we could compel Westcliff in some way," Daisy mused. "Trick him, or blackmail him, somehow."

"You can only blackmail a man if he's done something shameful that he wants to hide. And I doubt that stodgy, boring old Westcliff has ever done anything that's worthy of blackmail."

Daisy chuckled at the description. "He's not stodgy, boring, or even that old!"

"Mother says he's at least thirty-five. I'd say that is fairly old, wouldn't you?"

"I'll wager that most men in their twenties aren't nearly as fit as Westcliff."

As always, when a conversation turned to the subject of Westcliff, Lillian felt thoroughly provoked, not unlike the way she had felt in childhood when her brothers had tossed her favorite doll over her head, back and forth between them, while she cried for them to give it back to her. Why any mention of the earl should affect her this way was a question for which there was no answer. She dismissed Daisy's remark with an irritable shrug of her shoulders.

As they drew closer to the house, they heard a few happy yelps in the distance, followed by some youthful cheers that sounded like those of children playing. "What is that?" Lillian asked, glancing in the direction of the stables.

"I don't know, but it sounds as if someone is having an awfully good time. Let's go see."

"We don't have long," Lillian warned. "If Mother discovers that we're gone—"

"We'll hurry. Oh, please, Lillian!"

As they hesitated, a few more hoots and shouts of laughter floated from the direction of the stable yard, offering such a contrast to the peaceful scenery around them that Lillian's curiosity got the better of her. She grinned recklessly at Daisy. "I'll race you there," she said, and took off at a dead run.

Daisy hiked up her skirts and tore after her. Although Daisy's legs were far shorter than Lillian's, she was as light and agile as an elf, and she had nearly come even with Lillian by the time they had reached the stable yard. Puffing lightly from the effort of running up a long incline, Lillian rounded the outside of a neatly fenced paddock, and saw a group of five boys, varying in ages between twelve and sixteen, playing in the small field just beyond. Their attire identified them as stable boys. Their boots had been discarded beside the paddock, and they were running barefoot.

"Do you *see?*" Daisy asked eagerly.

Glancing over the group, Lillian saw one of them

brandishing a long willow bat in the air, and she laughed in delight. "They're playing rounders!"

Although the game, consisting of a bat, a ball, and four sanctuary bases arranged in a diamond pattern, was popular in both America and England, it had reached a level of obsessive interest in New York. Boys and girls of all classes played the game, and Lillian longingly remembered many a picnic followed by an afternoon of rounders. Warm nostalgia filled her as she watched a stable boy round the bases. It was clear that the field was often used for this purpose, as the sanctuary posts had been hammered deeply into the ground, and the areas between them had been trampled to form grass-free lanes of dirt. Lillian recognized one of the players as the lad who had loaned her the rounders bat for the wallflowers' ill-fated game two months earlier.

"Do you think they would let us play?" Daisy asked hopefully. "Just for a few minutes?"

"I don't see why not. That red-haired boy—he was the one who let us borrow the bat before. I think his name is Arthur . . ."

At that moment a low, fast pitch streaked toward the batter, who swung in a short, expert arc. The flat side of the bat connected solidly with the leather ball, and it came hurtling toward them in a bouncing drive that was referred to as a "hopper" back in New York. Running forward, Lillian scooped up the ball in her bare hands and fielded it expertly, throwing it to the boy who stood at the first sanctuary post. He caught it reflexively, staring at her with surprise. As the other boys noticed the pair of young women who stood beside the paddock, they all paused uncertainly.

Lillian strode forward, her gaze finding the red-haired

boy. "Arthur? Do you remember me? I was here in June—you loaned us the bat."

The boy's puzzled expression cleared. "Oh yes, Miss . . . Miss . . ."

"Bowman." Lillian gestured casually to Daisy. "And this is my sister. We were just wondering . . . would you let us play? Just for a little while?"

A dumbfounded silence ensued. Lillian gathered that while it had been acceptable to loan her the bat, allowing her into a game with the other stable boys was another thing entirely. "We're not all that bad, actually," she said. "We both used to play quite a lot in New York. If you're worried that we would slow your game—"

"Oh, it's not that, Miss Bowman," Arthur protested, his face turning as red as his hair. He glanced at his companions uncertainly before returning his attention to her. "It's just that . . . ladies of your sort . . . you can't . . . we're *in service,* miss."

"It's your off-time, isn't it?" Lillian countered.

The boy nodded cautiously.

"Well, it's our off-time too," Lillian said. "And it's only a little game of rounders. Oh, do let us play—we'll never tell!"

"Offer to show him your spitter," Daisy said out of the corner of her mouth. "Or the hornet."

Staring at the boys' unresponsive faces, Lillian complied. "I can pitch," she said, raising her brows significantly. "Fast balls, spit balls, hornet balls . . . don't you want to see how Americans throw?"

That intrigued them, she could see. However, Arthur said diffidently, "Miss Bowman, if someone was to see you playing rounders in the stable yard, we'd likely get the blame for it, and then—"

"No, you wouldn't," Lillian said. "I promise you, we'll take full responsibility if anyone catches us. I'll tell them that we left you no choice."

Though the group as a whole looked openly skeptical, Lillian and Daisy badgered and pleaded until they were finally allowed into the game. Taking possession of a worn leather-covered ball, Lillian flexed her arms, cracked her knuckles, and assumed a pitcher's stance as she faced the batter, who stood at the base designated Castle Rock. Shifting her weight to her left foot, she stepped into the throw, launching the ball in a fast, competent pitch. It landed with a stinging smack in the catcher's hand, while the batter swung and missed completely. A few admiring whistles greeted Lillian's effort.

"Not a bad arm for a girl!" was Arthur's comment, causing her to grin. "Now, miss, if you wouldn't mind, what was that hornet ball you were talking about?"

Catching the ball as it was thrown back to her, Lillian faced the batter again, this time gripping the ball with only her thumb and first two fingers. Drawing back, she raised her arm, then threw the ball with a snap of her wrist, giving it a spin that caused it to veer sharply inward just as it reached Castle Rock. The batter missed again, but even he exclaimed in appreciation for the hornet ball. On the next pitch, he finally connected with the ball, sending it to the west side of the field, where Daisy happily scampered after it. She hurled it to the player at the third sanctuary post, who leaped in the air to snatch it in his fist.

In just a few minutes, the fast-paced enjoyment of the game caused the players to lose all self-consciousness, and their drives and throws and full-bore runs became uninhibited. Laughing and crowing as loudly as the stable boys, Lillian was reminded of the careless freedom of

childhood. It was indescribable relief to forget, if only
for a little while, the innumerable rules and the stifling
propriety that had smothered them ever since they had
set foot in England. And it was such a glorious day, the
sun bright but so much gentler than it was in New York,
and the air soft and fresh as it filled her lungs.

"Your turn at bat, miss," Arthur said, raising a hand
for her to toss the ball to him. "Let's see if you can hit as
well as you throw!"

"She can't," Daisy informed him promptly, and Lillian made a hand gesture that caused the boys to roar in
scandalized delight.

Unfortunately it was true. For all her accuracy in
pitching, Lillian had never mastered the art of batting—
a fact that Daisy, who was a superior batter, took great
delight in pointing out. Picking up the bat, Lillian
gripped the handle like a hammer with her left hand, and
left the index finger of her right slightly open. Cocking
the bat over her shoulder, she waited for the pitch, timed
it with her narrowed gaze, and swung as hard as she was
able. To her frustration, the ball spun off the top of the
bat and went sailing over the catcher's head.

Before the boy could go in pursuit of it, the ball was
tossed back to the pitcher by some unseen source. Lillian
was perplexed as she saw Arthur's face suddenly blanch
to a shade of white that contrasted starkly with the fiery
locks of his hair. Wondering what could have put such a
look on his face, Lillian turned to glance behind her. The
catcher seemed to have stopped breathing as he too beheld the visitor.

For there, leaning casually against the paddock fence,
was none other than Marcus, Lord Westcliff.

Chapter 3

*C*ursing silently, Lillian gave Westcliff a sullen stare. He responded with a sardonic lift of one brow. Although he was clad in a tweed riding coat, his shirt was open at the throat, revealing the strong, sun-browned line of his neck. During their previous encounters, Westcliff had always been impeccably dressed and perfectly groomed. At the moment, however, his thick black hair was wind-tousled, and he was rather in need of a shave. Strangely, the sight of him like this sent a pleasant shiver through Lillian's insides and imparted an unfamiliar weakness to her knees.

Regardless of her dislike, Lillian had to acknowledge that Westcliff was an extremely attractive man. His features were too broad in some places, too sharp in others, but there was a rugged poetry in the structure of his face that made classical handsomeness seem utterly irrelevant. Few men possessed such deeply ingrained virility, a force of character that was too powerful to overlook. He was not only comfortable in his position of authority, he was obviously unable to function in any capacity other than as a leader. As a girl who had always been inclined to throw an egg in the face of authority, Lillian found Westcliff to be an unholy temptation. There had been few moments as satisfying as those when she had managed to annoy him beyond his ability to bear.

Westcliff's assessing gaze slid from her tumbled hair to the uncorseted lines of her figure, not missing the unbound shapes of her breasts. Wondering if he was going to give her a public dressing-down for daring to play rounders with a group of stable boys, Lillian returned his evaluating gaze with one of her own. She tried to look scornful, but that wasn't easy when the sight of Westcliff's lean, athletic body had brought another unnerving quiver to the pit of her stomach. Daisy had been right—it would be difficult, if not impossible, to find a younger man who could rival Westcliff's virile strength.

Still holding Lillian's gaze, Westcliff pushed slowly away from the paddock fence and approached.

Tensing, Lillian held her ground. She was tall for a woman, which made them nearly of a height, but Westcliff still had a good three inches on her, and he outweighed her by at least five stone. Her nerves tingled with awareness as she stared into his eyes, which were a shade of brown so intense that they appeared to be black.

His voice was deep, textured like gravel wrapped in velvet. "You should tuck your elbows in."

Having expected criticism, Lillian was caught offguard. "What?"

The earl's thick lashes lowered slightly as he glanced down at the bat that was gripped in her right hand.

"Tuck your elbows in. You'll have more control over the bat if you decrease the arc of the swing."

Lillian scowled. "Is there any subject that you're not an expert on?"

A glint of amusement appeared in the earl's dark eyes. He appeared to consider the question thoughtfully. "I can't whistle," he finally said. "And my aim with a trebuchet is poor. Other than that . . ." The earl lifted his hands in a helpless gesture, as if he was at a loss to come up with another activity at which he was less than proficient.

"What's a trebuchet?" Lillian asked. "And what do you mean, you can't whistle? Everyone can whistle."

Westcliff formed his lips into a perfectly round pucker and let out a soundless puff of air. They were standing so close that Lillian felt the soft touch of his breath against her forehead, stirring a few silken filaments of hair that had adhered to her damp skin. She blinked in surprise, her gaze falling to his mouth, and then to the open neck of his shirt, where his bronzed skin looked smooth and very warm.

"See? . . . Nothing. I've tried for years."

Bemused, Lillian thought of advising him to blow harder, and to press the tip of his tongue against the bottom row of his teeth . . . but somehow the thought of uttering a sentence with the word "tongue" in it to Westcliff seemed impossible. Instead she stared at him blankly and jumped a little as he reached out to her shoulders and turned her gently to face Arthur. The boy was standing several yards away with the forgotten rounders ball in his hand, watching the earl with an expression of awe mingled with dread.

Wondering if Westcliff was going to reprimand the

boys for allowing her and Daisy to play, Lillian said uneasily, "Arthur and the others—it wasn't their fault—I made them let us into the game—"

"I don't doubt it," the earl said over her shoulder. "You probably gave them no chance to refuse."

"You're not going to punish them?"

"For playing rounders on their off-time? Hardly." Removing his coat, Westcliff tossed it to the ground. He turned to the catcher, who was hovering nearby, and said, "Jim, be a good lad and help field a few balls."

"Yes, milord!" The boy ran in a flash to the empty space on the west side of the green beyond the sanctuary posts.

"What are you doing?" Lillian asked as Westcliff stood behind her.

"I'm correcting your swing," came his even reply. "Lift the bat, Miss Bowman."

She turned to look at him skeptically, and he smiled, his eyes gleaming with challenge.

"This should be interesting," Lillian muttered. Taking up a batter's stance, she glanced across the field at Daisy, whose face was flushed and eyes over-bright in the effort to suppress a burst of laughter. "My swing is perfectly fine," Lillian grumbled, uncomfortably aware of the earl's body just behind hers. Her eyes widened as she felt his hands slide to her elbows, pushing them into a more compact position. As his husky murmur brushed her ears, her excited nerves seemed to catch fire, and she felt a flush spreading over her face and neck, as well as other body parts that, as far as she knew, there were no names for.

"Spread your feet wider," Westcliff said, "and distribute your weight evenly. Good. Now bring your hands closer to your body. Since the bat is a few inches too long for you, you'll have to choke up on it—"

"I like holding it at the base."

"It's too long for you," he insisted, "which is why you pull your swing just before you hit the ball—"

"I like a long bat," Lillian argued, even as he adjusted her hands on the willow handle. "The longer the better, as a matter of fact."

A distant snicker from one of the stable boys caught her attention, and she glanced at him suspiciously before turning to face Westcliff. His face was expressionless, but there was a glitter of laughter in his eyes. "Why is that amusing?" she asked.

"I have no idea," Westcliff said blandly, and turned her toward the pitcher again. "Remember your elbows. Yes. Now, don't let your wrists roll—keep them straight, and swing in a level motion . . . no, not like that." Reaching around her, he stunned her by placing his hands right over hers and guiding her in the slow arc of a swing. His mouth was at her ear. "Can you feel the difference? Try again . . . is that more natural?"

Lillian's heart had begun a rapid rhythm that sent the blood in a dizzying rush through her veins. She had never felt so awkward, with the solid warmth of the man at her back, his sturdy thighs intruding in the light folds of her walking dress. His broad hands nearly enclosed hers completely, and she felt with surprise that there were calluses on his fingers.

"Once more," Westcliff coaxed. His hands tightened on hers. As their arms aligned, she felt the steely hardness of his biceps muscles. Suddenly she felt overwhelmed by him, threatened in a way that went far beyond physical influence. The air in her lungs seemed to expand painfully. She let out a swift, shallow breath, and another, and then she was released with disconcerting swiftness.

Stepping back, Westcliff stared at her intently, a frown disturbing the smooth plane of his forehead. It wasn't easy to distinguish the sable irises from his pupils, but Lillian had the impression that his eyes were dilated as if from the effects of some powerful drug. It seemed that he wanted to ask her something, but instead he gave her a curt nod and motioned for her to resume the batter's stance. Taking the catcher's place, he sank to his haunches and gestured to Arthur.

"Throw some easy ones to begin with," he called, and Arthur nodded, seeming to lose his apprehensiveness.

"Yes, milord!"

Arthur wound up and released a relaxed, straight pitch. Squinting in determination, Lilian gripped the bat hard, stepped into the swing, and turned her hips to lend more impetus to the motion. To her disgust, she missed the ball completely. Turning around, she gave Westcliff a pointed glance. "Well, your advice certainly helped," she muttered sarcastically.

"Elbows," came his succinct reminder, and he tossed the ball to Arthur. "Try again."

Heaving a sigh, Lillian raised the bat and faced the pitcher once more.

Arthur drew his arm back, and lunged forward as he delivered another fast ball.

Lillian brought the bat around with a grunt of effort, finding an unexpected ease in adjusting the swing to just the right angle, and she received a jolt of visceral delight as she felt the solid connection between the bat and the leather ball. With a loud crack the ball was catapulted high into the air, over Arthur's head, beyond the reach of those in the back field. Shrieking in triumph, Lillian dropped the bat and ran headlong toward the first sanctuary post, rounding it and heading toward second. Out of the corner of her eye, she saw Daisy hurtling across the field to scoop up the ball, and in nearly the same motion, throwing it to the nearest boy. Increasing her pace, her feet flying beneath her skirts, Lillian rounded third, while the ball was tossed to Arthur.

Before her disbelieving eyes, she saw Westcliff standing at the last post, Castle Rock, with his hands held up in readiness to catch the ball. *How could he?* After showing her how to hit the ball, he was now going to tag her out?

"Get out of my way!" Lillian shouted, running pell-mell toward the post, determined to reach it before he caught the ball. "I'm not going to stop!"

"Oh, I'll stop you," Westcliff assured her with a grin, standing right in front of the post. He called to the pitcher. "Throw it home, Arthur!"

She would go *through* him, if necessary. Letting out a warlike cry, Lillian slammed full-length into him, causing him to stagger backward just as his fingers closed over the ball. Though he could have fought for balance, he chose not to, collapsing backward onto the soft earth with Lillian tumbling on top of him, burying him in a heap of skirts and wayward limbs. A cloud of fine beige dust enveloped them upon their descent. Lillian lifted herself on his chest and glared down at him. At first she thought that he had been winded, but it immediately became apparent that he was choking with laughter.

"You cheated!" she accused, which only seemed to make him laugh harder. She struggled for breath, draw-

ing in huge lungfuls of air. "You're not supposed . . . to
stand in front . . . of the post . . . you dirty *cheater!*"

Gasping and snorting, Westcliff handed her the ball
with the ginger reverence of someone yielding a priceless
artifact to a museum curator. Lillian took the ball and
hurled it aside. "I was *not out,*" she told him, jabbing
her finger into his hard chest for emphasis. It felt as if
she were poking a hearthstone. "I was *safe,* do you . . .
hear me?"

She heard Arthur's amused voice as he approached
them. "Actually, miss—"

"Never argue with a lady, Arthur," the earl interrupted, having managed to regain his powers of speech,
and the boy grinned at him.

"Yes, milord."

"Are there ladies here?" Daisy asked cheerfully, coming from the field. "I don't see any."

Still smiling, the earl looked up at Lillian. His hair was
mussed, and his teeth were very white in his swarthy, dust-
streaked face. With his autocratic facade stripped away,
and his eyes sparkling with enjoyment, his grin was so unexpectedly engaging that Lillian experienced a curious
melting sensation inside. Hanging over him, she felt her
own lips curving in a reluctant smile. A loose lock of her
hair dangled free of its tether, sliding silkily over his jaw.

"What's a trebuchet?" she asked.

"A catapult. I have a friend who has a keen interest in
medieval weaponry. He . . ." Westcliff hesitated, a new
tension seeming to spread through his taut body as he
lay beneath her. "He recently built a trebuchet using an
ancient design . . . and enlisted me to help fire it . . ."

Lillian was entertained by the idea that the normally
reserved Westcliff was capable of such boyish antics. Re-

alizing that she was straddling him, she colored and began to wriggle off him. "Your aim was off?" she asked, striving to sound casual.

"The owner of the stone wall we demolished seemed to think so." The earl caught his breath sharply as her body slid away from his, and remained sitting on the ground even after she had gotten to her feet.

Wondering why he was staring at her so oddly, Lillian began to whack her dusty skirts with her hands, but it was impossible. Her clothes were a filthy mess. "Oh God," she murmured to Daisy, who was also rumpled and dirty, but not nearly to this extent. "How are we going to explain the state of our walking dresses?"

"I'll ask one of the maids to sneak them down to the laundry before Mother notices. Which reminds me—it's nearly time for us to awaken from our nap!"

"We'll have to hurry," Lillian said, glancing back at Lord Westcliff, who had put his coat back on and was now standing behind her. "My lord, if anyone asks you whether you've seen us . . . you will say that you haven't?"

"I never lie," he said, and she made an exasperated sound.

"Could you at least refrain from *volunteering* any information?" she asked.

"I suppose I could."

"How helpful you are," Lillian said in a tone that conveyed the opposite. "Thank you, my lord. And now if you will excuse us, we must run. Literally."

"Follow me, and I'll show you a shortcut," Westcliff offered. "I know a way through the garden and into the servants' entrance beside the kitchen."

Glancing at each other, the sisters nodded in unison

and hurried after him, waving distracted good-byes to Arthur and his friends.

As Marcus guided the Bowman sisters through the late-summer garden, he was annoyed by the way Lillian kept sidling ahead of him. She seemed physically incapable of following his lead. Marcus glanced at her covertly, taking note of the way her legs moved beneath the light muslin walking dress. Her stride was long and loose-limbed, unlike the practiced feminine sway that most women affected.

Silently Marcus reflected on his inexplicable reaction to her during the rounders game. As he had watched her, the vivid enjoyment in her expression had been completely irresistible. She had a coltish energy and an enthusiasm for physical activity that seemed to rival his own. It was not at all fashionable for young women in her position to exhibit such robust health and spirits. They were supposed to be shy and modest and restrained. But Lillian had been too compelling for him to ignore, and before he had quite known what was happening, he had joined the game.

The sight of her, so flushed and excited, had stirred up a few sensations that he would rather not have felt. She was prettier than he had remembered, and so entertaining in her prickly stubbornness that he had been unable to resist the challenge she presented. And at the moment when he had stood behind her and adjusted her swing, and felt her body press along his front, he had been keenly aware of a primal urge to drag her to some private place, flip up her skirts, and—

Forcing the thoughts away with a quiet sound of discomfort, he watched as Lillian strode ahead of him once more. She was filthy, her hair was tangled . . . and for some reason he couldn't stop thinking about what it had felt like to lie on the ground with her straddling him. She had been very light. Despite her height, she was a slender girl without much in the way of womanly curves. Not at all his preferred style. But he had wanted very much to catch her waist in his hands, and grind her hips down on his, and—

"This way," he said gruffly, shouldering past Lillian Bowman and keeping to the hedges and walls that concealed them from view of the house. He led the sisters beside paths lined with blue spires of salvia, ancient walls covered with red roses and brilliant puffs of hydrangea, and massive stone urns bursting with white violas.

"Are you certain that this is a shortcut?" Lillian asked. "I think the other way would have been much faster."

Unaccustomed to having his decisions questioned, Marcus shot her a cool glance as she came up beside him. "I know the way through my own estate gardens, Miss Bowman."

"Don't mind my sister, Lord Westcliff," Daisy said from behind them. "It's just that she's worried about what will happen if we're caught. We are supposed to be napping, you see. Mother locked us in our room, and then—"

"Daisy," Lillian interrupted tersely, "the earl doesn't want to hear about that."

"On the contrary," Marcus said, "I find myself quite interested in the question of how you managed to escape. The window?"

"No, I picked the lock," Lillian replied.

Tucking the information in the back of his mind, Marcus asked mockingly, "Did they teach you how to do that in finishing school?"

"We didn't attend finishing school," Lillian said. "I

taught myself how to pick locks. I've been on the wrong side of many a locked door since early childhood."

"How surprising."

"I suppose you never did anything worth being punished for," Lillian said.

"As a matter of fact, I was disciplined often. But I was seldom locked away. My father considered it far more expedient—and satisfying—to thrash me for my crimes."

"He sounds like a brute," Lillian remarked, and Daisy gasped behind them.

"Lillian, you should never speak ill of the dead. And I doubt the earl likes to hear you call his father names."

"No, he was a brute," Marcus said with a bluntness that matched Lillian's.

They came to an opening in the hedge, where a flagstone walk bordered the side of the manor. Motioning for the girls to be silent, Marcus glanced at the empty walk, eased them out into the partial concealment of a tall, narrow juniper, and gestured to the left side of the walk. "The kitchen entrance is over there," he murmured. "We'll go through there and take the staircase on the right to the second floor, and I'll show you the hallway that leads to your room."

The girls stared at him with brilliant smiles, both faces so similar and yet so different. Daisy had rounder cheeks, and an old-fashioned china doll prettiness that provided a somewhat incongruous setting for her exotic brown eyes. Lillian's face was longer and vaguely feline in cast, with tip-tilted eyes and a full, sweetly carnal mouth that made his heart thump an uncomfortable extra beat.

Marcus was still watching her mouth as she spoke. "Thank you, my lord," she said. "I trust we may depend on your silence about our game?"

Had Marcus been another kind of man, or had he entertained the merest flicker of romantic interest in either of the girls, he might have made use of the situation with some flirtatious little piece of blackmail. Instead he nodded and replied firmly, "You may depend on it."

Another cautious glance established that the flagstone walkway was still unoccupied, and the three of them walked out from the concealment of the juniper. Unfortunately, when they had reached the midway point between the hedge opening and the kitchen entrance, the sudden sound of voices echoed across the smooth slate-paved walkway and bounced gently off the manor wall. Someone was coming.

Daisy took off like a startled doe, reaching the kitchen entrance in a fraction of a second. Lillian, however, took the opposite tack, launching herself back toward the juniper. With no time to consider his actions, Marcus followed her just as a group of three or four figures appeared at the head of the walkway. Crowding with her in the narrow cavity between the juniper and the hedge, Marcus felt more than a bit ridiculous, hiding from guests on his own estate. However, his own dirty, dust-streaked condition was not something he cared to vaunt in company . . . and suddenly his thoughts were jumbled as he felt Lillian's arms clutching around the shoulders of his coat, pulling him deeper into the shadows. Pulling him against her. She was trembling . . . with fear, he thought at first. Shocked by his own protective reaction, he put his arm around her. But he quickly discovered that she was laughing silently, so inexplicably tickled by the situation that she had to muffle a series of squeaking gasps against his shoulder.

Smiling down at her quizzically, Marcus pushed back a straggle of chocolate-colored hair that had fallen over

her right eye. He squinted through a small aperture be-
tween the fragrant, thickly needled juniper branches.
Recognizing the men, who were slowly making their
way along the path as they discussed business matters,
Marcus ducked his head to whisper into Lillian's ear.
"Quiet. It's your father."

Her eyes widened, her laughter dissolving as she dug
her fingers reflexively into his coat. "Oh no. Don't let
him find me! He'll tell Mother."

Dipping his chin in a reassuring nod, Marcus kept his
arm around her, his mouth and nose near her temple.
"They won't see us. As soon as they pass, I'll take you
across the walkway."

She stayed very still, staring through the tiny spaces in
the juniper leaves, seeming not to realize that she was
locked against the Earl of Westcliff's body in what most
people would have described as an embrace. Holding her,
breathing against her temple, Marcus became aware of an
elusive scent, a faint flowery overture that he had vaguely
registered at the rounders field. Hunting for it, he found a
stronger concentration of the fragrance on her throat,
where it was blood-heated and intoxicating. His mouth
watered. Suddenly he wanted to touch his tongue to her
tender white skin, wanted to rip her dress down the front
and drag his mouth from her throat down to her toes.

His arm tightened around Lillian's narrow frame, and
his free hand compulsively sought her hips, exerting gentle but steady pressure to bring her closer against him.
Oh yes. She was the perfect height, so tall that minimal
adjustment was needed to match their bodies in just the
right way. Agitation filled him, igniting sensual fire in
the pulsing pathways of his veins. It would be so easy to
take her like this, just pull her dress up and kick her legs

apart. He wanted her a thousand ways, over him, under him, any part of him inside any part of her. He could feel the natural shape of her body beneath the thin dress, with no corset to mar the sleek line of her back. She stiffened a little as she felt his mouth touch her throat, and her breath caught in astonishment.

"What . . . what are you doing?" she whispered.

On the other side of the hedge, the four men paused as they became animated on the subject of stock manipulation, while Marcus's mind seethed with thoughts of an entirely different kind of manipulation. Dampening his dry lips with his tongue, he drew his head back and saw the confounded expression on Lillian's face. "I'm sorry," he breathed, fighting to regain his wits. "It's that smell . . . what is it?"

"Smell?" She looked utterly confused. "Do you mean my perfume?"

Marcus was distracted by the sight of her mouth . . . the plush, silky, rose-tinted lips that seemed to promise unspeakable sweetness. The scent of her invaded his nose repeatedly, in luxurious drifts that roused a fresh wave of fantastically lurid urges within his body. He hardened, his groin heating rapidly, while his heart thumped with unrivaled force. He couldn't think clearly. The effort to keep from groping her caused his hands to shake. Closing his eyes, he turned his face from hers, only to find himself nuzzling hungrily at her throat. She pushed at him a little, her sharp whisper at his ear. "What is the *matter* with you?"

Marcus shook his head helplessly. "I'm sorry," he rasped, even as he knew what he was about to do. "My God. Sorry—" His mouth clamped over hers, and he began to kiss her as if his life depended on it.

Chapter 4

It was the first time in Lillian's life that a man had ever kissed her without asking for permission. She wriggled and strained until Westcliff secured her more firmly against his body. He smelled like dust and horses and sunlight . . . and there was something else . . . a sweet, dry essence that reminded her of freshly mown hay. The pressure of his mouth increased, searching ardently until her lips were coaxed apart. She had never imagined kisses like these, deep, tenderly impatient caresses that seemed to sap her of strength until she closed her eyes and leaned into the hard support of his chest. Westcliff took instant advantage of her weakness, molding her against him until not an inch separated them, and her legs were parted by the intrusion of his powerful thigh.

The tip of his tongue played inside her mouth in sweeps of warmth that explored the edges of her teeth and the silken dampness beyond. Shocked by the intimacy, Lillian shrank backward, but he followed her, both his hands sliding up to cradle her head. She didn't know what to do with her tongue; she drew it back awkwardly as he played with her, harried and goaded and pleasured her until a shaking moan rose in her throat, and she pushed at him frantically.

His mouth broke from hers. Conscious of her father and his companions standing on the other side of the juniper, Lillian struggled to control her breathing, and watched their dark shapes through the heavy screen of verdant needles. The men proceeded along the pathway, oblivious to the embracing couple hidden at the garden entrance. Relieved that they were leaving, Lillian let out a shivering breath. Her heart hammered in her chest as she felt Westcliff's mouth slide along the fragile arch of her throat, tracing a simmering pathway of nerves. She writhed against him, still helplessly riding his thigh, and a brilliant bloom of heat began inside her.

"My lord," she whispered, "have you gone mad?"

"Yes. Yes." A velvety drag of his lips back to her mouth . . . another deeply marauding kiss. "Give me your mouth . . . your tongue . . . yes. Yes. So sweet . . . sweet . . ." His lips were hot and restless, shifting over hers in sensuous coercion, while his breath rushed against her cheek. Her lips and chin tingled from the scratchy bristle of his unshaven skin.

"My lord," she whispered again, jerking her mouth from his. "For God's sake—let go of me!"

"Yes . . . I'm sorry . . . just one more . . ." He sought her lips again, and she shoved at him as hard as she could. His chest was as hard as granite.

"Let go, you oaf!" Twisting wildly, Lillian managed to pry herself free of him. Her entire body tingled from the exquisite friction with his, even after they were separated.

As they stared at each other, she saw the haze of lust begin to dissipate from his expression, and his dark eyes widened with the dawning realization of what had just happened. "Holy hell," he whispered.

Lillian did not appreciate the way he stared at her, like a man beholding the fatal head of Medusa. She scowled at him. "I can find my own way to my room," she said curtly. "And *don't* try to follow me—I've had quite enough help from you today." Turning, she sped across the walkway, while he stared after with his jaw sagging.

By some miracle of God, Lillian managed to reach her room before her mother appeared to wake her daughters from their nap. Slipping through the partially open door, she closed it and hurriedly unfastened the front buttons of her gown. Daisy, who had already stripped down to her undergarments, went to the door and inserted a crimped pin beneath the knob to trick the lever and re-lock it.

"What took you so long?" Daisy asked, intent on her task. "I hope you're not angry that I didn't wait for you—I thought I should get back here and freshen up as quickly as possible."

"No," Lillian said distractedly, stepping out of her filthy gown. She deposited it at the bottom of the armoire and closed it out of sight. A sharp click signaled Daisy's success in relocking the door. Rapidly Lillian strode to the washstand, emptied the dirty water into the slop jar below, and poured fresh water into the bowl.

Washing her face and arms hastily, she blotted her skin with a length of clean toweling.

Suddenly a key turned in the lock, and both girls glanced at each other in alarm. They headed for their separate beds with running leaps, landing on the mattresses just as their mother entered the room. Fortunately the curtains were closed, making the light too ineffectual for Mercedes to detect any evidence of their activities. "Girls?" she asked suspiciously. "It is time for you to awaken now."

Daisy stretched and yawned loudly. "Mmmm . . . we've had a lovely nap. I feel *so* refreshed."

"As do I," Lillian said thickly, her head buried in her pillow, her heart pounding hard against the mattress.

"Now you must bathe and change into your evening gowns. I'll ring for the maids to draw a bath. Daisy, you will wear your yellow silk. Lillian, you must wear the green with the gold clips at the shoulders."

"Yes, Mother," they both said.

As Mercedes went back to the room next door, Daisy sat upright and stared at Lillian curiously. "Why were you so long in returning?"

Lillian rolled over and looked up at the ceiling, considering what had happened in the garden. She couldn't quite believe that Westcliff, who had always exhibited such disapproval of her, would have behaved in such a way. It made no sense. The earl had never displayed any hint of attraction to her before. In fact, this afternoon was the first occasion when they had actually managed to be civil to each other. "Westcliff and I were obliged to keep out of sight for a few minutes," Lillian heard herself say, while thoughts continued to click through her mind. "Father was among the group that came along the walkway."

"Oh Lord!" Daisy swung her legs over the side of her bed and stared at Lillian with an aghast grimace. "But Father didn't see you?"

"No."

"Well, that's a relief." Daisy frowned slightly, seeming to sense that there was a great deal being left unsaid. "It was quite sporting of Lord Westcliff not to give us away, wasn't it?"

"Sporting, yes."

A sudden smile curved Daisy's lips. "I think it was the funniest thing I've ever seen when he showed you how to swing the bat—I was certain that you were going to bash him with it!"

"I was tempted," Lillian replied darkly, standing from her own bed and going to pull the curtains open. As she jerked the heavy folds of lined damask to the side, a burst of afternoon sunlight invaded the room, causing tiny floating dust motes to sparkle in the air. "Westcliff looks for any excuse to demonstrate his superiority, doesn't he?"

"Was that what he was doing? It looked rather like he was trying to find an excuse to put his arms around you."

Startled by the comment, Lillian looked at her with narrowed eyes. "Why would you say a thing like that?"

Daisy shrugged. "There was something in the way he looked at you . . ."

"What way?" Lillian demanded, while panic began to flutter through her body like a thousand tiny wings.

"Just a sort of, well . . . *interested* way."

Lillian covered her turmoil with a scowl. "The earl

and I despise each other," she said tersely. "The only thing he is interested in is a potential business arrangement with Father." She paused and approached the vanity table, where her vial of perfume glittered in the ample fall of sunlight. Closing her fingers around the pear-shaped crystal vessel, she picked it up and rubbed her thumb across the stopper repeatedly. "However," she said hesitantly, "there is something I must tell you, Daisy. Something happened while Westcliff and I waited behind the hedgerow . . ."

"Yes?" Daisy's expression was alive with curiosity.

Unfortunately their mother chose that moment to sweep back into the room, followed by a pair of maids who laboriously dragged a folding slipper tub into the room in preparation for the bath. With their mother hovering over them, there was no opportunity for Lillian to speak to Daisy privately. And that was likely a good thing, as it allowed Lillian more time to ponder the situation. Slipping the vial of perfume into the reticule that she intended to carry that evening, she wondered if Westcliff had really been affected by her perfume. *Something* had happened to make him behave so strangely. And judging from the expression on his face when he realized what he had done, Westcliff had been shocked by his own behavior.

The logical thing to do was test this perfume. Put it through its paces, so to speak. A wry grin worked its way up to her mouth as she thought of her friends, who would probably be quite willing to help her conduct an experiment or two.

The wallflowers had been acquainted for approximately a year, always sitting against the wall during the dances. In retrospect, Lillian couldn't decide why it had taken so long for them to strike up a friendship. Perhaps one reason was that Annabelle was so beautiful, with hair the color of dark honey, and brilliant blue eyes, and a voluptuous, neatly turned figure. One couldn't imagine that such a goddesslike creature would ever condescend to be friends with mere mortals. Evangeline Jenner, on the other hand, was appallingly shy and possessed a stutter that made conversation incredibly difficult.

However, when it had finally become obvious that none of them would ever transcend their wallflower status by themselves, they had banded together to help one another find husbands, starting with Annabelle. Their combined efforts had succeeded in winning a husband for Annabelle, even though Simon Hunt wasn't the peer that she had originally set out to catch. Lillian had to admit that despite her initial misgivings over the match, Annabelle had made the right choice in marrying Hunt. Now, as the next oldest unmarried wallflower, it was Lillian's turn.

The sisters bathed and washed their hair, and then occupied separate corners of the room as the pair of maids helped them to dress. Following her mother's instructions, Lillian donned a gown of pale sea-green silk, with short, full sleeves and a bodice that was held together at the shoulders with gold clips. A detested corset had reduced her waist by two inches, while a bit of padding at the top enhanced her breasts until they formed a shallow cleavage. She was guided to the vanity table, where she sat wincing and flinching, her scalp smarting as a maid brushed the snarls from her hair and pinned it into an elaborate coiffure. Daisy, meanwhile, was subjected to similar torture as she was laced and padded and buttoned into a butter-colored gown with ruffles at the bodice.

Their mother hovered over them, anxiously muttering a stream of instructions about proper behavior. ". . . remember, English gentlemen do not like to hear a girl talk excessively, and they have no interest in your opinions. Therefore, I want the both of you to be as docile and quiet as possible. And do not mention any kind of sport! A gentleman may appear to find it amusing to hear you go on about rounders or lawn games, but inwardly they disdain a girl who discusses masculine subjects. And if a gentleman asks a question of you, find a way to turn it back to him, so that he will have the opportunity to tell you about his own experiences . . ."

"Another *thrilling* evening at Stony Cross Manor," Lillian muttered. Daisy must have heard her, for a muffled snort of amusement came from the other side of the room.

"What was that noise?" Mercedes asked crisply. "Are you paying attention to my advice, Daisy?"

"Yes, Mother. I couldn't breathe properly for a moment. I think my corset is too tight."

"Then don't breathe so deeply."

"Can't we loosen my stays?"

"No. British gentlemen prefer girls with very narrow waists. Now, where was I—oh yes, during dinner, if there is a lull in the conversation . . ."

Grimly enduring the lecture, which would undoubtedly be repeated in various forms during their stay at Westcliff's estate, Lillian stared into the looking glass. She felt agitated at the thought of facing Westcliff this evening. An image flashed through her mind, of his dark face lowering over hers, and she closed her eyes.

"Sorry, miss," the maid murmured, assuming that she had pinned a lock of hair too tightly.

"It's all right," Lillian replied with a rueful smile. "Tug away—I've got a hard head."

"That is a monumental understatement," came Daisy's rejoinder from the other side of the room.

As the maid continued to twist and pin her hair, Lillian's thoughts returned to Westcliff. Would he try to pretend that the kiss behind the hedgerow had never occurred? Or would he decide to discuss it with her? Mortified at the prospect, she realized that she needed to talk to Annabelle, who had come to know a great deal more about Westcliff since her marriage to his best friend, Simon Hunt.

Just as the last pin was being prodded into her coiffure, there came a tap on the door. Daisy, who was tugging on her elbow-length white gloves, hurried to answer it, ignoring Mercedes's protest that one of the maids should see to the door. Flinging it open, Daisy let out a happy exclamation at the sight of Annabelle Hunt. Lillian stood from her seat at the vanity and rushed over to her, and the three of them embraced. It had been a few days since they had seen each other at the Rutledge, the London hotel where both families resided. Soon the Hunts would move into a new house that was being built in Mayfair, but in the meanwhile the girls visited each other's suites at every opportunity. Mercedes objected occasionally, airing concerns about Annabelle's bad influence on her daughters—an amusing assertion, as it was clearly the other way around.

As usual Annabelle looked ravishing, in a pale blue satin gown that was tightly fitted to her shapely figure, with matching silk cord that laced up the front. The color of the gown deepened the rich blue of her eyes and flattered her peaches-and-cream complexion.

Annabelle drew back to look at both of them with glowing eyes. "How was your journey from London? Have you had any adventures yet? No, you couldn't possibly, you've been here less than a day—"

"We may have," Lillian murmured cautiously, mindful of her mother's keen ears. "I have to talk to you about something—"

"Daughters!" Mercedes interrupted, her tone strident with disapproval. "You haven't yet finished preparing for the soiree."

"I'm ready, Mother!" Daisy said quickly. "Look—all finished. I even have my gloves on."

"All I need is my reticule," Lillian added, darting to the vanity and snatching up the little cream-colored bag. "There—I'm ready too."

Well aware of Mercedes's dislike of her, Annabelle smiled pleasantly. "Good evening, Mrs. Bowman. I was hoping that Lillian and Daisy would be allowed to come downstairs with me."

"I'm afraid they will have to wait until I am ready," Mercedes replied in a frosty tone. "My two innocent girls require the supervision of a proper chaperone."

"Annabelle will be our chaperone," Lillian said brightly. "She's a respectable married matron now, remember?"

"I said a *proper* chaperone—" their mother argued, but her protests were abruptly cut off as the sisters left the room and closed the door.

"Dear me," Annabelle said, laughing helplessly, "that's the first time I've ever been called a 'respectable married matron'—it makes me sound rather dull, doesn't it?"

"If you were dull," Lillian replied, locking arms with

her as they strode along the hallway, "then Mother would
approve of you—"

"—and we would want nothing to do with you,"
Daisy added.

Annabelle smiled. "Still, if I'm to be the official chaperone of the wallflowers, I should set out some principal
rules of conduct. First, if any handsome young gentleman suggests that you sneak out to the garden with him
alone . . ."

"We should refuse?" Daisy asked.

"No, just make certain to tell me so that I can cover
for you. And if you happen to overhear some scandalous
piece of gossip that is not appropriate for your innocent
ears . . ."

"We should ignore it?"

"No, you should listen to *every word,* and then come
repeat it to me at once."

Lillian grinned and paused at the intersection between
two hallways. "Shall we try to find Evie? It won't be an
official wallflower meeting unless she's with us."

"Evie is already downstairs with her aunt Florence,"
Annabelle replied.

Both sisters exclaimed eagerly at the news. "How is
she? How does she look?"

"Oh, it's been forever since we've seen her!"

"Evie seems quite well," Annabelle said, sobering,
"though she is a bit thinner. And perhaps a little dispir-
ited."

"Who wouldn't be," Lillian said grimly, "after the
way she has been treated?"

It had been many weeks since any of them had seen
Evie, who was kept in seclusion by her late mother's
family. She was frequently locked away in solitude as

punishment for minor transgressions, and let out only under the strict supervision of her aunt. Her friends had speculated that living with such harsh and unloving relatives had contributed no small amount to Evie's difficult speech. Ironically, of all of the wallflowers, Evie was the one who least deserved such stern regulation. She was timid by nature, and inherently respectful of authority. From what they could gather, Evie's mother had been the rebel of the family, marrying a man well below her station. After she had died in childbirth, her daughter had been made to pay for her transgressions. And her father, whom Evie seldom had the opportunity to see, was in poor health and probably hadn't much longer to live.

"Poor Evie," Lillian continued moodily. "I'm strongly inclined to give her my turn as the next wallflower to marry—she needs the escape far more than I do."

"Evie's not ready yet," Annabelle said with a certainty that betrayed previous thought on the matter. "She's working on her shyness, but so far she can't even bring herself to have a conversation with a gentleman. Besides . . ." Mischief glimmered in her lovely eyes, and she slipped her arm around Lillian's narrow waist. "You're too old to put it off any longer, dear."

Lillian feigned a sour look in response, making her laugh.

"What was it that you wanted to tell me?" Annabelle asked.

Lillian shook her head. "Let's wait until we join Evie, or I'll end up having to repeat everything."

They made their way to the circuit of public rooms downstairs, where guests were milling about in elegant groups. Color was fashionable this year, at least for ladies' attire, and so the array of rich hues made the gathering appear like a flock of butterflies. The men were dressed in traditional black suits and white shirts, the only variation being the subtle differences in their soberly patterned vests and neckties.

"Where is Mr. Hunt?" Lillian asked Annabelle.

Annabelle smiled faintly at the mention of her husband. "I suspect he's visiting with the earl and a few of their friends." Her gaze sharpened as she caught sight of Evie. "There is Evie—and fortunately Aunt Florence doesn't seem to be hovering over her as usual."

Waiting alone, her absent gaze fixed on a gold-framed landscape painting, Evie seemed lost in private contemplation. Her shrinking posture was that of an apologetic cipher . . . it was clear that she did not feel herself to be part of the gathering, nor did she wish to be. Although no one ever seemed to look long enough at Evie to really notice her, she was actually quite beautiful—perhaps even more so than Annabelle—but in a completely unconventional way. She was freckled and red-haired, with large, round blue eyes and a mobile, full-lipped mouth that was utterly out of fashion. Her well-endowed figure was breathtaking, though the excessively modest gowns she was compelled to wear were distinctly unflattering. Moreover, her slump-shouldered posture did little to advertise her attractions.

Stealing forward, Lillian startled Evie by grasping her gloved hand and tugging her away. "Come," she whispered.

Evie's eyes lit with gladness at the sight of her. She hesitated and glanced uncertainly at her aunt, who was talking with some dowagers in the corner. Ascertaining that Florence was too absorbed in her conversation to notice, the four girls slipped from the parlor and hurried down the hallway like escaping prisoners. "Where are we going?" Evie whispered.

"The back terrace," Annabelle replied.

They went to the rear of the house and exited through a row of French doors that opened onto a broad flag-stoned terrace. Stretching the entire length of the house, the terrace overlooked the extensive gardens below. It looked like a scene from a painting, with orchards and beautifully kept walks and beds of rare flowers leading to the forest, while the Itchen River flowed below a nearby bluff that was defined by an ironstone wall.

Lillian turned toward Evie and hugged her. "Evie," she exclaimed, "I've missed you so! If you only knew of all the ill-conceived rescue plans we thought of to steal you away from your family. Why won't they let any of us come to visit you?"

"Th-they despise me," Evie said in a muffled voice. "I never realized h-how much until recently. It started when I tried to see my father. After they caught me, they locked me in my room for days, with h-hardly any food or water. They said I was ungrateful, and disobedient, and that my bad blood had finally risen to the fore. To them I'm n-nothing but a dreadful mistake that my mother made. Aunt Florence says it is my fault that she's dead."

Shocked, Lillian drew back to look at her. "She told you that? In those words?"

Evie nodded.

Without thinking, Lillian let out a few curse words that caused Evie to blanch. One of Lillian's more questionable accomplishments was the ability to swear as fluently as a sailor, acquired from much time spent with her grandmother, who had worked as a washwoman at the harbor docks.

"I know that it's not tr-true," Evie murmured. "I mean, m-my mother did die in labor, but I know that it wasn't my fault."

Keeping one arm around Evie's shoulders, Lillian walked with her to a nearby table on the terrace, while Annabelle and Daisy followed. "Evie, what can be done to get you away from those people?"

The girl shrugged helplessly. "My father is s-so ill. I've asked him if I could come to live with him, but he refuses. And he is too weak to keep my mother's family fr-from coming to take me back with them."

All four girls were silent for a moment. The unpleasant reality was that even though Evie was of an age to leave her family's custody voluntarily, an unmarried woman was in a precarious position. Evie would not inherit her fortune until her father's death, and in the meantime, she had no means to support herself.

"You can come live with me and Mr. Hunt at the Rutledge," Annabelle said suddenly, her voice filled with quiet determination. "My husband won't let anyone take you away if you don't wish it. He's a powerful man, and—"

"No." Evie was shaking her head before Annabelle had finished the sentence. "I would n-never do that to you . . . the imposition would be so . . . oh, *never*. And surely you must know how odd it w-would appear . . . the things that would be said . . ." She shook her head helplessly. "I've been considering something . . . my aunt Florence had an idea that I sh-should marry her son. Cousin Eustace. He's not a bad man . . . and it would allow me to live away from my other relatives . . ."

Annabelle's nose wrinkled. "Hmm. I know that's still done nowadays, first cousins marrying, but it does seem a bit incestuous, doesn't it? Any blood relation at all just seems so . . . *ugh*."

"Wait a minute," Daisy said suspiciously, coming to Lillian's side. "We've met Evie's cousin Eustace before. Lillian, do you remember the ball at Winterbourne House?" Her eyes narrowed accusingly. "He was the one who broke the chair, wasn't he, Evie?"

Evie confirmed Daisy's question with an inarticulate murmur.

"Good God!" Lillian exclaimed, "you are *not* considering marrying him, Evie!"

Annabelle wore a puzzled expression. "How did he break the chair? Does he have a foul temper? Did he throw it?"

"He broke it by *sitting* on it," Lillian said with a scowl.

"Cousin Eustace is rather l-large boned," Evie admitted.

"Cousin Eustace has more chins than I've got fingers," Lillian said impatiently. "And he was so busy filling his face during the ball that he couldn't be bothered to make conversation."

"When I went to shake his hand," Daisy added, "I came away with a half-eaten wing of roast chicken."

"He forgot that he was holding it," Evie said apologetically. "He did say he was sorry for ruining your glove, as I recall."

Daisy frowned. "That didn't bother me nearly as much as the question of where he was hiding the rest of the chicken."

Receiving a desperately imploring glance from Evie, Annabelle sought to calm the sisters' rising ferment. "We don't have much time," she counseled. "Let's discuss cousin Eustace when there is more leisure to do so. Meanwhile, Lillian, dear, wasn't there something you were going to tell us?"

It was an effective diversionary tactic. Relenting at the sight of Evie's distressed expression, Lillian temporarily abandoned the subject of Eustace and motioned for all of them to sit at the table. "It began with a visit to a perfume shop in London . . ." Accompanied by Daisy's occasional interjections, Lillian described the visit to Mr. Nettle's perfumery, and the concoction she had purchased, and its purported magical properties.

"Interesting," Annabelle commented with a skeptical smile. "Are you wearing it now? Let me smell it."

"In a moment. I haven't finished the story yet." Withdrawing the vial of perfume from her reticule, Lillian set it in the center of the table, where it sparkled gently in the diffused torchlight on the terrace. "I have to tell you about what happened today." She proceeded to relate the story of the impromptu rounders game that had taken place behind the stable yard, and Westcliff's unexpected appearance. Annabelle and Evie listened incredulously, both of them wide-eyed at the revelation that the earl had actually taken part in the game.

"It's no surprise that Lord Westcliff likes rounders," Annabelle commented. "He's a virtual fiend for outside activities. But the fact that he was willing to play with you . . ."

Lillian grinned suddenly. "Clearly his dislike was overridden by the overwhelming urge to explain everything that I was doing wrong. He started by telling me how I should correct my swing, and then he . . ." Her smile faded, and she was uncomfortably aware of a flush that spread rapidly over her skin.

"Then he put his arms around you," Daisy prompted in the avid silence that had settled over the table.

"He *what?*" Annabelle asked, her lips parting in amazement.

"Only to show me how to hold the bat properly." Lillian's dark brows drew together until they nearly met over the bridge of her nose. "Anyway, what occurred during the game doesn't matter—it was *after* the game that the surprise happened. Westcliff was guiding Daisy and me along the shortest route back to the house, but we were separated when Father and some of his friends came down the walkway. So Daisy sneaked on ahead, while the earl and I were obliged to wait behind the hedgerow. And while we were standing there together . . ."

The other three wallflowers leaned forward, all three gazes fastened on her without blinking.

"What happened?" Annabelle demanded.

Lillian felt the tips of her ears turn red, and it took surprising effort to force the words from her mouth. She stared hard at the little perfume bottle as she murmured, "He kissed me."

"Good Lord," Annabelle exclaimed, while Evie stared at her speechlessly.

"I knew it!" Daisy said. "I knew it!"

"How did you know—" Lillian began to argue, but Annabelle interrupted eagerly.

"Once? More than once?"

Thinking of the erotically linked chain of kisses, Lillian blushed even harder. "More than once," she admitted.

"Wh-what was it like?" Evie asked.

For some reason it hadn't occurred to Lillian that her friends would want a report on Lord Westcliff's sexual prowess. Annoyed by the insistent heat that was now making her cheeks and neck and forehead prickle, she cast her mind about for something to pacify them. For a moment the impression of Westcliff came to her with startling vividness . . . the hardness of his body, his warm, searching mouth . . . Her insides shifted as if they had been turned into molten metal, and suddenly she could not bring herself to admit the truth.

"Dreadful," she said, her feet fidgeting beneath the table. "Westcliff is the worst kisser I've ever encountered."

"*Ohhh . . .*" Daisy and Evie both breathed in disappointment.

Annabelle, however, gave Lillian a frankly doubtful look. "That's odd. Because I've heard quite a few rumors that Westcliff is very adept at pleasing a woman."

Lillian responded with a noncommittal grunt.

"In fact," Annabelle continued, "I attended a card party not a week ago, and one of the women at my table said that Westcliff was so superb in bed that he had ruined her for any other lover."

"Who said that?" Lillian demanded.

"I can't tell you," Annabelle said. "The statement was made in confidence."

"I don't believe it," Lillian replied grumpily. "Even in the circles that you move in, no one would be so brazen as to talk about such things in public."

"I beg to differ." Annabelle gave her a vaguely superior glance. "Married women get to hear much better gossip than unwed girls do."

"Drat," Daisy said enviously.

The table fell silent once again as Annabelle's amused

gaze locked with Lillian's glowering one. To Lillian's chagrin, she was the first to look away. "Out with it," Annabelle commanded, with the tremor of a sudden laugh in her voice. "Tell the truth—is Westcliff really so terrible at kissing?"

"Oh, I suppose he's tolerable," Lillian admitted grudgingly. "But that's not the point."

Evie spoke then, her eyes round with curiosity. "What is the p-point?"

"That Westcliff was driven to it—to kiss a girl he detests, namely me—by the smell of *that perfume.*" Lillian pointed at the tiny glimmering bottle.

The four girls regarded the vial with awe.

"Not really," Annabelle said disbelievingly.

"Really," Lillian insisted.

Daisy and Evie remained raptly silent, looking back and forth between the two of them as if they were viewing a tennis match.

"Lillian, for you, the most practical girl I've ever known, to claim that you have a perfume that acts as an aphrodisiac, is the most astonishing—"

"Aphrowhat?"

"A love potion," Annabelle said. "Lillian, if Lord Westcliff displayed any interest in you, it was not because of your perfume."

"What makes you so certain?"

Annabelle's brows lifted. "Has the perfume produced this effect in any other man of your acquaintance?"

"Not that I've noticed," Lillian admitted reluctantly.

"How long have you worn it?"

"About a week, but I—"

"And the earl is the only man it seems to have worked on?"

"There are other men who will respond to it," Lillian argued. "They just haven't had the opportunity to smell it yet." Seeing her friend's disbelief, she sighed. "I know how it sounds. I didn't believe a word that Mr. Nettle said about this perfume, until today. But I promise you, the moment that the earl got a whiff of it . . ."

Annabelle pinned her with a considering stare, clearly wondering if it could be true.

Evie spoke in the silence. "May I s-see it, Lillian?"

"Of course."

Reaching for the perfume vial as if it were some highly combustible explosive, Evie unstoppered it, brought it to her whimsically freckled nose, and sniffed. "I don't f-feel anything."

"I wonder if it works only on men?" Daisy mused aloud.

"What I'm wondering is," Lillian said slowly, "if any of *you* wore the perfume, would Westcliff be as attracted to you as he was to me?" She stared directly at Annabelle as she spoke.

Realizing what she was about to propose, Annabelle wore a look of comical dismay. "Oh no," she said, shaking her head vigorously. "I'm a married woman, Lillian, and very much in love with my husband, and I haven't the slightest interest in seducing his best friend!"

"You wouldn't have to seduce him, of course," Lillian said. "Just try some of the perfume and then go stand next to him, and see if he notices you."

"I'll do it," Daisy said enthusiastically. "In fact, I propose that we all wear the perfume tonight, and investigate whether it makes us more attractive to men."

Evie chortled at the idea, while Annabelle rolled her eyes. "You can't be serious."

Lillian gave her a reckless grin. "There's no harm in trying it, is there? Consider it a scientific experiment. You're merely collecting evidence to prove a theory."

A groan escaped Annabelle's lips as she watched the two younger girls shake out a few drops of the perfume to adorn themselves with. "This is the silliest thing I've ever done," she commented. "It's even more absurd than when we played rounders in our drawers."

"Knickers," Lillian said promptly, continuing their long-standing debate on the proper name for undergarments.

"Give me that." With a long-suffering expression, Annabelle held out her hand to receive the vial, and dampened her fingertip with the fragrant elixir.

"Use a little more," Lillian advised, watching in satisfaction as Annabelle dabbed the perfume behind her ears. "And put some on your neck too."

"I don't usually wear perfume," Annabelle said. "Mr. Hunt likes the smell of clean skin."

"He may prefer Lady of the Night."

Annabelle looked appalled. "Is that what this is called?"

"It's named after a night-blooming orchid," Lillian explained.

"Oh, good," Annabelle said sardonically. "I was afraid that it was named after a harlot."

Ignoring the remark, Lillian took the vial from her. After applying a few drops of the scent to her own throat and wrists, she tucked the vessel back into her reticule and stood from the table. "Now," she said in satisfaction, glancing at the wallflowers, "let's go find Westcliff."

Chapter 5

$\mathcal{U}$naware of the assault that would soon be launched against him, Marcus relaxed in the study with his brother-in-law, Gideon Shaw, and his friends Simon Hunt and Lord St. Vincent. They had gathered in the private room to talk before the formal dinner started. Leaning back in his chair behind the massive mahogany desk, he glanced at his pocket watch. Eight o'clock—time to join the company at large, especially as Marcus was the host. However, he remained still, and frowned at the watch's implacable face with the grimness of a man who had an unpleasant duty to perform.

He would have to speak to Lillian Bowman. With whom he had behaved like a madman today. Seizing her, kissing her in a berserk eruption of misguided passion . . . The thought of it made him shift uncomfortably in his chair.

Marcus's straightforward nature urged him to deal with the situation in a direct manner. There was only one possible solution to this dilemma—he would have to apologize for his behavior, and assure her that it would never happen again. He would be damned if he would spend the next month skulking through his own house in an effort to avoid the woman. Trying to ignore the whole thing was not feasible.

He only wished he knew why it had happened in the first place.

Marcus had been able to think of nothing else since that moment behind the hedgerow—his own astonishing breach of restraint, and even more bewildering, the primal satisfaction of kissing the annoying shrew.

"Pointless," came St. Vincent's voice. He was sitting on the corner of his desk, staring through the stereoscope. "Who gives a damn about views of landscapes and monuments?" St. Vincent continued lazily. "You need some stereocards featuring women, Westcliff. Now *there's* something worth viewing through this thing."

"I would think that you see enough of those in three-dimensional form," Marcus replied dryly. "Aren't you a bit preoccupied with the subject of female anatomy, St. Vincent?"

"You have your hobbies, I have mine."

Marcus glanced at his brother-in-law, who was politely expressionless, and Simon Hunt, who seemed amused by the exchange. The men were all remarkably different in character and origin. Their only common denominator was their friendship with Marcus. Gideon Shaw was that most contradictory of terms, an "American aristocrat," the great-grandson of an ambitious Yankee sea captain. Simon Hunt was an entrepreneur, a former butcher's son who was shrewd, enterprising, and trustworthy in every regard. Then there was St. Vincent, an unprincipled scoundrel and a prolific lover of women. He was always to be found at some fashionable party or gathering, staying only until the conversation became "tedious," which was to say that something meaningful or worthwhile was being discussed, and then he would leave in search of new revelry.

Marcus had never encountered a cynicism as deep-seated as St. Vincent's. The viscount almost never said what he meant, and if he ever felt a moment of compassion for anyone, he concealed it expertly. A lost soul, people sometimes called him, and it did seem likely that St. Vincent was beyond redemption. It was equally likely that Hunt and Shaw would not have tolerated St. Vincent's company were it not for his friendship with Marcus.

Marcus himself would have had little to do with St. Vincent were it not for his memories of the days when they had attended the same school. Time and again St. Vincent had proved himself to be a supportive friend, doing whatever was necessary to get Marcus out of a scrape, sharing packets of sweets from home with nonchalant benevolence. And he had always been the first by Marcus's side in a fight.

St. Vincent had understood what it was like to be despised by a parent, as his own father had been no better than Marcus's. The two boys had commiserated with dark humor, and had done what they could to help each other. In the years since they had left school, St. Vincent's character seemed to have eroded considerably, but Marcus was not one to forget past debts. Nor was he one to turn his back on a friend.

As St. Vincent lounged in the chair beside Gideon Shaw's, they presented a striking picture, the two of them fair-haired and abundantly favored by nature, yet so qualitatively different in appearance. Shaw was urbane and handsome, with an irreverent grin that beguiled all who saw it. His features were agreeably weathered with subtle signs that life, despite its bounty of material riches, had not always been easy for him. Whatever difficulties came his way, he handled them with grace and wit.

St. Vincent, by contrast, possessed an exotic male beauty, his eyes pale blue and catlike, his mouth edged with cruelty even when he smiled. He cultivated a manner of perpetual indolence that many London fashionables tried to emulate. Had it flattered him to dress like a dandy, St. Vincent undoubtedly would have. But he knew that ornamentation of any kind only served to distract from the golden splendor of his looks, and so he dressed with strict simplicity, in dark, well-tailored clothes.

With St. Vincent present in the study, the conversation naturally turned to the subject of women. Three days earlier a married lady of good standing in London society had reputedly tried to commit suicide when her affair with St. Vincent had ended. The viscount had found it convenient to escape to Stony Cross Park amid the furor of the scandal. "A ridiculous display of melodrama," St. Vincent scoffed, using the tips of his long fingers to play with the rim of his brandy snifter. "It's being said that she slit her wrists, when in reality she scratched them with a hatpin and then began screaming for a maidservant to help her." He shook his head in disgust. "Idiot. After all the pains we took to keep the affair secret, she does something like this. Now everyone in London knows, including her husband. And what did she hope to gain from it? If she sought to punish me for leaving her, she's going to suffer a hundred times more. People always blame the woman the most, especially if she's married."

"What of her husband's reaction?" Marcus asked, focusing at once on practical considerations. "Is it likely that he'll retaliate?"

St. Vincent's look of disgust deepened. "I doubt it, as he's twice her age and hasn't touched his wife in years. He's not likely to risk challenging me for the sake of her so-called honor. As long as she kept the thing quiet to spare him being labeled as a cuckold, he would have let her do as she pleased. But instead she's done everything possible to advertise her indiscretion, the little fool."

Simon Hunt stared at the viscount with calm inquiry. "I find it interesting," he said softly, "that you refer to the affair as *her* indiscretion rather than yours."

"It was," St. Vincent said emphatically. The lamplight played lovingly over the clever angles of his face. "I was discreet, and she was not." He shook his head with a world-weary sigh. "I should never have let her seduce me."

"She seduced you?" Marcus asked skeptically.

"I swear by all I hold sacred . . ." St. Vincent paused. "Wait. Since nothing is sacred to me, let me rephrase that. You'll just have to believe me when I say that she was the instigator of the affair. She dropped hints left and right, she began to appear everywhere I went, and she sent messages begging me to visit any time I chose, assuring me that she lived separately from her husband. I didn't even want her—I knew before I touched her that it was going to be a crashing bore. But it got to the point at which it was bad form to keep refusing her, and so I went to her residence, and she met me naked in the entrance hall. What was I supposed to do?"

"Leave?" Gideon Shaw suggested with a slight smile, staring at the viscount as if he were an entertaining occupant of the Royal Menagerie.

"I should have," came St. Vincent's glum acknowledgment. "But I've never been able to reject a woman who wants a tumble. And it had been a damned long time since I'd bedded anyone, at least a week, and I was—"

"A week is a long time to go without bedding someone?" Marcus interrupted, one brow arching.

"Are you going to claim that it's not?"

"St. Vincent, if a man has time to bed a woman more than once a week, he clearly doesn't have enough to do. There are any number of responsibilities that should keep you sufficiently occupied in lieu of . . ." Marcus paused, considering the exact phrase he wanted. "Sexual congress." A pronounced silence greeted his words. Glancing at Shaw, Marcus noticed his brother-in-law's sudden preoccupation with knocking just the right amount of ash from his cigar into a crystal dish, and he frowned. "You're a busy man, Shaw, with business concerns on two continents. Obviously you agree with my statement."

Shaw smiled slightly. "My lord, since my 'sexual congress' is limited exclusively to my wife, who happens to be your sister, I believe I'll have the good sense to keep my mouth shut."

St. Vincent smiled lazily. "It's a shame for a thing like good sense to get in the way of an interesting conversation." His gaze switched to Simon Hunt, who wore a slight frown. "Hunt, you may as well render your opinion. How often should a man make love to a woman? Is more than once a week a case for unpardonable gluttony?"

Hunt threw Marcus a vaguely apologetic glance. "Much as I hesitate to agree with St. Vincent . . ."

Marcus scowled as he insisted, "It is a well-known fact that sexual over-indulgence is bad for the health, just as with excessive eating and drinking—"

"You've just described my perfect evening, Westcliff," St. Vincent murmured with a grin, and returned his attention to Hunt. "How often do you and your wife—"

"The goings-on in my bedroom are not open for discussion," Hunt said firmly.

"But you lie with her more than once a week?" St. Vincent pressed.

"Hell, yes," Hunt muttered.

"And well you should, with a woman as beautiful as Mrs. Hunt," St. Vincent said smoothly, and laughed at the warning glance that Hunt flashed him. "Oh, don't glower—your wife is the last woman on earth whom I would have any designs on. I have no desire to be pummeled to a fare-thee-well beneath the weight of your ham-sized fists. And happily married women have never held any appeal for me—not when unhappily married ones are so much easier." He looked back at Marcus. "It seems that you are alone in your opinion, Westcliff. The values of hard work and self-discipline are no match for a warm female body in one's bed."

Marcus frowned. "There are more important things."

"Such as?" St. Vincent inquired with the exaggerated patience of a rebellious lad being subjected to an unwanted lecture from his decrepit grandfather. "I suppose you'll say something like 'social progress'? Tell me,

Westcliff . . ." His gaze turned sly. "If the devil proposed a bargain to you that all the starving orphans in England would be well-fed from now on, but in return you would never be able to lie with a woman again, which would you choose? The orphans, or your own gratification?"

"I never answer hypothetical questions."

St. Vincent laughed. "As I thought. Bad luck for the orphans, it seems."

"I didn't say—" Marcus began, and stopped impatiently. "Never mind. My guests are waiting. You are welcome to continue this wholly pointless conversation in here, or you may accompany me to the public receiving rooms."

"I'll go with you," Hunt said at once, unfolding his long body from the chair. "My wife will be looking for me."

"So will mine," Shaw said agreeably, rising also.

St. Vincent shot Marcus a glance of bright mischief. "God spare me from ever letting a woman put a ring through my nose—and worse, appearing so bloody pleased about it."

It was a sentiment that Marcus happened to agree with.

However, as the four men strolled negligently away from the study, Marcus couldn't help but reflect on the curious fact that Simon Hunt, who, aside from St. Vincent, had been the most dedicated bachelor Marcus had ever known, seemed unexpectedly content in the chains of marriage. Knowing more than anyone how tightly Hunt had clung to his freedom, and the scant number of positive relationships that he'd ever had with women, Marcus had been astonished by Hunt's willingness to surrender his autonomy. And to a woman like Annabelle, who at first had seemed little more than a shallow, self-absorbed husband hunter. But it had eventually become clear that an unusual degree of devotion existed between the pair, and Marcus had been forced to concede that Hunt had chosen well for himself.

"No regrets?" he murmured to Hunt as they strode down the hall, while Shaw and St. Vincent followed at a more leisurely pace.

Hunt glanced at him with a questioning smile. He was a big, dark-haired man, with the same sense of uncompromising masculinity and the same avid interest in hunting and sportsmanship that Marcus possessed. "About what?"

"Being led around by the nose by your wife."

That drew a wry grin from Hunt, and he shook his head. "If my wife does lead me around, Westcliff, it's by an altogether different body part. And no, I have no regrets whatsoever."

"I suppose there's a certain convenience in being married," Marcus mused aloud. "Having a woman close at hand to satisfy your needs, not to mention the fact that a wife is undoubtedly more economical than a mistress. There is, moreover, the begetting of heirs to consider . . ."

Hunt laughed at his effort to cast the issue in a practical light. "I didn't marry Annabelle for convenience. And although I haven't tabulated any numbers, I can assure you that she is *not* cheaper than a mistress. As for the begetting of heirs, that was the farthest thing from my mind when I proposed to her."

"Then why did you?"

"I would tell you, but not long ago you said that you hoped I wouldn't start—how did you put it?—'pollinate the air with maudlin sentiment.'"

"You believe yourself to be in love with her."

"No," Hunt countered in a relaxed manner, "I *am* in love with her."

Marcus lifted his shoulders in a brief shrug. "If believing that makes marriage more palatable to you, so be it."

"Good God, Westcliff . . ." Hunt murmured, a curious smile on his face, "haven't you ever been in love?"

"Of course. Obviously I have found that some women are preferable to others in terms of disposition and physical appearance—"

"No, no, no . . . I'm not referring to finding someone who is 'preferable.' I mean completely being absorbed by a woman who fills you with desperation, longing, ecstasy . . ."

Marcus threw him a disparaging glance. "I haven't time for that nonsense."

Hunt annoyed him by laughing. "Then love won't be a factor in the decision of whom you're going to marry?"

"Absolutely not. Marriage is too important an issue to be decided by mercurial emotions."

"Perhaps you're right," Hunt agreed easily. A bit too easily, as if he didn't really believe what he was saying. "A man like you should choose a wife in a logical manner. I will be interested in seeing how you accomplish it."

They reached one of the receiving rooms, where Livia was tactfully encouraging guests to prepare for the formal procession into the dining hall. As soon as she saw Marcus, she threw him a quick frown, for so far he had left her to deal with the assemblage on her own. He returned her shaming glance with an unrepentant one. Moving farther into the room, Marcus saw that Thomas Bowman and his wife, Mercedes, were standing immediately to his right.

Marcus shook hands with Bowman, a quiet and heavy-set man with a broomlike mustache of such thickness that it nearly atoned for the scarcity of hair on his head. When he was in society, Bowman displayed the perpetually distracted manner of someone who would rather be doing other things. It was only when the discussion came around to business—any kind of business—that his attention was engaged with rapier sharpness.

"Good evening," Marcus murmured, and bowed over Mercedes Bowman's hand. She was so thin that the knuckles and ridges beneath her glove formed a surface suitable for shredding carrots. She was an abrasive woman, a bundle of nerves and coiled aggressiveness. "Please accept my regrets for not being able to welcome you this afternoon," Marcus continued. "And allow me to say how agreeable your return to Stony Cross Park is."

"Oh, my lord," Mercedes trilled, "we are so *very* delighted to stay at your *magnificent* estate once again! And as to this afternoon—we thought nothing of your absence, other than to acknowledge that an important man like you, with so many concerns and responsibilities, must find innumerable demands made upon your time." One of her arms gestured in a way that reminded Marcus of the movements of a praying mantis. "Ah—I see my two lovely girls standing right over there—" Her voice raised even higher as she called to them, and motioned sharply for them to come to her. "*Girls!* Girls, look whom I've found. Come talk to Lord Westcliff!"

Marcus kept his face expressionless as he saw the raised brows of a few people standing nearby. Glancing in the direction of Mercedes's rapid gesticulations, he saw the Bowman sisters, who were both transformed from the dusty imps playing behind the stable yards earlier in the day. His gaze latched on to Lillian, who was dressed in a pale green gown, the bodice of which seemed to be held up only by a pair of little gold clips at the shoulders. Before he could control the direction of his wayward thoughts, he imagined detaching those clips and letting the green silk fall away from the creamy pale skin of her chest and shoulders—

Marcus dragged his gaze up to Lillian's face. Her shining sable hair was pinned neatly atop her head in an intricate mass that looked nearly too heavy for her slender neck to support. With her hair drawn completely away from her forehead, her eyes appeared more catlike than usual. As she looked back at him, a faint blush colored the crests of her cheeks, and she dipped her chin in a cautious nod. It was obvious that the last thing she wanted was to cross the room to them—to him—and Marcus could not blame her.

"There is no need to summon your daughters, Mrs. Bowman," he murmured. "They are enjoying the company of their friends."

"Their friends," Mercedes exclaimed scornfully. "If you mean that scandalous Annabelle Hunt, I can assure you that I do not condone—"

"I have come to hold Mrs. Hunt in the highest regard," Marcus said, giving the woman a level stare.

Taken aback by the pronouncement, Mercedes paled a little and hastily reversed herself. "If you, with your *superior* judgment, have chosen to esteem Mrs. Hunt, then I must certainly concur, my lord. In fact, I have always thought—"

"Westcliff," Thomas Bowman interrupted, having little interest in the subject of his daughters or whom they had befriended, "when will we have an opportunity to discuss the business matters that were brought up in our last correspondence?"

"Tomorrow, if you like," Marcus replied. "We've organized an early morning ride, followed by breakfast."

"I will forgo the ride, but I will see you at breakfast."

They shook hands, and Marcus took his leave of them with a shallow bow, turning to converse with other guests who sought his attention. Soon a newcomer joined the group, and they quickly made room for the diminutive figure of Georgiana, Lady Westcliff . . . Marcus's mother. She was heavily powdered, her silvery hair elaborately coiffured, and her wrists, neck, and ears heavily ornamented with brilliant jewels. Even her cane sparkled, the gilded handle paved with inset diamonds.

Some elderly women affected a crusty exterior but harbored a heart of gold underneath. The Countess of Westcliff was not one of those women. Her heart—the existence of which was highly arguable—was definitely not made of gold, or any remotely malleable substance. Physically speaking, the countess was not a beauty, nor had she ever been. If one were to replace her expensive garments with a plain broadcloth dress and apron, she would easily have been mistaken for an aging milkmaid. She had a round face; a small mouth; flat, birdlike eyes; and a nose of no remarkable shape or size. Her most distinguishing aspect was an air of peevish disenchantment, like that of a child who had just opened a wrapped birthday present to discover that it was the same thing she had received the year before.

"Good evening, my lady," Marcus said to his mother, regarding her with a wry smile. "We are honored that you have decided to join us this evening." The countess frequently eschewed well-populated dinners like this, preferring to take her meals in one of her private rooms upstairs. Tonight it seemed that she had decided to make an exception.

"I wanted to see if there were any interesting guests in this crowd," the countess replied somewhat grimly, her regal gaze sweeping the room. "From the looks of them, however, it seems the usual pack of dullards."

There were a few nervous titters and chortles from the group, as they chose—erroneously—to assume that the comment had been made in jest.

"You may wish to reserve your opinion until you've been introduced to a few more people," Marcus replied, thinking of the Bowman sisters. His judgmental mother would find no end of diversions in that incorrigible pair.

Adhering to the order of precedence, Marcus escorted the countess to the dining hall, while those of lower rank followed. Dinners at Stony Cross Park were famously lavish, and this one was no exception. Eight courses of fish, game, poultry, and beef were served, accompanied by fresh flower arrangements that were brought to the table with each new remove. They began with turtle soup, broiled salmon with capers, perch and mullet in cream, and succulent John Dory fish dressed with a delicate shrimp sauce. The next course consisted of peppered venison, herb-garnished ham, gently fried sweetbreads floating in steaming gravy, and crisp-skinned roast fowl. And so on and so forth, until the guests were stuffed and lethargic, their faces flushed from the constant replenishing of their wineglasses by attentive footmen. The dinner was concluded with a succession of platters filled with almond cheesecakes, lemon puddings, and rice soufflés.

Abstaining from dessert, Marcus drank a glass of port and entertained himself by stealing lightning-quick glances at Lillian Bowman. In the rare moments when she was still and quiet, Lillian looked like a demure young princess. But as soon as she began talking—making gestures with her fork and freely interrupting the men's conversation—all appearance of regalness dropped away. Lillian was far too direct, far too certain that what she said was interesting and worthy of being listened to. She made no attempt to seem impressed with the opinions of others, and she seemed incapable of being deferential to anyone.

After the rituals of port for the men, tea for the ladies, and a last few rounds of idle conversation, the guests dispersed. As Marcus walked slowly to the great hall with a group of guests that included the Hunts, he became aware that Annabelle was behaving a bit strangely. She walked so close to him that their elbows kept bumping, and she fanned herself enthusiastically even though the interior of the manor was quite cool. Squinting at her quizzically through the great puffs of scented air that she blew his way, Marcus asked, "Is it too warm in here for you, Mrs. Hunt?"

"Why, yes . . . do you feel warm too?"

"No." He smiled down at her, wondering why Annabelle abruptly stopped fanning and gave him a speculative gaze.

"Do you feel *anything*?" she asked.

Amused, Marcus shook his head. "May I ask what prompts your concern, Mrs. Hunt?"

"Oh, it's nothing. I just wondered if perhaps you might have noticed something different about me."

Marcus gave her a quick, impersonal inspection. "Your coiffure," he guessed. Having grown up with two sisters, he had learned that whenever they asked his opinion on their appearance, and refused to tell him why, it usually had something to do with their hairstyle. Though it was a bit inappropriate to discuss the personal appearance of his best friend's wife, Annabelle seemed to regard him in a brotherly light.

Annabelle grinned ruefully at his reply. "Yes, that's it. Forgive me if I am behaving a bit oddly, my lord. I fear I may have had a bit too much wine."

Marcus laughed quietly. "Perhaps some night air will clear your head."

Coming beside them, Simon Hunt caught the last remark, and he settled his hand at his wife's waist. Smiling, he touched his lips to Annabelle's temple. "Shall I take you out to the back terrace?"

"Yes, thank you."

Hunt went still, his dark head inclined toward hers. Although Annabelle couldn't see the arrested expression on her husband's face, Marcus noticed it, and wondered why Hunt suddenly looked so uncomfortable and distracted. "Excuse us, Westcliff," Hunt muttered, and pulled his wife away with unwarranted haste, forcing her to hurry to keep up with his ground-eating strides.

Shaking his head with a touch of bafflement, Marcus watched the pair's precipitate exit from the entrance hall.

"Nothing. Absolutely nothing," Daisy said glumly, wandering from the dining hall with Lillian and Evie. "I was seated between two gentlemen who couldn't have taken less interest in me. Either the perfume is a sham, or both of them are anosmic."

Evie gave her a blank look. "I . . . I'm afraid I'm not f-familiar with that word . . ."

"You would be if your father owned a soap company," Lillian said dryly. "It means that one has no sense of smell."

"Oh. Then my dinner p-partners must also have been anosmic. Because neither of them noticed me either. What about you, Lillian?"

"The same," Lillian replied, feeling both confounded and frustrated. "I suppose the perfume doesn't work after all. But I was so certain that it had an effect on Lord Westcliff . . ."

"Had you ever stood so close to him before?" Daisy asked.

"Of course not!"

"Then my guess is that simple proximity to you made him lose his head."

"Oh, well, obviously," Lillian said with self-deprecating sarcasm. "I'm a world-renowned temptress."

Daisy laughed. "I wouldn't discount your charms, dear. In my opinion, Lord Westcliff has always—"

But that particular opinion would forever go unheard, for as they reached the entrance hall, the three girls caught sight of Lord Westcliff himself. Leaning one shoulder against a column in a relaxed pose, he cut a commanding figure. Everything about him, from the arrogant tilt of his head to the physical confidence of his posture, bespoke the result of generations of aristocratic breeding. Lillian experienced an overpowering urge to sneak up to him and poke him in some ticklish place. She would have loved to make him roar with annoyance.

His head turned, and his gaze swept the three girls with polite interest before settling on Lillian. Then the look in his eyes became far less polite, and the interest took on a vaguely predatory quality that caused Lillian's breath to catch. She couldn't help remembering the feel of the hard-muscled body that was concealed beneath the impeccably tailored black broadcloth suit.

"He's t-terrifying," she heard Evie breathe, and Lillian glanced at her with sudden amusement.

"He's just a man, dear. I'm sure he orders his servants to help him put his trousers on one leg at a time, like everyone else."

Daisy laughed at her irreverence, while Evie looked scandalized.

To Lillian's surprise, Westcliff pushed away from the column and approached them. "Good evening, ladies. I hope you enjoyed the supper."

Tongue-tied, Evie could only nod, while Daisy responded animatedly, "It was splendid, my lord."

"Good." Although he spoke to Evie and Daisy, his gaze locked on to Lillian's face. "Miss Bowman, Miss Jenner . . . forgive me, but I had hoped to take your companion aside for a word in private. With your permission . . ."

"By all means," Daisy replied, giving Lillian a sly smile. "Take her away, my lord. We have no use for her at the moment."

"Thank you." Gravely he extended his arm to Lillian. "Miss Bowman, if you would be so kind?"

Lillian took his arm, feeling oddly fragile as he led her across the hall. The silence between them was awkward and question-fraught. Westcliff had always provoked her, but now he seemed to have acquired the knack of making her feel vulnerable—and she didn't like it at all. Stopping in the lee of a massive column, he turned to face her, and her hand dropped away from his arm.

His mouth and eyes were just two or three inches above her own, their bodies perfectly matched as they stood toe to toe. Her pulse became a soft, rapid tapping inside her veins, and her skin was suddenly covered in heat that presaged a burn, as if she were standing much too close to a fire. Westcliff's thick lashes lowered slightly over midnight-dark eyes as he noticed her heightened color.

"Miss Bowman," he murmured, "I assure you that in spite of what happened this afternoon, you have nothing to fear from me. If you have no objection, I would like to discuss it with you in a place where we won't be disturbed."

"Certainly," Lillian said calmly. Meeting him somewhere alone had the uncomfortable overtones of a lovers' tryst—which this would certainly not be. And yet she couldn't seem to control the nervous thrills that ran up and down her spine. "Where shall we meet?"

"The morning room opens onto an orangery."

"Yes, I know where that is."

"Shall we meet in five minutes?"

"All right." Lillian gave him a supremely unconcerned smile, as if she were quite accustomed to making clandestine arrangements. "I'll go first."

As she took her leave of him, she could feel his gaze on her back, and she knew somehow that he watched her every second until she was out of sight.

Chapter 6

*A*s Lillian walked into the orangery, she was suffused in the scent of . . . oranges. But lemons, bays, and myrtles also cast their fragrance extravagantly through the gently heated air. The tiled floor of the rectangular building was punctuated with iron grillwork vents that allowed the warmth of the stoves on the lower floor to waft evenly inside the room. Starlight shone through the glass ceiling and glittering windows, and illuminated the interior scaffolding that had been loaded with rows of tropical plants.

The orangery was shadowy, with only the flicker of torches outside to relieve the darkness. At the sound of a footstep, Lillian turned quickly to view the intruder. A flash of uneasiness must have revealed itself in her posture, for Westcliff made his voice low and reassuring. "It's just me. If you would rather meet in another place—"

"No," Lillian interrupted, mildly amused to hear one of the most powerful men in England refer to himself as "just me." "I like the orangery. It's my favorite place in the manor, actually."

"Mine also," he said, approaching her slowly. "For many reasons, not the least of which is the privacy it offers."

"You don't have much privacy, do you? With all the comings and goings at Stony Cross Park . . ."

"I manage to carve out sufficient time for solitude."

"And what do you do, when you're alone?" The entire situation was beginning to seem rather dreamlike, talking with Westcliff in the orangery, watching the glimmers of stray torchlight score across the harsh but elegant modeling of his face.

"I read," came his gravelly voice. "I walk. Occasionally I swim in the river."

She was suddenly grateful for the darkness, as the thought of his unclothed body sliding through the water caused her to flush.

Reading discomfort in her sudden silence, and mistaking the cause, Westcliff spoke gruffly. "Miss Bowman, I must apologize for what happened earlier today. I am at a loss to explain my behavior, other than to state that it was a moment of insanity that will never be repeated."

Lillian stiffened a little at the word "insanity." "Fine," she said. "I accept your apology."

"You may set your mind at ease with the knowledge that I do not find you desirable in any way whatsoever."

"I understand. Enough said, my lord."

"If the two of us were left alone on a deserted island, I would have absolutely no thought of approaching you."

"I realize that," she said shortly. "You don't have to go on and on about it."

"I just want to make it clear that what I did was a complete aberration. You are not the kind of woman whom I would ever be attracted to."

"All right."

"In fact—"

"You've made yourself *quite* clear, my lord," Lillian interrupted with a scowl, thinking that it was undoubtedly the most annoying apology she had ever received. "However . . . as my father always says, an honest apology comes with a price."

Westcliff shot her an alert glance. "Price?"

The air between them crackled with challenge. "Yes, my lord. It's no trouble for you to mouth a few words and then be done with it, is it? But if you were *truly* sorry for what you did, you would try to make amends."

"All I did was kiss you," he protested, as if she were making far too much of the incident.

"Against my will," Lillian said significantly. She adopted an expression of wounded dignity. "Perhaps there are some women who would welcome your romantic attentions, but I am not one of them. And I am not accustomed to being grabbed and forcefully subjected to kisses that I didn't ask for—"

"You participated," Westcliff retorted, wearing a Hades-like grimace.

"I did not!"

"You—" Seeming to realize that it was an unproductive argument, Westcliff broke off and swore.

"But," Lillian continued sweetly, "I might be willing to forgive and forget. If . . ." She paused deliberately.

"If?" he asked darkly.

"If you would do one small thing for me."

"And that would be?"

"Merely to ask your mother to sponsor my sister and me for the coming season."

His eyes widened in a most unflattering manner, as if the notion was outside the bounds of reason. "No."

"She might also instruct us on a few points of British etiquette—"

"*No.*"

"We need a sponsor," Lillian persisted. "My sister and I won't make headway in society without one. The countess is an influential woman, and well-respected, and her endorsement would guarantee our success. I'm certain that you could think of a way to convince her to help me—"

"Miss Bowman," Westcliff interrupted coldly, "Queen Victoria herself could not drag a pair of savage brats like you along the path of respectability. It's not possible. And pleasing your father is hardly enough incentive for me to put my mother through such hell as you are capable of creating."

"I thought you might say that." Lillian wondered if she dared follow her instincts and undertake a huge risk. Was there any chance that in spite of the wallflowers' lack of success with their perfume experiment this evening, it was still capable of working some magic on Westcliff? If not, she was about to make a terrible fool of herself. Taking a deep breath, she stepped closer to him. "Very well—you leave me no choice. If you don't agree to help me, Westcliff, I will tell everyone about what happened this afternoon. I daresay people will find no small amusement in the fact that the self-possessed Lord Westcliff cannot control his desire for a bumptious American girl with atrocious manners. And you won't be able to deny it—because you never lie."

Westcliff arched one brow, giving her a look that should have withered her on the spot. "You are overestimating your attractions, Miss Bowman."

"Am I? Then prove it."

Surely the feudal lords in Westcliff's extensive ancestry had worn an expression just like this when they had disciplined rebellious peasants. "How?"

Even in her present spirit of throwing caution to the wind, Lillian had to swallow hard before answering. "I dare you to put your arms around me," she said, "as you did earlier today. And we'll see if you have any more luck in controlling yourself this time."

The scorn in his gaze revealed exactly how pathetic he considered her challenge. "Miss Bowman, as it appears that I must put this plainly . . . I do not desire you. This afternoon was a mistake. One that will not be made again. Now if you will excuse me, I have guests to—"

"Coward."

Westcliff had begun to turn away, but the word caused him to swivel back to her with sudden incredulous fury. Lillian guessed that it was an accusation that had rarely, if ever, been leveled at him.

"What did you say?"

It required every inch of backbone she possessed to hold his icy gaze. "Clearly you're afraid to touch me. You're afraid that you might not be able to control yourself."

Looking away from her, the earl gave a slight shake of his head, as though suspecting that he must have misunderstood her. When he glanced back, his eyes were filled with active hostility. "Miss Bowman, is it so difficult for you to comprehend that I don't *want* to hold you?"

Lillian realized that he would not be making such a

fuss if he was completely confident in his own ability to resist her. Encouraged by the thought, she moved nearer to him, not missing the way his entire body seemed to tense. "The issue isn't whether you want to or not," she replied. "It's whether you'll be able to let go of me once you do."

"Incredible," he said beneath his breath, glaring at her with rank antagonism.

Lillian held still, waiting for him to pick up the gauntlet. As soon as he closed the remaining distance between them, her smile died away and her mouth felt oddly stiff, and her heart thumped hard at the base of her throat. One glance at his purposeful face revealed that he was going to do it. She had left him no choice but to try and prove her wrong. And if he did, she would never be able to look him in the face again. *Oh, Mr. Nettle,* she thought weakly, *your magic perfume had better work.*

Moving with infinite reluctance, Westcliff gingerly put his arms around her. The escalation of Lillian's heartbeat seemed to drive the air from her lungs. One of his broad hands settled between her tense shoulder blades, while the other pressed at the small of her back. He touched her with undue care, as if she were made of some volatile substance. And as he brought her body gently against his, her blood turned to liquid fire. Her hands fluttered in search of a resting place until her palms grazed the back of his coat. Flattening her palms on either side of his spine, she felt the flex of hard muscle even through the layers of silk-lined broadcloth and linen.

"Is this what you were asking for?" he murmured, his low voice at her ear.

Lillian's toes curled inside her slippers as his hot breath tickled her hairline. She responded with a wordless nod, feeling crestfallen and mortified as she realized that she had lost her gamble. Westcliff was going to show her how easy it was to release her, and then he would forever afterward subject her to ruthless mockery. "You can let me go now," she whispered, her mouth twisting in self-derision.

But Westcliff didn't move. His dark head dropped a little lower, and he drew in a breath that wasn't quite steady. Lillian perceived that he was taking in the scent of her throat . . . absorbing it with slow but ever-increasing greed, as if he were an addict inhaling lung-fuls of narcotic smoke. *The perfume*, she thought in bemusement. So it hadn't been her imagination. It was working its magic again. But why did Westcliff seem to be the only man to respond to it? Why—

Her thoughts were scattered as the pressure of his hands increased, causing her to shiver and arch.

"Damn it," Westcliff whispered savagely. Before she quite knew what was happening, he had pushed her up against a nearby wall. His fiercely accusing gaze moved from her dazed eyes to her parted lips, his silent struggle lasting another burning second, until he suddenly gave in with a curse and brought their mouths together with an impatient tug.

His hands adjusted the angle of her head, and he kissed her with gentle bites and nips, as if her mouth were an ex-otic delicacy to savor. Her knees weakened until she could hardly stand. This was Westcliff, she tried to re-mind herself . . . Westcliff, the man she hated . . . but as he sealed his mouth harder over hers, she couldn't stop herself from responding. Straining against him, she in-stinctively rose on her toes until their bodies were per-fectly aligned, the aching place between her thighs cradling the rigid bulge behind the buttoned fall of his trousers. Suddenly realizing what she had done, she flushed and tried to pull away, but he wouldn't let her. His hand clenched firmly over her bottom, holding her there while his mouth devoured hers with smoldering sensuality, licking deeply, exploring the damp silk of her inner cheeks. She couldn't seem to catch her breath . . . she gasped as she felt his free hand search the front of her bodice.

"I want to feel you," Westcliff muttered against her trembling lips, tugging in at the unrelenting obstruction of her padded basque. "I want to kiss you everywhere . . ."

Her breasts hurt inside her tightly cinched bodice. She was possessed by the insane urge to tear away the quilted lining of her corset and beg him to soothe her tormented flesh with his mouth and hands. Instead she threaded her fingers through the thick, slightly curling locks of his hair while he kissed her in a fever of rising need, until her thoughts were no longer coherent and she was shivering with desire.

Suddenly the heady stimulation ended, as Westcliff tore his mouth away and thrust her back against a fluted half column. Breathing raggedly, he half turned from her, and stood there with his fists clenched.

After a long time, Lillian collected herself sufficiently to speak. The perfume had worked rather too well. Her voice was thick and scratchy, as if she had just awoken from a long sleep. "Well. I . . . I suppose that answers my question. Now . . . as to my request for sponsorship . . ."

Westcliff did not look at her. "I'll think about it," he muttered, and strode from the orangery.

Chapter 7

"Annabelle, what happened to you?" Lillian asked the next morning, joining the other wallflowers at the farthest table on the back terrace for breakfast. "You look dreadful. Why aren't you wearing your riding habit? I thought you were going to try out the jumping course this morning. And why did you disappear so suddenly last night? It's not like you to simply vanish without saying—"

"I didn't have a choice in the matter," Annabelle said testily, folding her fingers around the delicate bowl of a porcelain teacup. Looking pale and exhausted, her blue eyes ringed with dark shadows, she swallowed a mouthful of heavily sweetened tea before continuing. "It was that blasted perfume of yours—as soon as he caught one whiff of it, he went berserk."

Shocked, Lillian tried to take in the information, her stomach plummeting. "It . . . it had an effect on Westcliff, then?" she managed to ask.

"Good Lord, not Lord Westcliff." Annabelle rubbed her weary eyes. "He couldn't have cared less what I smelled like. It was my *husband* who went completely mad. After he caught the scent of that stuff, he dragged me up to our room and . . . well, suffice it to say, Mr. Hunt kept me awake all night. *All night*," she repeated in sullen emphasis, and drank deeply of the tea.

"Doing what?" Daisy asked blankly.

Lillian, who was feeling a rush of relief that Lord Westcliff had not been attracted to Annabelle while she was wearing the perfume, gave her younger sister a derisive glance. "What do you think they were doing? Playing a few hands of Find-the-Lady?"

"Oh," Daisy said as comprehension dawned. She regarded Annabelle with unmaidenly curiosity. "But I was under the impression that you liked doing . . . *that* . . . with Mr. Hunt."

"Well, yes, of course I do, but . . ." Annabelle paused and turned red. "That is, when a man is aroused to that extremity—" She stopped as she realized that even Lillian was paying keen interest to her words. Being the only married member of the group, she possessed a knowledge of men and intimate matters that the others were exceedingly curious about. Generally Annabelle was quite forthcoming, but she drew the line at disclosing private details of her relationship with Mr. Hunt. Her voice lowered to a whisper. "Let's just say that my husband does not need the influence of some potion that increases his physical appetite even more."

"You're sure it was the perfume?" Lillian asked. "Perhaps something else set him off—"

"It was the perfume," Annabelle said unequivocally.

Evie broke in, looking puzzled. "But wh-why didn't it

stir Lord Westcliff when you wore it? Why did it affect only your husband, and n-no one else?"

"And why didn't anyone take any notice of Evie or me?" Daisy asked, disgruntled.

Annabelle drained her tea, poured some more, and carefully stirred a lump of sugar into her cup. Her heavy-lidded eyes regarded Lillian over the china rim. "What about you, dear? Did anyone take notice of you?"

"Actually . . ." Lillian studied the contents of her own teacup. "Westcliff did," she said grimly. "*Again.* Of all the luck. I've found an aphrodisiac that works only on a man whom I despise."

Annabelle choked on a swallow of tea, while Daisy clapped her hand over her own mouth to stifle a fit of laughter. After Annabelle's spasms of mingled coughing and giggling had subsided, she regarded Lillian with slightly watery eyes. "I can't begin to imagine how upset Westcliff must be to find himself so attracted to you when the both of you have always fought so terribly."

"I told him that if he wanted to make amends for his behavior, he could ask the countess to be our sponsor," Lillian said.

"Brilliant," Daisy exclaimed. "Did he agree?"

"He is lending some thought to the matter.

Leaning against the arm of her chair, Annabelle stared thoughtfully into the distant morning mist that enshrouded the forest. "I don't understand . . . Why would the perfume work only on Mr. Hunt and Lord Westcliff? And why would it have no effect on the earl when I wear it, whereas when you do . . ."

"Maybe the magical part," Evie speculated, "is that it h-helps it to find your true love."

"Balderdash," Lillian remarked, offended by the notion. "Westcliff is not my true love! He's a pompous, superior ass with whom I've never managed to have a civil conversation. And any woman unlucky enough to marry him will end up rotting here in Hampshire, having to account to him for everything she does. No, thank you."

"Lord Westcliff is hardly some fusty country gentleman," Annabelle said. "He stays at his house in London quite often, and he's invited everywhere. As for his superior manner—I suppose I can't argue with that. Except to say that when one becomes better acquainted with him, and he lets his guard down, he can be very engaging."

Lillian shook her head, her mouth hardening stubbornly. "If he is the only man this perfume will attract, I'll stop wearing it."

"Oh, don't!" Annabelle's eyes were suddenly sly and merry. "I should think you'd want to continue torturing him."

"Yes, wear it," Daisy urged. "We have no proof that the earl is the only man who will be seduced by your perfume."

Lillian glanced at Evie, who wore a faint smile. "Shall I?" she asked, and Evie nodded. "Very well," Lillian said. "If there is any chance of torturing Lord Westcliff, I should hate to miss it." She pulled the vial from the pocket of her riding skirts. "Does anyone want to try some more?"

Annabelle looked appalled. "No. Keep it far, *far* away from me."

The other two had already extended their hands. Lillian grinned and gave it to Daisy, who smoothed a few generous drops onto her wrists and tapped some behind her ears. "There," Daisy said with satisfaction. "That's twice as much as I used last night. If my true love is within a mile radius, he'll come running for me."

Evie received the bottle and applied some perfume to her throat. "Even if it doesn't w-work," she commented, "it's a very pretty scent."

Tucking the vial back into her pocket, Lillian stood from the table. She straightened the full chocolate-colored skirts of her riding habit, the longer side of which was caught up with a button to keep the hemline even while walking. On horseback, however, the skirt would be let down to drape attractively over the horse's side and cover her legs properly. Her hair was caught up in neatly pinned braids at the nape of her neck, with a small feather-trimmed hat perched atop her head. "It's time for the riders to gather at the stables." She raised her brows as she asked, "Aren't any of you going?"

Annabelle gave her a speaking glance. "Not after last evening."

"I don't ride well," Evie said apologetically.

"Neither do Lillian and I," Daisy said, leveling an admonishing stare at her older sister.

"Yes, I do," Lillian protested. "You know quite well that I can ride as well as any man!"

"Only when you ride *like* a man," Daisy retorted. Seeing Annabelle's and Evie's confusion, she explained. "Back in New York, Lillian and I rode astride most of the time. It's much safer, really, and far more comfortable. Our parents didn't mind as long as we rode on our own property, and wore strap-ankle breeches beneath our skirts. On the few occasions when we rode in the company of men, we went sidesaddle—but neither of us is very accomplished at it. Lillian is an excellent jumper when she rides astride. To my knowledge, however, she's never tried a jump on sidesaddle. And the balance is completely different, and the muscles that one uses are not the same, and this jumping course at Stony Cross Park—"

"Hush, Daisy," Lillian muttered.

"—is going to be very challenging, and I am fairly certain—"

"*Shut up,*" Lillian said in a fierce undertone.

"—that my sister is going to break her neck," Daisy finished, returning Lillian's glare with one of her own.

Annabelle looked troubled by the information. "Lillian, dear—"

"I have to go," Lillian said curtly. "I don't want to be late."

"I know for a fact that Lord Westcliff's jumping course is not appropriate for a novice."

"I'm not a novice," Lillian said through gritted teeth.

"There are some difficult jumps, with stiff bars at the top. Simon—that is, Mr. Hunt—took me through the course not long after it was built, and counseled me on how to approach the various jumps, and even then, it was very difficult. And if your riding position isn't perfect, you can interfere with the free movement of the horse's head and neck, and—"

"I'll be fine," Lillian interrupted coolly. "Heavens, Annabelle, I never knew you could be such a wet goose."

Inured by now to the sharpness of Lillian's tongue, Annabelle studied her defiant face. "Why is it necessary that you endanger yourself?"

"You should know by now that I never back down from a challenge."

"And that is an admirable quality, dear," came Annabelle's smooth reply. "Unless you're applying it to a pointless exercise."

It was the closest to an argument that they had ever come. "Look," Lillian said impatiently, "if I fall, you can give me a complete rake-down, and I'll listen to every word. But no one is going to stop me from riding today . . . and therefore the only pointless exercise is for you to wag your jaw about it."

Turning, she strode away, while she heard Annabelle's exasperated exclamation behind her, and Daisy's indistinct but resigned murmur, ". . . after all, it's her neck to break . . ."

After Lillian's departure, Daisy looked at Annabelle with an apologetic grimace. "I'm sorry. She didn't mean to sound sharp. You know how she is."

"There is no need for you to apologize," Annabelle said wryly. "Lillian is the one who should be sorry . . . though I suppose I'd have to go hang before she would ever say so."

Daisy shrugged. "There are times when my sister must suffer the consequences of her own actions. But one of the things I adore about her is that when she's proven wrong, she will admit it, and even make sport of herself."

Annabelle did not return the smile. "I adore her also, Daisy. So much that I can't let her walk blindly into danger—or in this case, ride straight toward it. It is obvious that she doesn't understand how dangerous that jumping course is. Westcliff is an experienced horseman, and as such, he had the course built to suit his own level of skill. Even my husband, who is a powerful rider, says that it is a challenge. And for Lillian to attempt it when she is not accustomed to jumping sidesaddle—" A frown shuttered her forehead. "The thought of her being hurt or killed in a fall is unbearable."

Evie spoke softly then. "M-Mr. Hunt is on the terrace. He's standing by the French doors."

The three of them glanced toward Annabelle's large,

dark husband, who was dressed in riding clothes. He stood with a group of three men who had approached him as soon as he had set foot on the back terrace. They all chuckled at some quip that Hunt had made—no doubt some off-color remark. Hunt was a man's man, and therefore well liked by the usual crowd at Stony Cross Park. A sardonic smile curved Hunt's lips as he glanced over the clusters of guests seated at the outdoor tables, while servants moved among them with platters of food and pitchers of fresh-squeezed juice. His smile changed, however, when he saw Annabelle, the cynicism transforming into a tenderness that made Daisy feel slightly wistful. It seemed as if something passed through the air between the couple, some intangible but intense connection that nothing could sever.

"Do excuse me," Annabelle murmured, standing. She went to her husband, who took her hand as soon as she reached him, and lifted it to press a kiss into her palm. Staring at her upturned face, he retained possession of her hand, and his head inclined toward hers.

"Do you think she is telling him about Lillian?" Daisy asked Evie.

"I hope so."

"Oh, he *must* handle the matter discreetly," Daisy said with a groan. "Any hint of confrontation, and Lillian will turn mulish."

"I imagine that Mr. Hunt will be very circumspect. He's known as a very effective negotiator in business matters, isn't he?"

"You're right," Daisy replied, feeling marginally better. "And he's accustomed to dealing with Annabelle, who has a rather fiery temperament herself." As they conversed, Daisy couldn't help noticing the odd phenomenon that happened whenever she and Evie were alone . . . Evie seemed to relax, and her stutter all but vanished.

Evie leaned forward, unselfconsciously graceful as she leaned her chin in the shallow cup of her hand and propped her elbow on the table. "What do you think is going on between them? Lillian and Lord Westcliff, I mean."

Daisy smiled ruefully, feeling a twinge of concern for her sister. "I think it frightened my sister yesterday to realize that she might find Lord Westcliff attractive. And she doesn't react well to being frightened—it usually makes her go off full-tilt and do something reckless. Hence her determination to go and kill herself on horseback today."

"But why would that frighten her?" Puzzlement colored Evie's expression. "I should think it would please Lillian to attract the notice of someone like the earl."

"Not when she knows that they would be at constant loggerheads with one another if anything were to come of it. And Lillian has no desire to be crushed by a man as powerful as Westcliff." Daisy sighed heavily. "I wouldn't want that for her either."

Evie nodded in reluctant agreement. "I . . . I suppose the earl would find it difficult to tolerate Lillian's colorful nature."

"Rather," Daisy said with a droll smile. "Evie, dear . . . I suppose it's tasteless of me to draw attention to it, but in the past minute your stammer has disappeared."

The red-haired girl tucked a shy smile in the concealment of her palm, and glanced at Daisy from beneath a sweep of auburn lashes. "I'm always much better when I'm away from home . . . away from my family. And it helps if I remember to talk slowly, and think about what

I'm going to say. But I'm worse when I'm tired, or when I have to speak to str-strangers. There's nothing more terrifying to me than going to a ball and facing a room full of people I don't know."

"Dear," Daisy said softly, "the next time you face a room full of strangers . . . you might tell yourself that some of them are just friends waiting to be found."

The morning was fresh and misty as riders congregated before the stables. There were approximately fifteen men, and two other women besides Lillian. The men were dressed in dark coats, breeches that ranged from fawn to mustard, and top boots. The women wore habits that were fitted closely to the waist, trimmed with braid, and finished with voluminous asymmetrical skirts that were buttoned on one side. Servants and stable boys moved among the crowd, bringing out horses and helping the riders to mount at one of three mounting blocks. Some guests had elected to bring their own horses, while others made use of the renowned stock of the Marsden stables. Although she had toured the stables on a previous visit, Lillian was struck anew by the beauty of the well-tended thoroughbreds that were led out to the waiting guests.

Lillian stood beside one of the mounting blocks in the company of Mr. Winstanley, an auburn-haired young man with attractive features but a weak chin, and two other gentlemen, Lord Hew and Lord Bazeley, who chatted amiably as they waited for their mounts to be brought around. Having little interest in the conversation, Lillian let her gaze wander idly around the scene until she saw Westcliff's lean form striding across the stable courtyard. His coat, though neatly tailored, had been abused by many wearings, and the leather of his top boots had been worn into butter-soft leniency.

Unwanted memories jolted her heart into a rapid rhythm. Her ears burned as she suddenly recalled his silky-rough whisper . . . *I want to kiss you everywhere* . . . Aware of uneasy stirrings within herself, she watched Westcliff approach a horse that had already been led out . . . an animal that Lillian remembered having seen before. The horse, named Brutus, was mentioned in nearly any conversation about equine matters. There was no hunter currently more admired in England than Brutus, a magnificent dark bay with an intelligent, workmanlike disposition. The bay's girth was deep, and his shoulders were muscular and heavily sloped, allowing him to travel easily over rough terrain and jump with remarkable proficiency. On the ground, Brutus had the discipline of a soldier . . . in the air, however, he soared as if he had wings.

"They say that with Brutus, Westcliff needs no second horse," remarked one of the guests.

Lillian, who stood at the mounting block, glanced at the speaker curiously. "What does that mean?"

The auburn-haired man smiled a bit incredulously, as though it were something everyone should know. "On a hunting day," he explained, "one usually rides his first horse in the morning, and then changes to a fresh replacement horse in the afternoon. But it seems that Brutus has the stamina and endurance of two horses."

"Like his owner," one of the others remarked, and they all chuckled.

Glancing around the scene, Lillian saw that Westcliff was involved in a conversation with Simon Hunt, who was quietly relating something that had caused a slight frown to appear on the earl's face. Standing beside his master, Brutus shifted and nuzzled the earl with rough affection, calming as Westcliff reached out to rub his nose.

Lillian was distracted as a stable boy, one of the ones who had engaged in the rounders game yesterday, brought a sleek gray to the mounting block. The boy winked conspiratorially at Lillian as she ascended to the top step. Winking back, she waited as the stable boy checked the tightness of the girth and the balance strap of the detested sidesaddle. Assessing the horse with an approving gaze, she noted that the gray was compact and refined, with flawless conformation and a look of lively intelligence. He was no more than thirteen hands high . . . a perfect lady's horse.

"What is his name?" Lillian asked. At the sound of her voice, one of the horse's ears pivoted toward her attentively.

"Starlight, miss. You'll do well with him—he's the best-mannered horse in the stables, next to Brutus."

Lillian patted the horse's silky neck. "You look like a gentleman, Starlight. I wish I could ride you properly instead of bothering with a silly old sidesaddle."

The gray inclined his head to glance at her with reassuring calmness.

"Milord made a point of telling me that if you were to ride, miss, you should be given Starlight," the stable boy said, seeming impressed by the fact that Westcliff himself had condescended to choose a mount for her.

"How kind," Lillian muttered, slipping her foot into the stirrup and hoisting herself lightly onto the three-pommeled saddle. She tried to sit squarely, with most of her weight carried on her right thigh and right seat bone. Her right leg hooked around a pommel with the toe pointing downward, while her left leg hung naturally in the stirrup. It was not uncomfortable at the moment, though Lillian knew that in a while her legs would ache from the unaccustomed position. Still, as she took the reins and leaned over to pat Starlight once more, she felt a thrill of enjoyment. She loved to ride, and this horse was superior to any in her family's stables.

"Er . . . miss . . ." the stable boy said in a low tone, and bashfully indicated her skirts, which were still buttoned. Now that Lillian was mounted, a good portion of her left leg was displayed.

"Thank you," she said, unfastening the large button at her hip to let the skirts drop over her leg. Satisfied that everything was as it should be, she gently urged the horse away from the mounting block, and Starlight responded immediately, sensitive to the slightest pressure of her boot heel.

Joining a group of riders who were heading toward the forest, Lillian felt a rush of anticipation at the thought of the jumping course. Twelve jumps in all, she had heard, all cleverly arranged on a track that wound through forest and field. It was a challenge that she was certain she could master. Even with the sidesaddle, she had a firm seat, her thigh snug against the curved leaping horn that would assist her balance. And the gray was a marvelously well-trained horse, spirited but obedient as he broke easily from a trot into a smooth gallop.

As Lillian neared the beginning of the course, she saw the first jump, a triangular coop that looked to be about two feet high and six feet across. "That will pose no problem for us, will it, Starlight?" she murmured to the horse. Slowing to a walk, they went toward the group of waiting riders. Before she reached them, however, she became aware of a rider coming up beside her. It was West-

cliff, seated on the dark bay, riding with an ease and econ-
omy of movement that caused the downy hairs on her
arms and the back of her neck to prickle, as it did whenever she saw a feat performed with stunning perfection.
She had to admit, the earl cut a dashing figure on a horse.

Unlike the other gentlemen present, Westcliff wore no
riding gloves. Remembering the gentle scrape of his cal-
lused fingers on her skin, Lillian swallowed hard and
avoided the sight of his hands on the reins. One cautious
glance at his face revealed that he was definitely dis-
pleased about something . . . the space between his dark
brows was notched, and his jaw had hardened into an
obdurate line.

Lillian summoned a carefree smile. "Good morning,
my lord."

"Good morning," came his quiet reply. He seemed to
consider his words carefully before he continued. "Are
you pleased with your mount?"

"Yes, he is splendid. It seems that I have you to thank
for choosing him."

Westcliff's mouth twisted slightly, as if the issue was of
no consequence. "Miss Bowman . . . it has come to my attention that you are not experienced at riding sidesaddle."

Her smile vanished from lips that suddenly felt frozen.
Recalling that Simon Hunt had been speaking to West-
cliff just a minute earlier, Lillian realized with a stab of
annoyance that Annabelle must have set this in motion.
Damn her for interfering, she thought, and scowled.
"I'll manage," she said tersely. "Think nothing of it."

"I'm afraid that I can't allow one of my guests to compromise her own safety."

Lillian watched her own gloved fingers tighten on the
reins. "Westcliff, I can ride as well as anyone else here.

And regardless of what you may have been told, I am not entirely unfamiliar with a sidesaddle. So if you will just leave me alone—"

"If I had been informed of this earlier, I might have found the time to take you around the course and judge your level of competence. As things stand, however, it's too late."

She absorbed his words, the firmness of his tone, the air of authority that rankled deeply. "You're telling me that I can't ride today?"

Westcliff held her gaze steadily. "Not on the jumping course. You are welcome to ride anywhere else on the estate. If you wish, I will assess your skills later in the week, and you might have another opportunity. Today, however, I can't allow it."

Unaccustomed to anyone telling her what she could and could not do, Lillian bit back a flood of offended accusations. Instead she managed to reply with tightly leashed calmness. "Your regard for my welfare is appreciated, my lord. But I would like to suggest a compromise. Watch me on the first two or three jumps, and if I don't seem to be managing them well, I'll abide by your decision."

"I don't compromise on issues of safety," Westcliff said. "You'll abide by my decision *now*, Miss Bowman."

He was being unfair. He was forbidding her to do something merely to display his power over her. Struggling to control her fury, Lillian felt the muscles around her mouth twitching. To her everlasting chagrin, she lost the battle with her temper.

"I can manage the jumps," she told him grimly. "I'll prove it to you."

Chapter 8

*B*efore Westcliff could react, Lillian dug her heel into Starlight's side and leaned over the saddle, her weight shifting to accommodate his sudden leap forward. The horse rallied at once, taking off at a full gallop. Clenching her thighs around the sidesaddle's pommels, Lillian felt her position weaken, her body pivoting as a result of what she was later to learn had been a "grip seat" that was a bit too tight. Gamely she adjusted the change in her hips' orientation just as Starlight approached the jump. She felt the rise of his forelegs and the tremendous force of his hindquarters pushing from the ground, giving her the momentary exhilaration of flying over the triangular barrier. As they landed, however, she had to fight for her seat, taking most of the impact on her right thigh and causing an unpleasant stinging pull. Still, she had done it, and very credibly.

Bringing the horse around with a triumphant smile, Lillian was aware of the surprised gazes of the assembled riders, who were no doubt wondering what had prompted the impulsive jump. All of a sudden she was startled by a blur of dark color beside her and a thunder of hooves. Confused, she had no opportunity to protest or defend herself as she was literally snatched from the saddle and thrown across a brutally hard surface. Dangling helplessly across Westcliff's rock-solid thighs, she was carried several yards away before he stopped the horse, dismounted, and dragged her to the ground with him. Her shoulders were caught in a bruising grip, and Westcliff's livid face was just inches from her own.

"Did you think to convince me of something with that asinine display?" he growled, giving her a brief shake. "The use of my horses is a privilege that I extend to my guests—a privilege you have just lost. From now on, don't even think of setting so much as a foot in the stables, or I will personally boot you off the estate."

White-faced with a rage that matched his, Lillian answered in a low, shaking voice. "Take your hands off me, you son of a bitch." To her satisfaction, she saw his eyes narrow at the profanity. But his painful grasp did not ease, and his breathing deepened to aggressive surges, as if he longed to do her violence. As her defiant gaze was imprisoned by his, she felt a searing charge of energy pass between them, an undirected physical impulse that made her want to strike him, hurt him, sink to the ground and roll with him in an outright brawl. No man had ever maddened her so. As they stood there glaring at each other, bristling with hostility, the heat between them increased until they were both flushed and quickened. Neither of them was aware of the congregation of dumbfounded onlookers in the near distance—they were too enmeshed in mutual antagonism.

A silky masculine voice interrupted their silent, lethal communion, slicing skillfully through the tension. "Westcliff . . . you didn't tell me that you would be providing entertainment, or I would have come out here earlier."

"Don't interfere, St. Vincent," Westcliff snapped.

"Oh, I wouldn't dream of it. I merely wanted to compliment you on the way you're handling the situation. Very diplomatic. Suave, even."

The gentle sarcasm caused the earl to release Lillian roughly. She staggered back a step, and was immediately caught at the waist by a pair of deft hands. Bemused, she looked up into the remarkable face of Sebastian, Lord St. Vincent, the infamous rake and seducer.

The intensifying sunlight burned off the mist and laced St. Vincent's dark gold hair with streaks of glittering pale amber. Lillian had seen him from a distance on many occasions, but they had never been introduced, and St. Vincent had always avoided the line of wallflowers at any ball he happened to be attending. At a distance, he was a striking figure. At close range, the exotic beauty of his features was nearly immobilizing. St. Vincent had the most extraordinary eyes she had ever seen, light blue and catlike, shaded with dark lashes and surmounted by tawny brows. His features were strong but refined, his skin gleaming like bronze that had been patiently polished for hours. Contrary to Lillian's expectations, St. Vincent looked wicked but not at all dissipated, his smile skillfully reaching through her anger and enjoining a tentative response. Such a plenitude of charm should have been illegal.

Switching his gaze to Westcliff's set face, St. Vincent arched one brow and asked lightly, "Shall I escort the culprit back to the manor, my lord?"

The earl nodded. "Get her out of my sight," he muttered, "before I'm moved to say something I'll regret."

"Go ahead and say it," Lillian snapped.

Westcliff took a step toward her, his expression thunderous.

Hastily St. Vincent tucked Lillian behind him. "Westcliff, your guests are waiting. And although I'm certain they're enjoying this fascinating drama, the horses are getting restless."

The earl seemed to undergo a brief but savage battle with his self-discipline before he managed to school his features into impassivity. He jerked his head in the direction of the manor in a silent command for St. Vincent to remove Lillian from the scene.

"May I take her back on my horse?" St. Vincent inquired politely.

"No," came Westcliff's stony reply. "She can damned well walk to the house."

St. Vincent motioned at once for a groom to take charge of the two abandoned horses. Giving his arm to a fuming Lillian, he gazed down at her with a twinkle in his pale eyes. "It's the dungeons for you," he informed her. "And I intend to personally apply the thumbscrews."

"I would prefer torture to *his* company any day," Lillian said, gathering up the long side of her skirt and buttoning it to walking length.

As they walked away, Lillian's back stiffened at the sound of Westcliff's voice. "You might stop by the icehouse on the way back. She needs cooling."

Fighting to marshal his emotions into some semblance of order, Marcus stared after Lillian Bowman with a gaze that should have singed the back of her riding jacket. He usually found it easy to step back from any situation and assess it objectively. In the past few minutes, however, every vestige of self-control had exploded.

As Lillian had ridden defiantly toward the jump, Marcus had seen her momentary loss of alignment, potentially fatal on a sidesaddle, and the instant expectation that she would fall had sent him reeling. At that speed, her spine or her neck could have snapped. And he had been powerless to do anything but watch. He had been abruptly cold with dread, nauseated from it, and when the little idiot had managed to land safely, the full sum of his fear had been transformed into blazing white fury. He had made no conscious decision to approach her, but suddenly they were both on the ground, and her narrow shoulders were in his hands, and all he wanted to do was crush her in his arms in a paroxysm of relief, and kiss her, and then dismember her with his bare hands.

The fact that her safety meant so much to him was . . . not something that he wanted to think about.

Scowling, Marcus went to the groom who held Brutus's reins, and took them from him. Lost in brooding contemplation, he was only dimly aware that Simon Hunt had quietly advised the guests to proceed with the jumping course without waiting for the earl to lead them.

Simon Hunt approached him on horseback, his face expressionless. "Are you going to ride?" he asked calmly.

For answer, Marcus swung up into the saddle, clicking softly as Brutus shifted beneath him. "That woman is intolerable," he grumbled, his gaze daring Hunt to offer an opinion to the contrary.

"Did you mean to goad her into taking the jump?" Hunt asked.

"I commanded her to do the exact opposite. You must have heard me."

"Yes, I and everyone else heard you," Hunt said dryly. "My question pertains to your tactics, Westcliff. It's obvious that a woman like Miss Bowman requires a softer approach than outright command. Moreover, I've seen you at the negotiating table, and your powers of persuasion are unmatched by anyone except perhaps Shaw. Had you chosen, you could have coaxed and flattered her to do your bidding in less than a minute. Instead you used all the subtlety of a bludgeon in the attempt to prove yourself her master."

"I've never noticed your gift for hyperbole before," Marcus muttered.

"And now," Hunt continued evenly, "you've thrown her over to St. Vincent's sympathetic care. God knows he'll probably rob her of her virtue before they even reach the manor."

Marcus glanced at him sharply, his smoldering ire undercut by sudden worry. "He wouldn't."

"Why not?"

"She's not his preferred style."

Hunt laughed gently. "Does St. Vincent have a preferred style? I've never noticed any similarities between the objects of his pursuit, other than the fact that they are all women. Dark, fair, plump, slender . . . he's remarkably unprejudiced in his affairs."

"Damn it all to hell," Marcus said beneath his breath, experiencing, for the first time in his life, the gnawing sting of jealousy.

Lillian concentrated on putting one foot in front of the other, when all she wanted was to head back to Westcliff and fling herself upon him in a mindless attack. "That arrogant, pompous *clodpole*—"

"Easy," she heard St. Vincent murmur. "Westcliff is in a thorough temper—and I wouldn't care to engage him in your defense. I can best him any day with a sword, but not with fists."

"Why not?" Lillian muttered. "You've got a longer reach than Westcliff."

"He's got the most vicious right hook I've ever encountered. And I have an unfortunate habit of trying to shield my face—which frequently leaves me open for gut punches."

The unashamed conceit behind the statement drew a reluctant laugh from Lillian. As the heat of anger faded, she reflected that with a face like his, one could hardly blame him for desiring to protect it. "Have you fought with the earl often?" she asked.

"Not since we were boys at school. Westcliff did everything a bit too perfectly—I had to challenge him now and then just to make certain that his vanity didn't become overinflated. Here . . . shall we take a more scenic route through the garden?"

Lillian hesitated, recalling the numerous stories that she had heard about him. "I'm not certain that would be wise."

St. Vincent smiled. "What if I promise on my honor not to make any advances to you?"

Considering that, Lillian nodded. "In that case, all right."

St. Vincent guided her through a small leafy grove, and onto a graveled path shaded by a row of ancient yews. "I should probably tell you," he remarked casu-

ally, "that since my sense of honor is completely deterio-
rated, any promise I make is worthless."

"Then I should tell you that *my* right hook is likely ten
times more vicious than Westcliff's."

St. Vincent grinned. "Tell me, darling, what happened
to cause bad blood between you and the earl?"

Startled by the casual endearment, Lillian thought of
reprimanding him, then decided to let it pass. After all, it
had been very nice of him to give up his morning ride to
escort her back to the manor. "I'm afraid it was a case of
hatred at first sight," she replied. "I think Westcliff is a
judgmental boor, and he considers me an ill-natured
brat." She shrugged. "Perhaps we're both right."

"I think neither of you is right," St. Vincent murmured.

"Well, actually . . . I am something of a brat," Lillian
admitted.

His lips twitched with barely suppressed humor. "Are
you?"

She nodded. "I like to have my way, and I'm very
cross when I don't get it. In fact, I've often been told that
my temperament is quite similar to that of my grandmother, who was a dockside washwoman."

St. Vincent seemed entertained by the notion of being
related to a washwoman. "Were you close to your
grandmother?"

"Oh, she was a ripping old dear. Foul-mouthed and
high-spirited, and she often said things that would make
you laugh until your stomach hurt. Oh . . . pardon . . . I
don't think I'm supposed to say the word 'stomach' in
front of a gentleman."

"I'm shocked," St. Vincent said gravely, "but I'll recover." Looking around them as if to ascertain that he

wouldn't be overheard, he whispered conspiratorially, "I'm not really a gentleman, you know."

"You're a viscount, aren't you?"

"That hardly goes hand-in-hand with being a gentleman. You don't know much about the peerage, do you?"

"I believe I already know more than I want to."

St. Vincent gave her a curious smile. "And here I thought you were intent upon marrying one of us. Am I mistaken, or aren't you and your younger sister a pair of dollar princesses brought over from the colonies to land titled husbands?"

"The *colonies?*" Lillian repeated with a chiding grin. "In case you hadn't heard, my lord, we won the Revolution."

"Ah. I must have forgotten to read the paper that day. But in answer to my question . . . ?"

"Yes," Lillian said, flushing a little. "Our parents brought us here to find husbands. They want to infuse the family line with blue blood."

"Is that what you want?"

"Today my sole desire is to *draw* some blue blood," she muttered, thinking of Westcliff.

"What a ferocious creature you are," St. Vincent said, laughing. "I pity Westcliff if he crosses you again. In fact, I think I should warn him . . ." His voice died away as he saw the sudden pain on her face, and heard the sharp intake of her breath.

A tearing agony went through Lillian's right thigh, and she would have stumbled to the ground had it not been for the support of his arm around her back. "Oh, damn it," she said shakily, clutching at her thigh. A twisting spasm in her thigh muscle caused her to groan through her clenched teeth. "Damn, damn—"

"What is it?" St. Vincent asked, swiftly lowering her to the path. "A leg cramp?"

"Yes . . ." Pale and shaking, Lillian caught at her leg, while her face contorted with agony. "Oh God, it hurts!"

He bent over her, frowning with concern. His quiet voice was threaded with urgency. "Miss Bowman . . . would it be possible for you to temporarily ignore everything you've heard about my reputation? Just long enough for me to help you?"

Squinting at his face, Lillian saw nothing but an honest desire to relieve her pain, and she nodded.

"Good girl," he murmured, and gathered her writhing body into a half-sitting position. He talked swiftly to distract her, while his hand slipped beneath her skirts with gentle expertise. "It will take just a moment. I hope to God that no one happens along to see this—it looks more than a bit incriminating. And it's doubtful that they would accept the traditional but somewhat overused leg-cramp excuse—"

"I don't care," she gasped. "Just make it go away."

She felt St. Vincent's hand slide lightly up her leg, the warmth of his skin sinking through the thin fabric of her knickers as he searched for the knotting, twitching muscle. "Here we are. Hold your breath, darling." Obeying, Lillian felt him roll his palm strongly over the muscle. She nearly yelped at the burst of searing fire in her leg, and then suddenly it eased, leaving her weak with relief.

Relaxing back against his arm, Lillian let out a long breath. "Thank you. That's much better."

A faint smile crossed his lips as he deftly tugged her skirts back over her legs. "My pleasure."

"That never happened to me before," she murmured, flexing her leg cautiously.

"No doubt it was a repercussion from your exploit in the sidesaddle. You must have strained a muscle."

"Yes, I did." Color burnished her cheeks as she forced herself to admit, "I'm not used to jumping on sidesaddle—I've only done it astride."

His smile widened slowly. "How interesting," he murmured. "Clearly my experiences with American girls have been entirely too limited. I didn't realize you were so delightfully colorful."

"I'm more colorful than most," she told him sheepishly, and he grinned.

"Much as I would love to sit here chatting with you, sweet, I had better return you to the house, if you're able to stand now. It will do you no good to spend too much time alone with me." He stood in an easy movement and reached down for her.

"It seems to have done me quite a bit of good," Lillian replied, allowing him to pull her up.

St. Vincent offered her his arm, and watched as she tested her leg. "Is it all right?"

"Yes, thank you," Lillian replied, taking hold of his arm. "You've been very kind, my lord."

He stared at her with an odd flicker in his pale blue eyes. "I'm not kind, darling. I'm only nice to people when I'm planning to take advantage of them."

Lillian responded with a carefree grin, daring to ask, "Am I in danger from you, my lord?"

Though his expression remained relaxed with good humor, his eyes were disturbingly intent. "I'm afraid so."

"Hmm." Lillian studied the chiseled edge of his profile, thinking that for all his posturing, he had not taken advantage of her helplessness a few moments ago. "You're awfully forthcoming about your evil intentions. It makes me wonder if I should really worry."

His only response was an enigmatic smile.

After parting company with Lord St. Vincent, Lillian climbed the steps to the spacious back terrace, where laughter and excited feminine chatter was resounding off the flagstones. Ten young women were standing around one of the tables, involved in some kind of game or experiment. They bent over a row of glasses that had been filled with various liquids, while one of them, who was blindfolded, cautiously dipped her fingers into one of them. Whatever the result was, it caused them all to squeal and giggle. A group of dowagers sat nearby, watching the proceedings with amused interest.

Lillian caught sight of her sister in the crowd, and wandered to her. "What is this?" she asked.

Daisy turned to view her with surprise. "Lillian," she murmured, slipping an arm around her waist, "why are you back early, dear? Did you have some difficulty at the jumping course?"

Lillian drew her aside while the game continued. "One could say that," she said tartly, and told her about the events of the morning.

Daisy's dark eyes turned round with dismay. "Good God," she whispered. "I can't imagine Lord Westcliff losing his head that way . . . and as for you . . . what were you thinking, to let Lord St. Vincent do such a thing?"

"I was in pain," Lillian whispered back defensively. "I couldn't think. I couldn't even *move*. If you'd ever had a muscle cramp, you would know how much it hurts."

"I would elect to lose my leg entirely before letting

someone like Lord St. Vincent near it," Daisy said beneath
her breath. After pausing to consider the situation, she
couldn't seem to keep from asking, "What was it like?"

Lillian smothered a laugh. "How should I know? By
the time my leg stopped hurting, his hand was gone."

"Drat." Daisy frowned slightly. "Do you suppose he'll
tell anyone?"

"Somehow I don't think he will. He seems to be a gentleman, in spite of his claims otherwise." A scowl settled
on Lillian's forehead as she added, "*Far* more of a gentleman than Lord Westcliff was today."

"Hmm. How did he know that you couldn't ride
sidesaddle?"

Lillian regarded her without rancor. "Don't play the
idiot, Daisy—it's perfectly obvious that Annabelle told
her husband, who then told Westcliff."

"You won't hold this against Annabelle, I hope. She
never intended for the issue to blow up the way it did."

"She should have kept her mouth shut," Lillian said
grumpily.

"She was afraid that you would take a tumble if you
jumped sidesaddle. We all were."

"Well, I didn't!"

"You might have, though."

Lillian hesitated, her scowl fading as honesty compelled her to admit, "There's no doubt that I would have,
eventually."

"Then you won't be cross with Annabelle?"

"Of course not," Lillian said. "It wouldn't be fair to
blame her for Westcliff's beastly behavior."

Looking relieved, Daisy tugged her back to the
crowded table. "Come, dear, you must try this game. It's
silly but quite fun." The girls, all of them unmarried,

and ranging in age from their early teens to mid-twenties, moved to make room for the pair of them. While Daisy explained the rules, Evie was blindfolded, and the other girls proceeded to change the positions of the four glasses. "As you can see," Daisy said, "one glass is filled with soap water, one with clear, and one with blue laundry water. The other, of course, is empty. The glasses will predict what kind of man you will marry."

They watched as Evie felt carefully for one of the glasses. Dipping her finger into the soap water, Evie waited for her blindfold to be drawn off, and viewed the results with chagrin, while the other girls erupted with giggles.

"Choosing the soap water means she will marry a poor man," Daisy explained.

Wiping off her fingers, Evie exclaimed good-naturedly, "I s-suppose the fact that I'm going to be m-married at all is a good thing."

The next girl in line waited with an expectant smile as she was blindfolded, and the glasses were repositioned. She felt for the vessels, nearly overturning one, and dipped her fingers into the blue water. Upon viewing her choice, she seemed quite pleased. "The blue water means she's going to marry a noted author," Daisy told Lillian. "You try next!"

Lillian gave her a speaking glance. "You don't really believe in this, do you?"

"Oh, don't be cynical—have some fun!" Daisy took the blindfold and rose on her toes to tie it firmly around Lillian's head.

Bereft of sight, Lillian allowed herself to be guided to the table. She grinned at the encouraging cries of the young women around her. There was the sound of the glasses being moved in front of her, and she waited with her hands half raised in the air. "What happens if I pick the empty glass?" she asked.

Evie's voice came near her ear. "You die a sp-spinster!" she said, and everyone laughed.

"No lifting the glasses to test their weight," someone warned with a giggle. "You can't avoid the empty glass, if it's your fate!"

"At the moment I *want* the empty glass," Lillian replied, causing another round of laughter.

Finding the smooth surface of a glass, she slid her fingers up the side and dipped them into the cool liquid. A general round of applause and cheering, and she asked, "Am I marrying an author, too?"

"No, you chose the clear water," Daisy said. "A rich, handsome husband is coming for you, dear!"

"Oh, what a relief," Lillian said flippantly, lowering the blindfold to peek over the edge. "Is it your turn now?"

Her younger sister shook her head. "I was the first to try. I knocked over a glass twice in a row, and made a dreadful mess."

"What does that mean? That you won't marry at all?"

"It means that I'm clumsy," Daisy replied cheerfully. "Other than that, who knows? Perhaps my fate has yet to be decided. The good news is that *your* husband seems to be on the way."

"If so, the bastard is late," Lillian retorted, causing Daisy and Evie to laugh.

Chapter 9

*U*nfortunately, the news of the altercation between Lillian and Lord Westcliff spread swiftly through the entire household. By early evening it had reached Mercedes Bowman's ears, and the result was not a pretty sight. White-eyed and shrill, Mercedes paced in front of her daughter in her room.

"Perhaps it could have been overlooked, had you simply made some inappropriate remark in Lord Westcliff's presence," Mercedes stormed, her skinny arms thrashing in wild gesticulations. "But for you to argue with the earl himself, and then to disobey him in front of everyone—do you realize how that makes us appear? You are not only ruining your own chances of marriage, but your sister's chances as well! Who would wish to marry into a family that must claim a . . . a *philistine* as one of their own?"

Feeling a stirring of shame, Lillian cast an apologetic glance at Daisy, who sat in the corner. Daisy shook her head slightly in reassurance.

"If you insist on behaving like a savage creature," Mercedes continued, "then I will be forced to take harsh measures, Lillian Odelle!"

Lillian sank lower on the settee at the sound of her hated middle name, the use of which always heralded some dire punishment.

"For the next week, you will not venture out of this room unless you are in my company," Mercedes said grimly. "I will monitor every action, every gesture, and every word that issues from your mouth, until I am convinced that you can be trusted to behave like a reasonable human being. It will be a shared punishment, for I find as little pleasure in your company as you find in mine. But I see no other alternative. And if you offer one word of protest, I shall double your punishment and make it a fortnight! During the times that you are not under my supervision, you will remain in this room, reading or meditating on your ill-advised conduct. Do you understand me, Lillian?"

"Yes, Mother." The prospect of being watched so closely for a week made Lillian feel like a caged animal. Repressing a howl of protest, she gazed mutinously at the flower-patterned carpet.

"The first thing you will do tonight," Mercedes continued, her eyes flashing in her narrow white face, "is apologize to Lord Westcliff for the trouble you caused earlier today. You will do it in my presence, so that I—"

"Oh no." Lillian sat up straight, glaring at her mother in open rebellion. "No. There is nothing that you or anyone can do to make me apologize to him. I'll die first."

"You will do as I say." Mercedes's voice lowered to a near growl. "You will apologize to the earl with abject humility, or you will not leave this room once for the rest of our stay here!"

As Lillian opened her mouth, Daisy interrupted hastily. "Mother, may I speak to Lillian privately, please? Just for a moment. *Please*."

Mercedes stared hard from one daughter to the other, shook her head as if wondering why she had been cursed with such unmanageable children, and strode from the room.

"She's truly angry this time," Daisy murmured in the dangerous silence that lingered in her wake. "I've never seen Mother in such a state. You may have to do as she asks."

Lillian stared at her in impotent fury. "I will not apologize to that superior ass!"

"Lilian, it would cost you nothing. Just say the words. You don't have to mean them. Just say, 'Lord Westcliff, I—' "

"I will not," Lillian repeated stonily. "And it *would* cost something—my pride."

"Is it worth being locked in this room, and having to miss all the soirees and suppers that everyone else will be enjoying? Please don't be stubborn! Lillian, I promise, I will help you think up some dreadful revenge on Lord Westcliff . . . something really evil. Just do what Mother wants for now—you may lose the battle, but you'll win the war. Besides . . ." Daisy searched desperately for another argument to sway her. "Besides, nothing would please Lord Westcliff more than for you to be locked away for the entire visit. You would be powerless to annoy or torment him. Out of sight, out of mind. Don't give him that satisfaction, Lillian!"

It was perhaps the only argument that had the power

to influence her. Frowning, Lillian stared at her sister's small ivory face, with its intelligent dark eyes and brows that were a shade too strongly marked. Not for the first time, she wondered how it was that the person most willing to join her reckless adventures was also the one who could most easily recall her to reason. Many people were often deceived by Daisy's frequent moments of whimsy, never suspecting the bedrock of ruthless common sense beneath the elfin facade.

"I'll do it," she said stiffly. "Though I'll probably choke on the words."

Daisy let out a huge sigh of relief. "I'll act as your intermediary. I'll tell Mother that you've agreed, and that she mustn't lecture you any further, or you might change your mind."

Lillian slumped on the settee, envisioning Westcliff's smug satisfaction when she was forced to deliver her apology. Damnation, it would be unbearable. Seething with animosity, she entertained herself by planning a series of complicated revenges against Westcliff, ending with the vision of him begging for mercy.

An hour later, the Bowman family proceeded from their room as one unit, led by Thomas Bowman. Their eventual destination was the dining hall, where another bombastic four-hour supper would be held. Having been recently apprised of his eldest daughter's shameful behavior, Thomas was in a state of barely contained fury, his mustache bristling above his set mouth.

Dressed in a pale lavender silk gown trimmed with spills of white lace at the bodice and short puffed sleeves, Lillian walked resolutely behind her parents, while her father's wrathful words floated back to her.

"The moment you become a handicap to a potential

business deal is the moment that I send you packing for New York. So far this husband-hunting sojourn in England has proved to be expensive and unproductive. I warn you, daughter, if your actions have disrupted my negotiations with the earl—"

"I'm sure they haven't," Mercedes interrupted frantically, as her dreams of attaining a titled son-in-law wobbled like a teacup poised on the edge of a table. "Lillian will apologize to Lord Westcliff, dear, and that will set everything to rights. You will see." Falling a half step behind him, she glanced over her shoulder to level a threatening glare at her elder daughter.

Part of Lillian felt like curling up into a ball of remorse, while the other part wanted to explode with resentment. Naturally her father would take exception to anyone and anything that threatened to interfere with his business . . . otherwise, he couldn't have cared less about her actions. All he had ever wanted of his daughters was for them to keep from bothering him. Had it not been for her three brothers, Lillian would have never known what it was like to receive even negligible crumbs of male attention.

"To ensure that you have the opportunity to properly ask the earl's pardon," Thomas Bowman said, pausing to glance at Lillian with hard, stone-colored eyes, "I have requested his indulgence in meeting us in the library before dinner. You will apologize to him then— both to my satisfaction and to his."

Coming to a dead halt, Lillian stared at him with wide eyes. Her resentment built in a hot, choking mass as she wondered if Westcliff had arranged this scenario as a lesson in humiliation. "Does he know why you've asked to meet him there?" she managed to ask.

"No. Nor do I believe that he expects an apology from

one of my notoriously ill-mannered daughters. However, if you do not deliver a satisfactory one, you will soon take your last glance of England from the deck of a steamer bound from New York."

Lillian was not fool enough to discount her father's words as an idle threat. His tone was utterly convincing in its grim imperative. And the thought of being forced to leave England, and worse, to be separated from Daisy . . .

"Yes, sir," she said, her jaw clenched.

The family proceeded along the hallway in strained silence.

As Lilly stewed, she felt her sister's small hand slip into hers. "It means nothing," Daisy whispered. "Just say it quickly and be done with—"

"Silence!" their father barked, and their hands fell apart.

Glumly preoccupied with her thoughts, Lillian took little notice of her surroundings as she accompanied her family to the library. The door had been left ajar, and her father gave the portal a single decisive rap before shepherding his wife and daughters into the room. It was a handsome library with a twenty-foot-high ceiling, movable staircases, and upper and lower galleries that contained acres of books. The scents of leather, vellum, and freshly waxed wood made the air richly pungent.

Lord Westcliff, who had been leaning over his desk with his hands braced on the age-worn surface, looked up from a sheaf of paperwork. He straightened, his black eyes narrowing as he saw Lillian. Dark, austere, and impeccably dressed, he was the perfect picture of an English aristocrat, with a perfectly knotted cravat and thick hair that had been ruthlessly brushed back from his forehead. It was suddenly impossible to reconcile the man who stood before her with the playful, unshaven brute who had let her knock him over on the rounders diamond behind the stable yard.

Ushering his wife and daughters into the room, Thomas Bowman spoke brusquely. "Thank you for agreeing to meet me here, my lord. I promise this won't take long."

"Mr. Bowman," Westcliff acknowledged in a low voice. "I did not anticipate the privilege of meeting with your family as well."

"I am afraid that the word 'privilege' is overstating the case," Thomas said sourly. "It seems that one of my daughters has behaved badly in your presence. She wishes to express her regret." He pushed his knuckles into the center of Lillian's back, prodding her toward the earl. "Go on."

A frown furrowed Westcliff's brow. "Mr. Bowman, it is not necessary—"

"You will allow my daughter to speak her piece," Thomas said, jabbing Lillian forward.

The atmosphere in the library was silent but volatile as Lillian lifted her gaze to Westcliff's. His frown had deepened, and with a spark of insight she understood that he did not want an apology from her. Not this way, with her father forcing her to do it in such a humiliating manner. Somehow that made it easier for her to apologize.

Swallowing hard, she stared directly into his fathomless dark eyes, the light picking out filaments of intense sable in the irises. "I am sorry about what happened, my lord. You have been a generous host, and you deserve far more respect than I showed you this morning. I should not have challenged your decision at the jumping course, nor should I have spoken to you as I did. I hope that you will accept my regrets, and know that they are sincere."

"No," he said softly.

Lillian blinked in confusion, thinking at first that he had rejected her apology.

"It is for me to apologize, Miss Bowman, not you," Westcliff continued. "Your spirited actions were provoked by a moment of high-handedness on my part. I cannot blame you for responding in such a way to my arrogance."

Lillian struggled to hide her astonishment, but it wasn't easy when Westcliff had just done the exact opposite of what she had expected. He had been given the perfect opportunity to quash her pride—and he had chosen not to. She could not understand it. What kind of game was he playing?

His gaze moved gently over her bewildered features. "Though I expressed it badly this morning," he murmured, "my concern for your safety was genuine. Hence the reason for my anger."

Staring at him, Lillian felt the ball of resentment that had lodged in her chest begin to dissolve. How nice he was being! And it didn't seem as if he was playing a part, either. He seemed genuinely kind and sympathetic. A sense of relief stole over her, and she was able to take a deep breath for the first time all day. "That wasn't the only reason for your anger," she said. "You also don't like to be disobeyed."

Westcliff laughed huskily. "No," he admitted with a slow smile, "I don't." The smile transformed the stern contours of his face, banishing his natural reserve and imparting an appeal that was a thousand times more potent than mere handsomeness. Lillian felt an odd, pleasant little chill chase over her skin.

"Now will I be allowed to ride your horses again?" she dared to ask.

"*Lillian!*" she heard her mother scold.

Westcliff's eyes glittered with amusement, as if he relished her audacity. "I wouldn't go that far."

Caught in the velvet snare of his gaze, Lillian became aware that their perpetual discord had changed into a kind of friendly challenge . . . tempered with something that felt almost . . . erotic. Good God. A few amiable words from Westcliff, and she was close to making a fool of herself.

Seeing that they had made peace, Mercedes bubbled over with enthusiasm. "Oh, dear Lord Westcliff, what a magnanimous gentleman you are! And you were not high-handed in the least—you were clearly moved by concern for my willful little angel, which is yet more proof of your infinite benevolence."

The earl's smile became sardonic as he slid a speculative gaze over Lillian, as if considering whether the phrase "willful little angel" was an apt description. Offering Mercedes his arm, he asked blandly, "May I escort you to the dining hall, Mrs. Bowman?"

Euphoric at the idea that everyone would see her being accompanied by Lord Westcliff himself, Mercedes accepted with a sigh of pleasure. As they undertook the journey from the study to the parlor where the dinner procession would be arranged, Mercedes launched into an excruciatingly prolonged discourse about her impressions of Hampshire, throwing in several little criticisms that were meant to be witty, but caused Lillian and Daisy to glance at each other in mute despair. Lord Westcliff received Mercedes's crass observations with careful politeness, the polish of his manners making hers appear even worse by contrast. And for the first time in Lillian's life, it occurred to her that perhaps her deliberate flouting of etiquette was not quite as clever as she had previously thought. Certainly she had no wish to become stuffy and reserved . . . but at the same time, it might not be such a bad thing to conduct herself with a bit more dignity.

No doubt Lord Westcliff was infinitely relieved to part company with the Bowmans when they arrived at the parlor, but he did not reveal it by word or gesture. Impassively wishing them a pleasant evening, he took his leave with a slight bow and made to join a group that included his sister Lady Olivia and her husband, Mr. Shaw.

Turning to Lillian, Daisy regarded her with wide eyes. "Why was Lord Westcliff so nice to you?" she whispered. "And why on earth did he offer Mother his arm, and escort us all the way here, and listen to her endless babbling?"

"I haven't the faintest idea," Lillian whispered back. "But clearly he has a high tolerance for pain."

Simon Hunt and Annabelle joined the group on the other side of the room. Absently smoothing the waist of her silvery-blue gown, Annabelle glanced over the crowd, caught Lillian's gaze, and made a distressed face. Obviously she had heard about the confrontation at the jumping course. *I'm sorry,* Annabelle mouthed. She seemed relieved as Lillian nodded in reassurance and sent her the silent message, *It's all right.*

Eventually they all proceeded into the dining hall, the Bowmans and the Hunts being among the last in line, as they were of very low rank. "Money always brings up the rear," Lillian heard her father say cryptically, and she guessed that he had little patience for the rules of precedence that were always so clearly defined on these occasions. It struck Lillian that on the occasions when the countess was absent, Lord Westcliff and his sister Lady Olivia tended to arrange things far less formally, encouraging the guests to enter the dining hall naturally instead of in a procession. With the countess attending, however, it appeared there would be strict adherence to tradition.

It seemed there were nearly as many footmen as there were guests, all of them clad in full dress livery of black plush breeches, a mustard-colored waistcoat, and a blue pigeon-tailed coat. They seated the guests deftly and poured wine and water without spilling a drop.

To Lillian's surprise, she had been seated near the head of Lord Westcliff's table, only three places away from his right hand. Occupying a place so close to the host was a mark of high favor, very seldom given to an unmarried girl with no rank. Wondering if the footman had make a mistake in seating her there, she glanced cautiously at the faces of those guests nearest her, and saw that they too were puzzled by her presence. Even the countess, who was being seated at the very end of the table, stared at her with a frown.

Lillian gave Lord Westcliff a questioning glance as he took his place at the head of the table.

One of his dark brows arched. "Is something amiss? You seem a bit perturbed, Miss Bowman."

The correct response would probably have been to blush and thank him for the unexpected honor. But as Lillian stared at his face, which was softened by the influence of candleglow, she found herself answering with brazen frankness. "I am wondering why I am sitting near the head of the table. In light of what happened this morning, I assumed you would have me seated all the way out on the back terrace."

There was a moment of utter silence as the guests around them registered shock that Lillian would so openly refer to the conflict between them. However, Westcliff astonished them all by laughing quietly, his gaze locked with hers. After a moment, the others joined in with forced chuckles.

"Knowing of your penchant for trouble, Miss Bowman, I have concluded that it is safer to keep you in my sight, and within arm's reach if possible."

His statement was delivered with matter-of-fact lightness. One would have to search very hard to find any innuendo in his tone. And yet Lillian felt a strange liquid ripple inside, sensation passing from one nerve to another like a flow of warm honey.

Lifting a glass of iced champagne to her lips, Lillian glanced around the dining hall. Daisy had been seated near the end of the table, talking animatedly and nearly knocking over a wine goblet as she gestured to emphasize her words. Annabelle was at the next table, seeming oblivious to the multitude of admiring masculine stares fastened on her. The men on either side of her were positively beaming at their good fortune at being seated next to such a ravishing companion, while Simon Hunt, located a few places away, regarded them with the baleful gaze of a very territorial male.

Evie, her aunt Florence, and Lillian's parents were included with the guests at the farthest table. As usual, Evie was saying very little to the men beside her, tongue-tied and nervous as she stared down at her plate. *Poor Evie,* Lillian thought sympathetically. *We'll have to do something about your blasted shyness.*

Reflecting on the subject of her unmarried brothers, Lillian wondered if there was any possibility of matching one of them with Evie. Perhaps she could find a way to induce one of them to come to England for a visit. God knew that any of them would be a better husband for Evie than her cousin Eustace. There was her oldest brother, Raphael, and the twins, Ransom and Rhys. A more robust group of young males could not be found. On the other hand, it seemed likely that any of the Bowman brothers would terrify Evie. They were good-natured men, but not what anyone would call refined. Or even civilized.

Her attention was diverted by the long line of footmen bringing in the first course; a parade of tureens filled with turtle soup, and silver platters bearing turbot dressed in lobster sauce, crawfish pudding, and herbed trout with stewed lettuce. It was the first of at least eight courses, which would be followed by several removes of dessert. Facing the prospect of yet another lengthy dinner, Lillian repressed a sigh and looked up to find Westcliff's subtly searching gaze on her. He said nothing, however, and Lillian found herself breaking the silence.

"Your hunter Brutus seems a very fine horse, my lord. I noticed that you used no whip or spurs with him."

The conversation around them faded, and Lillian wondered if she had made yet another faux pas. Perhaps an unmarried girl wasn't supposed to speak until someone addressed her directly. However, Westcliff answered readily. "I rarely use a whip or spurs with any of my stock, Miss Bowman. Usually I am able to obtain the results I want without them."

Lillian thought wryly that like everyone and everything else on the estate, the bay probably hadn't a thought of disobeying his master. "He seems to have a steadier temperament than the usual thoroughbred," she said.

Westcliff leaned back in his chair as a footman served

a portion of trout onto his plate. The flickering light played over the close-trimmed layers of his black hair . . . Lillian couldn't help but remember the feel of the heavy locks beneath her fingers.

"Brutus is a crossbred, actually. A mixture of thoroughbred and Irish draft."

"Really?" Lillian made no effort to conceal her surprise. "I would have thought you would ride only horses with pure pedigrees."

"Many prefer purebreds," the earl admitted. "But a hunter needs strong jumping ability, and the power to change direction easily. A crossbred like Brutus has all the speed and style of a thoroughbred, combined with the athletic prowess of an Irish draft."

The others at the table listened attentively. As Westcliff finished, a gentleman added jovially, "Superb animal, Brutus. Descendant of Eclipse, isn't he? One can always see the influence of the Darley Arabian . . ."

"It's very open-minded of you to ride a crossbred," Lillian murmured.

Westcliff smiled slightly. "I can be open-minded, on occasion."

"So I've heard . . . but I've never seen evidence of it until now."

Again, conversation stopped as the guests heard Lillian's provoking comments. Instead of becoming annoyed, Westcliff stared at her with unconcealed interest. Whether the interest was that of a man who found her attractive, or one who merely considered her an oddity of nature was difficult to determine. But it *was* interest.

"I've always tried to approach things in a logical manner," he said. "Which leads to the occasional break with tradition."

Lillian gave him a mocking grin. "You don't always find traditional ideas to be logical?"

Westcliff shook his head slightly, the gleam in his eyes growing brighter as he drank from a wineglass and watched her over the light-tricked crystal rim.

Another gentleman made some joking remark about curing Westcliff of his liberal views while the next course was brought out. The succession of curious bulky objects on silver platters was greeted with much fanfare and pleasure. There were four of them per table, twelve in all, set at measured intervals on small folding side tables, where under-butlers and head footmen proceeded to carve the offerings. The scent of spiced beef filled the air, while guests viewed the contents of the platters with murmurs of anticipation. Twisting a little in her seat, Lillian glanced at the platter nearest her, which was poised on a side table. She nearly recoiled in horror as she found herself looking into the charred features of an unrecognizable beast, with steam rising from its freshly baked skull.

Jerking in surprise, she heard the resultant clatter of silverware. A footman addressed her clumsiness immediately, laying out clean forks and spoons, and bending to retrieve the fallen utensils.

"Wh-what is that?" Lillian asked of no one in particular, unable to tear her gaze from the revolting sight.

"A calf's head," one of the ladies replied in a tone laden with condescending amusement, as if this was yet one more example of American backwardness. "A superior English delicacy. Don't say that you've never tried it?"

Struggling to make her face expressionless, Lillian shook her head wordlessly. She flinched as the footman pried open the calf's smoking jaws and sliced out the tongue.

"Some claim the tongue is the most delicious part," the lady continued, "while others swear that the brains are by far the most delectable. I will say, however, that without a doubt the eyes are the most exquisite tidbits."

Lillian's own eyes closed sickly at this revelation. She felt the rising sting of bile in her throat. She had never been an enthusiast for English cuisine, but as objectionable as she had found some dishes in the past, nothing had ever prepared her for the repulsive sight of the calf's head. Slitting her eyes open, she glanced around the room. It seemed that everywhere, calves' heads were being carved, opened and sliced. Brains were spooned out onto plates, throat sweetbreads were cut into thin slices . . .

She was going to be ill.

Feeling the blood drain from her face, Lillian looked toward the end of the table, where Daisy dubiously watched a few morsels being ceremoniously deposited on her plate. Slowly Lillian raised a corner of her napkin to her mouth. No. She couldn't let herself be ill. But the rich, oily smell of calf's head floated all around her, and as she heard the industrious clink of knives and forks being employed, and the appreciative murmuring of the diners, the sickness rose in choking waves. A small plate was settled in front of her, containing a few slices of . . . something . . . and a gelatinous eyeball with a conical base rolled lazily toward the rim.

"Sweet Jesus," Lillian whispered, sweat breaking out on her forehead.

A cool, calm voice seemed to cut through the cloud of nausea. "Miss Bowman . . ."

Desperately looking in the direction of the voice, she saw Lord Westcliff's impassive face. "Yes, my lord?" she asked thickly.

He seemed to choose his words with unusual care. "Forgive what may seem a somewhat eccentric request . . . but it occurs to me that now is the most opportune time to view a rare species of butterfly that abides on the estate. It comes out only at early evening, which is, of course, a departure from the usual pattern. You may recall my having mentioned it during a previous conversation."

"Butterfly?" Lillian repeated, swallowing repeatedly against a surge of nausea.

"Perhaps you might allow me to show you and your sister to the outdoor conservatory, where new hatchings have recently been sighted. To my regret, it would necessitate that we abstain from this particular remove, but we will return in time for you to enjoy the rest of the supper."

Several guests paused with their forks in mid-air, their expressions registering astonishment at Westcliff's peculiar request.

Realizing that he was giving her an excuse to leave the dining hall, with her sister accompanying them for propriety's sake, Lillian nodded. "Butterflies," she repeated breathlessly. "Yes, I would love to see them."

"So would I," came Daisy's voice from the other end of the table. She stood with alacrity, obliging all the gentlemen to courteously hoist themselves up from their chairs. "How considerate of you to remember our interest in the native insects of Hampshire, my lord."

Westcliff came to help Lillian from her chair. "Breathe through your mouth," he whispered. White-faced and sweating, she obeyed.

All gazes were upon them. "My lord," one of the gentlemen, Lord Wymark, said, "may I ask *which* rare species of butterfly you are referring to?"

There was a slight hesitation, and then Westcliff replied with grave deliberation. "The purple-spotted . . ." He paused before finishing, ". . . dingy-dipper."

Wymark frowned. "I fancy myself something of a lepidopterist, my lord. And while I know of the dingy-*skipper*, which is found only in Northumberland, I have never heard of the dingy-dipper."

There was a measured pause. "It's a hybrid," Westcliff said. "*Morpho purpureus practicus.* To my knowledge it has been observed only in the environs of Stony Cross."

"I should like to go have a glance at the colony with you if I may," Wymark said, setting his napkin on the table in preparation to rise. "The discovery of a new hybrid is always a remarkable—"

"Tomorrow evening," Westcliff said authoritatively. "The dingy-dippers are sensitive to the presence of humans. I would not wish to endanger such a fragile species. I think it best to visit them in small groups of two or three."

"Yes, my lord," Wymark said, obviously disgruntled as he settled back in his chair. "Tomorrow evening, then."

Gratefully Lillian took Westcliff's arm, while Daisy took the other, and they left the room with great dignity.

Chapter 10

$\mathcal{L}$illian was nearly overcome by nausea as Westcliff took her to an outdoor conservatory. The sky had turned plum-colored, the gathering darkness relieved only by starlight and the flares of newly lit torches. As the clean, sweet evening air swept over her, she gulped in deep breaths. Westcliff guided her to a cane-backed chair, exhibiting far more compassion than Daisy, who staggered against a column and shook with spasms of laughter.

"Oh . . . good Lord . . ." Daisy gasped, blotting tears of hilarity from her eyes, "your *face,* Lillian . . . you turned as green as a pea. I thought you were going to cast your crumpets in front of everyone!"

"So did I," Lillian said, shuddering.

"I take it you're not fond of calf's head," Westcliff murmured, sitting beside her. He extracted a soft white handkerchief from his coat and blotted Lillian's damp forehead.

"I'm not fond of anything," Lillian said queasily, "that stares back at me just before I'm supposed to eat it."

Daisy recovered her breath long enough to say, "Oh, don't carry on so. It only stared at you for a moment . . ." She paused and added, "Until its eyeballs were flipped out!" She convulsed with mirth once again.

Lillian glared at her howling sister and closed her eyes weakly. "For God's sake, do you have to—"

"Breathe through your mouth," Westcliff reminded her. The handkerchief moved over her face, absorbing the last traces of cold sweat. "Try putting your head down."

Obediently Lillian dropped her forehead to her knees. She felt his hand close over the chilled nape of her neck, massaging the stiff tendons with exquisite lightness. His fingers were warm and slightly rough-textured, and the gentle kneading was so pleasant that her nausea soon faded. He seemed to know exactly where to touch her, his fingertips discovering the most sensitive places on her neck and shoulders and nudging cleverly into the soreness. Holding still beneath his ministrations, Lillian felt her entire body relaxing, her breathing turning deep and even.

All too soon she felt him easing her back to an upright position, and she had to bite back a protesting moan. To her mortification, she wanted him to continue stroking her. She wanted to sit there all evening with his hand on her neck. And her back. And . . . other places. Her lashes lifted from her pale cheeks, and she blinked as she saw how close his face was to hers. Strange, how the severe lines of his features became more attractive every time she beheld them. Her fingers itched to skim along the bold edge of his nose, and the contours of his mouth, so stern and yet so soft. And the intriguing shadow of his night beard. All of it combined in a thoroughly masculine appeal. But most appealing of all were his eyes, black velvet warmed by torchlight, framed with straight lashes that cast shadows on the dramatic planes of his cheekbones.

Remembering his creative exposition on the subject of purple-spotted dingy-dippers, Lillian gave a little huff of amusement. She had always considered Westcliff an utterly humorless man . . . and in that, she had misjudged him. "I thought you never lied," she said.

His lips twitched. "Given the options of seeing you become ill at the dinner table, or lying to get you out of there quickly, I chose the lesser of two evils. Do you feel better now?"

"Better . . . yes." Lillian realized that she was resting in the crook of his arm, her skirts draped partially over one of his thighs. His body was solid and warm, perfectly matched to hers. Glancing downward, she saw that the fabric of his trousers had molded firmly around his muscular thighs. Unladylike curiosity awakened inside her, and she clenched her fingers against the urge to slide her palm over his leg. "The part about the dingy-dipper was clever," she said, dragging her gaze up to his face. "But inventing a Latin name for it was positively inspired."

Westcliff grinned. "I always hoped my Latin would be good for something." Shifting her a little, he reached into the pocket of his waistcoat and glanced at his watch. "We'll return to the dining hall in approximately a quarter hour. By that time the calves' heads should be removed."

Lillian made a face. "I hate English food," she exclaimed. "All those jellies and blobs, and wiggly puddings, and the game that is aged until by the time it's served, it is older than I am, and—" She felt a tremor of amusement run through him, and she turned in the half circle of his arm. "What is so amusing?"

"You're making me afraid to go back to my own dinner table."

"You should be!" she replied emphatically, and he could no longer restrain a deep laugh.

"Pardon," came Daisy's voice from nearby, "but I am going to take this opportunity to make use of the . . . the . . . oh, whatever the polite word is for it, I have no idea. I will meet you at the entrance of the dining hall."

Westcliff withdrew his arm from around Lillian, glancing at Daisy as if he had temporarily forgotten her presence.

"Daisy—" Lillian said uncomfortably, suspecting that her younger sister was inventing an excuse to leave them alone together.

Ignoring her, Daisy departed with an impish grin and a wave, slipping through the French doors.

As Lillian sat with Westcliff in a spill of shifting torchlight, she experienced a pang of nervousness. Although there might have been a dearth of rare hybrid butterflies outside, the ones in her stomach more than made up for it. Westcliff turned to face her more fully, one arm braced along the back of the cane settee.

"I spoke with the countess earlier today," he said, a smile still lurking at the corners of his lips.

Lillian was slow to respond, trying desperately to push away the image that had suddenly appeared in her mind, of his dark head bending over hers, his tongue penetrating the softness of her mouth . . . "About what?" she asked dazedly.

Westcliff responded with an eloquently sardonic glance.

"Oh," she murmured. "You must mean my . . . my request for her sponsorship . . ."

"Are we calling it a request?" Westcliff reached out to tuck a strand of loose hair neatly behind her ear. His fingertip brushed the outer edge, following the curve to the soft pad of her earlobe. "As I recollect, it bore a strong resemblance to extortion." He fingered the delicate lobe, his thumb smoothing over the tingling surface. "You never wear earrings. Why not?"

"I . . ." Suddenly she wasn't breathing properly. "My ears are very sensitive," she managed. "It hurts to clamp them with earbobs . . . and the thought of piercing them with a needle . . ." She stopped with a broken inhalation as she felt the tip of his middle finger investigating the shell of her ear, tracing the fragile inner structure. Westcliff let his thumb brush over the taut line of her jaw and the vulnerable softness beneath her chin, until she felt hot color spreading over her cheeks. They were sitting so close . . . it must be that he could smell her perfume. That was the only explanation for his loverlike touch on her face.

"Your skin is like silk," he murmured. "What were we talking about? . . . Oh yes, the countess. I managed to persuade her to sponsor you and your sister for the next season."

Lillian's eyes widened in astonishment. "You did? How? Did you have to bully her?"

"Do I strike you as the kind of man who would bully his sixty-year-old mother?"

"Yes."

A low laugh vibrated in his throat. "I have methods other than bullying," he informed her. "You just haven't seen them yet."

There was an implication in his words that she couldn't quite identify . . . but it filled her with a tingle of anticipation. "Why did you persuade her to help me?" she asked.

"Because I thought I might enjoy inflicting you on her."

"Well, if you're going to make me sound like some sort of plague—"

"And," Westcliff interrupted, "I felt obligated to make amends after my rough handling of you this morning."

"It wasn't all your fault," she said reluctantly. "I suppose I might have been somewhat provoking."

"Somewhat," he agreed dryly, his fingertips sliding behind her ear to the satiny edge of her hairline. "I should warn you that my mother's consent to the arrangement is not unconditional. If you push her too far, she'll balk. Therefore, I advise you to try to behave in her presence."

"Behave how?" Lillian asked, excruciatingly aware of the gentle exploration of his fingertip. If her sister didn't return soon, she thought dizzily, Westcliff was going to kiss her. And she wanted him to, so badly that her lips had begun to tremble.

He smiled at her question. "Well, whatever else you may do, don't—" He broke off suddenly, glancing at their surroundings as if he had become aware of someone's approach. Lillian could hear nothing except the rustle of the breeze that swept through the trees and scattered a few fallen leaves across the graveled pathways. However, in just a moment a lean, lithe form cut through the mosaic of torchlight and shadow, and the gleam of antiqued-gold hair identified the visitor as Lord St. Vincent. Westcliff withdrew his hand from Lillian immediately. The sensual spell was broken, and she felt the rush of warmth begin to fade.

St. Vincent's stride was long but relaxed, his hands buried casually in the depths of his coat pockets. He smiled at the sight of the pair on the bench, his gaze lingering on Lillian's face.

There was no doubt that this remarkably beautiful man, with the face of a fallen angel and eyes the color of heaven at daybreak, had occupied the dreams of many women. And been cursed by many a cuckolded husband.

It seemed an unlikely friendship, Lillian thought, glancing from Westcliff to St. Vincent. The earl, with his straightforward, principled nature, must certainly disapprove of his friend's wayward inclinations. But as often was the case, this particular friendship might be strengthened by their differences rather than being undermined by them.

Stopping before them, St. Vincent confided, "I would have found you sooner, but I was attacked by a swarm of dingy-dippers." His voice lowered with conspiratorial furtiveness. "And I don't wish to alarm either of you, but I had to warn you . . . they're planning to serve kidney pudding in the fifth course."

"I can manage that," Lillian said ruefully. "It is only animals served in their natural state that I seem to have difficulty with."

"Of course you do, darling. We're barbarians, the lot of us, and you were perfectly right to be appalled by the calves' heads. I don't like them either. In fact, I rarely consume beef in any form."

"Are you a vegetarian, then?" Lillian asked, having heard the word frequently of late. Many discussions had centered on the topic of the vegetable system of diet that was being promoted by a hospital society in Ramsgate.

St. Vincent responded with a dazzling smile. "No, sweet, I'm a cannibal."

"St. Vincent," Westcliff growled in warning, seeing Lillian's confusion.

The viscount grinned unrepentantly. "It's a good thing I happened along, Miss Bowman. You're not safe alone with Westcliff, you know."

"I'm not?" Lillian parried, tensing inwardly as she reflected that he never would have made the glib comment had he known of the intimate encounters between her and the earl. She didn't dare look at Westcliff, but she apprehended the immediate stillness of the masculine form so close to hers.

"No, indeed," St. Vincent assured her. "It's the morally upright ones who do the worst things in private. Whereas with an obvious reprobate such as myself, you couldn't be in safer hands. Here, you had better return to the dining hall under my protection. God knows what sort of lascivious scheme is lurking in the earl's mind."

Giggling, Lillian stood from the bench, enjoying the sight of Westcliff being teased. He regarded his friend with a slight scowl as he too rose to his feet.

Taking St. Vincent's proffered arm, Lillian wondered why he had bothered to come out here. Was it possible that he had some kind of interest in her? Surely not. It was generally known that marriageable girls had never been a part of St. Vincent's romantic history, and Lillian was obviously not the kind whom he would pursue for an affair. However, it was rather entertaining to find herself alone in the company of two men, one of them the most desirable bed partner in England, and the other the most eligible bachelor. She couldn't help grinning as she thought of how many girls would commit outright murder to be in her shoes at this very moment.

St. Vincent drew her away with him. "As I recall," he remarked, "our friend Westcliff forbade you to ride his horses, but he said nothing about a carriage drive. Will you consider accompanying me on a tour through the countryside tomorrow morning?"

As Lillian considered the invitation, she allowed for a brief silence in anticipation that Westcliff might have something to say on the matter. Naturally, he did.

"Miss Bowman will be occupied tomorrow morning." The earl's brusque voice came from behind them.

Lillian opened her mouth to deliver a sharp retort, but St. Vincent sent her a sideways glance as he opened the door, conveying a mischievous admonition to let him handle things. "Occupied with what?" he asked.

"She and her sister are meeting with the countess."

"Ah, what a magnificent old dragon," St. Vincent mused, drawing Lillian through the doorway. "I've always gotten along famously with the countess. Let me offer a bit of advice—she loves to be flattered, though she'll pretend otherwise. A few words of praise, and you'll have her eating out of your hand."

Lillian glanced over her shoulder at Westcliff. "Is that true, my lord?"

"I wouldn't know, as I've never bothered to flatter her."

"Westcliff considers flattery and charm a waste of time," St. Vincent told Lillian.

"So I've noticed."

St. Vincent laughed. "I shall propose a carriage drive for the day after tomorrow then. Does that sound agreeable?"

"Yes, thank you."

"Excellent," St. Vincent said, adding in an offhand manner, "unless, Westcliff, you have some other claim on Miss Bowman's schedule?"

"No claim at all," Westcliff said flatly.

Of course not, Lillian thought with sudden rancor. Obviously Westcliff had no desire for her company, unless it was to spare his guests the sight of watching her cast up her crumpets on the dinner table.

They rejoined Daisy, who raised her brows at the sight of St. Vincent and asked mildly, "Where did you come from?"

"Were my mother alive, you could ask her," he replied pleasantly. "But I doubt she knew."

"St. Vincent," Westcliff snapped for the second time that evening. "These are innocent girls."

"Are they? How intriguing. Very well, I'll try for propriety . . . What subjects may one discuss with innocent girls?"

"Hardly any," Daisy said glumly, making him laugh.

Before they reentered the dining hall, Lillian paused to ask Westcliff, "At what time shall I visit the countess tomorrow? And where?"

His gaze was opaque and cool. Lillian couldn't help but notice that his disposition seemed to have soured since the moment St. Vincent had invited her on a carriage drive. But why would that displease him? It would be laughable to assume that he was jealous, since she was the last woman in the world in whom he would entertain a personal interest. The only reasonable conclusion was that he feared that St. Vincent might try to seduce her, and he did not want to deal with the trouble that would ensue.

"Ten o'clock in the Marsden parlor," he said.

"I'm afraid that I am not familiar with that room—"

"Few people are. It is an upstairs parlor, reserved for the family's private use."

"Oh." She stared into his dark eyes, feeling grateful and confused. He had been kind to her, and yet their relationship could not, by any stretch of the imagination, be considered a friendship. She wished that she could rid herself of her growing curiosity about him. It had been much easier when she had been able to dismiss him as a self-important snob. However, he was far more complex than she had originally thought, revealing dimensions of humor, sensuality, and surprising compassion.

"My lord," she said, ensnared by his gaze. "I . . . I suppose I should thank you for—"

"Let's go in," he interrupted curtly, seeming eager to be out of her presence. "We've tarried long enough."

"Are you nervous?" Daisy whispered the next morning, as she and Lillian followed their mother to the door of the Marsden parlor. Although Mercedes had not been specifically invited to meet with the countess, she was bound and determined to be included in the visit.

"No," Lillian replied. "I'm certain we have nothing to fear as long as we keep our mouths shut."

"I've heard that she hates Americans."

"That's a pity," Lillian said dryly, "since both of her daughters married Americans."

"Quiet, the both of you," Mercedes whispered. Dressed in a silver-gray gown with a large diamond brooch at the throat, she gathered her hand into a tangle of sharp knuckles and rapped at the door. There was no sound from within. Daisy and Lillian glanced at each other with raised brows, wondering if the countess had decided not to meet with them after all. Frowning, Mercedes knocked at the door with increased force.

This time, a barbed voice penetrated the seams of mahogany paneling. "Stop that infernal hammering and enter!"

Wearing subdued expressions, the Bowmans entered the room. It was a small but lovely parlor, with walls covered in blue flowered paper and a large set of windows that revealed a view of the garden below. The Countess of Westcliff was arranged on a settee beneath the window, her throat swathed in ropes of rare black pearls, her fingers and wrists weighted with jewels. In contrast to the brilliant pale silver of her hair, the lines of her brows were dark and thick, set uncompromisingly low over her eyes. In feature and in form, she was completely bereft of angles; her face round, her figure run to plumpness. Silently Lillian reflected that Lord Westcliff must have inherited his father's looks, for there was little resemblance between him and his mother.

"I expected only two," the countess said with a hard look at Mercedes. Her accent was as clean and crisp as white icing on a tea cake. "Why are there three?"

"Your Grace," Mercedes began with a toadying smile, bobbing in an uncomfortable curtsy. "First let me tell you how deeply Mr. Bowman and I appreciate your condescension to my two angels—"

"Only a duchess may be addressed as 'Your Grace,'" the countess said, the corners of her mouth drawn downward as if by an excessive pull of gravity. "Did you intend that as mockery?"

"Oh *no*, Your . . . that is, my lady," Mercedes said

hastily, her face turning skull-white. "It was not mockery. Never that! I only wished to—"

"I will speak alone with your daughters," the countess said imperiously. "You may return in precisely two hours to collect them."

"Yes, my lady!" Mercedes fled the room.

Clearing her throat to camouflage a sudden irrepressible laugh, Lillian glanced at Daisy, who was also struggling to contain her amusement at seeing their mother so handily dispatched.

"What an unpleasant noise," the countess remarked, scowling at Lillian's throat clearing. "Kindly refrain from producing it again."

"Yes, my lady," Lillian said with her best attempt at humility.

"You may approach me," the countess commanded, looking from one to the other as they obeyed. "I watched you last evening, the both of you, and I witnessed a veritable catalogue of unseemly behavior. I am told that I must act as your sponsor for the season, which confirms my opinion that my son is determined to make my life as difficult as possible. Sponsoring a pair of maladroit American girls! I warn you, if you do not heed every word that I say, I will not rest until each of you is married to some sham continental aristocrat and sent to molder in the most godforsaken corners of Europe."

Lillian was more than a little impressed. As far as threats went, it was a good one. Stealing a glance at Daisy, she saw that her sister had sobered considerably.

"Sit," the countess spat.

They complied with all possible speed, occupying the

chairs that she indicated with a wave of her glittering hand. Reaching to the small table beside the settee, the countess produced a piece of parchment liberally covered with notes written in cobalt ink. "I have made a list," she informed them, using one hand to place a tiny pair of pince-nez spectacles on the abbreviated tip of her nose, "of the errors that were made by the two of you last evening. We will address it point by point."

"How could the list be that long?" Daisy asked in dismay. "The dinner lasted only four hours—how many mistakes could we have possibly made in that length of time?"

Staring at them stonily over the top edge of the parchment, the countess let the list unfold. Accordionlike, it opened . . . and opened . . . and opened . . . until the bottom edge brushed the floor.

"Bloody hell," Lillian muttered beneath her breath.

Overhearing the curse, the countess frowned until her brows formed an unbroken dark line. "If there were any room left on the parchment," she informed Lillian, "I would add that bit of vulgarity to it."

Repressing a long sigh, Lillian settled low in her chair.

"Sit up straight, if you please," the countess said. "A lady never allows her spine to touch the back of her chair. Now, we will begin with introductions. You have both displayed a lamentable habit of shaking hands. It makes one appear distastefully eager to ingratiate oneself. The accepted rule is not to shake hands but merely to bow when being introduced, unless the introduction is being made between two young ladies. And as we're on the subject of bowing, you must never bow to a gentleman to whom you have not been introduced, even if he is well-known to you by sight. Nor may you bow to a gentleman who has addressed a few remarks to you at the house of a mutual friend, or any gentleman with whom you have conversed with casually. A short verbal exchange does not constitute an acquaintanceship, and therefore must not be acknowledged with a bow."

"What if the gentleman has done you some service?" Daisy asked. "Picking up a fallen glove, or something like that."

"Express your thanks at the time, but do not bow to him in the future, as a true acquaintanceship has not been established."

"That sounds rather ungrateful," Daisy commented.

The countess ignored her. "Now, on to dinner. After your first glass of wine, you may not request another. When the host passes the wine decanter to his guests during dinner, it is for the benefit of the gentlemen, not the ladies." She glowered at Lillian. "Last night I heard you ask for your wineglass to be refilled, Miss Bowman. Very bad form."

"But Lord Westcliff refilled it without a word," Lillian protested.

"Only to spare you from drawing yet more undesirable attention to yourself."

"But why . . ." Lillian's voice faded to silence as she saw the countess's forbidding expression. She realized that if she was going to ask for explanations on every point of etiquette, it would be a long afternoon indeed.

The countess proceeded to explain dinner table conventions, including the proper way to cut an asparagus point, and the way to consume quail and pigeon. ". . . blancmange and pudding must be eaten with a fork, not a spoon," she was saying, "and much to my dismay, I observed you both using knives on your rissoles." She looked at them significantly, as though expecting them to wilt with shame.

"What are rissoles?" Lillian dared to ask.

Daisy answered cautiously, "I think they were the little brown patties with the green sauce on top."

"I rather liked those," Lillian mused.

Daisy regarded her with a sly smile. "Do you know what they were made of?"

"No, and I don't want to!"

The countess ignored the exchange. "All rissoles, patties, and other molded foods must be eaten only with a fork, and never with the aid of a knife." Pausing, she glanced over the list to find her place. Her birdlike eyes constricted to slits as she read the next item. "And now," she said, staring meaningfully at Lillian, "as to the subject of calves' heads . . ."

Groaning, Lillian covered her eyes with one hand and slid down in her chair.

Chapter 11

*T*hose who were accustomed to Lord Westcliff's usual purposeful stride would have been more than a little surprised to witness his slow meander from the study to the upstairs parlor. A letter was held lightly in his fingers, the contents of which had occupied his mind for the past few minutes. But as significant as the news was, it was not entirely responsible for his pensive mood.

Much as Marcus would have liked to deny it, he was filled with anticipation at the thought of seeing Lillian Bowman . . . and he was keenly interested in how she was managing his mother. The countess would make mincemeat of any average girl, but he suspected that Lillian would hold her own.

Lillian. Because of her, he was fumbling to retrieve his self-control like a boy scurrying to pick up a box of scattered matchsticks. He had an innate distrust of sentiment, particularly his own, and a profound aversion to anyone or anything that threatened his dignity. The

Marsden lineage was famously somber . . . generations of solemn men occupied with weighty concerns. Marcus's own father, the old earl, had rarely smiled. When he had, it had usually preceded something very unpleasant. The old earl had dedicated himself to erasing any nuance of frivolity or humor in his only son, and while he hadn't succeeded completely, he had left a forceful influence. Marcus's existence was shaped by relentless expectations and duties—and the last thing he needed was distraction. Particularly in the form of a rebellious girl.

Lillian Bowman was not a young woman whom Marcus would ever consider courting. He could not imagine Lillian living happily in the confines of the British aristocracy. Her irreverence and individuality would never allow her to blend smoothly into Marcus's world. Moreover, it was universally acknowledged that since both of Marcus's sisters had married Americans, it was imperative that he preserve the family's distinguished pedigree with an English bride.

Marcus had always known that he would end up married to one of the countless young women who came out each season, all of them so similar that it hardly seemed to matter which one he picked. Any of these shy, refined girls would suit his purposes, and yet he had never quite been able to bring himself to take an interest in them. Whereas Lillian Bowman had obsessed him from the first moment he had seen her. There was no logical reason for it. Lillian was not the most beautiful woman of his acquaintance, nor was she particularly accomplished. She was sharp-tongued and opinionated, and her headstrong nature was far more suitable for a man than a woman.

Marcus knew that he and Lillian were both too strong-willed, their characters designed to clash. The

conflict between them at the jumping course was a perfect example of why a union between them was impossible. But that did not change the fact that Marcus wanted
Lillian Bowman more than any other woman he had ever
known. Her freshness, her unconventionality, called to
him even as he struggled against the temptation she offered. He had begun to dream about her at night, of
playing and grappling with her, entering her warm,
thrashing body until she cried out in pleasure. And there
were other dreams, of lying with her in sensual stillness,
their flesh joined and throbbing . . . of swimming in the
river with her naked body gliding against his, her hair
trailing in wet mermaid tendrils over his chest and shoulders. Of taking her in the field as if she were a peasant
girl, rolling with her on the sun-warmed grass.

Marcus had never felt the bite of unspent passion as
keenly as he did now. There were many women who
would be entirely willing to satisfy his needs. All it
would take was a few murmurs and a discreet tap on the
bedroom door, and he would find himself in a pair of
welcoming female arms. But it seemed wrong to use one
woman as a substitute for someone that he couldn't have.

Drawing near the family parlor, Marcus paused beside
the half-open door as he heard his mother lecturing the
Bowman sisters. Her complaint appeared to hinge upon
the sisters' habit of speaking to the footmen who served
them at the dinner table.

"But why shouldn't I thank someone for doing me a
service?" he heard Lillian ask with genuine perplexity.
"It's polite to say thank you, isn't it?"

"You should no more thank a servant than you would
thank a horse for allowing you to ride it, or a table for
bearing the dishes you place upon it."

"Well, we're not discussing animals or inanimate objects, are we? A footman is a person."

"No," the countess said coldly. "A footman is a servant."

"And a servant is a person," Lillian said stubbornly.

The elderly woman replied in exasperation. "Whatever your view of a footman is, you must not thank him at dinner. Servants neither expect nor desire such condescension, and if you insist on putting them in the awkward position of having to respond to your remarks, they will think badly of you . . . as will everyone else. Do not insult me with that vapid stare, Miss Bowman! You come from a family of means—surely you employed servants at your New York residence!"

"Yes," Lillian acknowledged pertly, "but we talked to ours."

Marcus fought to suppress a sudden laugh. It had been rare, if ever, that he had heard anyone dare to spar with the countess. Knocking lightly at the door, he entered the room, interrupting a potentially caustic exchange. Lillian twisted in her chair to view him. The flawless ivory of her skin was burnished with pink at the crests of her cheeks. The sophisticated braided coil of her hair, pinned high on her head, should have made her appear older, but instead it seemed to emphasize her youth. Although she was motionless in the chair, an air of electric impatience seemed to surround her. She reminded him of a schoolgirl who was eager to escape her lessons and run outside.

"Good afternoon," Marcus said politely. "I trust your discussion is going well?"

Lillian gave him a speaking glance.

Sternly fighting a smile, Marcus delivered a formal

bow to his mother. "My lady, a letter has arrived from America."

His mother stared at him alertly, making no response even though she knew that the letter had to be from Aline.

Stubborn bitch, Marcus thought, cold annoyance settling in his chest. The countess would never forgive her older daughter for marrying a man of low descent. Aline's husband, McKenna, had once been in service, working for the family as a stable boy. While still in his teens, McKenna had gone to America to seek his fortune, and had returned to England as a wealthy industrialist. In the countess's view, however, McKenna's success would never atone for his common birth, and therefore she had objected violently to the marriage between McKenna and her daughter. Aline's obvious happiness meant nothing to the countess, who had developed hypocrisy to an art form. Had Aline simply had an affair with McKenna, the countess would have thought nothing of it. Becoming his wife, however, was an unpardonable offense.

"I thought you would wish to learn its contents at once," Marcus continued, coming forward to hand the letter to her.

He watched his mother's face grow taut. Her hands remained motionless in her lap, and her eyes were cold with displeasure. Marcus took a slightly malicious enjoyment in forcing her to confront a fact that she so obviously wished to disregard.

"Why don't you tell me the news?" she invited in a brittle voice. "It is obvious that you will not leave until you do."

"Very well." Marcus slipped the letter back into his pocket. "Congratulations, my lady—you are now a grandmother. Lady Aline has given birth to a healthy

boy, named John McKenna the second." He allowed a
fine edge of sarcasm in his tone as he added, "I'm certain
you will be relieved to know that she and the baby are
doing quite well."

On the periphery of his vision, Marcus saw the Bowman sisters exchange a puzzled glance, clearly wondering at the cause of the hostility that filled the air.

"How nice that our former stable boy has begotten a
namesake from my elder daughter," the countess remarked acidly. "This will be the first of many brats, I am
sure. Regrettably there is still no heir to the earldom . . .
which is your responsibility, I believe. Come to me with
news of your impending marriage to a bride of good
blood, Westcliff, and I will evince some satisfaction. Until then, I see little reason for congratulations."

Though he displayed no emotion at his mother's hard-
hearted response to the news of Aline's child, not to
mention her infuriating preoccupation with the begetting of an heir, Marcus was hard-pressed to hold back a
savage reply. In the midst of his darkening mood, he became aware of Lillian's intent gaze.

Lillian stared at him astutely, a peculiar smile touching her lips. Marcus arched one brow and asked sardonically, "Does something amuse you, Miss Bowman?"

"Yes," she murmured. "I was just thinking that it's a
wonder you haven't rushed out to marry the first peasant
girl you could find."

"Impertinent twit!" the countess exclaimed.

Marcus grinned at the girl's insolence, while the tightness in his chest eased. "Do you think I should?" he
asked soberly, as if the question was worth considering.

"Oh yes," Lillian assured him with a mischievous
sparkle in her eyes. "The Marsdens could use some new

blood. In my opinion, the family is in grave danger of becoming overbred."

"Overbred?" Marcus repeated, wanting nothing more than to pounce on her and carry her off somewhere. "What has given you that impression, Miss Bowman?"

"Oh, I don't know . . ." she said idly. "Perhaps the earth-shattering importance you attach to whether one should use a fork or spoon to eat one's pudding."

"Good manners are not the sole province of the aristocracy, Miss Bowman." Even to himself, Marcus sounded a bit pompous.

"In my opinion, my lord, an excessive preoccupation with manners and rituals is a strong indication that someone has too much time on his hands."

Marcus smiled at her impertinence. "Subversive, yet sensible," he mused. "I'm not certain I disagree."

"Do not encourage her effrontery, Westcliff," the countess warned.

"Very well—I shall leave you to your Sisyphean task."

"What does that mean?" he heard Daisy ask.

Lillian replied while her smiling gaze remained locked with Marcus's. "It seems you avoided one too many Greek mythology lessons, dear. Sisyphus was a soul in Hades who was damned to perform an eternal task . . . rolling a huge boulder up a hill, only to have it roll down again just before he reached the top."

"Then if the countess is Sisyphus," Daisy concluded, "I suppose we're . . ."

"The boulder," Lady Westcliff said succinctly, causing both girls to laugh.

"Do continue with our instruction, my lady," Lillian said, giving her full attention to the elderly woman as

Marcus bowed and left the room. "We'll try not to flatten you on the way down."

Lillian was troubled by a feeling of melancholy for the rest of the afternoon. As Daisy had pointed out, being lectured to by the countess was hardly a tonic for the soul, but Lillian's depression of the spirits seemed to stem from a deeper source than simply having spent too much time in the company of a bilious old woman. It had something to do with what had been said after Lord Westcliff had entered the Marsden parlor with the tidings of his newborn nephew. Westcliff had seemed pleased by the news, and yet not at all surprised by his mother's bitter reception. The rancorous exchange that had followed had impressed upon Lillian the importance—no, the necessity—that Westcliff marry a "bride of good blood," as the countess had phrased it.

A bride of good blood . . . one who knew how to eat a rissole and would never think of thanking the footman who had served it to her. One who would never make the mistake of crossing the room to speak to a gentleman, but stand docilely and wait for him to approach her. Westcliff's bride would be a dainty English flower, with ash-blond hair and a rosebud mouth, and a serene temperament. *Overbred,* Lillian thought with a touch of animosity toward the unknown girl. Why should it bother her so that Westcliff was destined to marry a girl who would blend flawlessly into his upper-class existence?

Frowning, she recalled the way the earl had touched her face last evening. A subtle caress, but wholly inappropriate, coming from a man who had absolutely no designs on her. And yet he hadn't seemed to be able to help himself. It was the effect of the perfume, she thought darkly.

She had anticipated such fun in torturing Westcliff with his own unwilling attraction to her. Instead it was rebounding on her in a most unpleasant way. *She* was the one being tortured. Every time Westcliff glanced at her, touched her, smiled at her, it provoked a feeling that she had never known before. A painful feeling of yearning that made her want impossible things.

Anyone would say that it was a ridiculous pairing, Westcliff and Lillian . . . especially in light of his responsibility to produce a purebred heir. There were other titled men who could not afford to be as selective as Westcliff, men whose inherited resources had dwindled, and therefore had need of her fortune. With the countess's sponsorship, Lillian would find some acceptable candidate, marry him, and be done with this eternal process of husband hunting. But—a new thought struck her—the world of the British aristocracy was quite small, and she would almost certainly be confronted with Westcliff and his English bride, again and again . . . The prospect was more than disconcerting. It was awful.

The yearning sharpened into jealousy. Lillian knew that Westcliff would never trúly be happy with the woman he was destined to marry. He would tire of a wife whom he could bully. And a steady diet of tranquillity would bore him abysmally. Westcliff needed someone who would challenge and interest him. Someone who could reach through to the warm, human man who was buried beneath the layers of aristocratic self-possession. Someone who angered him, teased him, and made him laugh.

"Someone like me," Lillian whispered miserably.

Chapter 12

A formal dress ball was held in the evening. It was a fine night, dry and cool, with the rows of tall windows opened to admit the outside air. The chandeliers scattered light over the intricately parqueted floor like glittering raindrops. Orchestra music filled the air in buoyant drifts, providing a perfect framework for the gossip and laughter of the guests.

Lillian did not dare accept a cup of punch, fearing that it would drip on her cream satin ball gown. The unadorned skirts fell in gleaming folds to the floor, while the narrow waist was cinched with a stiffened band of matching satin. The only ornamentation on the gown was an artful sprinkling of beads on the edge of her scoop-necked bodice. As she tugged a finger of her white glove more firmly over her little fingertip, she caught a glimpse of Lord Westcliff from across the room. He was dark and striking in his evening clothes, his white cravat pressed to the sharpness of a knife blade.

As usual, a group of men and women had gathered around him. One of the women, a beautiful blond with a voluptuous figure, leaned closer to him, murmuring something that brought a faint smile to his lips. He coolly observed the scene, appraising the gently milling assembly . . . until he saw Lillian. His gaze flicked over her in swift assessment. Lillian felt his presence so palpably that the fifteen yards or so between them might not have existed. Troubled by her own gauzy sensual awareness of the man standing across the room, she gave him a brief nod and turned away.

"What is it?" Daisy murmured, coming up beside her. "You look rather distracted."

Lillian responded with a wry smile. "I'm trying to remember everything the countess told us," she lied, "and keep it all straight in my head. Especially the bowing rules. If someone bows to me, I'm going to shriek and run in the opposite direction."

"I'm terrified of making a mistake," Daisy confided. "It was so much easier before I realized how many things I have been doing wrong. I'll be quite happy to be a wall-flower and sit safely at the side of the room this evening." Together they glanced at the row of semicircular niches running along one wall, each sided by slender pilasters and fitted with tiny velvet-covered benches. Evie sat alone in the farthest niche in the corner. Her pink dress clashed with her red hair, and she kept her head down as she sipped furtively from a cup of punch, every line of her posture proclaiming a disinclination to talk with anyone. "Oh, that won't do," Daisy said. "Come, let's pry the poor girl out of that niche and make her stroll with us."

Lillian smiled in agreement and made to accompany her sister. However, she froze with a sudden breath as she heard a deep voice near her ear. "Good evening, Miss Bowman."

Blinking with astonishment, she turned to face Lord Westcliff, who had crossed the room to her with surprising speed. "My lord."

Westcliff bowed over Lillian's hand and then greeted Daisy. His gaze returned to Lillian's. As he spoke, the light from the chandeliers played over the rich dark layers of his hair and the bold angles of his features. "You survived the encounter with my mother, I see."

Lillian smiled. "A better way to put it, my lord, is that she survived the encounter with us."

"It was obvious that the countess was enjoying herself immensely. She seldom encounters young women who don't wither in her presence."

"If I haven't withered in your presence, my lord, then I'm hardly going to wither in hers."

Westcliff grinned at that and then looked away from her, a pair of small creases appearing between his brows, as if he was contemplating some weighty matter. After a pause that seemed interminably long, his attention returned to Lillian. "Miss Bowman . . ."

"Yes?"

"Will you do me the honor of dancing with me?"

Lillian stopped breathing, moving, and thinking. Westcliff had never asked her to dance before, despite the multitude of occasions on which he should have asked out of gentlemanly politeness. It had been one of the many reasons that she had hated him, knowing that he considered himself far too superior, and her attractions too insignificant, for it to be worth the bother. And in her more spiteful fantasies, she had imagined a moment like this when he would have asked for a dance, and she would respond with a crushing refusal. Instead, she was astonished and tongue-tied.

"Do excuse me," she heard Daisy say brightly, "I must go to Evie . . ." And she sped away with all possible haste.

Lillian drew in an unsteady breath. "Is this a test that the countess has devised?" she asked. "To see if I remember my lessons?"

Westcliff chuckled. Gathering her wits, Lillian couldn't help but notice that people were staring at them, obviously wondering what she had said to amuse him. "No," he murmured, "I believe it's a self-imposed test to see if I . . ." He seemed to forget what he was saying as he stared into her eyes. "One waltz," he said gently.

Distrusting her own response to him, the magnitude of her desire to step into his arms, Lillian shook her head. "I think . . . I think that would be a mistake. Thank you, but—"

"Coward."

Lillian remembered the moment she had leveled the same charge at him . . . and she was no more able to resist the challenge than he. "I can't see why you should want to dance with me now, when you never have before."

The statement was more revealing than she had intended it to be. She cursed her own wayward tongue, while his speculative gaze wandered over her face.

"I wanted to," he surprised her by murmuring. "However, there always seemed to be good reasons not to."

"Why—"

"Besides," Westcliff interrupted, reaching out to take her gloved hand, "there was hardly a point in asking when your refusal was a foregone conclusion." Deftly he pressed her hand to his arm and led her toward the mass of couples in the center of the room.

"It was not a foregone conclusion."

Westcliff glanced at her skeptically. "You're saying that you would have accepted me?"

"I might have."

"I doubt it."

"I did just now, didn't I?"

"You had to. It was a debt of honor."

She couldn't help but laugh. "For *what*, my lord?"

"The calf's head," he reminded her succinctly.

"Well, if you hadn't served such a nasty object in the first place, I wouldn't have needed to be rescued!"

"You wouldn't have needed to be rescued if you didn't have such a weak stomach."

"You're not supposed to mention body parts in front of a lady," she said virtuously. "Your mother said so."

Westcliff grinned. "I stand corrected."

Enjoying their bickering, Lillian grinned back at him. Her smile died, however, as a slow waltz began and Westcliff turned her to face him. Her heart began to thump with unrestrained force. As she looked down at the gloved hand that he extended to her, she could not make herself take it. She could not let him hold her in public . . . she was afraid of what her face might reveal.

After a moment she heard his low voice. "Take my hand."

Dazed, she found herself obeying, her trembling fingers reaching for his.

Another silence passed, and then, softly, "Put your other one on my shoulder."

She watched her white glove settle slowly on his shoulder, the surface hard and solid beneath her palm.

"Now look at me," he whispered.

Her lashes lifted. Her heart gave a jolt as she stared

into his coffee-colored eyes, which were filled with dark warmth. Holding her gaze, Westcliff drew her into the waltz, using the momentum of the first turn to bring her closer to him. Soon they were lost in the midst of the dancers, circling with the lazy grace of a swallow's flight. As Lillian might have expected, Westcliff established a strong lead, allowing no chance of a misstep. His hand was firm at the small of her back, the other providing explicit guidance.

It was all too easy. It was perfect as nothing else in her life had ever been, their bodies moving in harmony as if they had waltzed together a thousand times before. Good Lord, he could dance. He led her into steps that she had never tried, reverse turns and cross steps, and it was all so natural and effortless that she gave a breathless laugh at the completion of a turn. She felt weightless in his arms, gliding smoothly within the parameters of his taut and graceful movements. Her skirts brushed his legs, wrapping and falling away in rhythmic repetition.

The crowded ballroom seemed to disappear, and she felt as if they were dancing alone, far away in some private place. Intensely aware of his body, the occasional touch of his warm breath on her cheek, Lillian drifted into a curious waking dream . . . a fantasy in which Marcus, Lord Westcliff, would take her upstairs after the waltz, and undress her, and lay her gently across his bed. He would kiss her everywhere, as he had once whispered . . . he would make love to her, and hold her while she slept. She had never wanted that kind of intimacy with a man before.

"Marcus . . ." she said absently, testing his name on her tongue. He glanced at her alertly. The use of some-one's first name was profoundly personal, far too intimate unless they were married or closely related. Smiling mischievously, Lillian turned the conversation into a more appropriate channel. "I like that name. It's not common nowadays. Were you named after your father?"

"No, after an uncle. The only one on my mother's side."

"Were you pleased to be his namesake?"

"Any name would have been acceptable, so long as it wasn't my father's."

"Did you hate him?"

Westcliff shook his head. "Something worse than that."

"What could be worse than hatred?"

"Indifference."

She stared at him with open curiosity. "And the countess?" she dared to ask. "Are you also indifferent to her?"

One corner of his mouth curled upward in a half smile. "I regard my mother as an aging tigress—one whose teeth and claws are blunted, but who is still capable of inflicting harm. Therefore I try to conduct all interactions with her at a safe distance."

Lillian gave him a mock-indignant scowl. "And yet you tossed me right into the cage with her this morning!"

"I knew you had your own set of teeth and claws." Westcliff grinned at her expression. "That was a compliment."

"I'm glad you told me so," she said dryly. "Otherwise I might not have known."

To Lillian's dismay, the waltz ended with one last sweet drawn-out note of a single violin. Amid the ensuing currents of dancers moving off the main floor, with others coming to replace them, Westcliff stopped abruptly. He was still holding her, she realized with a touch of confusion, and she took a hesitant step backward. Reflexively his arm hardened around her waist, and his fingers tightened in an instinctive attempt to keep her with him. Astonished by the action, and what it betrayed, Lillian felt her breath stop.

Checking his impulsiveness, Westcliff forced himself to release her. Still, she felt the force of desire radiating from him, as penetrating as the heat drafts of an entire forest on fire. And it was a mortifying thought that whereas her feelings for him were genuine, his might very well be the whimsical result of a perfume's aroma. She would have given anything not to be so attracted to him, when disappointment or even heartbreak was a foregone conclusion.

"I was right, wasn't I?" she asked huskily, unable to look at him. "It was a mistake for us to dance."

Westcliff waited so long to reply that she thought he might not. "Yes," he finally said, the single syllable roughened with some unidentifiable emotion.

Because he could not afford to want her. Because he knew as well as she that a pairing between them would be a disaster.

Suddenly it hurt to be near him. "Then I suppose this waltz will be our first and our last," she said lightly. "Good evening, my lord, and thank you for—"

"Lillian," she heard him whisper.

Turning from him, she walked away with a brittle smile, while goose bumps rose on the exposed skin of her neck and back.

The rest of the night would have been a misery for Lillian, had it not been for a timely rescue in the form of

Sebastian, Lord St. Vincent. He appeared beside her before she could join Evie and Daisy, who were sitting together on a velvet bench.

"What a graceful dancer you are, Miss Bowman."

After being with Westcliff, it seemed awkward to look up into the face of a man who was so much taller than she. St. Vincent stared at her with a promise of wicked enjoyment that she found difficult to resist. His enigmatic smile could have been offered to a friend or an enemy with equal ease. Lillian let her gaze slip downward to the slightly off-center knot of his cravat. There was a hint of disarray in his clothing, as if he had dressed with a bit too much haste after leaving a lover's bed—and meant to return there soon.

In answer to his easy compliment, Lillian smiled and shrugged a bit awkwardly, remembering too late the countess's admonition that ladies never shrugged. "If I appeared graceful, my lord, it was because of the earl's skill, not mine."

"You're too modest, sweet. I've seen Westcliff dance with other women, and the effect wasn't nearly the same. You seem to have patched up your differences with him quite nicely. Are you friends now?"

It was a harmless question, but Lillian sensed that his meaning was multilayered. She replied cautiously, while she noticed that Lord Westcliff was escorting an auburn-haired woman to the refreshment table. The woman was glowing with obvious pleasure at the earl's interest. A needle of jealousy stabbed through Lillian's heart. "I don't know, my lord," she said. "It's possible that your definition of friendship does not match mine."

"Clever girl." St. Vincent's eyes were like blue diamonds, pale and infinitely faceted. "Come, let me escort you to the refreshment table, and we'll compare our definitions."

"No, thank you," Lillian said reluctantly, even though she was parched with thirst. For her own peace of mind, she had to avoid Westcliff's proximity.

Following her gaze, St. Vincent saw the earl in the company of the auburn-haired woman. "Perhaps we'd better not," he agreed in a relaxed tone. "It would undoubtedly displease Westcliff to see you in my company. After all, he did warn me to stay away from you."

"He did?" Lillian frowned. "Why?"

"He doesn't want you to be compromised or otherwise harmed by association with me." The viscount slid her a baiting glance. "My reputation, you understand."

"Westcliff has no right to make any decisions about whom I associate with," Lillian muttered, swift anger burning through her. "The top-lofty, superior know-all, I'd like to—" She stopped and fought to marshal her rearing emotions. "I'm thirsty," she said tersely. "I want to go to the refreshment table. With you."

"If you insist," St. Vincent said mildly. "What shall it be? Water? Lemonade? Punch, or—"

"Champagne," came her grim reply.

"Whatever you desire." He accompanied her to the long table, which was surrounded by a long line of guests. Lillian had never known a purer sense of satisfaction than the moment Westcliff noticed that she was in St. Vincent's company. The line of his mouth hardened, and he stared at her with narrowed black eyes. Smiling defiantly, Lillian accepted a glass of iced champagne from St. Vincent and drank it in unladylike gulps.

"Not so fast, sweet," she heard St. Vincent murmur. "The champagne will go to your head."

"I want another," Lillian replied, dragging her attention away from Westcliff and turning toward St. Vincent.

"Yes. In a few minutes. You look a bit flushed. The effect is charming, but I think you've had enough for now. Would you like to dance?"

"I would love to." Giving her empty glass to a nearby footman with a tray, Lillian stared at St. Vincent with a deliberately dazzling smile. "How interesting. After a year of being a perpetual wallflower, I've received two invitations to dance in one night. I wonder why?"

"Well . . ." St. Vincent walked slowly with her to the crowd of dancers. "I'm a wicked man who can, on occasion, be just a bit nice. And I've been searching for a nice girl who can, on occasion, be just a bit wicked."

"And now you've found one?" Lillian asked, laughing.

"It would seem so."

"What were you planning to do, once you found the girl?"

There was an interesting complexity in his eyes. He seemed like a man who was capable of anything . . . and in her current reckless disposition, that was exactly what she wanted. "I will let you know," St. Vincent murmured. "Later."

Dancing with St. Vincent was an entirely different experience from dancing with Westcliff. There was not the sense of exquisite physical harmony, of movement without thought . . . but St. Vincent was smooth and accomplished, and as they circled the ballroom, he kept throwing out provocative comments that made her laugh. And he held her with assurance, with hands that, despite their respectful clasp, bespoke a wealth of experience with women's bodies.

"How much of your reputation is deserved?" she dared to ask him.

"Only about half . . . which makes me utterly reprehensible."

Lillian stared at him with quizzical amusement. "How could a man like you be friends with Lord Westcliff? You're so very different."

"We've known each other since the age of eight. And, stubborn soul that he is, Westcliff refuses to accept that I'm a lost cause."

"Why should you be a lost cause?"

"You don't want to know the answer to that." He interrupted the beginnings of her next question by murmuring, "The waltz is ending. And there is a woman near the gilded frieze who is watching us rather closely. Your mother, isn't she? Let me take you to her."

Lillian shook her head. "You had better part company with me now. Trust me—you don't want to meet my mother."

"Of course I do. If she is anything like you, I will find her captivating."

"If she is anything like me, I pray you will have the decency to keep your opinion to yourself."

"Have no fear," he advised lazily, easing her away from the dancing area. "I've never met a woman I didn't like."

"This is the last time you will ever make such a statement," she predicted dourly.

As St. Vincent escorted Lillian toward the group of gossiping women that included her mother, he said, "I'll invite her to accompany us on the carriage drive tomorrow, as you are in dire need of a chaperone."

"I don't *have* to have one," Lillian protested. "Men

and women may go for an unchaperoned drive as long as it's not a closed carriage and they're not gone for longer than—"

"You need a chaperone," he repeated with a gentle insistence that made her feel suddenly flustered and shy.

Thinking that his gaze couldn't possibly mean what she thought it meant, she laughed shakily. "Or else . . ." She tried to think of something daring to say. "Or else you'll compromise me?"

His smile, like everything else about him, was subtle and unhurried. "Something like that."

There was an odd but pleasant tickle at the back of her throat, as if she had swallowed a spoonful of treacle. St. Vincent wasn't behaving at all like the seducers that populated the silver-fork novels Daisy was so fond of. Those villainous characters, with their heavy mustaches and lecherous gazes, were prone to lie about their evil intentions until the revealing moment when they assaulted the virginal heroine and forced themselves upon her. St. Vincent, by contrast, seemed positively determined to warn her away from himself, and she could not quite picture him bestirring himself enough to force a girl to do anything against her will.

When Lillian made the introductions between her mother and St. Vincent, she saw the instant calculation in Mercedes's eyes. Mercedes viewed all eligible men of the peerage, regardless of age, appearance, or reputation, as potential prey. She would stop at nothing to ensure that each of her daughters married a title, and it mattered little to her if the man behind it was young and handsome, or old and senile. Having commissioned a private report on nearly every peer of note in England, Mercedes had memorized hundreds of pages of financial figures about the British aristocracy. As she stared at the elegant viscount who stood before her, one could almost see her riffle through the wealth of information in her brain.

Remarkably, however, in the course of the next few minutes Mercedes relaxed in St. Vincent's charming presence. He coaxed her into agreeing to the carriage drive, teased and flattered her, and listened to her opinions with such attentiveness that soon Mercedes began to blush and giggle like a girl in her teens. Lillian had never seen her mother behave that way with any other man. It quickly became obvious that whereas Westcliff made Mercedes nervous, St. Vincent had the opposite effect. He had a unique ability to make a woman—any woman, it seemed—feel attractive. He was far more polished than most American men, yet warmer and more accessible than English men. His allure was so compelling, in fact, that for a while Lillian forgot to glance around the room in search of Westcliff.

Taking Mercedes's hand in his, St. Vincent bent over her wrist and murmured, "Until tomorrow, then."

"Until tomorrow," Mercedes repeated, looking dazzled, and suddenly Lillian had a glimpse of what her mother must have looked like in her youth before disappointment had hardened her. A few women leaned toward Mercedes, and she turned to confer with them.

Bending his dark golden head, St. Vincent murmured close to Lillian's ear, "Would you care for that second glass of champagne now?"

Lillian nodded slightly, absorbing the pleasant mixture of fragrances that clung to him, the touch of expensive cologne, the hint of shaving soap, and the clean, clovelike essence of his skin.

"Here?" he asked softly. "Or in the garden?"

Realizing that he wanted her to steal away with him for a few minutes, Lillian felt a stirring of caution. Alone with St. Vincent in the garden . . . no doubt many an unwary girl's downfall had begun that way. Considering the proposition, she let her gaze wander until she caught sight of Westcliff taking a woman into his arms. Waltzing with her, just as he had with Lillian. The forever unattainable Westcliff, she thought, and anger filled her. She wanted distraction. And comfort. And the large, handsome male in front of her seemed willing to provide it.

"The garden," she said.

"Meet me in ten minutes, then. There is a mermaid fountain just beyond the—"

"I know where it is."

"If you can't manage to slip outside—"

"I will," she assured him, forcing a smile.

St. Vincent paused to view her with a shrewd but oddly compassionate gaze. "I can make you feel better, sweet," he whispered.

"Can you?" she asked dully, unwanted emotion staining her cheeks as red as poppies.

A promising glint appeared in his brilliant eyes, and he responded with a slight nod before taking his leave.

Chapter 13

*E*nlisting Daisy and Evie to cover for her, Lillian left the ballroom with them on the pretense of repairing their appearances. According to their swiftly devised plan, the two girls would wait on the back terrace as Lillian met with Lord St. Vincent in the garden. When they all returned to the ballroom, they would assure Mercedes that she had been with them the entire time.

"Are you qu-quite certain that it's safe for you to meet with Lord St. Vincent alone?" Evie asked as they walked to the entrance hall.

"Safe as houses," Lillian replied confidently. "Oh, he may try to take a liberty, but that's rather the point, isn't it? Besides, I want to see if my perfume works on him."

"It doesn't work on *anyone*," Daisy said morosely. "At least not when I'm wearing it."

Lillian glanced at Evie. "What about you, dear? Had any luck?"

Daisy answered for her. "Evie hasn't allowed anyone to get close enough to find out."

"Well, I'm going to give St. Vincent the opportunity to take a good long whiff of it. Heaven knows, this perfume should have *some* effect on a notorious rake."

"But if someone sees you—"

"No one will see us," Lillian interrupted with a touch of impatience. "If there is any man in England who is more experienced than Lord St. Vincent at sneaking around for a tryst, I'd like to know who."

"You had better be careful," Daisy warned. "Trysts are dangerous things. I've read about lots of them, and no good ever seems to come of them."

"It will be a very short tryst," Lillian assured her. "A quarter hour at most. What could happen in that amount of time?"

"From what Annabelle s-says," Evie said darkly, "a lot."

"Where *is* Annabelle?" Lillian asked, realizing that she had not seen her so far that evening.

"She wasn't feeling well earlier, poor thing," Daisy said. "She seemed a bit green around the gills. I'm afraid something at lunch may not have agreed with her."

Lillian made a face and shuddered. "No doubt it was something with eels or veal knuckles or chicken feet . . ."

Daisy grinned at her. "Don't, you'll make yourself ill. At any rate, Mr. Hunt is taking care of her."

They exited the French doors at the back of the entrance hall and walked out onto the empty flagstone terrace. Daisy turned to shake a finger waggishly at Lillian. "If you're gone for longer than a quarter hour, Evie and I will come looking for you."

Lillian responded with a low laugh. "I won't tarry."

She winked and smiled into Evie's worried face. "I'll be fine, dear. And just think of all the interesting things I'll be able to tell you when I return!"

"That's what I'm afr-fraid of," Evie replied.

Descending one side of the back staircase, Lillian picked up her skirts and ventured into the terraced gardens, past one of the ancient hedges that formed impenetrable walls around the lower levels. The torchlit garden was redolent with the colors and scents of autumn . . . gold and copper foliage, thick borders of roses and dahlias, flowering grasses and beds of fresh mulch that made the air pleasantly pungent.

Hearing the friendly splash of the mermaid fountain, Lillian followed a flagstone path to a little paved clearing illuminated by a lone torchlight. There was movement beside the fountain—one person, no, two people, closely entwined as they sat on one of the stone benches that surrounded the fountain. She stifled a gasp of surprise and drew back into the concealment of the hedge. Lord St. Vincent had told her to meet him here . . . but surely the man on the bench wasn't he . . . was it? Bewildered, Lillian crept forward a few inches to peer around the corner of the hedge.

It quickly became apparent that the couple was so involved in their love play that a passing stampede of elephants would have gone unnoticed by either of them. The woman's light brown hair had fallen loose, the waving locks hanging in the open void at the back of her partially unfastened gown. Her slim, pale arms loosely encircled his shoulders, and she breathed in shivering sighs as he tugged the sleeve of her gown from her shoulder and kissed the white curve. Lifting his head, he stared at her with a drowsy, impassioned gaze before leaning forward to take her mouth with his. Suddenly Lillian recognized the couple . . . it was Lady Olivia and her husband, Mr. Shaw. Mortified and curious, she drew back behind the hedge just as Mr. Shaw slid his hand into the back of his wife's gown. It was the most intimate scene that Lillian had ever witnessed.

And the most intimate sounds she had ever heard . . . soft gasps and love words, and an inexplicable gentle laugh from Mr. Shaw that caused Lillian's toes to curl. Her face was scorched with embarrassment as she inched quietly away from the clearing. She was not certain where to go or what to do now that the place for her own rendevous was already occupied. It had given her a strange feeling to witness the deeply passionate tenderness that existed between the Shaws. Love within marriage. Lillian had never dared to hope for such a thing for herself.

A large form appeared before her. Approaching slowly, he slid an arm behind her stiff shoulders and pressed a chilled glass of champagne into her fingers. "My lord?" Lillian whispered.

St. Vincent's soft murmur tickled her ear. "Come with me."

Willingly she allowed him to guide her along a darker path, which led to another lit clearing set with a ponderous circular stone table. A pear orchard beyond the clearing infused the air with the fragrance of ripening fruit. Keeping his arm around Lillian's shoulder, St. Vincent brought her forward. "Shall we stop here?" he asked.

She nodded and leaned her hip against the table, unable to look at him as she drank her champagne. Thinking of her near blunder into the private scene between the Shaws, she flushed deeply.

"Here now, you're not embarrassed, are you?" St. Vincent said, his voice gilded with amusement. "A little glimpse of . . . oh, come, that was nothing." He had removed his gloves—she felt the tips of his fingers slip beneath her chin, lightly nudging her face upward. "What a blush," he murmured. "Good Lord, I've forgotten what it's like to be so innocent. I doubt I ever was."

St. Vincent was mesmerizing in the torchlight. Shadows nestled lovingly beneath the fine planes of his cheekbones. The thick, layered locks of his hair were the bronzed gold of an ancient Byzantine icon. "They are married, after all," he continued, fitting his hands around her waist and lifting her into a seated position on the table.

"Oh, I . . . I don't disapprove," Lillian managed, draining her champagne. "In fact, I was thinking about how fortunate they are. They seem very happy together. And in light of the countess's aversion to Americans, I am surprised that Lady Olivia was allowed to marry Mr. Shaw."

"That was Westcliff's doing. He was determined not to let his mother's hypocritical views stand in the way of his sister's happiness. Considering her own scandalous past, the countess had little right to disapprove of her daughter's choice of whom to marry."

"The countess has a scandalous past?"

"Lord, yes. Her outward piety covers a wealth of private dissipation. It's why she and I get on so well. I'm the kind of man she used to have affairs with, back in her younger years."

The empty glass nearly dropped from Lillian's fingers. Setting the fragile vessel aside, she regarded St. Vincent with patent surprise. "She doesn't seem at all like the kind of woman who would have affairs."

"Haven't you ever noticed the lack of family resemblance between Westcliff and Lady Olivia? While the earl and his sister Lady Aline are legitimate issue, it is fairly common knowledge that Lady Olivia is not."

"Oh."

"But one can hardly blame the countess for infidelity," St. Vincent continued casually, "when one considers whom she was married to."

The subject of the old earl was one that interested Lillian keenly. He was a mysterious figure, and not one who anyone seemed particularly willing to discuss. "Lord Westcliff once told me that his father was a brute," she said, hoping that would induce St. Vincent to reveal more.

"Did he?" St. Vincent's eyes were bright with interest. "That's unusual. Westcliff never mentions his father to anyone."

"Was he? A brute, I mean."

"No," St. Vincent said softly. "Calling him a brute would be far too kind, as it implies a certain lack of awareness in one's own cruelty. The old earl was a devil. I know of only a fraction of his atrocities—and I don't wish to know any more." Leaning back on his hands, St. Vincent continued thoughtfully, "I doubt many people would have survived the Marsdens' style of parenting, which varied from benign neglect to utter fiendishness." He inclined his head, his features shrouded in shadow. "For most of my life I've watched Westcliff struggle not to become what his father wanted him to be. But he carries a burden of heavy expectations . . . and that guides his personal choices more often than he would wish."

"Personal choices such as . . ."

He looked at her directly. "Whom he will marry, for instance."

Understanding immediately, Lillian considered her reply with great care. "It's not necessary to warn me about that," she finally said. "I'm well aware that Lord Westcliff would never give a thought to courting someone like me."

"Oh, he's thought about it," St. Vincent stunned her by saying.

Lillian's heart stopped. "How do you know that? Has he mentioned something to you?"

"No. But it's obvious that he wants you. Whenever you're near, he can't tear his gaze from you. And when you and I were dancing tonight, he looked as if he wanted to skewer me with the nearest sharp object. However . . ."

"However . . ." Lillian prompted.

"When Westcliff finally marries, he will make the conventional choice . . . a malleable young English bride who will make no demands of him."

Of course. Lillian had never thought differently. But sometimes the truth was not easy to digest. And, maddeningly, there was nothing she could reasonably mourn over. She had never had anything to lose. Westcliff had never made a single promise, or expressed a single word of affection. A few kisses and a waltz did not even amount to a failed romance.

Why, then, did she feel so miserable?

Studying the minute alterations of her expression, St.

Vincent smiled sympathetically. "It will fade, sweet," he murmured. "It always does." Leaning down, he brushed his mouth over her hair until his lips reached the frail skin of her temple.

Lillian held still, knowing that if her perfume was going to work its magic on him, it would certainly be now. At this close distance, there was no way he could elude its effects. However, as he drew back, she saw that he was still calm and composed. There was nothing at all in his expression to indicate the near-violent passion that Westcliff had displayed toward her. *Bloody hell,* she thought with a flash of frustration. *What use is a perfume that only attracts the wrong man?*

"My lord," she asked softly, "have you ever wanted someone you couldn't have?"

"Not yet. But one can always hope."

She responded with a puzzled smile. "You *hope* to fall in love someday with someone you can't have? Why?"

"It would be an interesting experience."

"So would falling off a cliff," she said sardonically. "But I think one would rather learn about it from secondhand knowledge."

Laughing, St. Vincent levered himself off the table and turned to face her. "Perhaps you're right. We had better return you to the manor, my clever little friend, before your absence becomes too obvious."

"But . . ." Lillian realized that the interlude in the garden was apparently going to consist of nothing more than a stroll and a brief conversation. "That's all?" she blurted out. "You're not going to . . ." Her voice trailed into disgruntled silence.

Standing before her, St. Vincent rested his hands on the table, bracing them on either side of her hips without touching her. His smile was subtle and warm. "I assume you're referring to the advance I was supposed to make?" Deliberately he inclined his head until his breath caressed her forehead. "I've decided to wait, and let us both wonder a bit longer."

Crestfallen, Lillian wondered if he found her undesirable. For God's sake, according to the man's reputation, he would chase after anything in skirts. Whether she truly wanted him to kiss her or not was irrelevant in light of the larger issue, which was that she was being rejected by yet another man. Two rebuffs in one evening—that was a bit hard on anyone's vanity.

"But you promised to make me feel better," she protested, turning red with shame as she heard the supplicating note in her own voice.

St. Vincent laughed quietly. "Well, if you're going to start complaining . . . here. Something to think about."

His face lowered over hers, and his fingertips settled on her jaw, gently adjusting the angle of her head. Lillian's eyes closed, and she felt the silken pressure of his lips, moving over hers with compelling lightness. His mouth drifted in a slow, restive search, settling more firmly with each pass until her lips had parted for him. She had only begun to absorb the exotic promise of his kiss when it ended with a soft nuzzle of his mouth. Disoriented and breathless, she accepted the support of his hands on her shoulders until she was able to sit without toppling from the table.

Something to think about, indeed.

After helping her to descend to the ground, St. Vincent walked through the garden with her until they had reached the succession of terraces that led to the back balcony. They paused at the hedge. Moonlight limned the edges of his profile in silver as he looked into her up-turned face. "Thank you," he murmured.

Was he thanking her for the kiss? Lillian nodded uncertainly, thinking that perhaps it should have been the other way around. Even though the image of Westcliff still lingered moodily in the back of her mind, she didn't feel nearly as bleak as she had in the ballroom.

"You won't forget our carriage drive in the morning?" St. Vincent asked, his fingers sliding up the length of her gloves until he had found the bare parts of her upper arms.

Lillian shook her head.

St. Vincent frowned with mock concern. "Have I robbed you of the power of speech?" he asked, and laughed as she nodded. "Hold still, then, and I'll give it back to you." His head lowered swiftly, and he pressed a kiss to her mouth, sending a rush of tingling warmth through her veins. His long fingers cradled her cheeks as he gave her a questioning stare. "Is that better? Let me hear you say something."

She couldn't help but smile. "Good night," she murmured.

"Good night," he said with a smile full of whimsy, and turned her away from him. "You go in first."

When Sebastian, Lord St. Vincent exerted himself to be charming, as he did the following morning, Lillian doubted that any man on earth could be more appealing. Insisting that Daisy accompany them too, he met the three Bowman women in the entrance hall with a bouquet of roses for Mercedes. He escorted them outside to a black-lacquered curricle, gave a signal to the driver, and the well-sprung vehicle rolled smoothly along the graveled drive.

St. Vincent occupied the seat beside Lillian and kept all three women engaged with questions about their life in New York. It had been a long time, Lillian realized, since she and Daisy had discussed their birthplace with anyone. Hardly anyone in London society gave a fig about New York, or what was happening there. However, Lord St. Vincent proved to be such a receptive audience that soon story upon story was tumbling out.

Eagerly they told him about the row of stone mansions on Fifth Avenue, and about wintertime in Central Park, when the pond at Fifty-ninth Street had frozen over and weekly ice carnivals were held, and how it sometimes took a half hour to cross Broadway Avenue because of the ceaseless line of omnibuses and hackney coaches. And about the ice cream saloon on Broadway and Franklin, which dared to serve young ladies who were unaccompanied by male escorts.

St. Vincent seemed amused by their descriptions of Manhattanville excesses; the party they had once attended at which the ballroom had been filled with three thousand hothouse orchids, and the mania for diamonds that had begun with the discovery of new mines in South Africa, with the result that now everyone from the elderly to the smallest infants was bedecked in glittering gems. And of course the simple mandate given to every decorator . . . "More." More gilded molding, more bric-a-brac, more paint and decorative fabrics, until every room was filled from floor to ceiling.

At first Lillian felt rather nostalgic as she talked about the gaudy life she had once led. However, as the curricle passed acres of golden fields ready for harvest, and dark forests rustling with wildlife, she was aware of a surprising ambivalence regarding her former home. It had been an empty existence, really, with its endless pursuit of fashion and diversion. And London society seemed little better. She would never have thought that a place like Hampshire would appeal to her, but . . . *one could have a real life here,* she thought wistfully. A life she could inhabit fully, rather than always having to wonder about her unknown future.

Unaware that she had lapsed into silence, she stared absently at the passing scenery, recalled by St. Vincent's soft murmur.

"Lost your power of speech again?"

She looked up into his light, smiling eyes, while Daisy and Mercedes were chatting in the opposite seat, and she nodded.

"I know of an excellent cure," he told her, and she laughed self-consciously, while color flooded her cheeks.

Relaxed and in good humor after the carriage drive with Lord St. Vincent, Lillian only half heard her mother's prattling about the eligible viscount as they entered her room. "We'll have to find out more about him, of course, and I will consult the notes in our peerage report to see if there is something I have forgotten. If memory serves, however, he is in possession of a modest fortune, and his bearing and bloodlines are quite good . . ."

"I would not become too enthused over the idea of having Lord St. Vincent as a son-in-law," Lillian told Mercedes. "He trifles with women, Mother. I suspect the idea of marriage holds little appeal for him."

"So far," Mercedes countered, a scowl falling over the

foxlike contours of her face. "But he will have to marry eventually."

"Will he?" Lillian asked, unconvinced. "If so, I rather doubt that he would abide by the conventional notions of marriage. Fidelity, to start with."

Striding to a nearby window, Mercedes stared through the glinting glass panes with a pinched expression. Her delicate, almost skeletal fingers plucked at the heavy silk fringe of the window drapes. "All husbands are unfaithful in one way or another."

Lillian and Daisy glanced at each other with raised brows.

"Father isn't," Lillian replied smartly.

Mercedes responded with a laugh that sounded like crackling leaves being crushed underfoot. "Isn't he, dear? Perhaps he has stayed true to me physically—one can never be certain about these things. But his work has proved a more jealous and demanding mistress than a flesh-and-blood woman could ever be. All his dreams are invested in that collection of buildings and employees and legalities that absorb him to the exclusion of all else. If my competition had been a mortal woman, I could have borne it easily, knowing that passion fades and beauty lasts but an instant. But his company will never fade or sicken—it will outlast us all. If you have a year of your husband's interest and affection, it will be more than I have ever had."

Lillian had always been aware of the state of affairs between her parents—their lack of interest in each other could hardly be more obvious. But this was the first time that Mercedes had ever put it into words, and the brittleness of her tone caused Lillian to wince with pity.

"I'm not going to marry that kind of man," Lillian said.

"Illusions don't become a girl of your age. By the time I was twenty-four, I had borne two children. It is time for you to marry. And regardless of who your husband is, or what his reputation, you should not ask him to make promises that he may break."

"Then I take it that he may behave in any way he wishes, and treat me in whatever manner he sees fit, just so long as he is a peer?" Lillian retorted.

"That is correct," Mercedes said grimly. "After the investment your father has made in this venture . . . the clothes and the hotel bills, and all our other expenses . . . you have no choice, either of you, but to land an aristocratic husband. Furthermore, I will not return to New York in defeat and be made a laughingstock because my daughters failed to marry into the nobility." Jerking away from the window, she left the room, too preoccupied with her own angry thoughts to remember to lock the door, which stopped just short of meeting the doorjamb as it swung closed.

Daisy was the first to speak. "Does that mean that she wants you to marry Lord St. Vincent?" she asked ironically.

Lillian gave a humorless laugh. "She wouldn't care if I married a drooling, homicidal madman, as long as his bloodlines were noble."

Sighing, Daisy walked over to her and presented her back. "Help me with my gown and corset, will you?"

"What are you going to do?"

"I'm going to take these blasted things off and read a novel, and then I'm going to take a nap."

"You *want* to take a nap?" Lillian asked, having never known her sister to voluntarily rest in the middle of the day.

"Yes. Jolting about in the carriage gave me a headache, and now Mother has finished the job with all her talk of marrying peers." Daisy's frail shoulders were rigid in the confines of her walking dress. "You seem rather taken with Lord St. Vincent. What do you truly think of him?"

Lillian carefully pulled the succession of tiny loops from their carved ivory buttons. "He's amusing," she said. "And attractive. I would be tempted to dismiss him as a shallow good-for-naught . . . but every now and then I see signs of something beneath the surface . . ." She paused, finding it difficult to put her thoughts into words.

"Yes, I know." Daisy's voice was muffled as she bent to push down the heaps of delicate printed muslin from her hips to the floor. "And I don't like it, whatever it is."

"You don't?" Lillian asked in surprise. "But you were friendly to him this morning."

"One can't help but be friendly to him," Daisy admitted. "He has that quality that the hypnotists talk about. Animal magnetism, they call it. A natural force that draws people to oneself."

Lillian grinned and shook her head. "You read too many periodicals, dear."

"Well, Lord St. Vincent, regardless of his magnetism, seems to be the kind who is motivated entirely by self-interest, and therefore I don't trust him." Draping her discarded gown over a chair, Daisy tugged in determination at the framework of her corset, and sighed in relief as she pried it from her sylphlike body. If there was ever a girl who did not need a corset, it was Daisy. However, it simply wasn't proper for a lady to go without one. Eagerly Daisy tossed the corset to the floor, retrieved a book from the bedside table, and climbed onto the mattress. "I have a periodical, if you want to read too."

"No, thank you. I'm too restless to read, and I certainly couldn't sleep." Lillian cast a speculative glance at the partially open door. "I doubt Mother would notice if I slipped off to have a walk in the garden. She'll be poring over her peerage report for the next two hours."

There was no reply from Daisy, who had already become involved in the novel. Smiling at her sister's intent face, Lillian quietly left the room and went to the servants' entrance down the hall.

Entering the garden, she followed a path she had not taken before, paralleled by what seemed to be miles of immaculately trimmed yew hedge. The manor gardens, with their careful attention to structure and form, must look beautiful in the winter, she thought. After a light snow, the hedgerows and topiaries and statues would appear as if they had been coated in Christmas cake icing, while the limbs of the brown-leaved beeches would carefully hold wedges of ice and snow in their branches. Now, however, the winter seemed ages away from this russety September garden.

She passed a massive hothouse through which one could see trays of salad plants and containers of exotic vegetables. Two men conversed just outside the door, one of them squatting on his haunches before a row of wooden trays filled with drying tuber roots. Lillian recognized one of the men as the elderly master gardener. Progressing along the path beside the hothouse, Lillian couldn't help but notice that the man on the ground, who was dressed in rough trousers and a simple white shirt with no waistcoat, had an extremely athletic form, his position causing his garments to stretch over his backside in a most diverting way. He had picked up one of the tuber roots and was examining it critically, when he became aware that someone was approaching.

Standing, the man turned to face her. It *would* be Westcliff, Lillian thought, while her insides tangled in a knot of excitement. He monitored everything on his estate with the same meticulous care. Even a humble tuber root was not going to be allowed to dwell in comfortable mediocrity.

This version of Westcliff was the one she preferred to all others—the seldom seen version in which he was disheveled and relaxed, and mesmerizing in his dark virility. The open neck of his shirt revealed the edge of a fleece of curling hair. His trousers hung slightly loose on his lean waist, held up by a pair of braces that defined the hard line of his shoulders. If Lord St. Vincent possessed animal magnetism, Westcliff was nothing less than a lodestone, exerting such a pull on her senses that she felt her entire body tingle from its force. She wanted to go to him this very second, have him bear her to the ground with rough whole-mouthed kisses and impatient caresses. Instead she dipped her chin in a jerky nod in response to his murmured greeting, and quickened her pace along the path.

To her relief, Westcliff did not attempt to follow her, and her heartbeat soon slowed to its usual pace. Exploring her surroundings, she came to a wall that was nearly concealed by a tall hedge and great falls of ivy. It seemed that this particular section of the garden had been completely enclosed by towering walls. Curiously she walked along the hedge, but she could find no entrance to the private court. "There has to be a door," she murmured aloud. She stood back and stared at the wall before her, trying to find a break in the ivy. Nothing. Taking another tack, she went to the wall and reached through the spills of ivy, running her hands along the concealed sections of stone wall in search of a door.

There was a chuckle behind her, and she turned quickly at the sound.

It seemed that Westcliff had decided to follow her after all. As a perfunctory concession to propriety he had donned a dark waistcoat, but his shirt was still open at the throat, and his dusty trousers were rather the worse for wear. He came to her with a leisurely stride, a slight smile on his lips. "I should have known you'd try to find a way into the hidden garden."

Lillian was almost unnaturally aware of the quiet chatter of birds and the soft whisper of the breeze through the ivy. With his gaze holding hers, Westcliff approached . . . closer, closer, until their bodies were nearly touching. His fragrance drifted to her nostrils, the delicious mingling of sun-heated male skin and the singular dry sweetness that appealed to her so. Slowly he reached one arm around her, and her breath caught in the back of her throat as she shrank into the swishing ivy. She heard the metallic click of a latch.

"A bit more to the left and you would have found it," he said softly.

Blindly she turned in the half circle of his arm, watching as he pushed the ivy back and sent the door swinging gently inward.

"Go on," Westcliff urged. There was the slightest pressure of his hand at her waist, and he went with her into the garden.

Chapter 14

A wordless exclamation escaped Lillian's lips as she beheld a square patch of lawn that was surrounded on all sides by a butterfly garden. Every wall was bordered with rich tumbles of color, a profusion of wildflowers that were covered with delicate fluttering wings. The only furnishment in the garden was a circular bench in the center from which every part of the garden could be viewed. The sublime incense of sun-heated flowers floated to her nostrils, intoxicating her with their sweetness.

"It's called Butterfly Court," Westcliff said, closing the door. His voice was a stroke of unfinished velvet on her ears. "It's been planted with the flowers most likely to attract them."

Lillian smiled dreamily as she watched the tiny, busy forms hovering at the heliotrope and marigold. "What are those called? The orange and black ones."

Westcliff came to stand beside her. "Painted ladies."

"How does one refer to a group of butterflies? A swarm?"

"Most commonly. However, I prefer a more recent variation—in some circles it is referred to as a kaleidoscope of butterflies."

"A kaleidoscope . . . that's some kind of optical instrument, isn't it? I've heard of them, but never chanced to see one."

"I have a kaleidoscope in the library. If you like, I will show it to you later." Before she could reply, Westcliff pointed toward a huge fall of lavender. "Over there—the white butterfly is a skipper."

A sudden laugh bubbled in her throat. "A dingy-skipper?"

Answering amusement twinkled in his eyes. "No. Just the regular variety of skipper."

Sunlight glossed his heavy black hair and imparted a bronze sheen to his skin. Lillian's gaze fell to the strong line of his throat, and suddenly she was unbearably aware of the coiled force of his body, the contained masculine power that had fascinated her since the first time she had ever seen him. What would it feel like to be wrapped inside that potent strength?

"How lovely the lavender smells," she remarked, trying to distract her thoughts from their dangerous inclinations. "Someday I want to travel to Provence, to walk one of the lavender roads in summer. They say the stands of flowers are so far-reaching that the fields look like an ocean of blue. Can you imagine how beautiful it must be?"

Westcliff shook his head slightly, staring at her.

She wandered to one of the lavender stalks and touched the tiny violet-blue blossoms, and brought her scented fingertips to her throat. "They extract the essential oil by forcing steam through the plants and drawing off the liquid. It takes something like five hundred pounds of lavender plants to produce just a few precious ounces of oil."

"You seem quite knowledgeable on the subject."

Lillian's lips quirked. "I have a great interest in scents. In fact, I could help my father a great deal with his company, were he to allow it. But I'm a woman, and therefore my only purpose in life is to marry well." She wandered to the edge of the radiant wildflower bed.

Westcliff followed, coming to stand just behind her. "That puts me in mind of an issue that needs to be discussed."

"Oh?"

"You've been keeping company with St. Vincent of late."

"So I have."

"He is not a suitable companion for you."

"He is your friend, is he not?"

"Yes—which is why I know what he is capable of."

"Are you warning me to stay away from him?"

"As that would obviously be the supreme inducement for you to do otherwise . . . no. I am merely advising you not to be naive."

"I can manage St. Vincent."

"I'm sure you believe so." A thread of annoying condescension had entered his tone. "However, it is clear that you have neither the experience nor the maturity to defend yourself against his advances."

"So far *you* have been the only one I've needed to defend myself against," Lillian retorted, turning to face him. She observed with satisfaction that the shot had hit

its mark, causing a faint wash of color to edge his cheeks
and the well-defined bridge of his nose.

"If St. Vincent has not yet taken advantage of you,"
he replied with dangerous gentleness, "it is only because
he is waiting for an opportune moment. And in spite of
your inflated opinion of your own abilities—or perhaps
because of it—you are an easy mark for seduction."

"Inflated?" Lillian repeated in outrage. "I'll have you
know that I am far too experienced to be caught unaware by any man, including St. Vincent." To Lillian's
vexation, Westcliff seemed to recognize the exaggeration
for what it was, a smile gleaming in his sable eyes.

"I was mistaken, then. From the way you kiss, I assumed . . ." He deliberately left the sentence unfinished,
laying out bait that she was powerless to resist.

"What do you mean, 'from the way I kiss'? Are you
implying that there is something wrong? Something you
don't like? Something I shouldn't—"

"No . . ." His fingertips brushed her mouth, silencing
her. "Your kisses were very . . ." He hesitated as if the
right word eluded him, and then his attention seemed to
focus on the plush surface of her lips. "Sweet," he whispered after a long time, his fingers sliding across the un-
derside of her chin. Light as the touch was, he had to feel
the exquisite tension of her throat muscles. "But your response was not what I would have expected of an experienced woman."

His thumb rubbed across her lower lip, teasing it apart
from the top one. Lillian felt bemused and combative,
like a sleepy kitten who had just been awakened with a
tickling feather. She stiffened as she felt him slide a supportive arm behind her back. "What . . . what more was
I supposed to do? What could you have expected that I

didn't—" She stopped with a swift inhalation as his fingers followed the angle of her jaw, cupping the side of her face.

"Shall I show you?"

Reflexively she pushed at his chest in an attempt to loosen his hold. She might as well have tried to move an ironstone wall. "Westcliff—"

"You clearly have need of a qualified tutor." His warm breath touched her lips as he spoke. "Hold still."

Realizing that she was being mocked, Lillian pushed much harder, and found her wrists being twisted behind her back with astonishing ease, until the gentle weight of her breasts was thrust forward against his chest. Sputtering in protest, she felt his mouth cover hers, and she was instantly paralyzed by a flare of sensation that whipped through every muscle in her body until she was drawn up like a child's wooden puppet with knotted strings.

Folded inside his arms, compressed against the hard surface of his chest, she felt her breathing escalate into deep, uneven surges. Her lashes fell, the sunlight warm against the frail shelter of her lids. There was the slow penetration of his tongue, a melting intimacy that sent a hard shiver through her body. Feeling the movement, he sought to soothe her with long strokes of his palm over her back, even as his mouth played with hers. He searched more intensely, and the thrust of his tongue met with a bashful retreat that drew a low sound of amusement from his chest. Instantly offended, Lillian drew back, and he cupped his hand around the back of her head.

"No," he murmured. "Don't pull away. Open for me. Open . . ." His mouth was on hers again, coaxing and firm. Gradually understanding what he wanted of her, she let her tongue touch his. She felt the strength of his response, the urgency that flooded him, but he remained gentle as he explored her with drifting kisses. With her hands free, she could not stop herself from touching him, one hand flattening against the conditioned muscles of his back, the other rising to the column of his neck. His sun-darkened skin was smooth and hot, like freshly pressed satin. She investigated the forceful pulse in the hollow at the base of his throat, then let her fingers wander to the dark fleece that filled the open neck of his shirt.

Westcliff brought his warm hands up to her face, cupping her cheeks as he concentrated on her mouth, possessing her with hungry, soul-stealing kisses until she was too weak to stand. As her knees buckled, she felt his arms go around her again. He cradled her weak body, easing her to the thick carpet of grass underfoot. Lying halfway across her, his leg anchored in the heap of her skirts, he wedged a solid arm beneath her neck. His mouth sought hers, and this time she did not shy away from his restless searching, but opened to him fully. The world beyond the hidden garden vanished from her awareness. There was only this place, this patch of Eden, sunny and quiet and blazing with unearthly color. The mixed scents of lavender and warm male skin were all around her . . . too delicious . . . too compelling . . . Languidly she twined her arms around his neck, her hands sliding into the thick locks of his hair.

She felt a series of deft tugs at the front of her gown, and she lay passively beneath the clever workings of his hands, her body aching for his touch. Levering himself above her, he unhooked her corset and released her from the prison of laces and stays. She couldn't breathe deeply enough, or fast enough, her lungs striving to appease a desperate need for more oxygen. Caught in a tangle of confining clothes, she writhed to be free of them, and he held her down with a quiet murmur as he spread the edges of her corset wider and tugged at the delicate ribbon tie of her chemise.

The pale curves of her breasts were bared to the sun and the open air, and to the sloe-eyed gaze of the man who held her. He stared at the shallow rise of her chest, the pink buds of her nipples, and said her name softly as his head lowered. His mouth moved lightly against her skin, coasting up the taut hill of one breast and opening over the delicate tip. A sound of fearful pleasure was torn from her throat as she lay beneath him. The tip of his tongue circled the edge of her nipple, provoking it into unbearable sensitivity. Her hands gripped the impossibly hard muscles of his upper arms, her fingertips digging into the bulge of his biceps. Passion smoldered and flamed in ever-higher drafts, until she gasped and tried to twist away from him.

She breathed in quivering sobs as he kissed her mouth again. Her body, filled with unfamiliar pulses and rhythms, no longer seemed her own. "Westcliff . . ." Her mouth wandered unsteadily over the masculine scrape of his cheek, the edge of his jaw, and back to the softness of his lips. When the kiss ended, she turned her face to the side and gasped, "What do you want?"

"Don't ask that." His lips moved to her ear, and his tongue stroked into the tiny hollow behind the fragile lobe. "The answer . . ." Hearing the way her breath hastened, he lingered at her ear, tracing the fine edge with his tongue, nibbling at the folds within. "The answer is dangerous," he finally managed to say.

Wrapping her arms around his neck, she brought his mouth back to hers in a fiery open kiss that seemed to unravel his self-control.

"Lillian," he said unsteadily, "tell me not to touch you. Tell me it's enough now. Tell me——"

She kissed him again, greedily absorbing the heat and flavor of his mouth. A new urgency ignited between them, and his kisses became harder, more aggressive, until a surge of agonized need made her limbs heavy and weak. She felt her skirts being eased upward, the heat of sunlight penetrating the thin linen of her knickers. The careful weight of his hand descended to her knee, his palm covering the rounded joint. After a moment his hand slid upward. He gave her no opportunity to object, his mouth occupying hers with restless kisses, while his fingers skimmed the sleek line of her leg.

She jerked a little as he reached the swollen, tender flesh between her thighs, tracing the shape of her through the gauzy linen. A flush suffused her limbs and chest and face, and her heels dug into the lawn as she arched helplessly against his hand. He stroked her soothingly over the veil of linen. The thought of how those strong, slightly roughened fingers might feel against her skin caused her to moan with need. After what seemed an eternity of torment, he let his fingers enter the lace-edged slit of her undergarment. An agitated gasp escaped her as she felt herself being stroked and parted, his long fingers gliding through the silky dark curls. He fondled her with delicate idleness, as if he were playing with the petals of a half-open rose. One tantalizing fingertip brushed over the little peak that kindled with excitement, and all rational thought dissolved. He found the subtle spot where all her pleasure centered, and stroked her rhythmically, circling delicately, making her writhe in gathering desperation.

She wanted him, regardless of the consequences. She wanted his possession, and even the pain that would come with it. But with brutal suddenness, the weight of his body was lifted from hers, and Lillian was left tumbled and disoriented in the patch of velvety lawn. "My lord?" she asked breathlessly, managing to heave herself to a sitting position, with her clothes in wanton disarray.

He was sitting nearby, his arms braced on his bent knees. With something close to despair, she saw that he was once again in control of himself, whereas she was still trembling from head to toe.

His voice was cool and steady. "You've proved my point, Lillian. If a man you don't even like can bring you to this state, then how much easier would it be for St. Vincent?"

She started as if he had slapped her, and her eyes widened.

The transition from warm desire to a feeling of utter foolishness was not a pleasant one.

The devastating intimacy between them had been nothing but a lesson to demonstrate her inexperience. He had used it as an opportunity to put her in her place. Apparently she wasn't good enough to wed *or* to bed. Lillian wanted to die. Humiliated, she scrambled upward, clutching at her unfastened garments, and shot him a glare of hatred. "That remains to be seen," she choked out. "I'll just have to compare the two of you. And then if you ask nicely, perhaps I'll tell you if he—"

Westcliff pounced on her with startling swiftness,

shoving her back to the lawn and bracketing her tossing head between his muscular forearms. "Stay away from him," he snapped. "He can't have you."

"Why not?" she demanded, struggling as he settled more heavily between her flailing legs. "Am I not good enough for him either? Inferior breed that I am—"

"You're too good for him. And he would be the first to admit it."

"I like him all the better for not suiting your high standards!"

"Lillian—hold still, damn it—Lillian, look at me!" Westcliff waited until she had stilled beneath him. "I don't want to see you hurt."

"Has it ever occurred to you, you arrogant idiot, that the person most likely to hurt me might be *you*?"

Now it was his turn to recoil as if struck. He stared at her blankly, though she could practically hear the whirring of his agile brain as he sorted through the potential implications of her rash statement.

"Get off me," Lillian said sullenly.

He moved upward, straddling her slender hips, his fingers grasping the inner edges of her corset. "Let me fasten you. You can't run back to the manor half dressed."

"By all means," she replied with helpless scorn, "let's observe the proprieties." Closing her eyes, she felt him tugging her clothes into place, tying her chemise and rehooking her corset efficiently.

When he finally released her, she sprang from the ground like a startled doe and rushed to the entrance of the hidden garden. To her eternal humiliation, she couldn't find the door, which was concealed by the lavish spills of ivy coming over the wall. Blindly she thrust her hands into the trailing greenery, breaking two nails as she scrabbled for the doorjamb.

Coming up behind her, Westcliff settled his hands at her waist, easily dodging her attempts to throw him off. He pulled her hips back firmly against his and spoke against her ear. "Are you angry because I started making love to you, or because I didn't finish?"

Lillian licked her dry lips. "I'm angry, you bloody big hypocrite, because you can't make up your mind about what to do with me." She punctuated the comment with the hard jab of one elbow back against his ribs.

The sharp blow seemed to have no effect on him. With a mocking show of courtesy, he released her and reached for the concealed door handle, allowing her to escape the hidden garden.

Chapter 15

*A*fter Lillian fled the butterfly garden, Marcus struggled to cool his passions. He had nearly lost all control with Lillian, had almost taken her on the ground like a mindless brute. Only some infinitesimal gleam of awareness, weak as a candle flame in a storm, had kept him from ravishing her. An innocent girl, the daughter of one of his guests . . . Good Lord, he had gone mad.

Wandering slowly through the garden, Marcus tried to analyze a situation that he would never have expected to find himself in. To think that a few months ago he had mocked Simon Hunt for his excessive passion for Annabelle Peyton. He had not understood the power of obsession, had never felt its ferocious pull until now. He could not seem to reason himself out of it. It seemed that his will had been divorced from his intellect.

Marcus could not recognize himself in his reactions to Lillian. No one had ever made him feel this aware, this alive, as if her very presence heightened all his senses.

She fascinated him. She made him laugh. She aroused him unbearably. If only he could lie with her and find relief from this endless craving. And yet the rational part of his brain pointed out that his mother's assessment of the Bowman girls was on the mark. "Perhaps we can achieve a bit of superficial polish," the countess had said, "but my influence will certainly be no more than skin-deep. Neither of those girls is tractable enough to change in any significant way. The elder Miss Bowman, in particular. One could no more make a lady of her than one could change fool's-gold into the real substance. She is determined not to change."

Oddly, that was part of why Marcus was so drawn to Lillian. Her raw vitality, her uncompromising individuality, affected him like a wintry blast of air inside a stuffy house. However, it was dishonest of him, not to mention unfair, to continue his attentions to Lillian when it was obvious that nothing could come of them. No matter how difficult it was, he would have to leave her alone, as she had just asked.

The decision should have afforded him a certain measure of peace, but it didn't.

Brooding, he left the garden and went to the manor, noting against his will that the exquisite scenery around him seemed a bit muted, grayer, as if he viewed it through a dirty window. Inside, the atmosphere of the sprawling house seemed stale and dark. He felt as if he would never take real pleasure in anything again. Damning himself for the maudlin thoughts, Marcus headed to his private study, even though he was in dire need of a change of clothes. He strode through the open doorway and saw Simon Hunt seated at the desk, poring over a sheaf of legal documents.

Looking up, Hunt smiled and began to rise from the chair.

"No," Marcus said abruptly, with a staying motion of his hands. "I merely wanted a glance at the morning's deliveries."

"You look to be in foul humor," Hunt commented, settling back. "If it's about the foundry contracts, I've just written to our solicitor—"

"It's not that." Picking up a letter, Marcus broke the seal and glowered at it, perceiving that it was an invitation of some sort.

Hunt watched him speculatively. After a moment, he asked, "Have you reached a sticking point in your dialogue with Thomas Bowman?"

Marcus shook his head. "He seems receptive to the proposal I put forth about the enfranchisement of his company. I don't foresee any problems in securing an agreement."

"Then has it something to do with Miss Bowman?"

"Why do you ask?" Marcus countered warily.

Hunt responded with a sardonic look, as if the answer was too obvious to be voiced.

Slowly Marcus lowered himself to the chair on the other side of the desk. Hunt waited patiently, his undemanding silence encouraging Marcus to confide his thoughts. Although Hunt had always been a reliable sounding board on business and social matters, Marcus had never brought himself to discuss personal issues with him. Everyone else's issues, yes. His own, no.

"It's not logical for me to want her," he said at last, focusing his gaze on one of the stained-glass windows nearby. "It has all the makings of a farce. One can scarcely conceive of a more ill-suited pair."

"Ah. And as you've said previously, 'Marriage is too important an issue to be decided by mercurial emotions.'"

Marcus glanced at him with a scowl. "Have I ever mentioned how much I dislike your tendency to throw my own words back in my face?"

Hunt laughed. "Why? Because you don't want to take your own advice? I am compelled to point out, Westcliff, that had I heeded your counsel about marrying Annabelle, it would have been the greatest mistake of my life."

"At the time she was not a sensible choice," Marcus muttered. "It was only later that she proved herself to be worthy of you."

"But now you will admit that I made the right decision."

"Yes," Marcus replied impatiently. "One fails to see, however, how that applies to my situation."

"I was leading to the point that perhaps your instincts should play a part in the decision of whom to marry."

Marcus was genuinely offended by the suggestion. He stared at Simon Hunt as if he had gone mad. "Good God, man, what is the purpose of the intellect if not to deliver us from the folly of acting on instinct?"

"You rely on instinct all the time," Hunt chided.

"*Not* when it comes to decisions that have lifelong consequences. And in spite of my attraction to Miss Bowman, the differences between us would eventually result in misery for us both."

"I understand the differences between you," Hunt said quietly. As their gazes met, something in his eyes reminded Marcus that Hunt was a butcher's son who had climbed out of the middle class and made a fortune from nothing. "Believe me, I understand the challenges that Miss Bowman would face in such a position. But what if she is willing to accept them? What if she is willing to change herself sufficiently?"

"She can't."

"You do her an injustice by assuming that she could not adapt. Shouldn't she be allowed the chance to try?"

"Blast it, Hunt, I have no need of a devil's advocate."

"You were hoping for blind agreement?" Hunt asked mockingly. "Perhaps you should have sought someone of your own class for counsel."

"This has nothing to do with class," Marcus snapped, resenting the implication that his objections to Lillian stemmed from simple snobbery.

"No," Hunt agreed calmly, standing from the desk. "It's an empty argument. I think there is another reason you've decided not to pursue her. Something you won't admit to me, or possibly even to yourself." He went to the doorway and paused to give Marcus an astute glance. "As you contemplate the matter, however, you should be made aware that St. Vincent's interest in her is more than a passing fancy."

Marcus's attention was instantly captured by the statement. "Nonsense. St. Vincent has never had an interest in a woman beyond the limits of a bedroom."

"Be that as it may, I was recently informed by a reliable source that his father is selling off everything that isn't entailed. Years of indiscriminate spending and foolish investments have drained the family coffers—and St. Vincent will soon be deprived of his yearly allotment. He needs money. And the Bowmans' obvious desire for a titled son-in-law has hardly escaped him." Hunt allowed a skillfully timed pause before adding, "Whether or not Miss Bowman is suited to be the wife of a peer, she may very well marry St. Vincent. And if so, then he'll eventually come into his title and she will become a duchess. Fortunately for her, St. Vincent seems to have no qualms about her suitability for the position."

Marcus stared at him with furious astonishment. "I'll speak to Bowman," he growled. "Once I make him aware of St. Vincent's past, he'll put a stop to the courtship."

"By all means . . . if you think he'll listen. My guess is that he won't. A duke for a son-in-law, even a penniless one, is not a bad catch for a soap manufacturer from New York."

Chapter 16

To anyone who cared to notice, it was obvious during the last two weeks of the house party at Stony Cross Park that Lord Westcliff and Miss Lillian Bowman made a mutual effort to avoid each other's company as much as possible. It was equally obvious that Lord St. Vincent was partnering her with increasing frequency at the dances, picnics, and water parties that enlivened the pleasant autumn days in Hampshire.

Lillian and Daisy spent several mornings in the company of the Countess of Westcliff, who lectured, instructed, and tried in vain to instill them with an aristocratic perspective. Aristocrats never displayed enthusiasm, but rather detached interest. Aristocrats relied on subtle inflections of the voice to convey meaning. Aristocrats would say "relation" or "kinsman," rather than "relative." And they used the phrase "do be good enough" rather than ask "would you." Furthermore, it was mandatory that an aristocratic lady should never express herself directly, but instead hint gracefully at her meaning.

If the countess preferred one sister over the other, it was certainly Daisy, who proved far more receptive to the archaic code of aristocratic behavior. Lillian, on the other hand, made little effort to hide her scorn at social rules that were, in her opinion, completely pointless. Why did it matter if one slid the bottle of port across the table or simply handed it over, as long as the port reached its destination? Why were so many subjects forbidden to discuss, whereas others that held no interest for her must be visited in tedious repetition? Why was it better to walk slowly than at a brisk pace, and why must a lady try to echo a gentleman's opinions rather than offer her own?

She found a measure of relief in the company of Lord St. Vincent, who seemed not to give a damn about her mannerisms or what words she used. He was entertained by her frankness, and he was decidedly irreverent. Even his own father, the Duke of Kingston, was not exempt from St. Vincent's derision. The duke, it seemed, had no idea how to apply tooth powder to his toothbrush, or put on his stocking garters, as such tasks had always been done for him by his valet. Lillian could not help but laugh at the idea of such a pampered existence, leading St. Vincent to speculate in mock horror at the primitive life she must have led in America, having to live in a mansion that was identified with a dreaded *number* over the door, or having to comb one's own hair or tie one's own shoes.

St. Vincent was the most engaging man that Lillian had ever met. Beneath the layers of silken gentility, however, there was a hardness, an impenetrability, that could only have belonged to a very cold man. Or perhaps an extremely guarded one. Either way, Lillian knew intuitively that whatever kind of soul lurked inside this elegant creature, she would never find out. He was as beautiful and inscrutable as a sphinx.

"St. Vincent needs to marry into a fortune," Annabelle reported one afternoon, as the wallflowers sat beneath a tree, sketching and watercoloring. "According to Mr. Hunt, Lord St. Vincent's father, the duke, is soon to cut off his annual portion, as there is hardly any money left. There will be little for St. Vincent to inherit, I'm afraid."

"What happens when the money is gone?" Daisy asked, her pencil moving deftly across the paper as she sketched a view of the landscape. "Will St. Vincent sell some of his estates and properties when he becomes a duke?"

"That depends," Annabelle replied, picking up a leaf and inspecting the delicate vein pattern of its amber skin. "If most of the property he inherits is entailed, then no. But have no fear that he'll become a pauper—there are many families who will compensate him handsomely if he agrees to marry one of them."

"Mine, for example," Lillian said sardonically.

Annabelle watched her closely as she murmured, "Dear . . . has Lord St. Vincent mentioned anything to you about intentions?"

"Not a word."

"Has he ever tried to—"

"Heavens, no."

"He intends to marry you, then," Annabelle said with unnerving certainty. "If he were merely trifling, he would have tried to compromise you by now."

The silence that followed was gently fractured by the dry swish of the overhead leaves, and the scratch of Daisy's busy pencil.

"Wh-what will you do if Lord St. Vincent proposes?"

Evie asked, peeking at Lillian over the edge of her wooden watercolor case, the top half of which served as an easel as she balanced it on her lap.

Unthinkingly Lillian plucked at the grass beneath her, breaking the fragile blades with her fingers. Suddenly realizing that the activity was reminiscent of Mercedes, who had a nervous habit of pulling and tearing things, she stopped and tossed the bits of grass aside. "I'll accept him, of course," she said. The other three girls looked at her with mild surprise. "Why wouldn't I?" she continued defensively. "Do you realize how few dukes there are to be found? According to Mother's peerage report, there are only twenty-nine in all of Great Britain."

"But Lord St. Vincent is a shameless skirt chaser," Annabelle said. "I can't envision that as his wife, you would tolerate such behavior."

"All husbands are unfaithful in one way or another." Lillian tried to sound matter-of-fact, but somehow her tone came out defiant and surly.

Annabelle's blue eyes were soft with compassion. "I don't believe that."

"The next season hasn't even started," Daisy pointed out, "and now with the countess as our sponsor, we'll have much better luck this year than last. There's no need to marry Lord St. Vincent if you don't wish it—no matter what Mother says."

"I want to marry him." Lillian felt her mouth tighten into a stubborn line. "In fact, I will *live* for the moment when St. Vincent and I will attend a dinner as the Duke and Duchess of Kingston . . . a dinner that Westcliff will also be attending, and I will be escorted into the dining hall before him, as *my* husband's title will take precedence over his. I'll make Westcliff sorry. I'll make him wish—"

She broke off abruptly, realizing that her tone was far too sharp, betraying far too much. Stiffening her spine, she glared at some distant point on the landscape, and flinched as she felt Daisy's small hand settle between her shoulders.

"Perhaps by then you won't care anymore," Daisy murmured.

"Perhaps," Lillian agreed dully.

The next afternoon saw the estate mostly vacant of guests, as the majority of the gentlemen went to a local race meeting, to wager, drink, and smoke to their hearts' content. The ladies were conveyed in a succession of carriages to the village, where a traditional feast day would be attended by a touring company of London performers. Eager for the diversion of some light comedies and music, the female guests left the estate en masse. Although Annabelle, Evie, and Daisy all implored Lillian to come with them, she refused. The antics of a few traveling players held no appeal for her. She did not want to force herself to smile and laugh. She only wanted to walk alone outside . . . to walk for miles, until she was too weary to think about anything.

She went alone into the back garden, following the path that led to the mermaid fountain, which was set like a jewel in the middle of the paved clearing. A nearby hedge was covered with wisteria, appearing as if someone had draped a succession of pink tea cozies across the top of it. Sitting on the edge of the fountain, Lillian stared into the foamy water. She was not aware of anyone approaching until she heard a quiet voice from the path.

"What luck to find you in the first place I looked."

Glancing up with a smile, she beheld Lord St. Vincent. His golden-amber hair seemed to absorb the sunlight.

His coloring was unquestionably Anglo-Saxon, but the dramatic lines of his cheekbones, angled at a rather tigerish slant, and the sensuous fullness of his wide mouth gave him a singularly exotic appeal.

"Aren't you leaving for the race meeting?" Lillian asked.

"In a moment. I wanted to speak to you first." St. Vincent glanced at the space beside her. "May I?"

"But we're alone," she said. "And you always insist on a chaperone."

"Today I've changed my mind."

"Oh." Her smile held a slightly tremulous curve. "In that case, do have a seat." She colored as it occurred to her that this was the exact spot where she had seen Lady Olivia and Mr. Shaw embracing so passionately. From the glint in St. Vincent's eyes, it was apparent that he remembered too.

"Come the weekend," he said, "the house party will be over . . . and then it's back to London."

"You must be eager to return to the amusements of town life," Lillian remarked. "For a rake, your behavior has been surprisingly tame."

"Even we dissipated rakes need an occasional holiday. A constant diet of depravity would become boring."

Lillian smiled. "Rake or no, I have enjoyed your friendship these past days, my lord." As the words left her lips, she was surprised to realize that they were true.

"Then you think of me as a friend," he said softly. "That's good."

"Why?"

"Because I would like to continue seeing you."

Her heart quickened its pace. Although the remark

was not unexpected, she was caught off-guard nonetheless. "In London?" she asked inanely.

"Wherever you happen to be. Is that agreeable to you?"

"Well, of course, it . . . I . . . yes."

As he stared at her with those fallen-angel eyes and smiled, Lillian was forced to agree with Daisy's assessment of St. Vincent's animal magnetism. He looked like a man who was born to sin . . . a man who could make sinning so enjoyable that one hardly minded paying the price afterward.

St. Vincent reached for her slowly, his fingers sliding from her shoulders to the sides of her throat. "Lillian, my love. I'm going to ask your father for permission to court you."

She breathed unsteadily against the caressing framework of his hands. "I am not the only available heiress you could pursue."

His thumbs smoothed the gentle hollows of her cheeks, and his dark brown lashes half lowered. "No," he answered frankly. "But you're by far the most interesting. Most women aren't, you know. At least not out of bed." He leaned closer, until the heated touch of his whisper warmed her lips. "I daresay you'll be interesting *in* bed as well."

Well, here it was, Lillian thought dazedly—the long-awaited advance—and then her thoughts were muddled as his mouth moved over hers in a light caress. He kissed as if he were the first man who had ever discovered it, with a lazy expertise that seduced her by slow degrees. Even with her limited experience, she perceived that the kiss was wrought more of technique than emotion, but her stunned senses didn't seem to care as he drew a helpless response from her with every tender shift of his mouth. He built her pleasure at an unhurried pace, until she gasped against his lips and turned her head weakly away.

His fingers slid over the hot surface of her cheek, and he gently pressed her head to his shoulder. "I've never courted anyone before," he murmured, his lips playing near her ear. "Not for honorable purposes, at any rate."

"You're doing quite well for a beginner," she said against his coat.

Laughing, he eased away from her, and his warm gaze coasted over her flushed face. "You're lovely," he said softly. "And fascinating."

And wealthy, she added silently. But he was doing a very good job of convincing her that he desired her for more than financial reasons. She appreciated that. Forcing a smile to her lips, she stared at the enigmatic but charming man who might very well become her husband. *Your Grace,* she thought. That was what Westcliff would have to call her, once St. Vincent came into his title. First she would be Lady St. Vincent, and then the Duchess of Kingston. She would be above Westcliff socially, and she would never let him forget it. *Your Grace,* she repeated, comforting herself with the syllables. *Your Grace . . .*

After St. Vincent left her to go to the race meeting, Lillian wandered back to the manor. The fact that her future was finally taking shape should have relieved her, but instead she was filled with grim resolve. She entered the house, which was serene and silent. After the past weeks of seeing the place filled with people, it was strange to walk through the empty entrance hall. The hallways were quiet, with only the occasional passing of a lone servant to interrupt the stillness.

Pausing near the library, Lillian glanced into the large

room. For once it was unoccupied. She stepped inside the inviting room, with its two-story ceiling and the shelves lined with more than ten thousand books. The air was filled with the pleasant scents of vellum, parchment, and leather. What little wall space wasn't occupied with books had been crowded with framed maps and engravings. She decided to find a book for herself, a volume of light verse or some frivolous novel. However, with the acres of leather spines facing her, it was difficult to ascertain precisely where the novels were located.

As she passed before the shelves, Lillian discovered rows of history books, each of them sufficiently weighty to flatten an elephant. Atlases were next, and then a vast array of mathematical texts that would cure the most severe cases of insomnia. Near the end of one wall, a sideboard had been installed in a niche to fit flush with the bookshelves. A large engraved silver tray covered the top of the sideboard, bearing a collection of enticing bottles and decanters. The prettiest bottle, made of glass molded in a pattern of leaves, was half-filled with a colorless liquor. Her attention was caught by the sight of a pear inside the bottle.

Lifting the bottle, Lillian examined it closely and gently swirled the liquid until the pear lifted and turned with the motion. A perfectly preserved golden pear. This must be a variety of eau-de-vie, as the French called it . . . "water of life," a colorless brandy distilled from grapes, plums, or elderberries. Pears as well, it seemed.

Lillian was tempted to sample the intriguing beverage, but ladies never drank strong spirits. Especially not alone in the library. If she were caught, it would look very bad indeed. On the other hand . . . all the gentlemen were at the race meeting, the ladies had gone to the village, and most of the servants had been given the day off.

She glanced at the empty doorway, and then at the tantalizing bottle. A mantel clock ticked urgently in the silence. Suddenly she heard Lord St. Vincent's voice in her mind . . . *I'm going to ask your father for permission to court you.*

"Oh, hell," she muttered, and bent to rummage through the lower cabinet of the sideboard for a glass.

Chapter 17

"My lord."

At the sound of his butler's voice, Marcus looked up from his desk with a slight frown. He had been working for the past two hours on the amendments to a list of recommendations that would be presented to Parliament later in the year by a committee that he had agreed to serve on. If the recommendations were accepted, it would result in a substantial improvement to the house, street, and land drainage in London and its surrounding districts.

"Yes, Salter," he said brusquely, resenting the interruption. However, the old family butler knew better than to disturb him at his work unless something was significant enough to warrant it.

"There is a . . . a situation, my lord, that I felt certain you would wish to be informed of."

"What kind of situation?"

"It involves one of the guests, my lord."

"Well?" Marcus demanded, annoyed by the butler's diffidence. "Who is it? And what is he doing?"

"I am afraid the person is a 'she,' my lord. One of the footmen has just informed me that he saw Miss Bowman in the library, and she is . . . not well."

Marcus stood so suddenly that his chair nearly toppled over. "Which Miss Bowman?"

"I do not know, my lord."

"What do you mean, 'not well'? Is anyone with her?"

"I do not believe so, my lord."

"Is she hurt? Is she ill?"

Salter gave him a mildly harried stare. "Neither, my lord. Merely . . . not well."

Declining to waste time with further questions, Marcus left the room with a low curse, heading to the library with long strides that stopped just short of an outright run. What in God's name could have happened to Lillian or her sister? He was instantly consumed with worry.

As he hurried through the hallways, a host of irrelevant thoughts flashed through his mind. How cavernous the house seemed when it was devoid of guests, with its miles of flooring and infinite clusters of rooms. A grand, ancient house with the impersonal ambiance of a hotel. A house like this needed the happy shouts of children echoing through the halls, and toys littering the parlor floor, and the squeaky sounds of violin lessons coming from the music room. Marks on the walls, and teatime with sticky jam tarts, and toy hoops being rolled across the back terrace.

Until now Marcus had never considered the idea of marriage as anything other than a necessary duty to continue the Marsden line. But it had occurred to him lately that his future could be very different from his past. It could be a new beginning—a chance to create the kind of family he had never dared to dream of before. It startled him to realize how much he wanted that—and not with just any woman. Not with any woman he had ever met or seen or heard of . . . except for the one who was the complete opposite of what he should want. He was beginning not to care about that.

His hands gripped into white-knuckled balls, and his pace quickened. It seemed to take forever to reach the library. By the time he crossed the threshold, his heart was driving in sharp blows inside his chest . . . a rhythm that owed nothing to exertion and everything to panic. What he saw caused him to stop short in the center of the large room.

Lillian stood before a row of books, with a pile of them surrounding her on the floor. She was pulling rare volumes from the shelves one by one, examining each with a puzzled frown and then tossing it heedlessly behind her. She seemed oddly languid, as if she were moving under water. And her hair was slipping from its pins. She didn't look ill, precisely. In fact, she looked . . .

Becoming aware of his presence, Lillian glanced over her shoulder with a lopsided smile. "Oh. It's you," she said, her voice slurred. Her attention wandered back to the shelves. "I can't find anything. All these books are so *deadly* dull . . ."

Frowning in concern, Marcus approached her while she continued to chatter and sort through the books. "Not this one . . . nor this one . . . oh no, no, *no,* this one's not even in English . . ."

Marcus's panic transformed rapidly into outrage, followed swiftly by amusement. Damnation. If he had required additional proof that Lillian Bowman was utterly wrong for him, this was it. The wife of a Marsden would never sneak into the library and drink until she was, as his mother would phrase it, "a trifle disguised." Staring into her drowsy dark eyes and flushed face, Marcus amended the phrase. Lillian was not disguised. She was foxed, staggering, tap-hackled, top-heavy, shot-in-the-neck, staggering drunk.

More books sailed through the air, one of them narrowly missing his ear.

"Perhaps I could help," Marcus suggested pleasantly, stopping beside her. "If you would tell me what you're looking for."

"Something romantic. Something with a happy ending. There should always be a happy ending, shouldn' there?"

Marcus reached out to finger a trailing lock of her hair, his thumb sliding along the glowing satin filaments. He had never thought of himself as a particularly tactile man, but it seemed impossible to keep from touching her when she was near. The pleasure he derived from the simplest contact with her set all his nerves alight. "Not always," he said in reply to her question.

Lillian let out a bubbling laugh. "How very English of you. How you all love to suffer, with your stiff . . . stiff . . ." She peered at the book in her hands, distracted by the gilt on its cover. ". . . upper lips," she finished absently.

"We don't like to suffer."

"Yes, you do. At the very least, you go out of your way to avoid enjoying something."

By now Marcus was becoming accustomed to the unique mixture of lust and amusement that she always managed to arouse in him. "There's nothing wrong with keeping one's enjoyments private."

Dropping the book in her hands, Lillian turned to face him. The abruptness of the movement resulted in a sharp wobble, and she swayed back against the shelves even as he moved to steady her with his hands at her waist. Her tip-tilted eyes sparkled like an array of diamonds scattered over brown velvet. "It has nothing to do with privacy," she informed him. "The truth is that you don't *want* to be happy, bec—" She hiccupped gently. "Because it would undermine your dignity. Poor Wes'cliff." She regarded him compassionately.

At the moment, preserving his dignity was the last thing on Marcus's mind. He grasped the frame of the bookcase on either side of her, encompassing her in the half circle of his arms. As he caught a whiff of her breath, he shook his head and murmured, "Little one . . . what have you been drinking?"

"Oh . . ." She ducked beneath his arm and careened to the sideboard a few feet away. "I'll show you . . . wonderful, wonderful stuff . . . *this*." Triumphantly she plucked a nearly empty brandy bottle from the edge of the sideboard and held it by the neck. "Look what someone did . . . a pear, right inside! Isn' that clever?" Bringing the bottle close to her face, she squinted at the imprisoned fruit. "It wasn' very good at first. But it improved after a while. I suppose it's an ac"—another delicate hiccup— "acquired taste."

"It appears you've succeeded in acquiring it," Marcus remarked, following her.

"You won' tell anyone, will you?"

"No," he promised gravely. "But I'm afraid they're going to know regardless. Unless we can sober you in the next two or three hours before they return. Lillian, my angel . . . how much was in the bottle when you started?"

Showing him the bottle, she put her finger a third of the way from the bottom. "It was *there* when I started. I think. Or maybe there." She frowned sadly at the bottle. "Now all that's left is the pear." She swirled the bottle, making the plump fruit slosh juicily at the bottom. "I want to eat it," she announced.

"It's not meant to be eaten. It's only there to infuse the—Lillian, give the damned thing to me."

"I *am* going to eat it." Lillian tottered drunkenly away from him as she shook the bottle with increasing resolve. "If I can just get it out . . ."

"You can't. It's impossible."

"Impossible?" she scoffed, lurching to face him. "You have servants who can pull the brains from a calf's head, but they couldn' get one little pear out of a bottle? I doubt that. Send for one of your under-butlers—just give a whistle, and—oh, I forgot. You can't whistle." She focused on him, her eyes narrowing as she stared at his mouth. "That's the sillies' thing I ever heard. *Everyone* can whistle. I'll teach you. Right now. Pucker your lips. Like this. Pucker . . . see?"

Marcus caught her in his arms as she swayed before him. Staring down at her adorably pursed lips, he felt an insistent warmth invading his heart, overflowing and spilling past its fretted barriers. God in heaven, he was tired of fighting his desire for her. It was exhausting to struggle against something so overwhelming. Like trying not to breathe.

Lillian stared at him earnestly, seeming puzzled by his refusal to comply. "No, no, not like *that*. Like this." The bottle dropped to the carpet. She reached up to his mouth and tried to shape his lips with her fingers. "Rest your tongue on the edge of your teeth and . . . it's all about the tongue, really. If you're agile with your tongue, you'll be a very, very good"—she was temporarily interrupted as he covered her mouth with a brief, ravening kiss—"whistler. My lord, I can't talk when you—" He fitted his mouth to hers again, devouring the sweet brandied taste of her.

She leaned against him helplessly, her fingers sliding into his hair, while her breath struck his cheek in rapid, delicate puffs. A tide of sensual urgency rolled through him as the kiss deepened into full-blown compulsion. The memory of their encounter in the hidden garden had haunted him for days . . . the delicacy of her skin beneath his hands, her small, exquisite breasts, the enticing strength of her legs. He wanted to feel her wrapped around him, her hands clutching his back, her knees clamped around his hips . . . the silky-wet caress of her body as he moved inside her.

Pulling her head back, Lillian stared at him with wondering eyes, her lips damp and reddened. Her hands left his hair, her fingertips coming to the hard angles of his cheekbones, delicate strokes of coolness on the blazing heat of his skin. He bent his head, nuzzling his jaw against the pale silk of her palm. "Lillian," he whispered, "I've tried to leave you alone. But I can't do it anymore. In the past two weeks I've had to stop myself a thousand times from coming to you. No matter how often I tell myself that you are the most inappropriate . . ." He paused as she squirmed suddenly, twisting and craning her neck to look down at the floor. "No matter what I—Lillian, are you listening to me? What the devil are you looking for?"

"My pear. I dropped it, and—oh, there it is." She broke free of him and sank to her hands and knees, reaching beneath a chair. Pulling out the brandy bottle, she sat on the floor and held it in her lap.

"Lillian, forget the damned pear."

"How did it get *in* there, d'you think?" She poked her finger experimentally into the neck of the bottle. "I don' see how something so big could fit into a hole that small."

Marcus closed his eyes against a surge of aggravated passion, and his voice cracked as he replied. "They . . . they put it directly on the tree. The bud grows . . . inside . . ." He slitted his eyes open and squeezed them shut again as he saw her finger intruding deeper into the bottle. "Grows . . ." he forced himself to continue, "until the fruit is ripe."

Lillian seemed rather too impressed by the information. "They do? That is the cleverest, *cleverest* . . . a pear in its own little . . . oh no."

"What?" Marcus asked through clenched teeth.

"My finger's stuck."

Marcus's eyes flew open. Dumbfounded, he looked down at the sight of Lillian tugging on her imprisoned finger.

"I can't get it out," she said.

"Just pull at it."

"It hurts. It's throbbing."

"Pull harder."

"I can't! It's truly stuck. I need something to make it slippery. Do you have some sort of lubricant nearby?"

"No."

"Not *anything*?"

"Much as it may surprise you, we've never needed lubricant in the library before now."

Lillian frowned up at him. "Before you start to criticize, Wes'cliff, I should like to point out that I am not the first person ever to get her finger stuck in a bottle. It happens to people all the time."

"Does it? You must be referring to Americans. Because I've never seen an Englishman with a bottle stuck on his finger. Even a foxed one."

"I'm not foxed, I'm only—where are you going?"

"Stay there," Marcus muttered, striding from the room. As he went out into the hallway, he saw a housemaid approaching with a pail full of rags and cleaning supplies. The dark-haired maid froze as she saw him, intimidated by the sight of his scowling face. He tried to remember her name. "Meggie," he said curtly. "It *is* Meggie, isn't it?"

"Yes, milord," she said meekly, dropping her gaze.

"Do you have any soap or polish in that pail?"

"Yes, sir," she replied in confusion. "The housekeeper told me to polish the chairs in the billiards room—"

"What's it made of?" he interrupted, wondering if it contained any caustic ingredients. Seeing her increasing bewilderment, he clarified, "The polish, Meggie."

Her eyes turned round at the master's untoward interest in the mundane substance. "Beeswax," she said uncertainly. "An' lemon juice, an' a drop or two of oil."

"That's all?"

"Yes, milord."

"Good," he said with a decisive nod. "Let me have it, if I may."

Agog, the housemaid reached into the pail, pulled out a small pot of the waxy yellow concoction, and extended it to him. "Milord, if you wish for me to polish something—"

"That will be all, Meggie. Thank you."

She bobbed in a little curtsy, staring after him as if he had taken leave of his senses.

Returning to the library, Marcus saw Lillian lying on her back on the carpeted floor. His first thought was that she must have drifted into oblivion, but as he approached, he saw that she was holding a long wooden cylinder in her free hand, and squinting through one end. "I found it," she exclaimed in triumph. "The kaleidoscope. It's verrrry interesting. But not quite what I 'spected."

Silently he reached out, plucked the instrument from her hand, and gave her the other end to look through.

Lillian promptly gasped in amazement. "Oh, that's *lovely* . . . How does it work?"

"One end is fitted with strategically placed panels of silvered glass, and then . . ." His voice faded as she turned the thing toward him.

"My lord," she pronounced in solemn concern, viewing him through the cylinder, "you have three . . . hundred . . . eyes." She dissolved into a fit of giggles that shook her until she dropped the kaleidoscope.

Sinking to his knees beside her, Marcus said tersely, "Give me your hand. No, not that one. The one with the bottle on it."

She remained lying on her back as Marcus smeared a gob of the polish onto the exposed part of her finger. He rubbed the stuff into the seam where the bottle was clamped around her skin. Warmed by the heat of his palm, the scented wax released a heady burst of lemon fragrance, and Lillian breathed in the aroma with relish. "Oh, I like that."

"Can you pull it out now?"

"Not yet."

Making a sheath of his fingers, he continued to smooth the oily wax over her finger and the shaft of the bottle. Lillian relaxed at the gentle motion, seeming content to lie still and watch him.

He looked down at her, finding it difficult to resist the urge to climb over her prone body and kiss her senseless. "Would you mind telling me why you were drinking pear brandy in the middle of the afternoon?"

"Because I couldn' open the sherry."

His lips twitched. "What I meant was, why were you drinking at all?"

"Oh. Well, I was feeling rather . . . high-strung. And I thought it might help me to relax."

Marcus rubbed the base of her finger with soft, twisting strokes. "Why were you feeling high-strung?"

Lillian averted her face from him. "I don't want to talk about that."

"Hmm."

She looked back at him, her gaze narrowed. "What did you mean by that?"

"I meant nothing by it."

"You did. That was no ord'nary 'hmm.' It was a disapproving 'hmm.' "

"I was merely speculating."

"Gimme a guess," she challenged. "Your bes' guess."

"I think it has something to do with St. Vincent." He saw from the shadow that passed over her expression that his guess was on the mark. "Tell me what happened," he said, watching her closely.

"You know," she said dreamily, passing over his question, "you're not nearly as handsome as Lord St. Vincent."

"There's a surprise," he said dryly.

"But for some reason," she continued, "I never want to kiss him the way I do you." It was a good thing that she had closed her eyes, for if she had seen his expression, she might not have continued. "There is something about you that makes me feel terribly wicked. You make me want to do shocking things. Maybe it's because you're so proper. Your necktie is never crooked, and your shoes are always shiny. And your shirts are so starchy. Sometimes when I look at you, I want to tear off all your buttons. Or set your trousers on fire." She giggled helplessly. "I've so often wondered—are you ticklish, my lord?"

"No," Marcus rasped, his heart pounding beneath his starched shirt. Acute lust caused his flesh to burgeon heavily, his body eager to plunder the slender female form that was spread before him. His beleaguered sense of honor protested that he was not the kind of man who would take an inebriated woman to bed. She was helpless. She was a virgin. He would never forgive himself if he took advantage of her in this condition—

"It worked!" Lillian held up her hand and waved it victoriously. "My finger's out." Her lips curved in a sultry grin. "Why are you frowning?" Heaving herself to a sitting position, she caught at his shoulders for support. "That little crinkle you get between your brows . . . it makes me want to . . ." Her voice trailed away as she stared at his forehead.

"What?" Marcus whispered, his self-control nearly annihilated.

Still clinging to the support of his shoulders, Lillian rose to her knees. "To do this." Her lips pressed between his brows.

Marcus closed his eyes and gave a faint, desperate groan. He wanted her. Not merely to bed her—though at the moment that was certainly his uppermost thought—but in other ways as well. He could no longer deny that for the rest of his life, he would measure every other woman against her, and find them all lacking. Her smile, her sharp tongue, her temper, her infectious laugh, her body and spirit, everything about her struck a pleasurable chord in him. She was independent, willful, stubborn . . . qualities that most men did not desire in a wife. The fact that he did was as undeniable as it was unexpected.

There were only two ways to manage the situation. He could either continue trying to avoid her, which had been a spectacular failure so far, or he could simply give in. Give in . . . knowing that she would never be the placid, proper wife he had always envisioned having. In marrying her, he would defy a fate that had been scripted for him before he had even been born.

He would never be entirely certain what to expect from Lillian. She would behave in ways that he would not always understand, and she would bite back like a half-tamed creature whenever he tried to control her. She was a creature possessed of strong emotions and an even stronger will. They would quarrel. She would never allow him to become too comfortable, too settled.

Dear God, was that truly the future he wanted?

Yes. Yes. *Yes.*

Nuzzling the soft curve of her cheek, Marcus relished the hot surge of her brandy-scented breath on his face. He was going to take her. Firmly he slid both hands around her head, guiding her mouth to his. She made an inarticulate sound and returned the kiss with unmaidenly enthusiasm, so sweet and ardent in her response that he almost smiled. But the smile was lost in the luscious friction of their lips. He loved the way she responded to him, feasting on his mouth with a passion that equaled his own. Lowering her to the floor, he settled her into the crook of his arm and explored her mouth with deep, carnal strokes of his tongue. Her skirts bunched between them, frustrating their mutual attempts to press closer. Writhing like a cat, Lillian fought to push her hands inside his coat. They rolled slowly across the floor, first he on top, then she, neither of them caring as long as their bodies were entwined.

She was slim but strong, her limbs wrapping around him, her hands roaming impatiently over his back. Marcus had never experienced such intense arousal in his life, every cell in his body pervaded with heat. He had to get inside her. He had to feel, kiss, caress, taste every inch of her.

They rolled again, and the feel of a chair leg digging into Marcus's back temporarily recalled him to sanity. He realized that they were making love in one of the most frequented rooms of the house. This would not do. Swearing, he hauled Lillian up with him, clasping her hard against his body as they stood. Her soft mouth sought his, and he resisted with an unsteady laugh. "Lillian . . ." His voice was hoarse. "Come with me."

"Where?" she asked faintly.

"Upstairs."

He felt from the sudden tension of her spine that she understood what he intended. The brandy had loosened her inhibitions, but it had not robbed her of her wits. Not entirely, at any rate. She brought her light, hot fingers up to his cheek, staring into his eyes with glittering intensity. "To your bed?" she whispered. At his slight nod, she leaned forward and spoke against his mouth. "Oh yes . . ."

He sought her kiss-swollen lips with his own. She was so delicious, her mouth, her tongue . . . His breathing turned ragged, and he used the shifting pressure of his hands to mold her body to him. They staggered together until he braced one of his hands on a nearby bookshelf to secure their balance. He couldn't kiss her deeply enough. He needed more of her. More of her skin, her smell, her frantic pulse under his tongue, her hair wrapped around his fingers. He needed the flex and arch of her naked body under his, the scratch of her nails on his back, the shudder of her climax as her inner muscles clenched around him. He wanted to take her fast, slow, rough, easy . . . in infinite ways, in measureless passion.

Somehow he managed to lift his head long enough to say hoarsely, "Put your arms around my neck." And as she obeyed, he lifted her high against his chest.

Chapter 18

If this was a dream, Lillian thought a few minutes later, it was happening with amazing clarity. A dream, yes . . . she clung tightly to the notion. One could do anything one wished in a dream. There were no rules, no obligations . . . only pleasure. Oh, the pleasure . . . Marcus, undressing her, and himself, until their clothes were mingled in a heap on the floor, and he lifted her to a wide bed with cloud-soft pillows covered in slick white linen. This was definitely a dream, because people only made love in the dark, and afternoon sunlight was flooding the room.

Marcus was beside her, leaning over her, his mouth playing with hers in kisses so lazy and prolonged that she couldn't tell when one ended and another began. The length of his naked form pressed against hers, startling in its power, his flesh like steel beneath her exploring hands. Hard and yet satiny, and fever-hot . . . his body was a revelation. The springy hair on his chest tickled her bare breasts as he moved over her. He laid claim to every inch of her in a slow, erotic pilgrimage of kisses and caresses.

It seemed to her that his scent—and her own, for that matter—had altered in the heat of desire, acquiring a salty pungency that suffused every breath with erotic perfume. She buried her face against his throat, inhaling greedily. Marcus . . . this dream-Marcus was not a self-contained English gentleman, but a tender, audacious stranger who shocked her with the intimacies he demanded. Turning her onto her stomach, he nibbled his way down the length of her spine, his tongue finding places on her back that caused her to twitch in surprised pleasure. The warmth of his hand smoothed over her bottom. As she felt his fingertips probing the secret crevice between her thighs, she made a helpless sound, beginning to push up from the mattress.

Pressing her back down with a low murmur, Marcus separated the springy curls and entered her with one finger, teasing and circling the delicate flesh. She rested one side of her burning face against the snowy bed linens, gasping with pleasure. He purred against the back of her neck and moved to straddle her. The silken weight of his sex brushed against the inside of her leg while his hand played between her thighs, his touch devilishly light and gentle. Too gentle. She wanted more . . . she wanted anything . . . everything. Her heart raced, and she clutched handfuls of the linens, knotting them in her damp fists. A peculiar tension coiled within her, making her writhe beneath his powerfully muscled body.

Her breathless cries seemed to please him. He rolled her onto her back, his eyes glittering with dark fire. "Lillian," he whispered against her trembling mouth, "my angel, my love . . . does it ache right here?" His finger stroked inside her. "This sweet, empty place . . . do you want me to fill it?"

"Yes," she sobbed, wriggling to get closer to him. "Yes . . . Marcus, yes . . ."

"Soon." He dragged his tongue across her taut nipple.

She groaned as his tantalizing touch withdrew. Bewildered and frantic, she felt him slide lower, lower, tasting and nipping at her tense body, until . . . until . . .

Her breath caught with astonishment as his hands pushed her thighs wide, and the wet coolness of his tongue invaded the damp thicket of curls. Her hips arched high against his mouth. *He couldn't, he couldn't*, she thought dazedly, even as he licked deeper into her mound, the tip of his tongue circling in a sly, flirting torment that made her cry out. He wouldn't stop. He centered on the tiny peak of her sex, finding a rhythm that sent wildfire through her body, then pausing to probe the intricate folds until she groaned at the sensation of his tongue entering her.

"Marcus," she heard herself whispering brokenly, again and again, as if his name were an erotic incantation. "Marcus . . ." Her shaking hands descended to his head as she tried to urge him higher, to push his mouth where she needed it. Had she been able to find the words, she would have begged. Suddenly his mouth slid upward that small but crucial distance, clamping over her with sensuous precision, sucking and tonguing her without mercy. She let out a hoarse cry as a heavy tide of ecstasy swept over her, tumbling and washing her senses.

Marcus levered himself over her and cradled her in his arms, his mouth warm as he kissed her wet cheeks. Lillian held him tightly, her breath coming hard and fast. It still wasn't enough. She wanted his body, his soul, inside her own. Reaching down awkwardly, she touched the rigid length of his shaft and guided him to the damp cove between her thighs.

"Lillian . . ." His eyes were like molten obsidian. "If we do this, you need to understand how it will change things. We'll have to—"

"Now," she interrupted huskily. "Come inside me. *Now.*" She ran exploring fingertips from the root of the shaft to the swollen tip. Nuzzling the strong column of his throat, she bit him lightly. In a sudden blur of movement he pushed her to her back, his body lowering over hers. He pushed her legs wide. She felt a stinging pressure between her thighs, and her muscles tightened against the invasion.

Marcus reached between their bodies and found the peak of her sex, his fingertips kindling new pleasure in her sensitive flesh until she rocked upward in helpless reply. With each welcoming rise of her hips, she felt his insistent hardness pressing deeper, stretching her. And then he moved with an explicit thrust to sink fully inside her. Gasping in pained surprise, she held still, her hands clutching his hard, smooth back. Her flesh throbbed violently around his, a rim of tight-stretched soreness that would not ease despite her willingness to accept him. Murmuring for her to relax, he held still inside her with infinite patience, trying not to hurt her.

As he cuddled and kissed her, Lillian looked up into his tender dark eyes. As their gazes held, she felt her entire body loosening, all resistance draining away. His hand cupped beneath her bottom, lifting her as he began to move in a careful rhythm. "Is this all right?" he whispered.

Moaning, she wrapped her arms around his neck for answer. Her head fell back and she felt him kissing her throat, while her body opened fully to the slippery-hot intrusion. She began to squirm upward into the strokes of pleasure-pain, and it seemed that her movements enhanced his delight. His features went taut with excitement, while his breath scraped in his throat. "Lillian," he rasped, gripping her bottom more firmly. "My God, I can't . . . *Lillian* . . ." His eyes closed, and he groaned harshly as he reached his own climax, his sex throbbing palpably inside her.

Afterward he made to withdraw from her, but she clung to him, murmuring, "No. Not yet, please . . ." He rolled them both to their sides, their bodies still joined. Reluctant to let go of him, she hitched her slender leg high over his hip while his fingertips drifted over her back in exotic patterns. "Marcus," she whispered. "This *is* a dream . . . isn't it?"

She felt him smile drowsily against her cheek. "Go to sleep," he said, and kissed her.

When Lillian opened her eyes again, the afternoon light was considerably diminished, and the sky visible through the window was tinted with lavender. Marcus's lips wandered lightly from her cheek to her jaw, and his arm hooked beneath her shoulders, lifting her to a half-sitting position. Disoriented, she breathed in his familiar scent. Her mouth was parched, and her throat was stinging and dry, and when she tried to speak, her voice came out in a croak. "Thirsty."

The edge of a crystal glass pressed to her lips, and she drank gratefully. The liquid was cool and flavored with citrus and honey.

"More?"

As Lillian stared at the man who held her, she saw that he was fully dressed, his hair brushed into order, his complexion fresh from a recent washing. Her tongue felt thick and dry. "I dreamed . . . oh, I dreamed . . ."

But it rapidly became clear that it had not been a dream. Although Westcliff was properly clothed, she was naked in his bed, covered only by a sheet. "Oh God," she whispered, amazed and frightened by the realization of what she had done. Her head throbbed painfully. She pressed her aching temples with her fingers.

Turning a tray on the bedside table, Westcliff poured another glass of the refreshing liquid. "Does your head ache?" he asked. "I thought it might. Here." He gave her a thin paper packet, and she unfolded the end with trembling fingers. Tilting her head back, she poured the bitter contents of the packet to the back of her throat and washed it down with a gulp of the sweet beverage. The sheet slipped down to her waist. Flaming with mortification, she snatched it up with a gasp. Though Westcliff forbore to say anything, she saw from his expression that it was rather too late for modesty. She closed her eyes and moaned.

Taking the glass from her, Westcliff eased her down to the pillow and waited until she could bring herself to look at him once more. Smiling, he stroked her burning cheek with the backs of his knuckles. Wishing that he wouldn't appear so damned pleased with himself, Lillian scowled. "My lord—"

"Not yet. We'll talk after I've taken care of you."

She yelped with dismay as he pulled the sheet away from her body, exposing every inch of her skin to his gaze. "Don't!"

Ignoring her, Westcliff busied himself at the nightstand, pouring steaming water from a small jug into a creamware bowl. He dipped a cloth into the water, wrung it out, and sat beside Lillian. Realizing what he intended, she knocked his hand away reflexively. Pinning her with an ironic glance, he said, "If you're going to be coy at this point—"

"All right." Blushing wildly, she lay back and closed her eyes. "Just . . . get it over with."

The hot cloth pressed between her thighs, causing her to jerk in response. "Easy," he murmured, bathing her smarting flesh with tender care. "I'm sorry. I know it hurts. Lie still."

Lillian put her hand over her eyes, too mortified to watch as he molded another hot compress over the dull ache of her private parts. "Does that help?" she heard him ask. She nodded stiffly, unable to produce a sound. Westcliff spoke again, his voice colored with amusement. "I wouldn't have expected such modesty from a girl who frolics outdoors in her undergarments. Why are you covering your eyes?"

"Because I can't look at you while you're looking at me," she said plaintively, and he laughed. Removing the compress, he freshened it with a new splash of scalding water.

Lillian peered at him from beneath her fingers as he pressed the soothing hot cloth between her legs once more. "You must have rung for a servant," she said. "Did he—or she—see anything? Does anyone know that I'm with you?"

"Only my valet. And he knows better than to say a word to anyone about my . . ."

As he hesitated, obviously searching for the right word, Lillian said tensely, "Exploits?"

"This wasn't an exploit."

"A mistake, then."

"However you define it, the fact is that we must deal with the situation in an appropriate manner."

That sounded ominous. Removing her hand from her eyes, Lillian saw that when Westcliff withdrew the cloth, it was dotted with blood. Her blood. Her stomach felt hollow, and her heart pounded in an anxious tempo. Any young woman knew that when she slept with a man outside the bonds of wedlock, she was ruined. The word "ruined" had such an intractable feel to it . . . as if she had been permanently spoiled. Like the banana at the bottom of the fruit bowl.

"All we have to do is keep anyone from finding out," she said warily. "We'll pretend it never happened."

Westcliff drew the sheet up to her shoulders and leaned over her, his hands placed on either side of her shoulders. "Lillian. We've slept together. That is not something that can be dismissed."

She was suffused with sudden panic. "I can dismiss it. And if I can, then you—"

"I took advantage of you," he said, making the worst attempt she had ever seen at trying to appear remorseful. "My actions were unforgivable. However, the situation being what it is—"

"I forgive you," Lillian said quickly. "There, it's settled. Where are my clothes?"

"—the only solution is for us to marry."

A proposal from the Earl of Westcliff.

Any unmarried woman in England, upon hearing these words from this man, would have wept with gratitude. But it felt all wrong. Westcliff wasn't proposing because he truly wanted to, or because she was the woman he desired above all others. He was proposing out of obligation.

Lillian eased herself to a sitting position. "My lord," she asked unevenly, "is there any reason *other* than the fact that we just slept together that has moved you to propose to me?"

"Obviously you are attractive . . . intelligent . . . you will undoubtedly bear healthy children . . . and there are benefits to an alliance between our families . . ."

Spying her clothes, which had been neatly draped over a chair by the hearth, Lillian crawled from the bed. "I must get dressed." She winced as her feet touched the floor.

"I'll help you," Westcliff said at once, striding to the chair.

She remained by the bedside, her hair tumbling over her breasts and down to the small of her back. Carrying the clothes to her and laying them on the bed, Westcliff let his gaze sweep over her. "How lovely you are," he murmured. He touched her bare shoulders and let his fingers slide down to her elbows. "I'm sorry to have caused you pain," he said softly. "It won't be as difficult for you the next time. I don't want you to fear it . . . or to fear me. I hope you'll believe that I—"

"Fear *you*?" she said without thinking. "Good God, I would never do that."

Easing her head back, Westcliff looked at her while a slow smile spread across his face. "No, you wouldn't," he agreed. "You'd spit in the devil's eye if it suited you."

Unable to decide whether the comment was admiring or critical, Lillian shrugged away from him uneasily. She reached for her clothes and fumbled to dress herself. "I don't want to marry you," she said. It wasn't true, of course. But she could not ignore the feeling that it must not happen this way . . . that she shouldn't accept a proposal that was so obviously duty-driven.

"You have no choice," he said from behind her.

"Of course I do. I daresay Lord St. Vincent will accept me in spite of my lack of virginity. And if he doesn't, my parents are hardly going to toss me out into the streets. I'm sure you will be relieved to know that I release you from all obligation." Snatching her knickers from the bed, she bent to pull them on.

"Why do you mention St. Vincent?" he asked sharply. "Has he proposed to you?"

"Is that so difficult to believe?" Lillian retorted, tying the tapes of her knickers. She reached for her chemise. "He has asked for permission to approach my father, actually."

"You can't marry him." Westcliff watched with a scowl as her head and arms emerged from the chemise.

"Why not?"

"Because you're mine now."

She made a scoffing sound, even though she felt her heart give an extra beat at his possessiveness. "The fact that I slept with you does not constitute ownership."

"You could be breeding," he pointed out with ruthless satisfaction. "This very moment, my child might be growing in your belly. That constitutes something of a claim, I should think."

Lillian felt her knees quiver, although her tone matched his for coolness. "We'll find out eventually. In the meantime, I'm turning down your offer. Except that you haven't really made an offer, have you?" She shoved her bare foot into one of her stockings. "It was more like a command."

"Is *that* what this is about? That I haven't worded things to your satisfaction?" Westcliff shook his head impatiently. "Very well. Will you marry me?"

"No."

His face turned thunderous. "Why not?"

"Because sleeping together isn't sufficient reason to chain ourselves together for the rest of our lives."

He arched one brow with impeccable arrogance. "It's sufficient for me." Picking up her corset, he handed it to her. "Nothing you say or do will alter my decision. We're going to marry, and soon."

"It may be your decision, but it isn't mine," Lillian retorted, sucking in her breath as he took hold of the laces and tugged them deftly. "And I would like to hear what the countess will say when she is told that you intend to bring yet one more American into the family!"

"She'll have an apoplectic fit," Marcus replied calmly, tying her corset laces. "She'll go on a screaming tirade, at the end of which she'll probably faint. And then she'll go to the continent for six months, and refuse to write to any of us." Pausing, he added with relish, "How I'm looking forward to it."

Chapter 19

"Lillian. Lillian, dear . . . you must wake up. Here, I've sent for tea." Daisy stood over her bed, her small hand gently shaking Lillian's shoulder.

Grumbling and stirring, Lillian squinted up at her sister's face. "I don't want to wake up."

"Well, you must. Things are happening, and I thought you should be prepared."

"Things? What things?" Lillian lurched upward and put her hand to her aching forehead. One glance at Daisy's small, concerned face caused her heart to thump unpleasantly.

"Sit back against the pillow," Daisy replied, "and I'll give you your tea. There."

Accepting the cup of steaming liquid, Lillian painstakingly gathered her thoughts, which were as fuzzy and scattered as rolls of carded wool.

She had a vague memory of Marcus secreting her in her room last evening, where a warm bath and a helpful housemaid waited for her. She had bathed and changed into a fresh nightgown, and had popped into bed before her sister had returned from the festivities in the village. After a long, dreamless sleep, she might have convinced herself that the events of the previous night had never happened, if it wasn't for the lingering soreness between her thighs.

What now? she wondered anxiously. He had said that he intended to marry her. In the light of day, however, he might very well reconsider the offer. And she was not certain whether it was what she wanted. If she had to spend the rest of her life feeling like an unwanted obligation that had been forced upon Marcus . . .

"What 'things' are happening?" she asked.

Daisy sat on the edge of the bed, facing her. She was wearing a blue morning gown, her hair pinned untidily at the nape of her neck. Her concerned gaze fastened on Lillian's weary features. "About two hours ago, I heard some kind of to-do in Mother and Father's room. It seems that Lord Westcliff asked Father to meet with him privately—in the Marsden parlor, I believe—and then later Father returned, and I poked my head in to ask what was going on. Father wouldn't explain, but he seemed quite excited, and Mother was having conniptions about something, laughing and crying, and so Father sent for some spirits to calm her. I don't know what was said between Lord Westcliff and Father, but I rather hoped that you would—" Daisy broke off as she saw that Lillian's cup was rattling on the saucer. Hastily she reached over to take the tea from Lillian's nerveless hands. "Dear, what is it? You look so strange. Did something happen yesterday? Did you do something that Lord Westcliff took exception to?"

Lillian's throat closed hard around a wild laugh. She had never felt this way before, caught in the perilous margin between anger and tears. The anger won out. "Yes," she said, "something happened. And now he's using it to force his will on me, whether or not I wish it. To go behind my back and arrange everything with Father . . . Oh, I won't stand for this! I can't!"

Daisy's eyes turned as round as dinner plates. "Did you ride one of Lord Westcliff's horses without permission? Is that it?"

"Did I . . . God, no, if only that were it." Lillian buried her scarlet face in her hands. "I slept with him." Her voice filtered through the cold screen of her fingers. "Yesterday, while everyone was gone from the estate."

A shocked silence greeted the bald confession. "You . . . but . . . but I don't see how you could have . . ."

"I was drinking brandy in the library," Lillian said dully. "And he found me. One thing led to another, and then I was in his bedroom."

Daisy digested the information in wordless astonishment. She tried to speak, then took a sip of Lillian's discarded tea and cleared her throat. "I suppose when you say you slept with him, it was more than just a nap?"

Lillian shot her a withering glance. "Daisy, don't be a pea wit."

"Do you think he'll do the honorable thing and make an offer for you?"

"Oh yes," Lillian said bitterly. "He'll turn 'the honorable thing' into a big fat bludgeon and batter me over the head with it until I surrender."

"Did he say that he loves you?" Daisy dared to ask.

Lillian made a scornful sound. "No, he didn't utter a single word to that effect."

A puzzled frown creased her sister's forehead. "Lillian . . . is it that you're afraid he only wants you because of the perfume?"

"No, I . . . oh God, I didn't even consider that, I've been too scattered . . ." Groaning, Lillian snatched the nearest pillow and crammed it over her face as if she could smother herself. Which, at the moment, didn't sound half bad.

Thick as the pillow was, it didn't completely muffle Daisy's voice. "Do you *want* to marry him?"

The question caused a stab of pain in Lillian's heart. Tossing the pillow aside, she muttered, "Not like this! Not with him making the decision with no regard for my feelings, and claiming that he's only doing it because I've been compromised."

Daisy considered her words thoughtfully. "I don't believe Lord Westcliff will characterize it that way," she said. "He doesn't seem like the kind of man who would take a girl to bed, or marry her, unless he truly wanted to."

"One could only wish," Lillian said grimly, "that it mattered to him what *I* wanted." She left the bed and went to the washstand, where her own haggard reflection glowered back at her from the looking glass. Pouring water from the pitcher into the bowl, she splashed her face and scrubbed at her skin with a soft square of toweling. A fine cloud of cinnamon powder wafted into the air as she uncapped the small tin and dipped her toothbrush into it. The crisp bite of cinnamon banished the sour, pasty feeling from her mouth, and she rinsed her mouth vigorously until her teeth were as clean and smooth as glass. "Daisy," she said, glancing over her shoulder, "would you do something for me?"

"Yes, of course."

"I don't want to talk to Mother or Father just now. But I have to know for certain if Westcliff really did offer to marry me. If you could manage to find out—"

"Say no more," Daisy replied promptly, striding to the door.

By the time Lillian had finished her morning ablutions and had buttoned a white cambric robe over her nightgown, her younger sister had returned. "There was no need to ask," Daisy reported ruefully. "Father is gone, but Mother is staring into a glass of whiskey and humming wedding music. And she looks positively blissful. I would say beyond a doubt that Lord Westcliff made an offer."

"The bastard," Lillian muttered. "How dare he leave me out of everything as if I were incidental to the whole business?" Her eyes narrowed. "I wonder what he's doing now? Probably ensuring that all the loose ends are tied. Which means that the next person he'll want to speak to is—" She broke off with an inarticulate sound, while rage pumped through her until it seemed to steam from her pores. Controlling wretch that he was, Westcliff would not leave it to her to end her friendship with Lord St. Vincent. She would not be allowed the dignity of a proper farewell. No, Westcliff would take care of everything himself, while Lillian was left as helpless as a child in the face of his machinations. "If he is doing what I think he is," she growled, "I will brain him with a fireplace iron!"

"What?" Daisy was obviously bewildered. "What do you think he—*no*, Lillian, you can't leave the room in your nightclothes!" She went to the doorway and whispered loudly as her older sister stormed into the hallway. "Lillian! *Please* come back! Lillian!"

The hem of Lillian's white gown and robe billowed

behind her like the sails of a ship as she stalked through the hallway and descended the great staircase. It was still early enough that most of the guests were abed. Lillian was too incensed to care who saw her. Furiously she charged past a few startled servants. By the time she reached Marcus's study, she was breathing heavily. The door was closed. Without hesitation she burst through it, sending it crashing into the wall as she crossed the threshold.

Just as she had suspected, Marcus was there with Lord St. Vincent. Both men turned toward the interruption.

Lillian stared into St. Vincent's impassive face. "How much has he told you?" she demanded without preamble.

Adopting a neutral and pleasant facade, St. Vincent replied softly, "He's told me enough."

She switched her gaze to Marcus's unrepentant countenance, perceiving that he had delivered his information with the lethal efficiency of a battlefield surgeon. Having decided on his course, he was pursuing it aggressively to ensure victory. "You had no right," she said in seething fury. "I won't be manipulated, Westcliff!"

Deceptively relaxed, St. Vincent stepped away from the desk and came to her. "I wouldn't advise wandering about in dishabille, darling," he murmured. "Here, allow me to offer my—"

However, Marcus had already approached Lillian from behind and had placed his coat around her shoulders, concealing her night garments from the other man's view. Angrily she tried to knock the coat away. Marcus clamped it firmly on her shoulders and pulled her stiff body back against his. "Don't make a fool of yourself," he said close to her ear. She arched furiously away from him.

"Let go! I will have my say with Lord St. Vincent. He and I both deserve that much. And if you try to stop me, I'll simply do it behind your back."

Reluctantly Marcus released her and stood aside with his arms folded across his chest. Despite his outward composure, Lillian sensed the presence of some strong emotion inside him, one that he was not entirely successful at controlling. "Then talk," Marcus said curtly. From the stubborn set of his jaw, it was obvious that he had no intention of allowing them a moment's privacy.

Lillian reflected that there were few women who would ever be foolhardy enough to think that they could manage this arrogant, bullheaded creature. She feared that she might be one of them. She shot him a narrow-eyed glance. "Do try to keep from interrupting, will you?" she asked smartly, and turned her back to him.

Maintaining a nonchalant facade, St. Vincent half sat on the desk. Lillian frowned pensively, wanting very much to make him understand that she had not intentionally deceived him. "My lord, please forgive me. I didn't intend—"

"Sweet, there's no need for an apology." St. Vincent studied her with a lazy thoroughness that seemed to unearth her private thoughts. "You did nothing wrong. I know well enough how easy it is to seduce an innocent." After a skillful pause, he added blandly, "Apparently Westcliff does too."

"See here—" Marcus began, bristling.

"This is what happens when I try to be a gentleman," St. Vincent interrupted. He reached out to touch a long lock of Lillian's hair as it streamed over her shoulder. "Had I resorted to my usual tactics, I'd have seduced you ten times over by now, and you would be mine. But it seems I placed too much confidence in Westcliff's much-vaunted sense of honor."

"It was no more his fault than mine," Lillian said, determined to be honest. She saw from his expression, however, that he did not believe her.

Rather than dispute the point, St. Vincent released the lock of hair and spoke with his head inclined toward hers. "Love, what if I were to tell you that I still want you, regardless of what may have occurred between you and Westcliff?"

She could not hide her astonishment at the question.

Behind her, it seemed that Marcus could hold his silence no longer, his voice crackling with annoyance. "What you desire is irrelevant, St. Vincent. The fact of the matter is that she's mine now."

"By virtue of an essentially meaningless act?" St. Vincent countered coolly.

"My lord," Lillian said to St. Vincent, "it . . . it was not meaningless to me. And it is possible that there might be consequences. I could not marry one man while carrying another's child."

"My love, it is done all the time. I would accept the child as mine."

"I can't listen to much more of this," came Marcus's warning growl.

Ignoring him, Lillian stared at St. Vincent in open apology. "I couldn't. I'm sorry. The die has been cast, my lord, and I can do nothing to reverse it. But . . ." She reached out impulsively and gave him her hand. "But in spite of what has happened, I hope that I will be counted among your friends."

With a curious smile, St. Vincent gripped her hand warmly before releasing it. "There is only one circumstance in which I can imagine refusing you anything, sweet . . . and this is not it. Of course I will stand your friend." Looking over her head, he met Westcliff's gaze with a dark smile that promised the matter was not yet finished. "I don't believe that I will stay for the remainder of the house party," he said blandly. "Though I should not like for my precipitate departure to cause any gossip, I'm not certain that I will adequately be able to conceal my, er . . . disappointment, and therefore it is probably best that I leave. No doubt we'll have much to discuss when next we meet."

Marcus watched with narrowed eyes as the other man departed, closing the door behind him.

In the smoldering silence that followed, Marcus brooded over St. Vincent's comments. "Only one circumstance in which he would refuse you . . . what does that mean?"

Lillian rounded on him with a furious scowl. "I don't know and I don't care! You have behaved abominably, and St. Vincent is ten times the gentleman you are!"

"You wouldn't say that if you knew anything about him."

"I know that he has treated me with respect, whereas you regard me as some kind of pawn to be pushed this way and that—" She thumped both of her fists hard on his chest as he took her in his arms.

"You wouldn't be happy with him," Marcus said, disregarding her struggles as easily as if she were a writhing cat he had caught by the scruff of the neck. The coat he had placed around her shoulders fell to the floor.

"What makes you think I would be any better off with *you?*"

He clamped his hands around her wrists, and twisted

her arms behind her back, giving a grunt of surprise as she stomped hard on his instep. "Because you need me," he said, drawing in his breath as she squirmed against him. "Just as I need you." He crushed his mouth on hers. "I've needed you for years." Another kiss, this one deep and drugging, his tongue searching her intimately.

She might have continued to grapple with him had he not done something that surprised her. He released her wrists and wrapped his arms around her, holding her close in a warm, tender embrace. Caught off-guard, she went still, her heart thumping madly.

"It wasn't a meaningless act for me either," Marcus said, his raspy whisper tickling her ear. "Yesterday I finally realized that all the things I thought were wrong about you were actually the things I enjoyed most. I don't give a damn what you do, so long as it pleases you. Run barefoot on the front lawn. Eat pudding with your fingers. Tell me to go to hell as often as you like. I want you just as you are. After all, you're the only woman aside from my sisters who has ever dared to tell me to my face that I'm an arrogant ass. How could I resist you?" His mouth moved to the soft cushion of her cheek. "My dearest Lillian," he whispered, easing her head back to kiss her eyelids. "If I had the gift of poetry, I would shower you with sonnets. But words have always been difficult for me when my feelings are strongest. And there is one word in particular that I can't bring myself to say to you . . . 'goodbye.' I couldn't bear the sight of you walking away from me. If you won't marry me for the sake of your own honor, then do it for the sake of everyone who would have to tolerate me otherwise. Marry me because I need someone who will help me to laugh at myself. Because someone has to teach me how to whistle. Marry me, Lillian . . . because I have the most irresistible fascination for your ears."

"My ears?" Bewildered, Lillian felt him duck his head to nip at the pink tip of her earlobe.

"Mmmm. The most perfect ears I've ever seen." As he traced the inner crevice of her ear with his tongue, his hand slid from her waist to her breast, savoring the shape of her figure unregulated by corset stays. She was keenly aware of her own nakedness beneath the gown as he touched her breast, his fingers curving over the soft, small shape until the nipple gathered tightly into his palm. "These too," he murmured. "Perfect . . ." Absorbed in caressing her, he unfastened the tiny buttons of her robe.

Lillian felt her pulse begin to thunder, her breath mingling in rapid puffs with his. She remembered the hard planes of his body brushing lightly over hers as they had made love, the consummate fit between them, the sliding flex of muscle and sinew beneath her hands. Her skin tingled with the memory of his touch, and the clever explorations of his mouth and fingers that had reduced her to shivering need. No wonder he was so cool and cerebral during the day—he saved all his sensuality for bedtime.

Stirred by his closeness, she caught at his wrists. There was still much they had to discuss . . . issues too important for either of them to ignore. "Marcus," she said breathlessly, "don't. Not just now. It only muddles things further, and—"

"For me it makes everything clear."

His hands slid to either side of her face, cradling her cheeks with yearning gentleness. His eyes were so much darker than her own, with only the faintest glimmer of deepest amber to betray that they were not black but brown. "Kiss me," he whispered, and his mouth found hers, catching at her top lip and then the lower, in nuzzling half-open caresses that sent rich quivers of response all the way down to her toes. The floor seemed to move beneath her feet, and she grasped his shoulders for balance. He covered her mouth more firmly with his, the moist pressure disorienting her with a fresh shock of pleasure.

Continuing to kiss her, he helped her to wrap her arms around his neck, and caressed her shoulders and back, and when it became apparent that her legs were quivering, he eased her to the carpeted floor. His mouth wandered to her breast, catching the tip as he licked at it through the fragile white cambric. Colors dazzled her eyes, deep red and blue and gold, and she realized dazedly that they were lying in a patch of sunlight that had been enriched by the row of rectangular stained-glass windows. It dappled her skin in lavish hues as if she were caught beneath an unraveling rainbow.

Marcus took hold of the front of her nightgown, tugging impatiently at the two sides until buttons popped and went scattering across the carpet. His face looked different to her; softer, younger, his skin tinted with the flush of desire. No one had ever stared at her this way, with a fiery absorption that blocked out every other awareness. Bending over her exposed breast, he licked the pearly-white skin until he found the bud of deep pink, and closed his mouth over it.

Lillian panted and arched, pushing her body upward, straining with the need to enfold him completely. She reached for his head, her fingers slipping into the thick black hair. Understanding the unspoken plea, he nibbled the tip of her breast, using his teeth and tongue with tormenting gentleness. One of his hands rucked up the front of her gown and slid to her stomach, the tip of his ring finger delicately circling her navel. A fever of desire consumed her as she writhed in the pool of colored light-spill from the window. His fingers slid lower, to the verge of tight, silky curls, and she knew that as soon as he touched the little peak half hidden in the folds of her sex, she would reach a summit of blinding pleasure.

All of a sudden, he drew his hand away, and Lillian whimpered in protest. Cursing, Marcus tucked her body beneath his and pulled her face into his shoulder just as the door opened.

In a moment of frozen silence breached only by her ragged breaths, Lillian peered out from the concealing shelter of Marcus's body. She saw with a start of fright that someone was standing there. It was Simon Hunt. A ledger book and a few folders secured with black ribbon were clasped in his hands. Blank-faced, Hunt lowered his gaze to the couple on the floor. To his credit, he managed to retain his composure, though it must have been difficult. The Earl of Westcliff, known to his acquaintances as an eternal proponent of moderation and self-restraint, was the last man Hunt would have expected to be rolling on the study floor with a woman clad in her nightgown.

"Pardon, my lord," Hunt said in a carefully controlled voice. "I did not anticipate that you would be . . . meeting . . . with someone at this hour."

Marcus skewered him with a savage stare. "You might try knocking next time."

"You're right, of course." Hunt opened his mouth to add something, appeared to think better of it, and cleared his throat roughly. "I'll leave you here to finish your, er . . . conversation." As he withdrew from the room, however, it seemed that he couldn't keep from ducking his head back in and asking Marcus cryptically, "Once a week, did you say?"

"Close the door behind you," Marcus said icily, and Hunt obeyed with a smothered sound that sounded suspiciously like laughter.

Lillian kept her face against Marcus's shoulder. As mortified as she had been on the day that he had seen her playing rounders in her knickers, this was ten times worse. She would never be able to face Simon Hunt again, she thought, and groaned.

"It's all right," Marcus murmured. "He'll keep his mouth shut."

"I don't care whom he tells," Lillian managed to say. "I'm not going to marry you. Not if you compromised me a hundred times."

"Lillian," he said, a sudden tremor of laughter in his voice, "it would be my greatest pleasure to compromise you a hundred times. But first I would like to know what I've done this morning that is so unforgivable."

"To begin with, you talked to my father."

His brows lifted a fraction of an inch. "*That* offended you?"

"How could it not? You've behaved in the most high-handed manner possible by going behind my back and trying to arrange things with my father, without one word to me—"

"Wait," Marcus said sardonically, rolling to his side and sitting up in an easy movement. He reached out with a broad hand to pull Lillian up to face him. "I was not being high-handed in meeting with your father. I was adhering to tradition. A prospective bridegroom usually approaches a woman's father before he makes a formal proposal." A gently caustic note entered his voice as he added, "Even in America. Unless I've been misinformed?"

The clock on the mantel dispensed a slow half-minute before Lillian managed a grudging reply. "Yes, that's how it's usually done. But I assumed that you and he had already made a betrothal agreement, regardless of whether or not it was what *I* wanted—"

"Your assumption was incorrect. We did not discuss any details of a betrothal, nor was anything mentioned about a dowry or a wedding date. All I did was ask your father for permission to court you."

Lillian stared at him with surprised chagrin, until another question occurred to her. "What about your discussion with Lord St. Vincent just now?"

Now it was Marcus's turn to look chagrined. "That was high-handed," he admitted. "I should probably say that I'm sorry for it. However, I'm not. I couldn't risk the possibility that St. Vincent might convince you to marry him instead of me. So I felt it necessary to warn him away from you." He paused before continuing, and Lillian noticed an unusual hesitancy in his manner. "A few years ago," he said, not quite looking at her, "St. Vincent took an interest in a woman with whom I was . . . involved. I wasn't in love with her, but in time it was possible that she and I might have—" He stopped and shook his head. "I don't know what would have come of the relationship. I never had the opportunity to find out. When St. Vincent began to pursue her, she left me for him." A humorless smile edged his lips. "Predictably, St. Vincent tired of her within a few weeks."

Lillian stared compassionately at the severe line of his

profile. There was no trace of anger or self-pity in the scant recitation, but she sensed that he had been hurt by the experience. For a man who valued loyalty as Marcus did, a friend's betrayal and a lover's perfidy must have been hard to bear. "And yet you remained friends with him?" she asked, her voice softening.

He replied in a careful monotone. It was obvious that he found it difficult to speak of personal matters. "Every friendship has its scars. And I believe that if St. Vincent had understood the strength of my feelings for the woman, he would not have pursued her. In this case, however, I could not allow the past to repeat itself. You're too . . . important . . . to me."

Jealousy had darted through Lillian at the thought of Marcus having feelings for another woman . . . and then her heart stopped with a jolt as she wondered what level of significance she should place on the word "important." Marcus had the Englishman's innate dislike of wearing his emotions on his sleeve. But she realized that he was trying very hard to open his closely guarded heart to her, and that perhaps a little encouragement on her part might yield some surprising results.

"Since St. Vincent obviously has the advantage in looks and charm," Marcus continued evenly, "I reasoned that I could only weigh the balance with sheer determination. Which is why I met with him this morning to tell him—"

"No, he doesn't," Lillian protested, unable to help herself.

Marcus looked at her then, his gaze quizzical. "Pardon?"

"He doesn't have the advantage over you," Lillian informed him, her face reddening as she discovered that it was hardly any easier for her to reveal what was in her heart than it was for him. "You are very charming when it suits you. And as for your looks . . ." Her blush deepened until she felt heat pouring off her. "I find you very attractive," she blurted out. "I . . . I always have. I would never have slept with you last night unless I wanted you, no matter how much brandy I had drunk."

A sudden smile touched his mouth. Reaching out to her gaping bodice, he pulled it together gently, and stroked the backs of his knuckles against the rosy surface of her throat. "Then I may assume that your objections to marrying me are predicated more on the idea of being forced, rather than deriving from any personal prejudice?"

Absorbed in the pleasure of his caress, Lillian gave him a bemused glance. "Hmm?"

A soft laugh escaped him. "What I'm asking is, would you consider becoming my wife if I promised that you wouldn't be forced into it?"

She nodded cautiously. "I . . . I might consider it. But if you're going to behave like some medieval lord and try to browbeat me into doing what you want—"

"No, I won't try to browbeat you," Marcus said gravely, though she saw a flicker of amusement in his eyes. "It's obvious that such tactics wouldn't work. I've met my match, it seems."

Mollified by the statement, Lillian felt herself relax a little. She didn't even protest when he reached out to pull her into his lap, her long legs dangling over his. A warm hand slid beneath her gown to her hip in a clasp that was more comforting than sensual, and he stared at her shrewdly. "Marriage is a partnership," he said. "And since I've never entered a business partnership without first negotiating terms, we'll do the same in this situation. Just you and I, in private. No doubt there will be a few points of contention—but you will find that I am well versed in the art of compromise."

"My father will insist on having the final say about the dowry."

"I wasn't speaking of financial matters. What I want from you is something your father can't negotiate."

"You intend for us to discuss things like . . . our expectations of each other? And where we are to live?"

"Precisely."

"And if I said that I did not want to reside in the country . . . that I prefer London to Hampshire . . . you would agree to live at Marsden Terrace?"

He regarded her speculatively as he replied. "I would make some concessions to that effect. Though I would have to return here frequently to manage the estate. I gather you're not fond of Stony Cross Park?"

"Oh no. That is . . . I like it very much. My question was hypothetical."

"Even so, you are accustomed to the pleasures of town life."

"I would want to live here," Lillian insisted, thinking of the beauty of Hampshire, the rivers and forests, the meadows where she could envision playing with her children. The village with its eccentric characters and shopkeepers, and the local festivals that enlivened the leisurely pace of country life. And the estate manor itself, grand and yet intimate, with all its nooks and corners to nestle in during rainy days . . . or amorous nights. She couldn't help blushing as she reflected that

the owner of Stony Cross Park was by far its most compelling attraction. Life with this vital man, no matter
where they resided, would never be dull.

"Of course," she continued pointedly, "I would be far
more disposed to take up residence in Hampshire were I
ever allowed to ride again."

The statement met with a barely suppressed laugh. "I'll
have a groomsman saddle Starlight for you this very
morning."

"Oh, *thank you*," she said sardonically. "Two days
before the house party ends, you're giving me permission
to ride. Why now? Because I slept with you last night?"

A lazy grin curved his mouth, and his hand moved
stealthily over her hip. "You should have slept with me
weeks ago. I would have given you full run of the estate."

Lillian bit the insides of her cheeks to keep from smiling back at him. "I see. In this marriage I will be obliged
to barter my sexual favors whenever I want something
from you."

"Not at all. Although . . ." A teasing light appeared in
his eyes. "Your favors do seem to put me in an agreeable
disposition."

Marcus was flirting with her, relaxed and bantering in
a way that she had never seen him before. Lillian would
wager that few people would recognize the dignified Earl
of Westcliff in the man who was lounging on the carpet
with her. And as he shifted her more comfortably in his
arms, and drew his hand along her calf, ending with a
gentle squeeze of her narrow ankle, Lillian was aware of
a delight that went far beyond physical sensation. Her
passion for him seemed to dwell within her very bones.

"Would we get on well together, do you think?" she
asked dubiously, daring to play with the knot of his

necktie, loosening the gray watered-silk fabric with her fingertips. "We're opposites in nearly every regard."

Inclining his head, Marcus nuzzled the tender inside of her wrist, his lips brushing the blue-tinted veins that lay like fine lacework beneath the skin. "I am coming to believe that taking a wife who is exactly like myself would be the worst conceivable decision I could make."

"Perhaps you're right," Lillian mused, letting her fingertips curl into the gleaming close-cut hair at the side of his head. "You need a wife who won't let you have your way all the time. One who . . ." She paused with a little shiver as his tongue touched a delicate spot near her inner elbow. "Who," she continued, struggling to gather her thoughts, "would be willing to take you down a notch when you become too pompous . . ."

"I am never pompous," Marcus said, drawing the edge of her gown away from the vulnerable curve of her throat.

Her breath hitched as he began to kiss the wing of her collarbone. "What would you call it when you carry on as if you always know best, and anyone who disagrees with you is an idiot?"

"Most of the time, the people who disagree with me do happen to be idiots. I can't help that."

A breathless laugh escaped her, and she let her head rest back on his arm as his mouth traveled to the side of her neck. "When shall we negotiate?" she asked, surprised by the throatiness of her own voice.

"Tonight. You'll come to my room."

She gave him a skeptical glance. "This wouldn't be a ruse to lure me into a situation in which you would take unscrupulous advantage of me?"

Drawing back to look at her, Marcus answered

gravely. "Of course not. I intend to have a meaningful discussion that will put to rest any doubts you may have about marrying me."

"Oh."

"And then I'm going to take unscrupulous advantage of you."

Lillian's smile was compressed between their lips as he kissed her. She realized that it was the first time she had ever heard Marcus make a rakish remark. He was usually too straitlaced to exhibit the kind of irreverence that came so naturally to her. Perhaps this was a small sign of her influence on him.

"But for now . . ." Marcus said, "I have a logistical problem to solve."

"What problem?" she asked, shifting a little as she became aware of the aroused tension of his body beneath her.

He smoothed the pad of his thumb over her lips, lightly massaging, shaping her mouth. As if he couldn't help himself, he stole one last kiss. The deep, yearning strokes of his mouth caused her lips to tingle, sensation spilling and sliding all through her, and she was left breathless and weak in his arms. "The problem is how to take you back upstairs," Marcus whispered, "before anyone else sees you in your nightgown."

Chapter 20

It was unclear whether Daisy had been the one to "spill the beans," as they said in New York, or whether the news had come from Annabelle, who had perhaps been informed by her husband of the scene in the study. All Lillian could be certain of, as she joined the other wallflowers for a mid-morning nuncheon in the breakfast room, was that *they knew.* She could see it in their faces—in Evie's abashed smile, and Daisy's conspiratorial air, and Annabelle's studied casualness. Lillian blushed and avoided their collective gaze as she sat at the table. She had always maintained a cynical facade, using it as a defense against embarrassment, fear, loneliness . . . but at the moment she felt unusually vulnerable.

Annabelle was the first to break the silence. "What a dull morning it's been so far." She lifted her hand to her mouth with a gracefully manufactured yawn. "I do hope someone can manage to enliven the conversation. Any gossip to share, by chance?" Her teasing gaze arrowed to Lillian's discomfited expression. A footman approached to fill Lillian's teacup, and Annabelle waited until he had left the table before continuing. "You've made rather a late appearance this morning, dear. Didn't you sleep well?"

Lillian slitted her eyes as she stared at her gleefully mocking friend, while she heard Evie choke on a mouthful of tea. "As a matter of fact, no."

Annabelle grinned, looking entirely too cheerful. "Why don't you tell us your news, Lillian, and then I'll share mine? Though I doubt that mine will be half as interesting."

"You seem to know everything already," Lillian muttered, trying to drown her embarrassment with a large draft of tea. Succeeding only in burning her tongue, she set her cup down and forced herself to meet Annabelle's gaze, which had softened in amused sympathy.

"Are you all right, dear?" Annabelle asked gently.

"I don't know," Lillian admitted. "I don't feel at all like myself. I'm excited and glad, but also somewhat . . ."

"Afraid?" Annabelle murmured.

The Lillian of a month ago would have died by slow torture rather than admit to one moment of fear . . . but she found herself nodding. "I don't like being vulnerable to a man who is not generally known for his sensitivity or softheartedness. It's fairly obvious that we're not well-suited in temperament."

"But you are attracted to him physically?" Annabelle asked.

"Unfortunately, yes."

"Why is that a misfortune?"

"Because it would be so much easier to marry a man

with whom one shared a detached friendship, rather
than . . . than . . ."

All three young women leaned toward her intently.
"R-rather than what?" Evie asked, wide-eyed.

"Rather than flaming, clawing, lurid, positively inde-
cent passion."

"Oh my," Evie said faintly, drawing back in her chair,
while Annabelle grinned and Daisy stared at her with en-
raptured curiosity.

"This from a man whose kisses were 'merely tolerable'?" Annabelle asked.

A grin tugged at Lillian's lips as she looked down into
the steaming depths of her tea. "Who would have
guessed that such a starched and buttoned-up sort could
be so different in the bedroom?"

"With you, I imagine he can't help himself,"
Annabelle remarked.

Lillian looked up from her cup. "Why do you say that?"
she asked warily, fearing for a moment that Annabelle was
making a reference to the effects of her perfume.

"The moment you enter the room, the earl becomes
far more animated. It is obvious that he is fascinated by
you. One can hardly have a conversation with him, as he
is constantly straining to hear what you are saying, and
watching your every movement."

"Does he?" Pleased by the information, Lillian strove to
appear nonchalant. "Why have you never mentioned it
before?"

"I didn't want to meddle, since there seemed a possibility that you preferred Lord St. Vincent's attentions."

Lillian winced and leaned her forehead on her hand.
She told them about the mortifying scene between her-

self and Marcus and St. Vincent that morning, while they reacted with sympathy and shared discomfort.

"The only thing that prevents a feeling of compassion for Lord St. Vincent," Annabelle said, "is the certain knowledge that he has broken many hearts and caused many tears in the past—and therefore it is only just that he should know how it feels to be rejected."

"Nevertheless, I feel as if I misled him," Lillian said guiltily. "And he was so nice about it. Not one word of reproach. I couldn't help but like him for it."

"Be c-careful," Evie suggested softly. "From what we've heard of Lord St. Vincent, it doesn't seem in character that he should concede so easily. If he approaches you again, promise that you will not agree to go somewhere alone with him."

Lillian stared at her concerned friend with a smile. "Evie, you sound positively cynical. Very well, I promise. But there is no need to worry. I don't believe that Lord St. Vincent is foolish enough to make an enemy of someone as powerful as the earl." Desiring a change of subject, she turned her attention to Annabelle. "Now that I've shared my news, it's time for yours. What is it?"

With her eyes dancing, and the sunlight moving over her light satiny hair, Annabelle looked all of twelve years old. Her gaze darted to the side to confirm that they were not being overheard. "I'm almost positive that I'm expecting," she whispered. "I've had signs recently . . . queasiness and sleepiness . . . and this is the second month that I seem to have missed my courses."

They all gasped with delight, and Daisy surreptitiously reached across the table to squeeze Annabelle's hand. "Dear, that is the most wonderful news! Does Mr. Hunt know?"

Annabelle's smile turned rueful. "Not yet. I want to be absolutely certain when I tell him. And I want to keep it from him as long as possible."

"Why?" Lillian asked.

"Because as soon as he knows, he will be so overprotective that I won't be allowed to go anywhere on my own."

Knowing what they did of Simon Hunt and his passionate absorption with all things Annabelle, the wallflowers silently agreed. Once Hunt learned of the coming baby, he would hover over his pregnant wife like a hawk.

"What a triumph," Daisy exclaimed, keeping her voice low. "A wallflower last year, a mother this year. Everything is turning out beautifully for you, dear."

"And Lillian is next," Annabelle added with a smile.

Lillian's raw nerves stung with a mixture of pleasure and alarm at the words.

"What is it?" Daisy murmured to her sotto voce, while the other two conversed excitedly about the coming baby. "You look worried. Having doubts? . . . I suppose that is only natural."

"If I marry him, we're guaranteed to fight like cats and dogs," Lillian said tensely.

Daisy smiled at her. "Is it possible that you are dwelling too much on your differences? I have a suspicion that you and the earl may be more alike than you know."

"In what ways could we possibly be alike?"

"Just consider it," her younger sister advised with a grin. "I'm sure you'll come up with something."

Having summoned both his mother and sister to the Marsden parlor, Marcus stood before them with his hands clasped behind his back. He found himself in the unfamiliar position of trusting his own heart, rather than following the dictates of reason. That wasn't at all like a Marsden. The family was renowned for its long line of coldly practical antecedents, with the exception of Aline and Livia. Marcus, for his part, had followed the typical Marsden pattern . . . until Lillian Bowman had entered his life with all the subtlety of a hurricane.

Now the commitment he was making to a headstrong young woman was bringing Marcus a sense of peace he had never known before. An amused grimace tugged at the small muscles of his face as he wondered how to tell the countess that she would finally have a daughter-in-law—who happened to be the last girl she would ever have selected for the position.

Livia sat in a nearby chair while the countess, as always, occupied the settee. Marcus could not help but be struck by the difference in their gazes, his sister's warm and expectant, his mother's flat and wary.

"Now that you have roused me from my midday rest," the countess said tartly, "I beg you speak your piece, my lord. What news have you to deliver? What matter is so imperative that I must be summoned at so inconvenient an hour? Some inconsequential missive about that ill-begotten brat of your sister's, I suppose. Well, out with it!"

Marcus's jaw hardened. All inclinations to break the news in a gentle fashion had vanished at the uncharitable reference to his nephew. Suddenly he took great satisfaction in the prospect of informing his mother that every single one of her grandchildren, including the future heir to the title, would be half American.

"I'm sure you will be pleased to learn that I have

heeded your advice and finally chosen a bride," he said smoothly. "Although I have not yet made a formal proposal to her, I have good reason to believe that she will accept when I do."

The countess blinked in surprise, her composure faltering.

Livia stared at him with a wondering smile. There was a sudden wicked enjoyment in her eyes that inclined Marcus to think she had guessed at the identity of the unnamed bride. "How lovely," she said. "Have you finally found someone who will tolerate you, Marcus?"

He grinned back at her. "It would seem so. Though I suspect it would behoove me to hasten the wedding plans before she comes to her senses and flees."

"Nonsense," the countess said sharply. "No woman would flee from the prospect of marrying the Earl of Westcliff. You possess the most ancient title in England. On the day you marry, you will bestow on your wife more peerage dignities than any uncrowned head on the face of the earth. Now, tell me whom you have decided on."

"Miss Lillian Bowman."

The countess made a disgusted sound. "Enough of this witless humor, Westcliff. Tell me the girl's name."

Livia fairly wriggled with delight. Beaming at Marcus, she leaned closer to her mother and said in a loud stage whisper, "I think he's serious, Mother. It really is Miss Bowman."

"It cannot be!" The countess looked aghast. One could practically see the capillaries bursting in her cheeks. "I demand that you renounce this piece of insanity, Westcliff, and come to your senses. I will not have that atrocious creature as my daughter-in-law!"

"But you will," Marcus said inexorably.

"You could have your pick of any girl here or on the continent . . . girls of acceptable lineage and bearing . . ."

"Miss Bowman is the one I want."

"She could never fit into the mold of a Marsden wife."

"Then the mold will have to be broken."

The countess laughed harshly, the sound so ugly that Livia clenched the arms of her chair to keep from clapping her hands over her ears. "What madness has possessed you? That Bowman girl is a mongrel! How can you think of burdening your children with a mother who will undermine our traditions, scorn our customs, and make a mockery of basic good manners? How could such a wife serve you? Good God, Westcliff!" Pausing, the enraged woman labored to catch her breath. Glancing from Marcus to Livia, she exploded, "What is the source of this family's infernal obsession with Americans?"

"What an interesting question, Mother," Livia said drolly. "For some reason none of your offspring can stand the thought of marrying one of their own kind. Why do you suppose that is, Marcus?"

"I suspect the answer would not be flattering to any of us," came his sardonic reply.

"You have a responsibility to marry a girl of good blood," the countess cried, her face twisting. "The only reasons for your existence are to further the family lineage and preserve the title and its resources for your heirs. And you have failed miserably so far."

"*Failed?*" Livia interrupted, her eyes flashing. "Marcus has quadrupled the family fortune since Father died, not to mention improving the lives of every servant and tenant on this estate. He has sponsored humanitarian bills in Parliament and created employment for more than a hundred men at the locomotive works, and moreover he has been the kindest brother one could ever—"

"Livia," Marcus murmured, "there is no need to defend me."

"Yes, there is! After all you have done for everyone else, why shouldn't you marry a girl of your own choosing—a spirited and perfectly lovely girl, I might add—without having to endure Mother's silly speeches about the family lineage?"

The countess trained a vicious gaze on her youngest child. "You are ill-qualified to participate in any discussion of the family lineage, child, in light of the fact that you scarcely qualify as Marsden issue. Or must I remind you that you were the result of a single night's dalliance with a visiting footman? The late earl had no choice but to accept you in lieu of being labeled a cuckold, but still—"

"Livia," Marcus interrupted tersely, extending a hand to his sister, who had turned white. The news was far from a surprise to her, but the countess had never dared to voice it openly until now. Rising to her feet, Livia came to him at once, her eyes blazing in her pale face. Marcus curved a protective arm around her back and pulled her close as he murmured in her ear. "It's best if you leave now. There are things that must be said—and I won't have you caught in the crossfire."

"It's all right," Livia said with only a slight tremor in her voice. "I don't mind the things she says . . . She lost the power to hurt me long ago."

"But I mind them on your behalf," he replied gently. "Go find your husband, Livia, and let him comfort you, while I deal with the countess."

Livia looked up at him then, her face much calmer. "I'll go find him," she said. "Though I don't need comfort."

"Good girl." He kissed the top of her head.

Surprised by the show of affection, Livia chuckled a little and stepped back from him.

"What are you whispering about?" the countess demanded testily.

Marcus ignored her as he walked his sister to the door, and closed it quietly behind her. When he turned to face the countess, his face was grim. "The circumstances of Livia's birth do not reflect on her character," he said. "They reflect on yours. I don't give a damn if you chose to dally with a footman or even if you bore his issue . . . but I mind very much that you should shame Livia for it. She's lived beneath the shadow of your wrongdoing for her entire life, and paid dearly for your past indulgences."

"I will not apologize for my needs," the countess snapped. "In the absence of your father's affections, I had to take my pleasures where I found them."

"And you let Livia take the brunt of the blame." His mouth twisted. "Though I saw the way she was maltreated and neglected as a child, I could do nothing to protect her at the time. But now I can. There will be no further mention of this subject to her. *Ever.* Do you understand?"

Despite the quiet timbre of his voice, his volcanic fury must have communicated itself to her, for she did not protest or argue. She only swallowed hard and nodded.

A full minute passed as both of them marshaled their emotions into order. The countess was the first to launch an offensive. "Westcliff," she said in a controlled manner, "has it occurred to you that your father would have despised that Bowman girl and everything she represents?"

Marcus stared at her blankly. "No," he said at length,

"it had not occurred to me." His late father had been absent from his thoughts for so long that Marcus hadn't thought to wonder what his impression of Lillian Bowman might be. The fact that his mother supposed it would matter to him was astonishing.

Assuming that she had given him cause for second thought, the countess pressed on with increasing determination. "You always desired to please him," she continued, "and you often did, though he rarely acknowledged it. Perhaps you won't believe me when I say that underneath it all, your father had only your best interests in mind. He wished to mold you into a man who was worthy of the title, a powerful man who would never be taken advantage of. A man like himself. And for the most part he succeeded."

The words were intended to flatter Marcus. They had the opposite effect, striking him like an ax blow to the chest. "No, he didn't," he said hoarsely.

"You know what kind of woman he would want to sire his grandchildren," the countess said. "The Bowman girl is unworthy of you, Westcliff, unworthy of your name and your blood. Imagine a meeting between the two of them . . . her and your father. You know how he would have loathed her."

Marcus suddenly imagined Lillian confronting his devil of a father, who had awed and terrified everyone he had ever encountered. There was no doubt in his mind that Lillian would have reacted to the old earl with her customary flippancy. She would not have feared him for a second.

At his continued silence, the countess spoke in a softer tone. "Of course she has her charms. I can well understand the attractions that those of the lower order can hold for us—they sometimes appeal to our desire for the exotic. And there is no surprise in the fact you, like all men, crave variety in your female pursuits. If you want her, then by all means have her. The solution is obvious: after you both have married other people, you and she may have an affair until you tire of her. Our kind always finds love outside of marriage—it is better that way, you will see."

The room was unnaturally quiet, while Marcus's mind seethed with soul-corroding memories and bitter echoes of voices long since silenced. Though he despised the role of a martyr and had never cast himself in that light, he could not help but reflect that for most of his life, his own needs had gone largely unaddressed as he had shouldered his responsibilities. Now he had finally found a woman who offered all the warmth and enjoyment that had been so long overdue him . . . and damn it all, he had a right to demand the support of family and friends, no matter what private reservations they might have. His thoughts ventured into darker territory as he considered the earliest years of his life, when his father had sent away anyone for whom Marcus had felt an attachment. To keep him from being weak. To keep him from being dependent on anyone other than himself. It had established a pattern of isolation that had ruled Marcus's entire life until now. But no longer.

As for his mother's suggestion, that he have an affair with Lillian when they were both married to other people, the idea offended Marcus down to the bottom of his soul. It would be nothing but a perverse imitation of the honest relationship that they both deserved.

"Listen well," he said when he could finally trust himself to speak. "Before this conversation began, I was fully determined to make her my wife. But were it possible to increase my resolve, your words just now would have done it. Do not doubt me when I say that Lillian Bowman is the *only woman on this earth* whom I would ever consider marrying. Her children will be my heirs, or else the Marsden line stops with me. From now on my overriding concern is her well-being. Any word, gesture, or action that threatens her happiness will meet with the worst consequences imaginable. You will never give her cause to believe that you are anything but pleased by our marriage. The first word I hear to the contrary will earn you a very long carriage ride away from the estate. Away from England. Permanently."

"You can't mean what you are saying. You are in a temper. Later, when you have calmed yourself, we will—"

"I'm not in a temper. I'm in deadly earnest."

"You've gone mad!"

"No, my lady. For the first time in my life I have a chance at happiness—and I will not lose it."

"You fool," the countess whispered, trembling visibly with fury.

"Whatever comes of it, marrying her will be the least foolish thing I've ever done," he replied, and took his leave of her with a shallow bow.

Chapter 21

*L*ater that morning Annabelle excused herself from the breakfast room with an apologetic murmur. "I'm feeling rather green again," she said. "I believe I shall retire to my room for just a little while. Fortunately Mr. Hunt is out riding, and he won't know that I'm taking a nap."

"I'll w-walk with you to your room," said Evie in concern.

"Oh, Evie, dear, there's no need . . ."

"It will be the perfect excuse to avoid Aunt Florence, wh-who is probably looking for me."

"Well, in that case, thank you." Battling a wave of nausea, Annabelle leaned gratefully on Evie's arm as they departed.

Lillian and Daisy made to follow the pair.

"I don't think she will be able to keep the news from Mr. Hunt for long, do you?" Daisy whispered.

"Not at this rate," Lillian whispered back. "I'm certain he must suspect something, since Annabelle is usually as healthy as a horse."

"Perhaps. However, I have heard that men are sometimes oblivious to such matters . . ."

As they left the breakfast room, they saw Lady Olivia walking along the hallway, her pretty face wreathed with a perturbed expression. It was odd to see her frowning, as she was usually a singularly cheerful woman. Lillian wondered what had happened to upset her.

Glancing up, Lady Olivia saw the pair of sisters, and her face cleared. A warm smile came to her lips. "Good morning."

Although Lady Olivia was only two or three years older than Lillian, she seemed infinitely more worldly-wise, possessing the eyes of a woman who had known great sadness in her past. It was that sense of unknown experiences, so far beyond Lillian's own, that had always made her feel a bit awkward around Lady Olivia. Though the earl's sister was a charming conversationalist, one had the perception that there were questions that should not be asked, and subjects that were sensitive.

"I was going to the orangery," Lady Olivia said.

"We shan't stop you, then," Lillian replied, fascinated by the faintest trace of resemblance to Westcliff in the woman's face . . . nothing distinctive, but a certain look about the eyes, and the smile . . .

"Do come with me," Lady Olivia urged. Seeming to obey a sudden impulse, she reached out for Lillian's hand, her small fingers wrapping around Lillian's much longer ones. "I've just had the most interesting conversation with the earl. I would love to discuss it with you."

Oh good God. He had told his sister, then. And very

possibly his mother. Lillian shot a glance of veiled panic at her sister, who proved to be no help whatsoever.

"I'm heading to the library for a novel," Daisy announced brightly. "The one I'm reading now is something of a disappointment, and I don't care to finish it."

"Go to the last row on the right, two shelves from the floor," Lady Olivia advised. "And look behind the books in front. I've hidden my favorite novels there—wicked stories that no innocent girl should read. They'll corrupt you immeasurably."

Daisy's dark eyes lit up at the information. "Oh, thank you!" She scampered away without a backward glance, while Lady Olivia grinned.

"Come," she said, tugging Lillian through the breakfast room. "If we're to be sisters, there are some things you will want to know. I'm an invaluable source of information, and I'm feeling quite gabby at the moment."

Amused, Lillian went with her to the orangery, which branched off from the breakfast room. It was warm and fragrant, with the noonday sun approaching and heat coming from the grillwork vents in the floor.

"It's not entirely certain that we will be sisters," Lillian remarked, sitting beside her on a cane bench with a curved French back. "If the earl implied that something has been agreed upon—"

"No, he didn't go that far. However, he did express some rather serious intentions toward you." Lady Olivia's hazel-green eyes were bright with smiling inquiry, and yet there was a watchful quality in them. "No doubt I should be restrained and tactful, but I simply can't bear it, I have to ask . . . Are you going to accept him?"

Lillian, who was never at a loss for words, found herself stammering as badly as Evie. "I . . . I . . ."

"Forgive me," Lady Olivia said, taking pity on her. "As those who know me best will attest, I love to go charging into other peoples' affairs. I hope I haven't offended you."

"No."

"Good. I never seem to get on well with people who are easily offended."

"Neither do I," Lillian confessed, her shoulders relaxing, and they both smiled. "My lady, the situation being what it is—although you may not know the details, unless the earl—"

"No," Lady Olivia reassured her gently. "As always, my brother was closemouthed about the details. He is an annoyingly private man who adores tormenting inquisitive people like myself. Go on."

"The truth is that I want to accept him," Lillian said frankly. "But I do have a few reservations."

"Of course you do," Lady Olivia said promptly. "Marcus is an overwhelming man. He does everything well, and he makes certain that everyone is aware of it. One can't approach the simplest of endeavors, such as brushing your teeth, without having him advise whether you should begin with the molars or incisors."

"*Yes.*"

"A dreadfully trying man," Lady Olivia continued, "who insists on seeing things in absolutes—right or wrong, good or bad. He is opinionated and overbearing, not to mention incapable of admitting that he is ever wrong."

It was clear that Lady Olivia would have gone on at length about Marcus's flaws, but Lillian experienced a sudden rush of defensiveness. After all, it wasn't quite fair to paint such a harsh portrait of him. "All that may be true," she said, "but one has to give Lord Westcliff credit for being honest. He always keeps his word. And even when he is overbearing, he is only trying to do what he thinks is best for other people."

"I suppose . . ." Lady Olivia said dubiously, and that encouraged Lillian to expound on the subject.

"Moreover, a woman who married Lord Westcliff would never have to fear him straying. He would be faithful to her. He would make her feel safe, because he would always take care of her and never lose his head in an emergency."

"But he is rigid," Lady Olivia insisted.

"Not really—"

"And cold-natured," Lady Olivia said with a regretful shake of her head.

"Oh no," Lillian argued, "not in the *least*. He is the most—" She stopped abruptly, turning scarlet as she saw Lady Olivia's satisfied smile. She had just been neatly cornered.

"Miss Bowman," Lady Olivia murmured, "you sound like a woman in love. And I fervently hope that you are. Because it has taken so long for Marcus to find you . . . and it would break my heart for his sake, if his love went unrequited."

Lillian flinched at the sudden violent thump of her heart. "He doesn't love me," she said unevenly. "At least he hasn't said anything to that effect."

"I'm not surprised. My brother tends to express his feelings with actions rather than words. You'll have to be patient with him."

"So I'm discovering," Lillian replied darkly, and the other woman laughed.

"I've never known him quite as well as my older sister,

Aline, does. They are much closer in age, and she was his main confidante until she left for America with her husband. It was Aline who explained quite a lot to me about Marcus whenever I was ready to murder him."

Lillian was very still as she listened attentively to the low, sweetly mellow voice. She had not realized until this very moment how much she wanted to understand Marcus. Never before had she comprehended why lovers were preoccupied with collecting keepsakes; letters, locks of hair, a lost glove, a ring. But now she knew how it felt to be obsessed by someone. She was filled with the compulsive desire to know the smallest details about a man who seemed so utterly straightforward and yet was practically unknowable.

Lady Olivia draped an arm across the camelback of the settee, and stared thoughtfully at the plant-laden scaffolding beside them. "There are things that Marcus will never reveal to anyone about his past, as he considers it unmanly to complain, and he would rather die by slow inches than be the object of sympathy. And if he ever finds out that I've told you anything, he'll have my head."

"I'm good at keeping secrets," Lillian assured her.

Lady Olivia gave her a quick smile, then studied the tip of her own shoe as it peeped from the ruffled hem of her skirts. "You'll fit in well with the Marsdens, then. We're nothing if not a secretive lot. And none of us likes to dwell on the past. Marcus, Aline, and I all suffered in different ways from the actions of my parents, neither of whom, in my opinion, was ever fit to have children. My mother has never been interested in anyone other than herself, or anything beyond what might affect her directly. And my father never gave a damn about either of his daughters."

"I'm sorry," Lillian said sincerely.

"No, his indifference was a blessing, and we knew it. It was far worse for Marcus, who was the victim of my father's insane notions of how to raise the Westcliff heir." Although Lady Olivia's voice was quiet and even, Lillian felt a chill run through her, and she rubbed her hands over her sleeves to soothe the prickling flesh of her arms. "My father tolerated nothing less than perfection in his son. He set ridiculously high standards in every aspect of Marcus's life, and punished him terribly if ever he failed to meet them. Marcus learned to endure a thrashing without shedding a tear or displaying one hint of rebellion, for if he did, the punishment was doubled. And Father was merciless when he discovered any weakness. I once asked Aline why Marcus has never been very fond of dogs . . . she told me that when he was a child, he was afraid of a pair of wolfhounds that Father kept as pets. The dogs sensed his fear, and hence were aggressive with him, barking and snarling whenever they saw him. When Father discovered how much Marcus feared them, he locked him alone in a room with them, to force him to confront what he was most afraid of. I can't imagine what it must have been like for a five-year-old boy to be shut away with those beasts for hours." She smiled bitterly. "Trust my father to give literal meaning to the phrase 'thrown to the dogs.' At the moment he should have protected his son, he chose instead to put him through hell."

Lillian stared at her without blinking. She tried to speak, to ask something, but her throat had become very tight. Marcus was so eternally confident and self-assured that it was impossible to envision him as a frightened child. And yet so much of his reserve must have come from the painful lesson at an early age that there was no one to help him. No one to safeguard him against his fears. Ridiculously, though Marcus was now a full-grown man in his prime, she longed to comfort the little boy he had been.

"My father wished for his heir to be independent and hard-hearted," Lady Olivia continued, "so that no one could ever take advantage of him. And therefore whenever he saw that Marcus had become fond of someone, a favorite nanny, for example, she was dismissed at once. My brother discovered that to display affection for anyone would result in their being sent away. He became distant with all those whom he loved but did not want to lose, including Aline and myself. From what I understand, things improved for Marcus when he was sent away to school, where his friends became a makeshift family."

So that was why Marcus had remained a steadfast friend to St. Vincent, Lillian thought. "Did your mother never interfere on her children's behalf?" she asked.

"No, she was too preoccupied with her own affairs."

They were both silent for a time. Lady Olivia waited patiently for Lillian to speak, seeming to understand that she was trying to absorb what she had been told. "What a relief it must have been when the old earl passed away," she murmured.

"Yes. A sad statement of a man's life, that the world should have been so improved by his absence."

"He did not succeed in his attempts to make your brother cold and heartless."

"No, indeed," Lady Olivia murmured. "I'm glad you can see that, my dear. Marcus has come so far, and yet he is still very much in need of . . . lightness."

Rather than ease her curiosity about Marcus, the con-

versation had only awakened more questions, a deluge
of them. However, her acquaintance with Lady Olivia
was still too new and untested for her to be certain how
far her questions could go before they were gently dismissed. "To your knowledge, my lady," Lillian finally
ventured, "has Lord Westcliff ever seriously considered
marrying someone before? I am aware that there once
was a woman for whom he had feelings . . ."

"Oh, that . . . it was nothing, really. Marcus would
have tired of her quickly had Lord St. Vincent not stolen
her away. Believe me, had Marcus wished to fight for
her, she would have been his for the taking. What he
never seemed to understand—what the rest of us saw—
was that it was all a ploy on her part to arouse his jealousy, and induce him to marry her. But her plan failed
because Marcus wasn't really interested in her. She was
one of a string of women who . . . well, as you can
guess, Marcus has never lacked for female attention.
He's a bit spoiled in that way, having had women practically fall into his arms ever since he came of age." She
threw Lillian a laughing glance. "I'm sure he has found
it refreshing to encounter a woman who actually dares
to disagree with him."

"I'm not certain that 'refreshing' would be his first
choice of words," Lillian replied wryly. "However, when
I don't like something that he's done, I do not hesitate to
tell him so."

"Good," Lady Olivia returned. "That is precisely
what my brother needs. There are few women—or men,
for that matter—who ever contradict him. He is a strong
man who requires an equally strong wife to balance his
nature."

Lillian found herself needlessly smoothing the skirts of

her pale green gown as she remarked carefully, "If Lord Westcliff and I did marry . . . he would face many objections from relatives and friends, wouldn't he? Especially from the countess."

"His friends would never dare," Lady Olivia replied at once. "As for my mother . . ." She hesitated and then said frankly, "She has already made it clear that she does not approve of you. I doubt she ever will. However, that leaves you in very large company, as she disapproves of nearly everyone. Does it worry you that she opposes the match?"

"It tempts me beyond reason," Lillian said, causing Lady Olivia to erupt with laughter.

"Oh, I do like you," she gasped. "You must marry Marcus, as I would love above all else to have you as a sister-in-law." Sobering, she stared at Lillian with a warm smile. "And I have a selfish reason for hoping that you will accept him. Although Mr. Shaw and I have no immediate plans to move to New York, I know that day will not be long in coming. When that happens, I should be relieved to know that Marcus is married and has someone to care for him, with both his sisters living so far away." She stood from the bench, straightening her skirts. "The reason I've told you all of this is because I wanted you to understand why it is so difficult for Marcus to abandon himself to love. Difficult, but not impossible. My sister and I have finally managed to break free of the past, with the help of our husbands. But Marcus's chains are the heaviest of all. I know that he is not the easiest man to love. However, if you could bring yourself to meet him halfway . . . perhaps even a bit more than halfway . . . I believe you would never have cause to regret it."

* * *

The estate was swarming with industrious servants, who
reminded one of bees in a hive as they undertook the
complicated chore of packing their masters' and mis-
tresses' belongings. The general company would depart
the day after tomorrow, though some were already taking their leave. Few were inclined to make an early departure, however, as no one wanted to miss the large
farewell ball that would be held on the last evening of
the house party.

Lillian was thrown into frequent proximity with her
mother, who was supervising (or harassing, as it might
more accurately be said) a pair of housemaids in their la-
borious efforts to fold and pack hundreds of articles into
the great leather-bound steamer trunks that had been
brought up by the footman. After the stunning turn of
events in the past day or two, Lillian fully expected her
mother to plot out her every word and gesture in the effort to secure a betrothal with Lord Westcliff. However,
Mercedes was surprisingly quiet and indulgent, seeming
to choose her words with extreme care whenever she and
Lillian spoke. On top of that, she did not mention Westcliff at all.

"What is the matter with her?" Lillian asked Daisy,
bewildered by her mother's docile manner. It was nice
not to have to scrap and spar with Mercedes, but at the
same time, now was when Lillian would have expected
Mercedes to mow her over like a charging horse brigade.

Daisy shrugged and replied puckishly, "One can only
assume that since you've done the opposite of everything
she has advised, and you seem to have brought Lord
Westcliff up to scratch, Mother has decided to leave the

matter in your hands. I predict that she will turn a deaf ear and a blind eye to anything you do, so long as you manage to keep the earl's interest."

"Then . . . if I steal away to Lord Westcliff's room later this evening, she won't object?"

Daisy gave a low laugh. "She would probably help you to sneak up there, if you asked." She gave Lillian an arch glance. "Just what are you going to do with Lord Westcliff, alone in his room?"

Lillian felt herself flush. "Negotiate."

"Oh. Is that what you call it?"

Biting back a smile, Lillian narrowed her eyes. "Don't be saucy, or I won't tell you the lurid details later."

"I don't need to hear them from you," Daisy said airily. "I've been reading the novels that Lady Olivia recommended . . . and now I daresay I know more than you and Annabelle put together."

Lillian couldn't help laughing. "Dear, I'm not certain that those novels are entirely accurate in their depiction of men, or of . . . of *that.*"

Daisy frowned. "In what way are they not accurate?"

"Well, there's not really any sort of . . . you know, lavender mist and the swooning, and all the flowery speeches."

Daisy regarded her with sincere disgruntlement. "Not even *a little* swooning?"

"For heaven's sake, you wouldn't want to swoon, or you might miss something."

"Yes, I would. I should like to be fully conscious for the beginning, and then I should like to swoon through the rest of it."

Lillian regarded her with startled amusement. "Why?"

"Because it sounds dreadfully uncomfortable. Not to mention revolting."

"It's not."

"Not what? Uncomfortable, or revolting?"

"Neither," Lillian said in a matter-of-fact tone, though she was struggling not to laugh. "Truly, Daisy. I would tell you if it were otherwise. It's lovely. It really is."

Her younger sister contemplated that, and glanced at her skeptically. "If you say so."

Smiling to herself, Lillian thought about the evening ahead of her, and felt a thrill of eagerness at the prospect of being alone with Marcus. Her conversation in the orangery with Lady Olivia had given her a greater understanding of how remarkable it was that Marcus had let his guard down with her to the extent that he already had.

Perhaps it wasn't a certainty that their relationship would be filled with turmoil. It took two to argue, after all. It was possible that she could find ways to decide when something was worth fighting over, or when she should simply dismiss it as unimportant. And Marcus had already shown signs of being willing to accommodate her. There had been that apology in the library, for example, when Marcus could have crushed her pride, and had chosen not to. Those were not the actions of an uncompromising man.

If only she were a bit more artful, like Annabelle, Lillian thought that she might have a better chance at managing Marcus. But she had always been too blunt and straightforward to possess any feminine wiles. *Ah, well,* she thought wryly, *I've gotten this far without any wiles . . . I suppose I'll do fine if I just blunder on ahead the way I've been doing.*

Idly sorting through some articles on the dresser in the corner, Lillian set aside the necessities that would have to remain unpacked until their departure the day after next. Her silver-backed brush, a rack of pins, a fresh pair of gloves . . . she paused as her fingers closed around the vial of perfume that Mr. Nettle had given her. "Oh dear," she murmured, sitting on the spindly velvet-upholstered chair. She stared at the glittering vial that was cradled in her palm. "Daisy . . . am I obligated to tell the earl that I used a love potion on him?"

Her younger sister seemed appalled by the very idea. "I should say not. What reason would you have to tell him?"

"Honesty?" Lillian suggested.

"Honesty is overrated. As someone once said, 'Secrecy is the first essential in affairs of the heart.' "

"It was the Duc de Richelieu," said Lillian, who had read the same book of philosophy during their school-room lessons. "And the accurate quote is, 'Secrecy is the first essential in affairs of the *State*.' "

"He was French, though," Daisy argued. "I'm sure he meant the heart as well."

Lillian laughed and glanced at her sister affectionately. "Perhaps he did. But I don't want to keep secrets from Lord Westcliff."

"Oh, very well. But heed my words—it wouldn't be a true love affair if you didn't have a few little secrets."

Chapter 22

At a suitably late hour, when some of the guests had retired and others were lingering downstairs in the card room and the billiards room, Lillian crept from her chamber with the intention of meeting Marcus. She tiptoed along the hallway, and stopped short as she saw a man standing against a wall at the juncture of two wide corridors. The man stepped forward, and she immediately recognized him as Marcus's valet.

"Miss," he said calmly, "milord bid me to show you the way."

"I know the way. And *he* knows that I know the way. What the devil are you doing here?"

"Milord did not wish for you to wander through the house unaccompanied."

"Naturally," she said. "I could be accosted by someone. Seduced, even."

Seemingly inured to sarcasm, when it was perfectly

obvious that she was not going to the earl's room for a chaste visit, the valet turned to lead the way.

Fascinated by his reserve, Lillian couldn't help asking, "So . . . is it often that you are required to escort unmarried ladies to Lord Westcliff's private rooms?"

"No, miss," came his unflappable reply.

"Would you tell me if it were otherwise?"

"No, miss," he said in exactly the same tone, and she grinned.

"Is the earl a good master?"

"He is an excellent master, miss."

"I suppose you would say that even if he was an ogre."

"No, miss. In that case I would merely say that he was an acceptable master. When I say that he is an excellent master, however, I mean precisely that."

"Hmm." Lillian was encouraged by the valet's words. "Does he talk to his servants? Thank them for doing a good job, that sort of thing?"

"No more than is appropriate, miss."

"Which is to say never?"

"More accurate would be to say not usually, miss."

Since the valet seemed disinclined to talk after that, Lillian followed him in silence to Marcus's room. He accompanied her to the threshold, scratched at the door with the tips of his fingers, and waited for a response from within.

"Why do you do that?" Lillian whispered. "That scratching business. Why don't you knock?"

"The countess prefers a scratch to a knock, as it is more soothing to her nerves."

"Does the earl prefer you to scratch at his door?"

"I doubt very much he cares one way or the other, miss."

Lillian frowned thoughtfully. In the past she had heard other servants scratching their employers' doors, and it had always struck her American ears as being a bit odd . . . rather like a dog scuffling to be let in from outside.

The door opened, and Lillian felt a rush of pure gladness at the sight of Marcus's dark face. His expression was impassive, but his eyes were glowing with warmth. "That will be all," he said to the valet, staring at Lillian's face as he reached out to draw her past the threshold.

"Yes, milord." The valet disappeared with tactful speed.

Closing the door, Marcus stared at Lillian, the spark in his eyes burning brighter, a smile now lurking at the corners of his lips. He looked so handsome, with his austere features lit by the mingled glow of the lamp and the hearth, that a sweet shiver went through her. Rather than his usual tied-and-buttoned attire, he had gone without a coat, and his white shirt was open at the throat, revealing a glimpse of smooth brown skin. She had kissed that triangular hollow at the base of it . . . she had let her tongue play across it . . .

Ripping her thoughts from the scalding memory, Lillian glanced away from him. Immediately she felt his lean fingers come up to her hot cheek, guiding her face back to his. The tip of his thumb slid over her chin. "I wanted you today," he said softly.

Her heart escalated into a rapid thump, and the cheek beneath his caressing fingertips tautened with a smile. "You didn't so much as glance in my direction even once during supper."

"I was afraid to."

"Why?"

"Because I knew that if I did, I wouldn't be able to keep from making you into my next course."

Lillian's lashes lowered as she let him ease her closer, his hand sliding over the length of her spine. Her breasts and waist felt swollen within the insulating grip of her corset, and she suddenly longed to be rid of it. Taking as deep a breath as the stays would allow, she became aware of a sweetly spicy scent in the air.

"What is that?" she murmured, drawing in the fragrance. "Cinnamon and wine . . ." Turning in the circle of his arms, she looked around the spacious bedroom, past the poster bed to the small table that had been set near the window. There was a covered silver dish on the table, from which a few traces of sweet-scented steam were still visible. Perplexed, she twisted back to look at Marcus.

"Go and find out," he said.

Curiously Lillian went to investigate. Taking hold of the cover's handle, which had been wrapped with a linen napkin, she lifted the lid, letting a soft burst of intoxicating fragrance into the air. Momentarily puzzled, Lillian stared at the dish, and then burst out laughing. The white porcelain dish was filled with five perfect pears, all standing on end, their skin gleaming and ruby-red from having been poached in wine. They sat in a pool of clear amber sauce that was redolent of cinnamon and honey.

"Since I couldn't obtain a pear from a bottle for you," came Marcus's voice from behind her, "this was the next best alternative."

Lillian picked up a spoon and dug into one of the melting-soft pears, lifting it to her lips with relish. The bite of warm, wine-soaked fruit seemed to dissolve in her mouth, the spiced honey sauce causing a tingle in the back of her throat. "Mmmm . . ." She closed her eyes in ecstasy.

Looking amused, Marcus turned her to face him. His gaze fell to the corner of her lips, where a stray drop of honey sauce glittered. Ducking his head, he kissed and licked away the sticky drop, the caress of his mouth causing a new pleasurable ache deep inside her. "Delicious," he whispered, his lips settling more firmly, until she felt as if her blood were flowing in streams of white-hot sparks. She dared to share the taste of wine and cinnamon with him, tentatively exploring his mouth with her tongue, and his response was so encouraging that she wrapped her arms around his neck and pressed herself closer. *He* was delicious, the taste of his mouth clean and sweet, the feel of his lean, solid body immeasurably exciting. Her lungs expanded with shaky-hot breaths, restrained by the clench of her corset stays, and she broke the kiss with a gasp.

"I can't breathe."

Wordlessly Marcus turned her around and unfastened the gown. Reaching her corset, he untied the laces and loosened them with a series of expert tugs, until the stays expanded and Lillian gulped in relief. "Why did you lace so tightly?" she heard him ask.

"Because the dress wouldn't fasten otherwise. And because, according to my mother, Englishmen prefer their women to be narrow-waisted."

Marcus snorted as he eased her back to face him. "Englishmen prefer women to have larger waists in lieu of fainting from lack of oxygen. We're rather practical that way." Noticing that the sleeve of her unfastened gown had slipped over her white shoulder, he lowered his mouth to the smooth curve. The silken brush of his lips against her skin caused her to tremble, and she nestled close to him, while sensations wavered inside her like images in sun-warmed water. Blindly she reached up to his hair, her fingers thrilling at the feel of the coarse silken locks. The rhythm of her heart drove free and hard inside her chest, and she moved restlessly in his arms as he kissed his way up to her throat.

"Lillian." His voice was husky and rueful. "This is too soon. I promised you . . ." Pausing, he stole a kiss from the tender hollow beneath her ear. "Promised . . ." he continued doggedly, "that we would negotiate your terms."

"Terms?" she asked vaguely, clasping his head in her hands and urging his mouth back to hers.

"Yes, I—" Marcus broke off to kiss her lips, slanting his mouth over hers with twisting pressure. She explored his neck and face, her fingertips passing over the strong lines of his cheekbones and jaw, the taut sinew of his neck. The smell of his skin intoxicated her with every breath. She wanted to press herself against him until there was not an inch of space left between them. Suddenly she could not kiss him hard enough, long enough.

As he felt her escalating wildness, Marcus forcibly eased her back, ignoring her whimper of protest. His own breath knocked sharply in his throat, and it seemed to require great effort to sort through his disordered thoughts. "Little one . . ." His hands rubbed gentle circles on her back and shoulders to soothe her. "Softly. Softly. You can have everything you want. You don't have to fight for it."

Lillian nodded jerkily. She had never been so aware of the difference in their respective experience, realizing

that he was able to restrain his intense passion, whereas
she was utterly overwhelmed. His mouth touched her
burning forehead and followed the wing of her brow.
"It's better for you . . . for both of us . . . to make it last
longer," he murmured. "I don't want to take you in
haste."

She found herself nudging strongly against his face,
his hands, like a cat demanding to be stroked.

One of his palms slipped into the open back of her
gown, seeking the skin above the edge of her corset, and
a sigh escaped him as he felt her downy softness. "Not
yet," he said in a rough whisper, though whether he was
talking to himself or to her was unclear. He clasped the
vulnerable curve of her neck in one strong hand, and
bent to feast on her parted lips, her chin, the front of her
throat. "You're so sweet," he said raggedly.

She couldn't help but grin, even in the flush of desire.
"Am I?"

Marcus sought her mouth with another hungering
kiss. "Very sweet," he confirmed huskily. "Though if I
were a lesser man, you'd have torn my head off by
now."

The words drew a low laugh from her. "Now I understand the attraction between us. We're a danger to
everyone but each other. Like a pair of ill-tempered
hedgehogs." She paused as a thought occurred to her,
and she pulled away from him. "Speaking of attraction . . ." Her legs were a bit unsteady, and she wandered to the ready support of the bed. Standing against
one of the heavy carved posts, she murmured, "I have
something to confess."

Marcus followed her, the light limning the sleek, superbly toned lines of his body. The fashionable looseness

of his trousers, which lightly followed the shape of his lean form, did little to conceal the powerful muscles beneath. "That doesn't surprise me." He rested one hand on the post just above her head, his posture relaxed. "Am I going to like this confession or not?"

"I don't know." She reached into the hidden pocket of her gown, concealed in the deep folds of her skirts, and found the vial of perfume. "Here."

"What is it?" Receiving the vial, Marcus opened it and inhaled the scent. "Perfume," he said, his gaze questioning as it returned to her face.

"Not just any perfume," Lillian replied apprehensively. "It's the reason you were first attracted to me."

He sniffed it again. "Oh?"

"I purchased it from an old perfumer in London. It's an aphrodisiac."

Sudden laughter flickered in his eyes. "Where did you learn that word?"

"From Annabelle. And it's true," Lillian told him earnestly, "it really is one. It has a special ingredient that the perfumer told me would attract a suitor."

"What special ingredient?"

"He wouldn't tell me what it was. But it worked. Don't laugh, it did! I noticed its effect on you the day that we played rounders, when you kissed me behind the hedgerow. Don't you remember?"

Marcus seemed entertained by the notion, but it was clear that he did not believe that he had been seduced by a perfume. He passed it beneath his nose again, and murmured, "I remember having noticed the scent. But I was attracted to you for many other reasons long before that day."

"Liar," she accused. "You hated me."

He shook his head. "I never hated you. I was bothered, plagued, and tormented by you, but that's not at all the same thing."

"The perfume works," she insisted. "Not only did you respond to it, but Annabelle tried it on her husband—and she swears that he kept her up all night as a result."

"Sweetheart," Marcus said wryly, "Hunt has behaved like a boar in rut around Annabelle since the first day they met. It's typical behavior for him, where she is concerned."

"But it wasn't typical behavior for you! You had absolutely no interest in me until I wore this scent, and the first time you got a whiff of it—"

"Are you claiming," he interrupted, his eyes like black velvet, "that I would have a similar reaction to any woman who wears it?"

Lillian opened her mouth to reply, then closed it abruptly as she recalled that he hadn't displayed any interest when the other wallflowers had tried it. "No," she admitted. "But it does seem to make quite a bit of difference with me."

A slow smile curved his lips. "Lillian, I've wanted you every moment since I first held you in my arms. And it has nothing to do with your damned perfume. However"—he inhaled the scent one last time before replacing the tiny stopper—"I do know what the secret ingredient is."

Lillian stared at him with wide eyes. "You do not!"

"I do," he said smugly.

"What a know-all," Lillian exclaimed with laughing annoyance. "Perhaps you're guessing at it, but I assure you that if *I* can't figure out what it is, you certainly couldn't—"

"I know *conclusively* what it is," he informed her.

"Tell me, then."

"No. I think I'll let you discover it on your own."

"Tell me!" She pounced on him eagerly, thumping him hard on the chest with her fists. Most men would have been driven back by the solid blows, but he only laughed and held his ground. "Westcliff, if you don't tell me this instant, I'll—"

"Torture me? Sorry, that won't work. I'm too accustomed to it by now." Lifting her with shocking ease, he tossed her onto the bed like a sack of potatoes. Before she could move an inch, he was on top of her, purring and laughing as she wrestled him with all her might.

"I'll make you give in!" She hooked a leg around his and shoved hard at his left shoulder. The childhood years of fighting with her boisterous brothers had taught her a few tricks. However, Marcus countered every move easily, his body a mass of steely, flexing muscles. He was very agile, and surprisingly heavy. "You're no challenge at all," he teased, allowing her to roll atop him briefly. As she sought to pin him, he twisted and levered himself over her once more. "Don't say that's your best effort?"

"Cocky bastard," Lillian muttered, renewing her efforts. "I could win . . . if I didn't have a gown on . . ."

"Your wish may yet be granted," he replied, smiling down at her. After another few moments, he held her down on the mattress, taking care not to hurt her in their love play. "That's enough," he said. "You're tiring. We'll call it an even match."

"Not yet," she panted, still determined to best him.

"For God's sake, you little savage," he said in amusement, "it's time to give up."

"Never!" She strained wildly against him, her weary arms trembling.

"Relax," came his caressing murmur, and her eyes widened as she felt the hardness of his body between her thighs. She gasped, her struggles fading. "Softly, now . . ." He pulled the front of her gown down, momentarily trapping her arms. "Easy," he whispered.

Lillian went still, her blood pumping violently as she stared up at him. The light was uncertain in this part of the room, the bed swathed in shadow. Marcus's dark form moved over hers, his hands turning her this way and that as he eased the gown from her body, and unhooked her corset. And then suddenly she was breathing, breathing, too loudly, too fast, and the soothing stroke of his palm down the front of her body only agitated her further.

Her skin had become so sensitive that the feel of the open air seemed to chafe her, her entire body tingling and prickling. She began to shiver as he peeled away her chemise, her stockings and drawers, the occasional soft graze of his knuckles or fingertips causing her to start.

Marcus stood by the bed, staring at her intently as he removed his own clothes with leisurely slowness. His elegantly sculpted body was becoming familiar to her now, as was the aching excitement that penetrated every inch of her tender flesh. She moaned a little as he joined her on the mattress, gathering her against the warm fleece of his chest. Feeling the continuous tremors that ran through her, he drew his hand over the pale length of her back and cupped the taut shape of her bottom. Everywhere he touched her, she felt waves of intense relief followed by a deeper, more pleasurable ache.

He kissed her slowly, deeply, licking into the silky recesses of her mouth until she groaned with pleasure. Moving down to her breasts, he covered them with light, half-open kisses, touching her nipples with fleeting strokes of his tongue. He coaxed and courted her as if she weren't already flushed and trembling with desire, as if she weren't breathing in pleading sobs for him to ease the pangs of need. When her breasts were swollen and her nipples had contracted to hard tips, he took one peak into his mouth and began to tug firmly, while his hand settled on her stomach.

She felt a tightening coil inside, a gathering urgency that drove her mad. Her own hand shook violently as she grasped his, and brought it to the damp tangle of curls between her thighs. He smiled against her breast, and moved to the other nipple, pulling it into the moist velvet of his mouth. Time seemed to stop as she felt his fingers searching delicately, parting the springy locks, then grazing over the wet, intricately couched peak of her sex. *Ahhh* . . . his caresses were gossamer-light as he stroked her with delicate insistence, first teasing, then assuaging, then teasing again, until she cried out in helpless release, her hips jerking hard against his hand.

Cuddling her protectively, Marcus caressed her quivering limbs. He whispered endearments against her half-open mouth, words of adoration and lust, while his hands moved over her body in reverent forays. Lillian wasn't aware of the exact moment when his touch became more arousing than soothing, but gradually she felt him layering sensation upon sensation. Her heartbeat launched into a new urgent pattern, and she shifted uneasily beneath him. He parted her legs and pushed her knees up a little, and entered her slowly. She flinched at the intimate soreness of the invasion. He was so hard, above her, inside her, that her flesh tightened instinctively, but nothing could stop the thick, heavy slide. He kept his thrusts easy and deep, nudging into the tight clasp of her sex with utter tenderness. Every movement seemed to draw a thrill of pleasure from the depths of her body, and soon she relaxed until the pain had tapered to a barely discernible twinge. She felt hot all over, feverish and desperate as she sensed the approach of another climax. Suddenly he astonished her by withdrawing.

"Marcus," she whimpered, "oh God, don't stop, please—"

Hushing her with his mouth, he lifted and turned her carefully until she was lying on her stomach. Dazed and shaking, she felt him push a pillow beneath her hips, and then another, until she was propped up high and open as he knelt between her thighs. His fingers stroked and spread the folds of her sex, and then he was pushing inside her again, and her moans became uncontrollable. Helplessly she turned her head to the side, her cheek pressed against the mattress, while her twisting hips were steadied in the firm grasp of his hands. He thrust even deeper than before, probing and stroking and pleasuring her with a measured rhythm . . . deliberately pushing her over the edge of sanity. She begged, sobbed, groaned, even cursed, and she heard him laugh softly as he drove her into a shattering burst of rapture. Her body clenched around his sex in throbbing contractions, milking a climax from him until a deep growl was torn from his throat.

Panting, Marcus lowered his body over hers, his mouth at the nape of her neck, his sex still buried inside her.

Resting passively beneath him, licking her swollen lips, Lillian mumbled, "And you called *me* a savage." She caught her breath as he chuckled, the hair on his chest rubbing like rough-napped velvet against her back.

* * *

Although Lillian was pleasantly tired from their love-making, the last thing she wanted to do was sleep. She was filled with wonder at the discoveries she was making about the man she had once disdained as stodgy and boring, who had turned out to be neither. She was beginning to recognize that Marcus possessed a softer side that few people were ever allowed to see. And she sensed that he cared about her, though she was afraid to speculate on that, as the feelings that seemed to be pouring from her own heart had become alarmingly intense.

After Marcus had wiped her perspiring body with a cool, damp cloth, he dressed her in his discarded shirt, which held the scent of his skin. He brought her a plate containing a poached pear, and a glass of sweet wine, and even allowed her to feed him a few bites of the silky-soft fruit. When her appetite was sated, Lillian set aside the empty plate and spoon, and turned to snuggle against him. He rose on one elbow and looked down at her, his fingers playing idly in her hair.

"Are you sorry that I wouldn't let St. Vincent have you?"

She gave him a puzzled smile. "Why would you ask such a thing? Surely you're not having pangs of conscience."

Marcus shook his head. "I am merely wondering if you had any regrets."

Surprised and touched by his need for reassurance, Lillian toyed with the dark curls on his chest. "No," she said frankly. "He is attractive, and I do like him . . . but I didn't want him."

"You did consider marrying him, however."

"Well," she admitted, "it did cross my mind that I would like to be a duchess—but only to spite you."

A smile flashed across his face. He retaliated with a punishing nip at her breast, causing her to yelp. "I couldn't have borne it," he admitted, "seeing you married to anyone but me."

"I don't think Lord St. Vincent will have any difficulty finding another heiress to suit his purposes."

"Perhaps. But there aren't many women with fortunes comparable to yours . . . and none with your beauty."

Smiling at the compliment, Lillian crawled halfway over him and hitched one leg over his. "Tell me more. I want to hear you wax lyrical about my charms."

Levering himself to a sitting position, Marcus lifted her with an ease that made her gasp, and settled her until she straddled his hips. He stroked a fingertip along the pale skin that was exposed at the open vee of the shirt. "I never wax lyrical," he said. "Marsdens are not a poetic sort. However . . ." He paused to admire the sight of the long-limbed young woman who sat astride him while her hair trailed to her waist in tangled streamers. "I could at least tell you that you look like a pagan princess, with your tangled black hair and your bright, dark eyes."

"And?" Lillian encouraged, linking her arms loosely around his neck.

He set his hands at her slender waist and moved them down to grasp her strong, sleek thighs. "And that every erotic dream I've ever had about your magnificent legs pales in comparison to the reality."

"You've dreamed about my legs?" Lillian wriggled as she felt his palms slide up her inner thighs in a lazy, teasing path.

"Oh yes." His hands disappeared beneath the drooping hem of the shirt. "Wrapped around me," he murmured, his tone deepening. "Gripping tightly as you rode me . . ."

Lillian's eyes widened as she felt his thumbs stroking the fragile outer folds of her sex. "What?" she asked faintly, and drew a ragged breath as she felt him open her with gentle massaging strokes. His fingers were doing something wicked, their artful movements concealed by the shirt. She shivered and watched his intent face as he used both hands to toy with her, some fingers filling her, others flirting skillfully with the sensitive little crest that seemed to burn at his touch. "But women don't . . ." she said in breathless confusion. "Not that way. At least . . . *oh . . . ah* . . . I've never heard . . ."

"Some do," he murmured, teasing her in a way that caused her to moan. "My reckless angel . . . I think I'll have to show you."

In her innocence, she didn't comprehend until he lifted her again, and positioned her, and helped her to slide along the rigid, engorged length of his arousal until she was fully impaled on him. Shocked beyond words, Lillian made a few tentative movements, obeying the low murmur of his voice and the patient guidance of his hands on her hips. After a while she found a rhythm. "That's it," Marcus said, now sounding breathless. "That's the way . . ." Reaching beneath the shirt once more, he found the aching nub beneath the hood of her sex. He circled it with his thumb in an electrifying counterpoint to her downward thrusts, with a soft pressure that sent new heat dancing across her nerves. His steady gaze held hers, drinking in the sight of her pleasure, and the realization of how utterly focused he was on her caused the ecstasy to ripen until she shuddered in hard, deep-seated spasms, her body and heart and mind filled with him. Gripping her waist, Marcus held her firmly as he ground upward, letting his own pleasure pump and surge through her.

Feeling witless and utterly drained, Lillian let herself collapse over him, her head coming to rest on the center of his chest. His heart pounded and thundered beneath her ear for long minutes before it eased into something approaching a normal rhythm. "My God," he muttered, his arms sliding around her, then falling away as if even that required too much effort. "Lillian. Lillian."

"Mmm?" She blinked drowsily, experiencing an overwhelming need to sleep.

"I've changed my mind about negotiating. You can have whatever you want. Any conditions, anything that's in my power to accomplish. Just put my mind at ease and say you'll be my wife."

Lillian managed to lift her head and stare into his heavy-lidded eyes. "If this is an example of your bargaining ability," she said, "I'm rather worried about your corporate affairs. You don't surrender this easily to your business partners' demands, I hope."

"No. Nor do I sleep with them."

A slow grin spread across her face. If Marcus was willing to take a leap of faith, then she would do no less. "Then to put your mind at ease, Westcliff . . . yes, I'll be your wife. Though I warn you . . . you may be sorry you didn't negotiate when you learn my conditions later. I may want a board position on the soap company, for example . . ."

"God help me," he muttered, and with a deep sigh of contentment, he fell asleep.

Chapter 23

Lillian stayed in Marcus's bed for most of the night. She woke up now and then to find herself enveloped in the heat of his body and the soft layers of linen and silk and wool. Marcus must have been exhausted from their lovemaking, for there was no sound and little movement from him. As morning approached, however, he was the first to awaken. Lost in a contented slumber, Lillian protested as he roused her.

"It's almost daybreak," Marcus whispered in her ear. "Open your eyes. I have to take you to your room."

"No," she said groggily. "In a few minutes. Later." She tried to burrow back into his arms. The bed was so warm, and the air was cold, and she knew that the floor would feel like ice beneath her feet.

Marcus kissed the top of her head and eased her to a sitting position. "Now," he insisted gently, rubbing circles on her back. "The maid will be up to light the grate . . . and many of the guests will go shooting this morning, which means they will rise soon."

"Someday," Lillian said grumpily, huddling against his powerful chest, "you'll have to explain why men find it such an unholy joy to go outside before it's light, and wander through muddy fields to kill small animals."

"Because we like to test ourselves against nature. And more importantly, it gives us an excuse to drink before noon."

She smiled and nuzzled into his shoulder, rubbing her lips against the sleek male skin. "I'm cold," she whispered. "Lie with me under the covers."

Marcus groaned at the temptation she offered, and forced himself to leave the bed. Lillian immediately tunneled beneath the covers, clutching the soft folds of Marcus's shirt more tightly around herself. However, he returned soon, fully dressed, and he dug her out of the bedclothes. "There's no use complaining," he said, wrapping her in one of his robes. "You're going back to your room. You can't be seen with me at this hour."

"Are you afraid of scandal?" Lillian asked.

"No. However, it is in my nature to behave with discretion whenever possible."

"Such a gentleman," she mocked, holding her arms up as he tied the belt of the robe. "You should marry a girl of equal discretion."

"Ah, but they're not half so entertaining as the wicked ones."

"Is that what I am?" she asked, draping her arms around his shoulders. "A wicked girl?"

"Oh yes," Marcus said softly, and covered her mouth with his.

*   *   *

Daisy awakened to a scratching sound at the door. Squinting her eyes open, she saw by the color of the light that it was still early morning, and that her sister was busy at the dressing table, brushing snarls from her hair. Sitting up and pushing her own hair from her eyes, she asked, "Who could that be?"

"I'll see." Already dressed in a dark red corded-silk day gown, Lillian went to the door and opened it a few inches. From what Daisy could see, a housemaid had come to deliver a message. A murmured conversation ensued, and though Daisy could not quite hear their words, she heard the mild surprise in her sister's voice, followed by an edge of annoyance. "Very well," Lillian said crisply. "Tell her I will. Though I hardly see the need for all this skulking about."

The housemaid disappeared, and Lillian closed the door, frowning.

"What?" Daisy asked. "What did she tell you? Who sent her?"

"It was nothing," Lillian replied, and added with heavy irony, "I'm not supposed to say."

"I overheard something about skulking."

"Oh, it's just a bothersome piece of business that I have to take care of. I'll explain it later this afternoon—no doubt I'll have some highly entertaining and colorful story to tell."

"Does it involve Lord Westcliff?"

"Indirectly." Lillian's frown cleared, and suddenly she looked radiantly happy. Perhaps more so than Daisy had ever seen her. "Oh, Daisy, it's revolting, the way I want to fawn all over him. I'm afraid that I'm going to do something dreadfully silly today. Burst into song or something. For God's sake, don't let me."

"I won't," Daisy promised, smiling back at her. "Are you in love, then?"

"That word is not to be mentioned," Lillian said swiftly. "Even if I were—and I am not admitting anything—I would never be the first to say it. It's a matter of pride. And there's every chance that he won't say it back, but just respond with a polite 'thank you,' in which case I would have to murder him. Or myself."

"I hope the earl is not equally as stubborn as you," Daisy commented.

"He isn't," Lillian assured her. "Although he thinks he is." Some private memory caused her to chortle, clasping a hand to her forehead. "Oh, Daisy," she said with devilish glee, "I'm going to be such an abominable countess."

"Let's not put it that way," Daisy said diplomatically. "Rather, we'll say 'unconventional countess.'"

"I can be any kind of countess I want," Lillian said, half in delight, half in wonder. "Westcliff said so. And what's more . . . I actually think he means it."

After a light breakfast of tea and toast, Lillian went out to the back terrace of the manor. Resting her elbows on the balcony, she stared at their extensive gardens with their carefully edged paths, and broad margins of low box hedges lavished with roses, and ancient manicured yews that provided so many delightful hidden places to explore. Her smile faded as she reflected that at this moment, the countess was waiting for her at Butterfly Court, after having sent one of the housemaids to deliver her summons.

The countess desired a private talk with Lillian . . . and it was not a good sign that she wished to meet at such a distance from the manor. Since the countess often had difficulty walking, and either used a cane or chose on occasion to be pushed about in a wheeled chair, going to the hidden garden was an arduous undertaking. It would have been far simpler and more sensible if she had wanted to meet in the upstairs Marsden parlor. But perhaps what the countess wished to say was so private—or so loud—that she did not want to risk the possibility of being overheard. Lillian knew exactly why the countess had requested that she tell no one about their meeting. If Marcus found out, he would insist on delving thoroughly into the matter afterward—something that neither woman wanted. Besides, Lillian had no intention of hiding behind Marcus. She could face the countess on her own.

She fully expected a tirade, of course. Her acquaintance with the woman had taught her that the countess had a sharp tongue and did not seem to set any limit as to how wounding her words might be. But that didn't matter. Every syllable the countess uttered would roll off Lillian like raindrops down a window, because she was secure in the knowledge that nothing could stop her marriage to Marcus. And the countess would have to realize that it was in her own best interest to have a cordial relationship with her daughter-in-law. Otherwise, they were capable of making life equally unpleasant for each other.

Lillian smiled grimly as she descended the long flight of steps that led to the gardens, and walked out into the cool morning air. "I'm coming, you old witch," she muttered. "Do your worst."

The door to Butterfly Court was ajar when she reached it. Squaring her shoulders, Lillian composed her features into cool unconcern, and strode inside. The countess was alone in the hidden garden, with no servant nearby to attend her. She sat on the circular garden bench as if it were a throne, her jeweled walking stick resting beside her. As expected, her expression was stony, and for a brief moment Lillian was almost tempted to laugh at the reflection that the woman resembled a tiny warrior, prepared to accept nothing less than uncontested victory.

"Good morning," Lillian said pleasantly, approaching her. "What a lovely place you've chosen for us to meet, my lady. I do hope the walk from the house was not too strenuous for you."

"That is my own concern," the countess replied, "and none of yours."

Although there was no discernible expression in her fish-flat black eyes, Lillian was aware of a sudden slithery chill. It wasn't quite fear, but an instinctive trepidation that she had never felt in their previous encounters. "I was merely expressing an interest in your comfort," Lillian said, holding up her hands in a mocking gesture of self-defense. "I won't provoke you with any further attempts at friendliness, my lady. Go right ahead and speak your piece. I am here to listen."

"For your own sake, and for my son's, I hope that you do." An icy brittleness layered the countess's words, and yet at the same time she sounded vaguely perplexed, as if disbelieving that there was a necessity of saying these things at all. No doubt of all the controversies she had experienced in her lifetime, this was one she had never expected. "Had I imagined that a girl of your commonness would be capable of attracting the earl, I would have put a stop to this far earlier. The earl is not in full possession of his faculties, or it would never have come to this madness."

As the silver-haired woman paused to draw breath, Lillian heard herself asking quietly, "Why do you call it madness? A few weeks ago you allowed that I might be able to catch a British peer. Why not the earl himself? Are you objecting mostly because of your personal dislike, or—"

"Stupid girl!" the countess exclaimed. "My objections stem from the fact that no one in the past fifteen generations of Marsden heirs has married outside the aristocracy. And my son will *not* be the first earl to do so! You understand nothing about the importance of blood—you, who come from a country that has no traditions, no culture, and no vestige of nobility. If the earl marries you, it will be not only his failure, but mine, and the downfall of every man and woman related to the Marsden escutcheon."

The pomposity of the statement nearly drew a jeering laugh from Lillian . . . except that she began to understand, for the first time, that Lady Westcliff's belief in the inviolability of the Marsdens' noble lineage was nearly religious in its fervor. As the countess worked to restore her tattered composure, Lillian wondered how, if at all, she might bring the issue down to a personal level, and appeal to the countess's deeply buried feelings for her son.

Emotional candor was seldom easy for Lillian. She preferred to make clever comments, or cynical ones, as it had always seemed far too risky to speak from the heart. This was important, however. And perhaps she owed an attempt at sincerity to the woman whose son she would soon wed.

Lillian spoke with awkward slowness. "My lady, I know that deep down you must desire your son's happiness. I wish you could understand how much I want the same thing for him. It is true that I am not noble, nor am I accomplished in the ways that you would prefer . . ." She paused with a self-derisive smile as she added, "Nor am I precisely certain of what an escutcheon is. But I think . . . I think I could make Westcliff happy. At least I could ease his cares a little . . . and I will not be a complete madcap, I swear it. If you believe nothing else, please know that I would never want to embarrass him, or to offend you—"

"I will listen to no more of this puling rubbish!" the countess exploded. "Everything about you offends me. I would not have you as a servant on my estate, much less the mistress of it! My son cares nothing for you. You are merely a symptom of his past grievances against his father. You are a rebellion, a useless retaliation against a ghost. And when the novelty of his vulgar bride wears thin, the earl will come to despise you as I do. But by then it will be too late. The lineage will be ruined."

Lillian remained expressionless, though she felt the color drain from her face. No one, she realized, had ever looked at her with real hatred until now. It was clear that the countess wished every ill upon her short of death—perhaps not even barring that. Rather than shrink, cry, or protest, however, Lillian found herself launching a counterattack. "Maybe he wants to marry me as a retaliation against *you,* my lady. In which case I am delighted to serve as the means of reprisal."

The countess's eyes bulged. "You dare!" she croaked.

Although Lillian was tempted to say more, she half feared it would send the countess into apoplexy. And, she thought wryly, killing a man's mother was not a good way to begin a marriage. Biting back more barbed words, she gave the countess a slitted glance. "We've made our positions clear, I suppose. Though I had hoped for a different outcome to our conversation, I will allow that the news is still something of a shock. Perhaps in time we shall come to some kind of understanding."

"Yes . . . we will." There was a soft hiss in the woman's voice, and Lillian had to resist an instinctive urge to step back as she saw the malevolence in her gaze. Suddenly feeling chilled and befouled by the ugliness of their exchange, Lillian wanted nothing more than to be as far away from her as possible. But the countess could do nothing to her, she reminded herself, as long as Marcus wanted her.

"I will marry him," she insisted calmly, feeling the need to make that point clear.

"Not as long as I am living," the countess whispered. Levering herself upward, she grasped her cane and used it to steady her balance. Mindful of the woman's physical frailty, Lillian nearly went to help her. However, the woman gave her such a venomous glare that Lillian held back, half suspecting the countess might lash out with the cane.

The gentle morning sun broke through the delicate veil of mist that hung over the butterfly garden, and a few painted ladies unfolded their wings to flutter over the half-open flower cups. It was such a beautiful garden, and such an incongruous setting for the poisonous words that had been exchanged. Lillian followed the older woman's tedious progress out of Butterfly Court.

"Let me open the door for you," Lillian offered. The countess waited regally, then crossed the threshold of Butterfly Court. "We might have met at a more convenient place," Lillian couldn't resist commenting. "After all, we can fight just as easily inside the manor, where you wouldn't have to walk nearly so far."

Ignoring her, Lady Westcliff continued to walk away. And then she said something curious, not bothering to direct the comment over her shoulder, but to the side, as if she were speaking to someone else. "You may proceed."

"My lady?" Lillian questioned, puzzled, and she made to follow her outside the hidden garden.

With brutal quickness, she was smothered in a blur of movement, seized from behind in a crushing grip. Before she could move or speak, something was clamped over her mouth and nose. Her eyes flew wide in bewildered fear, and she tried to flail, and her lungs moved in a painful attempt to draw in air. The thing over her face, clenched tightly by a large hand, was saturated with a sickly-sweet fluid, its fumes shooting into her nostrils, her throat, chest, head . . . a swift, noxious billow that caused her to collapse piece by piece, like a tower of painted wooden blocks. Losing control of her arms and legs, she sank into a fathomless darkness, her eyes closing as the sun turned black.

Returning from a late breakfast that had been held at the lakeside pavilion after the morning's shooting, Marcus paused at the nadir of the great staircase at the back of the manor. One of the shooting party, an elderly man who had been a friend of the family for the past twenty-five years, had sought his attention, wishing to complain about another of the guests. "He shot out of turn," the old man said heatedly, "not once, not twice, but *thrice*. And to make matters worse, he claimed to have downed one of the birds that *I* shot. Never in all my years of

hunting at Stony Cross Park have I encountered such unspeakable boorishness—"

Marcus interrupted with grave politeness, promising
that not only would he speak to the offensive guest, but
that the elderly man would certainly be invited to return
next week to hunt or shoot at his leisure. Somewhat mollified, the affronted old man left Marcus with a few last
grumbles about ill-behaved guests with no conception of
gentlemanly manners in the field. Smiling ruefully, Marcus ascended the steps to the back terrace. He saw Hunt,
who had also just returned, standing with his head bent
toward his wife. Annabelle looked distinctly worried
about something, whispering to Hunt and curling her
fingers into the sleeve of his coat.

As he reached the top step, Marcus was approached
by Daisy Bowman and her friend Evie Jenner, who, as
usual, could not quite bring herself to meet his gaze.
Making a shallow bow, Marcus smiled at Daisy, for
whom he thought he could easily develop a brotherly affection. The slightness of her form and her sweetly exu-
berant spirit reminded him of Livia in her younger years.
At the moment, however, the usual brightness of her expression had been dulled, and her cheeks were bereft of
color.

"My lord," Daisy murmured, "I am relieved that you
have returned. There is a . . . a private matter that is
causing us some concern . . ."

"How may I be of service?" Marcus asked immediately. A light breeze ruffled through his hair as he bent
his head over hers.

Daisy hardly seemed to know how to explain. "It's my
sister," she told him tensely. "She can't be found anywhere. The last I saw her was about five hours ago. She

left on some errand and wouldn't explain what it was. When she did not return, I took it upon myself to look for her. And the other wallflowers—that is, Evie and Annabelle—they have been searching, too. Lillian is nowhere to be found in the manor, nor in the gardens. I even walked as far as the wishing well, to see if she'd gone there on some whim. It's not like her to disappear like this. Not without me, at any rate. Perhaps it is too soon to worry, but . . ." She paused and frowned, as if she were trying to reason herself out of her concern but found herself unable. "Something is very wrong, my lord. I can feel it."

Marcus kept his face expressionless, though inside he felt a violent stab of worry. His mind busily riffled through the possible explanations for her absence, from the frivolous to the extreme, and yet nothing seemed to make sense. Lillian was not a silly fool who might have wandered away from the house and become lost, nor, despite her love of pranks, would she play this kind of game. Neither did it seem likely that she had gone visiting somewhere, as she knew no one in the village, and she would not have left the estate on her own. Was she injured in some way? Had some illness overtaken her?

His heart thundering anxiously, he kept his voice calm as he glanced from Daisy's small face to Evie Jenner's. "Is it possible that she went to the stables and—"

"N-no, my lord," Evie Jenner said. "I've already gone there to ask, and all of the horses are there, and none of the stable hands have s-seen Lillian today."

Marcus nodded briefly. "I'll organize a thorough search of the house and grounds," he said. "She'll be found within the hour."

Seeming comforted by his brusque manner, Daisy let out an unsteady sigh. "What can I do?"

"Tell me more about the errand she went on." Marcus stared intently into her round, gingerbread-colored eyes. "What was your conversation prior to her leaving?"

"One of the housemaids came to deliver a message to her this morning, and—"

"At what time?" Marcus interrupted tersely.

"Approximately eight o'clock."

"Which housemaid?"

"I don't know, my lord. I could hardly see a thing, as the door was scarcely opened as they spoke. And the maid wore a mobcap, so I can't even tell you the color of her hair."

During the conversation, they were joined by Hunt and Annabelle.

"I'll question the housekeeper and the housemaids," Hunt said.

"Good." Filled with an explosive need for action, Marcus muttered, "I'll start the grounds search." He would gather a group of servants and a few male guests, including Lillian's father, to help. Rapidly he calculated the length of time that Lillian had been absent, and the distance she could have traveled on foot across relatively rugged terrain. "We'll begin with the gardens, and broaden it to a ten-mile radius around the manor." Catching Hunt's gaze, he jerked his head toward the doors, and they both made to depart.

"My lord," came Daisy's anxious voice, delaying him briefly. "You will find her, won't you?"

"Yes," he said without hesitation. "And then I'm going to strangle her."

That drew a tense smile from Daisy, and she watched him as he strode away.

Marcus's mood progressed from biting frustration to unendurable worry during the lengthening afternoon. Thomas Bowman, grimly convinced that his daughter was up to some bit of mischief making, joined a party of riders who searched the nearby woodland and surrounding meadows, while another group of volunteers went down the bluff to the river. The bachelors' house, the gatehouse, the caretaker's house, the icehouse, the chapel, conservatory, wine cellar, stable and stable yard were all meticulously inspected. It seemed that every inch of Stony Cross Park had been covered, with nothing, not so much as a footprint or discarded glove, to indicate what might have happened to Lillian.

While Marcus rode through the wood and fields until Brutus's sides were wet and his mouth flecked with foam, Simon Hunt remained inside the manor to methodically question the servants. He was the only man Marcus trusted to perform the task with the same ruthless efficiency that he himself would have used. Marcus, for his part, didn't want to speak patiently with anyone. He wanted to knock heads together and choke the information he wanted from someone's helpless throat. Knowing that Lillian was somewhere out there, lost or perhaps hurt, filled him with an unfamiliar emotion, hot as lightning, cold as ice . . . a feeling he gradually identified as fear. Lillian's safety was too important to him. He could not tolerate the thought that she was in a situation in which he was unable to help her. Unable, even, to find her.

"Will you order the ponds and lake to be dragged, milord?" asked the head footman, William, after a rapid account of the search so far. Marcus looked at him blankly, while a buzzing in his ears grew sharper, more piercing, and the hammer of his own pulse caused his veins to hurt. "Not yet," he heard himself say in a surprisingly even voice. "I'm going to my study to confer with Mr. Hunt. You will find me there if anything occurs in the next few minutes."

"Yes, milord."

Striding to his study, where Hunt had been questioning the servants one at a time, Marcus entered the room without knocking. He saw Hunt seated at the broad mahogany desk, his chair angled to face a housemaid who perched on the other chair. She struggled to her feet at the sight of Marcus, and managed to bob a nervous curtsy. "Sit," he said tersely, and whether it was his tone, his harsh expression, or merely his presence, she burst into tears. Marcus's alert gaze shot to Simon Hunt, who was staring at the housemaid with a calm, terrible tenacity.

"My lord," Hunt said quietly, his gaze unswerving from the maid's streaming countenance as she wept into her sleeve, "after interviewing this young woman—Gertie— for some minutes, it has become apparent that she may have some useful information to share regarding Miss Bowman's undisclosed errand this morning, and her subsequent disappearance. However, I believe that a fear of being dismissed may be inducing Gertie to hold her silence. If you, as her employer, might provide some guarantee—"

"You won't be dismissed," Marcus said to the maid in a hard voice, "if you tell me your information at this very moment. Otherwise, not only will you find yourself dismissed, I will see to it that you are prosecuted as an accessory to Miss Bowman's disappearance."

Gertie stared at him with bulging eyes, her weeping fading rapidly as she answered with a terrified stutter. "M-mi lord . . . I-I was sent to give Miss Bowman a message this morning, but I weren't supposed to tell no one . . . she was to meet in secret, in Butterfly Court . . . and she said if I was to say a word of it, I would be sacked—"

"Sent by whom?" Marcus demanded, his blood teeming with fury. "To meet with whom? Tell me, damn it!"

"I was sent by the countess," Gertie whispered, appearing awestruck by whatever it was she saw in his face. "By Lady Westcliff, milord."

Before the last word had left her lips, Marcus had left the room, charging toward the grand staircase in murderous fury.

"Westcliff!" Simon Hunt bellowed, following him at a dead run. "Westcliff . . . damn you, wait . . ."

Marcus only quickened his pace, taking the stairs three at a time. More than anyone on earth, he knew what the countess was capable of . . . and his soul was smothered in a black cloud of horror at the knowledge that—one way or another—he might already have lost Lillian.

Chapter 24

$\mathcal{L}$illian was aware of being jostled with irritating repetition. Slowly she comprehended that she was being conveyed in a carriage, swaying and jolting over the road at high speed. A terrible smell saturated everything . . . some kind of potent solvent, like turpentine. Stirring in confusion, she realized that her ear was pressed hard against an unyielding pillow stuffed with some highly condensed substance. She felt so horribly ill, as if she had been poisoned. With each breath she took, her throat burned. Nausea spread through her in repeated waves. She moaned in protest, while her clouded mind worked to disentangle itself from unpleasant dreams.

Cracking her eyes open, she saw something above her . . . a face that seemed to dart out at her and disappear at random. She tried to ask something, to find out what was happening, but her brain seemed to have been disconnected from the rest of her body, and though she was vaguely aware of speaking, the words that came from her mouth were gibberish.

"Shhh . . ." A long-fingered hand moved over her head, massaging her scalp and temples. "Rest. You'll come out of it soon, darling. Just rest, and breathe."

Confused, Lillian closed her eyes and tried to harness her brain into some fragile imitation of its usual process. After a while, she connected the voice to an image. "Sainvincen . . ." she mumbled, her tongue not quite moving properly in her mouth.

"Yes, love."

Her first lurching impulse was one of relief. A friend. Someone who would help her. But the relief turned hollow as her instincts shuffled in restless warning, and she rolled her head on what turned out to be St. Vincent's thigh. The nauseating smell overwhelmed her . . . it was in her nose and on her face, the fumes stinging her eyes, and she lifted her fingers to claw at her skin in an instinctive attempt to scratch it off.

St. Vincent caught her wrists, murmuring, "No, no . . . I'll help you. Put your hands down, love. There's a good girl. Drink some of this. Only a sip, or it won't stay down." The nozzle of something—a flask, a skin, a bottle, perhaps—pressed against her lips, and cool water trickled into her mouth. She swallowed gratefully, and held still as a damp cloth moved over her cheeks and nose and jaw.

"Poor sweet," St. Vincent murmured, wiping her throat, then moving to her forehead. "The idiot who brought you to me must have given you twice as much ether as was needed. You should have awakened long before now."

Ether. The idiot who brought you to me . . . The first

glimmer of understanding came to her, and Lillian stared up at him hazily, perceiving only the lean outlines of his face and the color of his hair, dark gold like the gilding of an antique Slavic icon. "Can't see . . ." she whispered.

"That should improve in a few minutes."

"Ether . . ." Lillian puzzled over the word, which sounded familiar. She had encountered it before, in some apothecary shop or another. Ether . . . sweet vitriol . . . used as an intoxicant, and occasionally as an aid to medical procedures. "Why?" she asked, uncertain if her uncontrollable trembling was the result of ether poisoning, or the realization that she was lying helpless in the arms of an enemy.

Though she still couldn't clearly see the expression on St. Vincent's face, she heard the gravely apologetic note in his voice. "I had no choice in the manner of your delivery, darling, or I would have made certain that you had been treated more gently. All I was told was that if I wanted you, I should come to collect you without delay, else you would be disposed of in some other manner. Knowing the countess, I wouldn't have been surprised if she had elected to drown you like a cat in a sack."

"Countess," Lillian repeated faintly, still finding it difficult to maneuver her thick, swollen tongue. Saliva kept flooding her mouth, an aftereffect of the ether. "Westcliff . . . tell him . . ." Oh, how she wanted Marcus. She wanted his deep voice and loving hands, and the hard warmth of his body against hers. But Marcus didn't know where she was, or what had happened to her.

"You've met with a change of fate, my pet," St. Vincent said softly, stroking her hair again. It seemed that he could read her thoughts. "There's no point in asking for Westcliff . . . you're out of his reach now."

Lillian floundered and strained to sit up, but all she succeeded in was nearly rolling onto the floor of the carriage.

"Easy," St. Vincent murmured, holding her in place with only the lightest pressure on her shoulders. "You're not ready to sit on your own yet. No, don't. You'll make yourself ill."

Though she despised herself for it, Lillian couldn't prevent a whimper of distress as she collapsed back into his lap, her head falling weakly against his thigh. "What are you doing?" she managed to ask, panting for breath and striving to keep down her gorge. "Where are we going?"

"To Gretna Green. We're going to marry, sweet."

It was difficult to think past the nausea and the instant panic. "I won't cooperate," Lillian finally whispered, swallowing and swallowing.

"I'm afraid you will," he replied evenly. "I know of several methods to solicit your participation, though I would prefer not to cause you unnecessary pain. And after the ceremony, an expedient consummation will make the union permanent."

"Westcliff won't accept it," she croaked. "No matter what you do. He'll . . . he'll take me away from you."

St. Vincent's voice was soft. "He will have no legal right to you by then, sweet. And I've known him far longer than you have, which is why I know that he won't want you after I've taken you."

"Not if it's rape," Lillian choked, flinching as she felt the easy slide of his palm over her shoulder. "He wouldn't blame me."

"It won't be rape," St. Vincent said gently. "If I know one thing, darling, it's how to . . . well, I won't boast. But rather than quibble over technicalities, I can assure you that although Westcliff won't blame you, neither will he chance the possibility of his wife giving birth to another man's bastard. Nor would he be able to accept a woman who has been defiled. He will—with reluctance, of course—inform you that it would probably be best for all parties concerned to leave things as they are. And then he'll go on to marry the proper English girl that he should have chosen in the first place. Whereas you"—his finger traced the curve of her trembling cheek— "will do just fine for me. I daresay your family will reconcile themselves to me fairly soon. They're the sort to make a virtue of necessity."

Lillian did not happen to agree with his analysis, at least where Marcus was concerned. She had a good deal more faith in his loyalty than that. However, it wasn't a theory that she cared to test—especially the unwilling consummation part. She lay still for a long minute, discovering to her relief that her vision was clearing, and her nausea had eased slightly, though the pools of bitter saliva kept collecting in her mouth. Now that her initial confusion and the first flush of panic were over, she was able to harness her sluggish mind sufficiently to think. Though part of her longed to explode with rage, she couldn't see much benefit for herself in that. Much better to recover her wits, and try to think rationally.

"I want to sit up," she said flatly.

St. Vincent seemed admiring and surprised by her calmness. "Slowly, then, and allow me to support you until you get your bearings."

Showers of white and blue sparks veiled Lillian's vision as she felt him maneuver her until she was braced in the corner of the carriage. More saliva, a surge of weakness, and then she managed to collect herself. Her dress was unfastened, she saw, with the front gaping open to the waist to reveal the crumpled chemise underneath. Her heart kicked anxiously at the discovery, and she tried unsuccessfully to tug the edges of the gown together. Her accusing gaze lifted to St. Vincent's face. His expression was grave, but his eyes were light and smiling. "No, I haven't ravished you," he murmured. "Yet. I prefer my victims to be conscious. However, your breathing was weak, and I feared the mixture of an ether overdose and a very tight corset might be the finish of you. I removed the corset, but I couldn't quite fasten your gown."

"More water," Lillian said raspily, and took a cautious sip from the leather skin that he handed to her. She stared at St. Vincent stonily, searching for any vestige of the charming companion she had known at Stony Cross Park. All she could see were the dispassionate eyes of a man who would hesitate at nothing to get what he wanted. He possessed no principles, no sense of honor, no human weakness. She could cry, scream, beg, and none of it would move him. He would stop at nothing, even rape, to achieve his ends.

"Why me?" she asked in a monotone. "Why not make off with some other unwilling girl who has some money?"

"Because you were the most convenient option. And financially speaking, you're by far the most well endowed."

"And you want to strike at Westcliff," she said. "Because you're jealous of him."

"Darling, that's going a bit too far. I wouldn't trade places with Westcliff and his infernal load of obligations for all the world. I merely want to improve my own circumstances."

"And therefore you are willing to take a wife who will hate you?" Lillian asked, rubbing her eyes, which felt filmy and sticky. "If you think I would ever forgive you, you're a vain, self-centered idiot. I'll do everything in my power to make you miserable. Is that what you want?"

"At the moment, pet, all I want is your money. Later we'll discover ways in which I might be able to soften your feelings toward me. Failing that, I can always deposit you in some remote country estate where the only entertainment is watching the cows and sheep through the window."

Lillian's head pounded and throbbed. She moved her fingers to her temples and pressed them firmly in an effort to ease the ache. "Don't underestimate me," she said with her eyes closed, while her heart felt like a cold, hard stone in her chest. "I will make your life hell. I may even murder you."

A gentle, mirthless laugh greeted her statement. "No doubt someone will, someday. It may as well be my own wife."

Lillian fell silent, squeezing her eyes tighter over a threatening prickle of useless tears. She would not cry, however. She would wait for an opportune moment . . . and if murder was what was required for her to escape him, she would happily oblige.

By the time Marcus had reached the countess's private suite of rooms, with Simon Hunt in close pursuit, the commotion had attracted the attention of half the household. Intent on reaching the malicious bitch who was his mother, Marcus was only vaguely aware of the stunned faces of the servants he passed. He ignored Simon Hunt's exhortations to calm himself, to keep from tearing off in a fury, to behave rationally. Never in his life had Marcus been so far beyond the reach of sanity.

Reaching the door of his mother's apartments, Marcus found it locked. He rattled the handle violently. "Open it," he bellowed. "Open it now!"

Silence, and then a maid's frightened reply from within. "Milord . . . the countess bade me to tell you that she is resting."

"I'll send her to her eternal fucking rest," Marcus roared, "if this door isn't opened *now*."

"Milord, please—"

He drew back three or four paces and hurled himself against the door, which shook on its hinges and partially gave with a splintering sound. There were fearful cries in the hallway from a pair of female guests who happened to witness the astonishing display of raging frenzy. "Dear God," one exclaimed to the other, "he's gone berserk!"

Marcus drew back again and lunged at the door, this time sending chunks of paneling flying. He felt Simon Hunt's hands grasp him from behind, and he whirled with his fist drawn back, ready to launch an attack on all fronts.

"Jesus," Hunt muttered, retreating a step or two with his hands raised in a defensive gesture. His face was taut and his eyes were wide, and he stared at Marcus as if he were a stranger. "Westcliff—"

"Stay the hell out of my way!"

"Gladly. But let me point out that if our positions were reversed, you would be the first to tell me to keep a cool—"

Ignoring him, Marcus swerved back to the door and targeted the disjointed lock with a powerful, accurately aimed blow of his boot heel. The housemaid's scream shot through the doorway as the ruined portal swung open. Bursting into the receiving room, Marcus charged toward the bedchamber, where the countess sat in a chair by a small hearth fire. Fully dressed and swathed in ropes of pearls, she stared at him with amused disdain.

Breathing heavily, Marcus advanced on her with bloodlust racing through his veins. It was certain that the countess had no idea that she was in mortal danger, or she would not have received him so calmly.

"Full of animal spirits today, are we?" she asked. "Your descent from gentleman to savage brute has been accomplished so very quickly. I must offer Miss Bowman my compliments on her efficacy."

"What have you done with her?"

"Done with her?" Her expression taunted him with its innocent perplexity. "What the devil do you mean, Westcliff?"

"You met with her at Butterfly Court this morning."

"I never walk that far from the manor," the countess said haughtily. "What a ridiculous asser—" She let out a strident cry as Marcus seized her, his fingers wrapping around the pearl ropes and tightening them around her throat.

"Tell me where she is, or I'll snap your neck like a wishbone!"

Simon Hunt seized him from behind once more, determined to prevent a murder from occurring. "Westcliff!"

Marcus closed his hand in a harder grip around the pearls. He glared without blinking into his mother's face, not missing the flicker of vindictive triumph that lurked in her eyes. He did not take his gaze from hers even as he heard his sister Livia's voice.

"Marcus," she said urgently. "Marcus, listen to me! You have my permission to throttle her later. I'll even help. But at least wait until we've found out what she's done."

Marcus tightened the tension of the pearls until the elderly woman's eyes seemed to protrude from their shallow sockets. "Your only value to me," he said in a low tone, "is your knowledge of Lillian Bowman's whereabouts. If I can't obtain that from you, I'll send you to the devil. Tell me, or I'll choke it from you. And believe that I have enough of my father in me to do it without a second thought."

"Oh yes, you have him in you," the countess said raspily. As his hold on her necklace loosened marginally, she smiled with malevolent enjoyment. "I see that all pretenses of being nobler, better, wiser than your father have finally vanished. That Bowman creature has poisoned you without your even being—"

"Now!" he roared.

For the first time, she began to look uneasy, though no less self-righteous. "I will admit, I met with Miss Bowman this morning at Butterfly Court—where she told me of her intentions to run away with Lord St. Vincent. She has decided to elope with him."

"That's a lie!" came Livia's outraged cry, while a burst of agitated female voices came from the direction of the doorway . . . the wallflowers, who seemed to be vigorously denying the statement.

Marcus released the countess as if he had been burned. His first reaction was a piercing relief that Lillian was still alive. However, the relief was followed immediately by the awareness that she was far from safe. In light of St. Vincent's need of a fortune, it made perfect

sense for him to abduct Lillian. Marcus turned from his
mother, never wanting to look at her again, unable to
bring himself to speak to her. His gaze locked with Simon Hunt's. Predictably, Hunt was already making
rapid calculations. "He'll take her to Gretna Green, of
course," Hunt murmured, "and they'll have to travel
east to the main road in Hertfordshire. He won't risk
traveling the back ways and getting mired in mud, or
having the wheels damaged from broken road. From
Hertfordshire it will be approximately forty-five hours to
Scotland . . . and at a speed of ten miles per hour, with
occasional stops for fresh relay horses . . ."

"You'll never overtake them," the countess cried with
a cackling laugh. "I told you I would have my way,
Westcliff!"

"Oh, shut up, you evil hag!" cried Daisy Bowman impatiently from the doorway, her eyes huge in her pale
face. "Lord Westcliff, shall I run to the stables and tell
them to saddle a horse?"

"Two horses," Simon Hunt said resolutely. "I'm going with him."

"Which ones—"

"Ebony and Yasmin," Marcus replied. They were his
best Arabians, bred for speed over long distance. They
were not as lightning-fast as thoroughbreds, but they
would endure a punishing pace for hours, traveling at
least three times as fast as St. Vincent's coach.

Daisy disappeared in a flash, and Marcus turned to
his sister. "See that the countess is gone by the time I return," he said curtly. "Pack whatever she needs, and get
her off the estate."

"Where do you wish me to send her?" Livia asked,
pale but composed.

"I don't give a damn, so long as she knows not to return."

Realizing that she was being banished, and most likely exiled, the countess rose from her chair. "I will not be disposed of in this manner! I won't have it, my lord!"

"And tell the countess," Marcus said to Livia, "that if the slightest harm comes to Miss Bowman, she had better pray that I never find her."

Marcus strode from the room, shoving through a small crowd that had gathered in the hallway. Simon Hunt followed, pausing only to murmur briefly to Annabelle and press a kiss to her forehead. She stared after him with an anxious frown, biting her lip to keep from calling after him.

After a lengthy pause, the countess was heard to mutter, "It matters not what becomes of me. I am content in the knowledge that I have prevented him from befouling the family lineage."

Livia turned to give her mother a half-pitying, half-contemptuous glance. "Marcus never fails," she said softly. "Most of his childhood was spent learning to overcome impossible odds. And now that Marcus has finally found someone worth fighting for . . . do you really think he would let anything stop him?"

Chapter 25

*D*espite her fear and worry, the residual effects of the ether caused Lillian to sleep as she sat with her head resting against the side of the velvet-upholstered wall of the carriage. The eventual cessation of movement caused her to awaken. Her back hurt, and her feet were cold and numb. Rubbing her sore eyes, she wondered if she had been dreaming. She willed herself to awaken in the quiet little bedroom at Stony Cross Park . . . or better yet, the spacious bed she had shared with Marcus. Opening her eyes, she saw the interior of St. Vincent's carriage, and her heart plummeted.

Her fingers shook as she reached out to lift the window curtain with a clumsy motion. It was early evening, the dying sun casting a last harsh glitter through a scant grove of oak trees. The carriage had stopped in front of a coaching inn, with a sign, THE BULL AND MOUTH, hanging beside the front entrance. It was a large inn capable of stabling perhaps a hundred horses, with three conjoined buildings to house the many travelers who made use of the main turnpike road.

Aware of a movement on the seat beside her, Lillian began to turn, and stiffened as she felt both her wrists being caught neatly behind her back. "What—" she asked, at the same time that cold metal rings were snapped smoothly around her wrists. She tugged at her arms, but they were fastened securely. Handcuffs, she realized. "You bastard," she said, her voice trembling with fury. "You coward. You bloody—" Her voice was muffled as a wad of fabric was shoved into her mouth, and a gag was gently cinched over it.

"Sorry," St. Vincent murmured in her ear, not sounding at all penitent. "You shouldn't tug at your wrists, pet. You'll bruise them needlessly." His warm fingers closed over her icy fists. "An interesting toy, this," he murmured, a fingertip slipping beneath the metal cuff to stroke her wrist. "Some women of my acquaintance have a great fondness for it." Turning her rigid body in his arms, he smiled as he saw the angry bewilderment in her expression. "My innocent . . . it will be a great pleasure to tutor you."

Pushing at the gag with her dry tongue, Lillian could not help reflecting on how beautiful and treacherous a creature he was. A villain should be black-haired and wart-covered and as monstrous on the outside as he was on the inside. It was vastly unjust that a soulless beast like St. Vincent should be graced with such handsomeness. "I'll return momentarily," he told her. "Be still— and try not to cause trouble."

The smug ass, Lillian thought bitterly, while the rising pressure of panic caused her throat to tighten. She watched without blinking as St. Vincent opened the door and swung down from the carriage. A gathering semidarkness enclosed her as evening fell. Forcing herself to breathe regularly, Lillian tried to think above her fear. Surely there would come a moment, an opening, when she would have a chance to escape. All she had to do was wait.

Her absence at Stony Cross Park would have been noticed many hours ago. They would be searching for her . . . wasting time, worrying . . . and all the while, the countess would be waiting in silent complacency, satisfied in the knowledge that she had handily dispatched of at least one troublesome American. What was Marcus thinking at this moment? What was he—no, she couldn't allow herself to dwell on the thought, for it had caused her eyes to sting, and she would not let herself cry. St. Vincent would not have the satisfaction of seeing any evidence of weakness.

Twisting her hands in the cuffs, Lillian tried to figure out what kind of locking mechanism fastened them, but in her current position, it was useless. Relaxing back against the seat, she glared at the door until it opened once more.

St. Vincent climbed back into the carriage and signaled the driver. The vehicle jolted slightly as it was drawn to the yard behind the coaching inn. "In a moment I will take you upstairs to a room where you can see to your private needs. Regrettably we haven't time for a meal, but I can promise you a decent breakfast on the morrow."

When the carriage stopped once more, St. Vincent grasped her waist and pulled her toward him, his blue eyes glittering appreciatively at the glimpse of her breasts through the thin chemise, while the front of her dress gaped open. Covering her with his coat to conceal the sight of the handcuffs and gag, he slung her over his shoulder. "Don't even think of struggling or kicking," she heard him say, the sound of his voice muffled by the layer of broadcloth. "Or I may decide to delay our journey while I demonstrate precisely what my paramours find so delightful about handcuffs."

Held in check by the credible threat of rape, Lillian held still as he carried her outside the carriage, crossing through the back courtyard of the inn to an outside staircase. Someone he passed must have asked a question about the prone woman slung over St. Vincent's shoulder, for he said with a rueful laugh, "My light-o'-love is a bit tap-hackled, I'm afraid. A weakness for gin. Turns her nose up at good French brandy and goes for blue ruin, the little pea wit." The comments elicited a hearty masculine guffaw, and Lillian simmered in mounting fury. She counted the number of steps St. Vincent ascended . . . twenty-eight, with one landing between the flights. They were on the upper level of the building, with one door that led to a row of rooms inside. Nearly smothering beneath the coat, Lillian tried to guess how many doors they might have passed as St. Vincent proceeded along the hallway. They entered a room, and St. Vincent closed the door with his foot.

Carrying Lillian to the bed, he carefully unloaded her, removed the coat, and pushed back the wild locks of hair that had fallen over her flushed face.

"I want to make certain they're hitching up a decent team," St. Vincent murmured, his eyes as brilliantly faceted as gemstones, and just as cold. "I'll return soon."

Lillian wondered if he ever felt a genuine emotion about anyone or anything, or if he simply moved through life like an actor on a stage, manufacturing whatever expressions served his purposes. Something in her searching gaze caused his slight smile to fade, and his manner turned businesslike as he withdrew something from the inside of his coat. A key, she saw, with a sting of sudden excitement in her chest. Pushing her to her side, St. Vincent unlocked the handcuffs. She could not prevent a sigh of relief as her arms were freed. Her emancipation was short-lived, however. Gripping her wrists, he controlled her arms with maddening ease, lifting them to the iron rods of the bed's headboard to refasten them. Although Lillian tried to make the task as difficult as possible for him, she had not yet regained her strength.

Stretched before him on the bed, with her arms over her head, Lillian watched him warily, her mouth working beneath the gag. St. Vincent raked her prone body with an insolent glance, making it clear to both of them that she was completely at his mercy. *Please, God, don't let him* . . . Lillian thought. She did not look away from him, nor did she shrink, sensing somehow that part of what had kept her safe from him so far was her lack of visible fear. A painful knot gathered in her throat as St. Vincent lifted a practiced hand to the exposed skin of her upper chest, and stroked the edge of her chemise. "Would that we had time to play," he said lightly. Watching her face, he slid his fingers to the curve of her breast and fondled until he felt the nipple harden at his touch. Shamed and enraged, Lillian breathed rapidly through her nostrils.

Slowly St. Vincent removed his hand and stood back from the bed. "Soon," he murmured, though it was unclear whether he meant his return from the inn's stable yard or his intention to sleep with her.

Lillian closed her eyes and listened to the sound of his footsteps across the floor. The door opened and closed, followed by the click of the lock being turned from outside. Shifting on the mattress, Lillian craned her neck to squint at the handcuffs that secured her to the bed. They were made of steel, welded with a chain in the middle, and engraved with the words *Higby-Dumfries #30, Warranted Wrought/British Made.* Each cuff was fastened with a hinge and separate lock, affixed to the chain with tangs that had been bent through the locking bolt ends and welded to the bodies of the cuffs.

Squirming higher on the bed, Lillian managed to grasp one of the pins that had remained in her tumbled coiffure, and pulled it from her hair. She straightened the pin, curved one end of it with a twist of her fingers, and inserted it into the lock, prying for a tiny lever inside. The end of the hairpin kept slipping off the lever, which turned out to be quite difficult to trick. Swearing as the hairpin bent from the pressure, Lillian extracted it, straightened it, and tried once more, while steadily exerting pressure with the back of one wrist against the inner rim of the cuff. All at once she heard a sharp click, and the cuff fell open.

She sprang from the bed as if it were on fire, and scrambled for the door with the handcuffs dangling from one wrist. Ripping off the gag and spitting the sodden wad of cloth from her mouth, she tossed the articles aside and set to work on the door. With the aid of another hairpin, she picked the lock with practiced skill. "Thank God," she whispered as the door opened. Hearing voices and sounds from the tavern below, she calculated that her chances of finding a sympathetic stranger to help her were far better inside the inn, rather than in the stable yard where footmen and drivers milled. A quick glimpse of the hallway to ascertain that no one was coming, and then she darted over the threshold.

Conscious of her disheveled gown and open bodice, Lillian yanked the edges of her gown together as she hurried to the building's interior staircase. Her heart hammered painfully, and her head filled with noise. She was suffused with a mad desperation that made her feel capable of anything. It seemed that her body obeyed some force outside her own will, causing her feet to fly along the stairs with reckless momentum.

Reaching the bottom, Lillian rushed into the main room of the inn. People halted in mid-conversation, turning toward her with mildly startled expressions. Spying a large desk and a grouping of chairs in one corner, with four or five well-dressed gentlemen standing in a half circle nearby, Lillian approached them hurriedly. "I need to speak to the innkeeper," she said without preamble. "Or a manager. Anyone who can help me. I need—"

She broke off abruptly as she heard her name being called, and glanced over her shoulder, fearing that St. Vincent had discovered her escape. Her entire body stiffened in battle readiness. But there was no sign of St. Vincent, no betraying gleam of golden-amber hair.

She heard the voice again, a deep sound that penetrated to her soul. "Lillian."

Her legs quivered beneath her as she saw a lean, dark-haired man coming from the front entryway. *It can't be*, she thought, blinking hard to clear her vision, which must surely have been playing tricks on her. She stumbled a little as she turned to face him. "Westcliff," she whispered, and took a few hesitant steps forward.

The rest of the room seemed to vanish. Marcus's face was pale beneath its tan, and he stared at her with searing intensity, as if he feared she might disappear. His stride quickened, and as he reached her, she was seized and caught in a biting grip. He wrapped his arms around her, pulling her hard against him. "My God," he muttered, and buried his face in her hair.

"You came," Lillian gasped, trembling all over. "You found me." She couldn't conceive how it was possible. He smelled of horses and sweat, and his clothes were chilled from the outside air. Feeling her shiver, Marcus drew her tightly inside his coat, murmuring endearments against her hair.

"Marcus," Lillian said thickly. "Have I gone mad? Oh, please be real. Please don't go away—"

"I'm here." His voice was low and shaken. "I'm here, and I'm not going anywhere." He drew back slightly, his midnight gaze scouring her from head to toe, his hands searching urgently over her body. "My love, my own . . . have you been hurt?" As his fingers slid along her arm, he encountered the locked manacle. Lifting her wrist, he stared at the handcuffs blankly. He inhaled sharply, and his body began to shake with primitive fury. "Goddamn it, I'll send him to hell—"

"I'm fine," Lillian said hastily. "I haven't been hurt."

Bringing her hand to his mouth, Marcus kissed it roughly, and kept her fingers against his cheek while his breath struck her wrist in swift repetitions. "Lillian, did he . . ."

Reading the question in his haunted gaze, the words he couldn't yet bring himself to voice, Lillian whispered scratchily, "No, nothing happened. There wasn't time."

"I'm still going to kill him." There was a deadly note in his voice that made the back of her neck crawl. Seeing the open bodice of her gown, Marcus released her long enough to pull off his coat and place it over her shoulders. He suddenly went still. "That smell . . . what is it?"

Realizing that her skin and clothes still retained the noxious scent, Lillian hesitated before replying. "Ether," she finally said, trying to form her trembling lips into a reassuring smile as she saw his eyes dilate into pools of black. "It wasn't bad, actually. I've slept through most of the day. Other than a touch of queasiness, I'm—"

An animal growl came from his throat, and he pulled her against him once more. "I'm sorry. I'm so sorry. Lillian, my sweet love . . . you're safe now. I'll never let anything happen to you again. I swear it on my life. You're safe." He took her head in his hands, and his mouth slid over hers in a kiss that was brief, soft, and yet so shockingly intense that she swayed dizzily. Closing her eyes, she let herself rest against him, still fearing that none of this was real, that she would awaken to find herself with St. Vincent once more. Marcus whispered comforting words against her parted lips and cheeks, and held her with a grip that seemed gentle but could not have been broken by the combined efforts of ten men. Glancing out from the secure depths of his embrace, she saw the tall form of Simon Hunt approaching.

"Mr. Hunt," she said in surprise, while Marcus's lips drifted over her temple.

Hunt slid a concerned glance over her. "Are you all right, Miss Bowman?"

She had to twist a little to avoid Marcus's exploring mouth as she replied breathlessly. "Oh yes. Yes. As you can see, I am unharmed."

"That is a great relief," Hunt returned with a smile. "Your family and friends have all been quite distraught over your absence."

"The countess—" Lillian began, and stopped short, wondering how to explain the magnitude of the betrayal to Marcus. However, as she looked into his eyes, she saw the infinite concern in their gleaming sable depths, and she wondered how she could ever have thought him unfeeling.

"I know what happened," Marcus said softly, smoothing the wild mane of her hair. "You won't ever have to see her again. She'll be gone for good by the time we return to Stony Cross Park."

Even with the questions and worries that flooded her, Lillian was overcome with sudden exhaustion. The waking nightmare had come to a precipitate end, and it seemed that for now there was nothing more she could do. She waited docilely, her cheek resting against the steady support of Marcus's shoulder, only half hearing the conversation that ensued.

". . . have to find St. Vincent . . ." Marcus was saying.

"No," Simon Hunt said emphatically, "*I'll* find St. Vincent. You take care of Miss Bowman."

"We need privacy."

"I believe there is a small room nearby—more of a vestibule, actually . . ."

But Hunt's voice trailed away, and Lillian became aware of a new, ferocious tension in Marcus's body. With a lethal shift of his muscles, he turned to glance in the direction of the staircase.

St. Vincent was descending, having entered the rented room from the other side of the inn and found it empty. Stopping midway down the stairs, St. Vincent took in the curious tableau before him . . . the clusters of bewildered onlookers, the affronted innkeeper . . . and the Earl of Westcliff, who stared at him with avid bloodlust.

The entire inn fell silent during that chilling moment, so that Westcliff's quiet snarl was clearly audible. "By God, I'm going to butcher you."

Dazedly Lillian murmured, "Marcus, wait—"

She was shoved unceremoniously at Simon Hunt, who caught her reflexively as Marcus ran full-bore toward the stairs. Instead of skirting around the banister, Marcus vaulted the railings and landed on the steps like a cat. There was a blur of movement as St. Vincent attempted a strategic retreat, but Marcus flung himself upward, catching his legs and dragging him down. They grappled, cursed, and exchanged punishing blows, until St. Vincent aimed a kick at Marcus's head. Rolling to avoid the blow of his heavy boot, Marcus was forced to release him temporarily. The viscount lurched up the stairs, and Marcus sprang after him. Soon they were both out of sight. A crowd of enthusiastic men followed, shouting advice, exchanging odds, and exclaiming in excitement over the spectacle of a pair of noblemen fighting like spurred roosters.

White-faced, Lillian glanced at Simon Hunt, who wore a faint smile. "Aren't you going to help him?" she demanded.

"Oh no. Westcliff would never forgive me for interrupting. It's his first tavern brawl." Hunt's gaze flickered over Lillian in friendly assessment. She swayed a little, and he placed a large hand on the center of her back and guided her to the nearby grouping of chairs. A cacophony of noise drifted from upstairs. There were heavy thudding sounds that caused the entire building to shake, followed by the noises of furniture breaking and glass shattering.

"Now," Hunt said, ignoring the tumult, "if I may have a look at that remaining handcuff, I may be able to do something about it."

"You can't," Lillian said with weary certainty. "The key is in St. Vincent's pocket, and I've run out of hairpins."

Sitting beside her, Hunt took her manacled wrist, regarded it thoughtfully, and said with what she thought
was rather inappropriate satisfaction, "How fortunate. A
pair of Higby-Dumfries number thirty."

Lillian gave him a sardonic glance. "I take it you are a
handcuff enthusiast?"

His lips twitched. "No, but I do have a friend or two in
law enforcement. And these were once given as standard
issue to the New Police, until a design flaw was discovered. Now one may find a dozen pair of Higby-Dumfries
in any London pawnshop."

"What design flaw?"

For answer, Hunt adjusted the locked cuff on her wrist,
with the hinge and lock facing downward. He paused at
the sound of more furniture breaking from upstairs, and
grinned at Lillian's gathering scowl. "I'll go," he said
mildly. "But first . . ." He withdrew a handkerchief from
his pocket with one hand, inserting it between her wrist
and the steel cuff as a makeshift inner padding. "There.
That may help to cushion the force of the blow."

"Blow? What blow?"

"Hold still."

Lillian squeaked in dismay as she felt him lift her
manacled wrist high over the desk and bring it down
sharply on the bottom of the hinge. The whack served to
jar the lever mechanism inside the lock, and the cuff
snapped open as if by magic. Stunned, Lillian regarded
Hunt with a half smile as she rubbed her bare wrist.
"Thank you. I—"

There was another crashing sound, this time coming
from directly overhead, and a chorus of excited bellows
from the onlookers caused the walls to tremble. Above it
all, the innkeeper could be heard complaining shrilly

that his building would soon be reduced to matchsticks.

"Mr. Hunt," Lillian exclaimed, "I do wish that you would try to be of some use to Lord Westcliff!"

Hunt's brows lifted into mocking crescents. "You don't actually fear that St. Vincent is getting the better of him?"

"The question is not whether I have sufficient confidence in Lord Westcliff's fighting ability," Lillian replied impatiently. "The fact is, I have *too much* confidence in it. And I would rather not have to bear witness at a murder trial on top of everything else."

"You have a point." Standing, Hunt refolded his handkerchief and placed it in his coat pocket. He headed to the stairs with a short sigh, grumbling, "I've spent most of the day trying to stop him from killing people."

Lillian never fully remembered the rest of that evening, only half conscious as she stood against Marcus. He kept his hard arm locked firmly around her back to support her drooping weight. Although he was disheveled and a bit bruised, Marcus radiated the primal energy of a healthy male who had come fresh from a fight. She gathered that he was making a great many demands, and that everyone seemed eager to please him. It was agreed that they would lodge at The Bull and Mouth for the night, with Hunt departing for Stony Cross Park at first light. In the meanwhile, Hunt went to load St. Vincent, or what was left of him, into his carriage and send him to his London residence. It seemed that St. Vincent would not be prosecuted for his misdeeds, as that would only serve to inflate the episode into a massive scandal.

With all the arrangements made, Marcus carried Lillian to the largest guest room in the building, where a bath and food were sent up as quickly as possible. It was sparely furnished but very clean, with an ample bed covered in pressed linen and soft, faded quilts. An old copperplate slipper tub was set before the hearth and filled by two chambermaids carrying steaming kettles. As Lillian waited for the bathwater to cool sufficiently, Marcus bullied her into eating a bowl of soup, which was quite tolerable, though its ingredients were impossible to identify. "What are those little brown chunks?" Lillian asked suspiciously, opening her mouth reluctantly as he spooned more in.

"It doesn't matter. Swallow."

"Is it mutton? Beef? Did it originally have horns? Hooves? Feathers? Scales? I don't like to eat something when I don't know what—"

"More," he said inexorably, pushing the spoon into her mouth again.

"You're a tyrant."

"I know. Drink some water."

Resigning herself to his domineering ways—just for one night—Lillian finished the light meal. The food gave her a new surge of strength, and she felt invigorated as Marcus pulled her into his lap. "Now," he said, cuddling her against his chest, "tell me what happened, from the beginning."

Before long Lillian found herself talking animatedly, almost chattering, as she described her encounter with Lady Westcliff at Butterfly Court, and the events that occurred afterward. She must have sounded overwrought, for Marcus occasionally interrupted the stream of rapid words with soothing murmurs, his manner interested and infinitely gentle. His mouth brushed over her hair, his warm breath filtering down to her scalp. Gradually she relaxed against him, her limbs feeling heavy and loose.

"How did you persuade the countess to confess so

quickly?" she asked. "I would have thought she would have held out for days. I would have thought she would rather die than admit anything—"

"I'm afraid that was the choice I gave her."

Her eyes widened. "Oh," she whispered. "I'm sorry, Marcus. She is your mother, after all—"

"Only in the most technical sense of the word," he said dryly. "I felt no filial attachment to her before now, but if I had, it would surely have been extinguished after today. She's done enough harm for one lifetime, I think. We'll try keeping her in Scotland from now on, or perhaps somewhere abroad."

"Did the countess tell you what was said between her and me?" Lillian asked tentatively.

Marcus shook his head, his mouth twisting. "She told me that you had decided to elope with St. Vincent."

"*Elope?*" Lillian repeated in shock. "As if I deliberately . . . as if I had chosen him over—" She stopped, aghast, as she imagined how he must have felt. Although she had not shed a single tear during the entire day, the thought that Marcus might have wondered for a split second if yet another woman had left him for St. Vincent . . . it was too much to bear. She burst into noisy sobs, startling herself as well as Marcus. "You didn't believe it, did you? My God, please say you didn't!"

"Of course I didn't." He stared at her in astonishment, and hastily reached for a table napkin to wipe at the stream of tears on her face. "No, no, don't cry—"

"I love you, Marcus." Taking the napkin from him, Lillian blew her nose noisily and continued to weep as she spoke. "I love you. I don't mind if I'm the first one to say it, nor even if I'm the only one. I just want you to know how very much—"

"I love you too," he said huskily. "I love you too. Lillian . . . Please don't cry. It's killing me. Don't."

She nodded and blew into the linen folds again, her complexion turning mottled, her eyes swelling, her nose running freely. It appeared, however, that there was something wrong with Marcus's vision. Grasping her head in his hands, he pressed a hard kiss to her mouth and said hoarsely, "You're so beautiful."

The statement, though undoubtedly sincere, caused her to giggle through her last hiccupping sobs. Wrapping his arms around her in an embrace that was just short of crushing, Marcus asked in a muffled voice, "My love, hasn't anyone ever told you that it's bad form to laugh at a man when he's declaring himself?"

She blew her nose with a last inelegant snort. "I'm a hopeless case, I'm afraid. Do you still want to marry me?"

"Yes. Now."

The statement shocked her out of her tears. "What?"

"I don't want to return with you to Hampshire. I want to take you to Gretna Green. The inn has its own coach service—I'll hire one in the morning, and we'll reach Scotland the day after tomorrow."

"But . . . but everyone will expect a respectable church wedding . . ."

"I can't wait for you. I don't give a damn about respectability."

A wobbly grin spread across Lillian's face as she thought of how many people would be astonished to hear such a statement from him. "It smacks of scandal, you know. The Earl of Westcliff rushing off for an anvil wedding in Gretna Green . . ."

"Let's begin with a scandal, then." He kissed her, and she responded with a low moan, clinging and arching against him, until he pushed his tongue deeper, molding his lips tighter over hers, feasting on the warm, open silkiness of her mouth. Breathing heavily, he dragged his lips to her quivering throat. "Say, 'Yes, Marcus,'" he prompted.

"Yes, Marcus."

His eyes were dark and incandescent as he stared at her, and she sensed that there was a multitude of things he wanted to tell her. However, all he said was, "It's time for your bath."

She could have done it herself, but Marcus insisted on undressing her, and bathing her as if she were a child. Relaxing in his care, she watched his dark face through the soft veil of mist that rose from the bath. His movements were deliberately slow as he soaped and rinsed her body until she was pink and glowing. Lifting her from the slipper tub, he dried her with a length of toweling. "Raise your arms," he murmured.

She glanced askance at the worn-looking garment in his hand. "What is that?"

"A nightgown from the innkeeper's wife," he replied, pulling it over her head. Lillian pushed her arms through the sleeves and sighed at the scent of clean flannel settling around her. The gown was an indistinguishable color, and it was far too large for her, but she felt comforted by its worn, soft folds.

Curling up in the bed, Lillian watched as Marcus bathed and dried himself, the muscles in his back rippling, his superbly fit body a pleasure to behold. An irresistible smile curved her lips as she reflected that this extraordinary man belonged to her . . . and she would never be quite certain how she had won his well-guarded heart. Marcus extinguished the lamp and came to bed, and Lillian cuddled against him eagerly as he slid beneath the covers. His scent rushed over her, fresh, edged with the crispness of soap and the faintest hints of sun and salt. She wanted to drown in the wonderful smell of him, she wanted to kiss and touch every inch of his body. "Make love to me, Marcus," she whispered.

His shadowy form loomed over her while his hand played in her hair. "My love," he said, a note of tender amusement in his voice, "since this morning you've been threatened, drugged, abducted, handcuffed, and carried halfway across England. Haven't you had enough for one day?"

She shook her head. "I was a bit tired before, but now I've gotten my second wind. I couldn't possibly sleep."

For some reason that made him laugh.

His body lifted away from hers. She thought at first that he meant to move to the other side of the bed, but then she felt the hem of her nightgown being raised. Her bare legs tingled as the cool air brushed over her skin. Her breath quickened. The thick cotton was drawn higher, higher, until her breasts were exposed, the tips hardening. His mouth was soft and hot as it descended to her skin, searching and nuzzling, finding places of unexpected sensation; the ticklish place at the side of her ribs, the velvet undercurve of her breast, the delicate rim of her navel. When Lillian tried to caress him, her hands were gently pushed to her sides, until she understood that he meant her to lie completely still. Her breaths turned even and deep, the muscles in her stomach and legs quivering as pleasure chased like drops of quicksilver over her body.

Marcus nibbled and kissed his way to the secret dampness between her thighs, and her legs spread easily at his touch. She was open and utterly vulnerable, every nerve sizzling with aching excitement. A high, faint sound escaped her throat as he licked into the dark triangle, bolts of delight running through her with each stroke of his tongue along the rosy, slippery-soft skin. His tongue danced and tickled and opened her, and then he settled in for minutes of sweetly rhythmic teasing, until sensation weighted her limbs and her breath came in weak cries. Finally he slipped his fingers deeply inside her, and she groaned, struggling, climaxing, shuddering as if she might come apart from pleasure.

Dazed, she felt him pull down her nightgown. "Your turn now," she mumbled, her head settling on his shoulder as he gathered her against him. "You haven't . . ."

"Sleep," he whispered. "I'll have my turn tomorrow."

"I'm still not tired," she insisted.

"Close your eyes," Marcus said, his hand moving to her bottom in a circling caress. He brushed his mouth over her forehead and her fragile eyelids. "Rest. You'll need to regain your strength . . . because once we're married, I won't be able to leave you alone. I'll want to love you every hour, every minute of the day." He nestled her more closely against him. "There is nothing on earth more beautiful to me than your smile . . . no sound sweeter than your laughter . . . no pleasure greater than holding you in my arms. I realized today that I could never live without you, stubborn little hellion that you are. In this life and the next, you're my only hope of happiness. Tell me, Lillian, dearest love . . . how can you have reached so far inside my heart?" He paused to kiss her damp silken skin . . . and smiled as the wisp of a feminine snore broke the peaceful silence.

Epilogue

To the Right Honorable the Countess of Westcliff
Marsden Terrace, Upper Brook Street, no.2
London

Dear Lady Westcliff,

It was both an honor and a delight to receive your letter. I beg to offer congratulations at the glad tidings of your recent marriage. Though you have modestly professed that the match with Lord Westcliff is all to your advantage, I must take the liberty of disagreeing. Having had the fortune of making your acquaintance, I can attest that the advantage belongs to the earl in winning the hand of such a charming and accomplished young lady—

"*C*harming?" Daisy interrupted dryly. "Oh, he knows you so little."

"And accomplished," Lillian reminded her in a superior tone, before turning back to the letter from Mr. Nettle. "He goes on to write . . . *'Perhaps if your younger sister were more like you, she might also find someone to marry.'* "

"He did not write that!" Daisy exclaimed, leaping over an ottoman and making a grab for the letter, while Lillian defended herself with a shriek of laughter. Annabelle, who sat in a nearby chair, smiled over the rim of her teacup as she sipped the brew in hopes of settling her stomach. She had already confided her intention to tell her husband about her pregnancy that evening, as it was becoming more and more difficult to conceal her condition.

The three of them sat in the parlor of Marsden Terrace. A few days earlier, Lillian and Marcus had returned to Hampshire from their "blacksmith's marriage," as such affairs were called in Gretna Green. She had been silently gratified to find that the countess had indeed been spirited off the estate, with all traces of her presence removed. *Dowager* countess, Lillian corrected herself, rather unnerved every time she realized that *she* was now the Countess of Westcliff. Now Marcus had taken her to London, where he was visiting the locomotive works with Mr. Hunt and attending to other necessary business. In a matter of days the Westcliffs would leave for a hastily arranged honeymoon in Italy . . . and as far away as possible from Mercedes Bowman, who had not yet ceased complaining about having been robbed of the large society wedding she had intended for her daughter.

"Oh, do get off me, Daisy," Lillian cried good-naturedly, shoving at her younger sister. "I admit it, I made up that last part. Stop it, you'll rip the thing to shreds. Now where was I?" Assuming an expression of dignity befitting an earl's wife, Lillian held up the letter and continued importantly. "Mr. Nettle went on to deliver a number of lovely compliments, and wished me well with the Marsden family—"

"Did you tell him that your mother-in-law tried to dispose of you?" Daisy asked.

"And then," Lillian continued, ignoring her, "he answered my question about the perfume."

Both young women glanced at her in surprise. Annabelle's blue eyes turned round with curiosity. "You asked him about the secret ingredient?"

"For God's sake, what is it?" Daisy demanded. "Tell! Tell!"

"You might be a bit disappointed in the answer," Lillian said, turning sheepish. "According to Mr. Nettle, the secret ingredient is . . . nothing."

Daisy looked outraged. "There is no secret ingredient? It isn't a real love potion? I've been *marinating* myself in it for no reason?"

"Here, I'll read his explanation. 'Your success in capturing the heart of Lord Westcliff was purely the result of your own magic, and the essential addition to the fragrance was, in fact, yourself.'" Laying the letter in her lap, Lillian grinned at her sister's annoyed expression. "Poor Daisy. I'm sorry that it wasn't real magic."

"Drat," Daisy grumbled. "I should have known."

"The odd thing is," Lillian continued thoughtfully, "Westcliff *did* know. The night I told him about the perfume, he said he knew conclusively what the secret ingredient was. And this morning, before I showed him the letter from Mr. Nettle, he told me his answer—which turned out to be correct." A slow smile crossed her face. "The arrogant know-all," she muttered lovingly.

"Wait until I tell Evie," Daisy said. "She will be as disappointed as I am."

Annabelle glanced at her with a pucker marring her pretty forehead. "Has she replied to your letter yet, Daisy?"

"No. Evie's family has her under lock and key again. I doubt they'll let her send or receive letters. And what worries me is that before they left Stony Cross Park, her aunt Florence was giving out very forceful hints that a betrothal to cousin Eustace is in the works."

The other two groaned. "Over my dead body," Lillian said grimly. "You realize we'll have to resort to creative measures if we're to pry Evie out of her family's clutches and find a good match for her."

"We will," came Daisy's confident reply. "Believe me, dear, if we can find a husband for you, we can do *anything*."

"That does it," Lillian said, and sprang from the settee to advance menacingly toward her with an upraised cushion.

Giggling, Daisy scrambled behind the nearest piece of furniture and cried, "Remember, you're a countess! Where's your dignity?"

"I've misplaced it," Lillian informed her, and chased after her with glee.

Meanwhile . . .

"Lord St. Vincent, there is a visitor at the door. I informed her that you were not at home, but she is most insistent that she be allowed to see you."

The library was dark, and cold, except for a small spill of feeble light that came from the hearth. The fire

would soon burn out . . . yet Sebastian could not seem
to rouse himself sufficiently to add another log, no matter that there was a small stack of wood within each
reach. A blazing conflagration fit to burn the house
down would still not have been enough to warm him. He
was empty and numb, a body without a soul, and he
prided himself on it. It took rare talent for a man to sink
to his current level of depravity.

"At this hour?" Sebastian murmured without interest,
staring not at his butler, but at the cut-crystal brandy
snifter in his hand. He rolled the stem idly in his long fingers. There was no question as to what the unidentified
woman wanted. But though he was otherwise without
prospects for the evening, Sebastian realized that for
once he was not in the mood for a tumble.

"Send her away," he said coolly. "Tell her my bed is
already occupied."

"Yes, milord." The butler left, and Sebastian settled into
his chair once more, stretching his long legs before him.

He finished the brandy in his snifter with an efficient
swallow as he contemplated his most immediate problem . . . money, or the lack thereof. His creditors were
becoming aggressive in their demands, and a wide array
of debts could not be ignored much longer. Now that his
efforts to gain a badly needed fortune from Lillian Bowman had failed, he would need to get the money from
someone else. He knew some wealthy women who might
be induced to loan him some capital in return for the personal favors he could deliver so well. Or another option
was to—

"Milord?"

Sebastian looked up with a scowl. "For God's sake,
what is it?"

"The woman will not leave, milord. She is intent on seeing you."

An exasperated sigh left him. "If she's that bloody desperate, send her in. Though she had best be warned that a quick fuck and an even quicker good-bye are all I'm game for tonight."

A young, nervous voice came from behind the butler, betraying the fact that the persistent visitor had followed him inside. "That is not quite what I had in mind." She slipped around the servant and came into the room, her form wrapped in a heavy hooded cloak.

Obeying the flicker of Sebastian's eyes, the butler vanished, leaving them alone.

Sebastian rested his head on the back of his chair, regarding the mysterious figure with an emotionless gaze. The idle thought crossed his brain that she could be holding a pistol beneath the cloak. Perhaps she was one of the many women who had threatened to kill him in the past . . . one who had finally screwed up the courage to make good on her promise. He bloody well didn't give a damn. She could shoot him with his blessing, as long as she did it properly and didn't botch the job. Remaining relaxed in his seat, he murmured, "Take down your hood."

A slender white hand reached up, and she complied. The hood slipped away from hair so vividly red that it eclipsed the embers in the fireplace.

Sebastian shook his head in bemusement as he recognized the young woman. The ridiculous creature from the house party at Stony Cross Park. A shy, stammering twit, whose red hair and voluptuous figure might make her tolerable company as long as she kept her mouth shut. They had never actually spoken. Miss Evangeline

Jenner, he recalled. She had the largest, roundest eyes he had ever seen, rather like the eyes of a wax doll . . . or a young child. Her gaze touched gently on his face, not missing the shadows of bruises that had resulted from the fight with Westcliff.

Feather wit, Sebastian thought contemptuously, wondering if she had come to rail at him for abducting her friend. No. Even she couldn't be that stupid, risking her virtue, or for all she knew, her life, appearing unaccompanied at his house.

"Come to see the devil in his lair, have you?" he asked.

She came closer, her expression intent and oddly fearless. "You're not the devil. You're only a man. A very fl-flawed one."

For the first time in days Sebastian felt a faint urge to smile. A flicker of reluctant interest stirred in him. "Just because the tail and horns aren't visible, child, doesn't mean you should discount the possibility. The devil comes in many guises."

"Then I'm here to make a Faustian bargain." Her speech was very slow, as if she had to think over every word before she spoke. "I have a proposition for you, my lord."

And she drew closer to the hearth, emerging from the darkness that surrounded them both.

Now, a special peek . . .
You won't want to miss
DEVIL IN WINTER
The third title in the fabulous
"Wallflowers" series
Coming March 2006
by Lisa Kleypas
Only from Avon Books

London, 1843

$\mathscr{A}$s Sebastian, Lord St. Vincent, stared at the young woman who had just barged her way into his London residence, it occurred to him that he may have tried to abduct the wrong heiress last week.

Although kidnapping had not, until recently, been on Sebastian's long list of villainous acts, he really should have been more clever about it.

In retrospect, Lillian Bowman had been a foolish choice, though at the time she had seemed the perfect solution to Sebastian's dilemma. Her family was wealthy, whereas Sebastian was titled and in financial straits. And Lillian herself had promised to be an entertaining bed partner, with her dark-haired beauty and her fiery temperament. He should have chosen far less spirited prey. Lillian, a lively American heiress, had put up fierce resistance to his plan until she had been rescued by her fiancé, Lord Westcliff.

Miss Evangeline Jenner, the lamblike creature who now stood before him, was as unlike Lillian Bowman as possible. Sebastian regarded her with veiled contempt, pondering what he knew of her. Evangeline was the only child of Ivo Jenner, the notorious London gambling club owner, and a mother who had run off with him—only to quickly realize her mistake. Though Evangeline's mother had come from decent lineage, her father was little better than gutter scum. Despite the inglorious pedigree, Evangeline might have made a decent enough match if not for her crippling shyness, which resulted in a torturous stammer.

Sebastian had heard men say grimly that they would wear a hairshirt until their skin was bloody rather than attempt a conversation with her. Naturally Sebastian had done his utmost to avoid her whenever possible. That had not been difficult. The timid Miss Jenner was wont to hide in corners. They had never actually spoken directly—a circumstance that had appeared to suit them both quite well.

But there was no avoiding her now. For some reason Miss Jenner had seen fit to come uninvited to Sebastian's home at a scandalously late hour. To make the situation even more compromising, she was unaccompanied—and spending more than a half minute alone with Sebastian was sufficient to ruin any girl. He was debauched, amoral, and perversely proud of it. He excelled at his chosen occupation—that of degenerate seducer—and he had set a standard that few rakes could aspire to.

Relaxing in his chair, Sebastian watched with deceptive idleness as Evangeline approached. The library was dark except for a small fire in the hearth, its flickering light playing gently over the young woman's face. She didn't look to be more than twenty, her complexion fresh, her eyes filled with the kind of innocence that never failed to arouse his disdain. Sebastian had never valued nor admired innocence.

Though the gentlemanly thing would have been for him to rise from his chair, there seemed little point in making polite gestures under the circumstances. Instead, he motioned to the other chair beside the hearth with a negligent wave of his hand.

"Have a seat if you like," he said. "Though I shouldn't plan to stay long if I were you. I'm easily bored, and your reputation is hardly that of a scintillating conversationalist."

Evangeline didn't flinch at his rudeness. Sebastian couldn't help wondering what kind of upbringing had inured her so thoroughly to insult, when any other girl would have flushed or burst into tears. Either she was a pea wit, or she had remarkable nerve.

Removing her cloak, Evangeline draped it over one arm of the velvet-upholstered chair, and sat without grace or artifice. *Wallflower*, Sebastian thought, recalling that she was friends not only with Lillian Bowman, but also with Lillian's younger sister Daisy, and Annabelle Hunt. The group of four young women had sat at the side of numerous balls and soirees all last season, a band of perpetual wallflowers. However, it seemed that their bad luck had changed, for Annabelle had finally managed to catch a husband, and Lillian had just brought Lord Westcliff up to scratch. Sebastian doubted that their good fortune would extend to this bumbling creature.

Though he was tempted to demand her purpose in visiting him, Sebastian feared that might set off a round of prolonged stammering that would torment them both.

He waited with forced patience, while Evangeline appeared to consider what she was about to say. As the silence drew out, Simon watched her in the gamboling firelight and realized, with some surprise, that she was attractive. He had never really looked at her directly, only receiving the impression of a frowsy, red-haired girl with bad posture. But she was lovely.

As Sebastian stared at her, he became aware of a slight tension building in his muscles, tiny hairs rising on the back of his neck. He remained relaxed in his chair, though the tips of his fingers made slight depressions in the soft-napped velvet upholstery. He found it odd that he had never noticed her, when there was a great deal worth noticing. Her hair, the brightest shade of red he had ever seen, seemed to feed on the firelight, glowing with incandescent heat. The slender wings of her brows and the heavy fringe of her lashes were a darker shade of auburn, while her skin was that of a true redhead, fair and a bit freckled on the nose and cheeks. Sebastian was amused by the festive scattering of little gold flecks, sprinkled as if by the whim of a friendly fairy. She had unfashionably full lips that were colored a natural rose and large, round blue eyes . . . pretty but emotionless eyes, like those of a wax doll.

"I r-received word that my friend Miss Bowman is now Lady Westcliff," Evangeline remarked in a careful manner. "She and the earl went on to Gr-Gretna Green after he . . . dispatched of you."

" 'Beat me to a pulp' would be a more accurate choice of words," Sebastian said pleasantly, knowing that she couldn't help but notice the shadowy bruises on his jaw from Westcliff's righteous pummeling. "He didn't seem to take it well, my borrowing of his betrothed."

"You k-kidnapped her," Evangeline countered calmly. " 'Borrowing' implies that you intended to give her back."

Sebastian felt his lips curve with his first real smile in a long time. She wasn't a simpleton, apparently. "Kidnapped, then, if you're going to be precise. Is that why you've come to visit, Miss Jenner? To deliver a report on the happy couple? I'm weary of the subject. You had better say something interesting soon, or I'm afraid you'll have to leave."

"You w-wanted Miss Bowman because she is an heiress," Evangeline said. "And you need to marry someone with money."

"True," Sebastian acknowledged easily. "My father, the duke, has failed in his one responsibility in life: to keep the family fortune intact so he can pass it on to me. My responsibility, on the other hand, is to pass my time in profligate idleness and wait for him to die. I've been doing my job splendidly. The duke, however, has not. He's made a botch of managing the family finances, and at present he is unforgivably poor and, even worse, healthy."

"My father is rich," Evangeline said without emotion. "And dying."

"Congratulations." Sebastian studied her intently. He did not doubt that Ivo Jenner had a considerable fortune from the gambling club. Jenner's was a place where London gentlemen went for gaming, good food, strong drink, and inexpensive whores. The atmosphere was one of extravagance tinged with a comfortable degree of shabbiness. Nearly twenty years earlier, Jenner's had been a second-rate alternative to the legendary Craven's, the grandest and most successful gaming club that England had ever known.

However, when Craven's had burned to the ground and its owner had declined to rebuild, Jenner's club had inherited a flood of wealthy patrons by default, and it had risen to its own position of prominence. Not that it could ever be compared to Craven's. A club was largely a reflection of its owner's character and style, both of which Jenner was sorely lacking. Derek Craven had been, indisputably, a showman. Ivo Jenner, by contrast, was a ham-fisted brute, an ex-boxer who never excelled at anything, but by some miraculous whim of fate had become a successful businessman.

And here was Jenner's daughter, his only child. If she was about to make the offer that Sebastian suspected, he could not afford to refuse it.

"I don't want your c-congratulations," Evangeline said in response to his earlier remark.

"What *do* you want, child?" Sebastian asked softly. "Get to the point, if you please. This is becoming tedious."

"I want to be with my father for the last few days of his l-life. My mother's family won't allow me to see him. I've tried to run away to his club, but they always catch me, and then I'm punished. I w-will not go back to them this time. They have plans that I intend to avoid—at the cost of my own life, if necessary."

"And those plans are?" Sebastian prodded idly.

"They are trying to force me to marry one of my cousins. Mr. Eustace Stubbins. He cares n-nothing for me, nor I for him . . . but he is a willing pawn in the family's scheme."

"Which is to gain control of your father's fortune when he dies?"

"Yes. At first I considered the idea, because I thought

that Mr. Stubbins and I could have our own house . . . and I thought . . . life might be bearable if I could live away from the r-rest of them. But Mr. Stubbins told me that he has no intention of moving anywhere. He wants to stay under the family's roof . . . and I don't think I can survive there much longer." Faced with Sebastian's seemingly incurious silence, she added quietly, "I believe they mean to k-kill me after they've gotten my father's money."

Sebastian's gaze did not move from her face, though he kept his tone light. "How inconsiderate of them. Why should I care?"

Evangeline did not rise to his baiting, only gave him a steady stare that was evidence of an innate toughness Sebastian had never before encountered in a woman. "I'm offering to marry you," she said. "I want your protection. My father is too ill and weak to help me, and I will not be a burden to my friends. I believe they would offer to harbor me, but even then I would always have to be on guard, fearing that my relations would manage to steal me away and force me to do their will. An unmarried woman has little recourse, socially or legally. It isn't f-fair . . . but I can't afford to go tilting at windmills. I need a h-husband. You need a rich wife. And we are both equally desperate, which leads me to believe that you will agree to my pr-proposition. If so, then I should like to leave for Gretna Green tonight. Now. I'm certain that my relations are already looking for me."

The silence was charged and heavy as Sebastian contemplated her with an unfriendly gaze. He didn't trust her. And after the debacle of last week's thwarted abduction, he had no wish to repeat the experience.

Carnival Pride℠
April 2 - 9, 2006.

7 Day Exotic Mexican Riviera Itinerary

DAY	PORT	ARRIVE	DEPART
Sun	Los Angeles/Long Beach, CA		4:00 P.M.
Mon	"Book Lover's" Day at Sea		
Tue	"Book Lover's" Day at Sea		
Wed	Puerto Vallarta, Mexico	8:00 A.M.	10:00 P.M.
Thu	Mazatlan, Mexico	9:00 A.M.	6:00 P.M.
Fri	Cabo San Lucas, Mexico	7:00 A.M.	4:00 P.M.
Sat	"Book Lover's" Day at Sea		
Sun	Los Angeles/Long Beach, CA	9:00 A.M.	

ports of call subject to weather conditions

TERMS AND CONDITIONS

PAYMENT SCHEDULE:
50% due upon booking
Full and final payment due by February 10, 2006

Acceptable forms of payment are Visa, MasterCard, American Express, Discover and checks. The cardholder must be one of the passengers traveling. A fee of $25 will apply for all returned checks. Check payments must be made payable to **Advantage International, LLC and sent to: Advantage International, LLC, 195 North Harbor Drive, Suite 4206, Chicago, IL 60601**

CHANGE/CANCELLATION:
Notice of change/cancellation must be made in writing to Advantage International, LLC.

Change:
Changes in cabin category may be requested and can result in increased rate and penalties. A name change is permitted 60 days or more prior to departure and will incur a penalty of $50 per name change. Deviation from the group schedule and package is a cancellation.

Cancellation:

181 days or more prior to departure	$250 per person
121 - 180 days or more prior to departure	50% of the package price
120 - 61 days prior to departure	75% of the package price
60 days or less prior to departure	100% of the package price (nonrefundable)

US and Canadian citizens are required to present a valid passport or the original birth certificate and state issued photo ID (drivers license). All other nationalities must contact the consulate of the various ports that are visited for verification of documentation.

We strongly recommend trip cancellation insurance!

For complete details call 1-877-ADV-NTGE or visit www.AuthorsAtSea.com

- -

For booking form and complete information
go to www.AuthorsAtSea.com or call 1-877-ADV-NTGE

Complete coupon and booking form and mail both to:
Advantage International, LLC,
195 North Harbor Drive, Suite 4206, Chicago, IL 60601